Preface

While this novel is primarily a work of fiction, it was originally written to highlight the worst-case scenario of a nuclear holocaust. The radiation effects on the human body and the land and struggles the survivors would face has been thoroughly researched and drawn from numerous non-fiction books and documents. While such a scenario is extremely unlikely its ramifications, if played out, give fertile ground for thought…

NUCLEAR MIDNIGHT

Nuclear Midnight

"from a nightmare scenario a new world is forged"

ROBERT COLE

Published by Robert Cole
Copyright 2015

Acknowledgements

To Rosey, my partner, and friend, who shared the tedium of the research and the agony of the writing.

To my mother, who endured the proofreading of the manuscript.

POST HOLOCAUST BRITAIN

Contents

CHAPTER 1

Toward the east, a plane banked sharply against the swollen
nimbus clouds of the storm as the pilot waited for his
clearance to land. The storm was already over Singapore,
rumbling and spitting lightning bolts as it threw itself against
the glistening glass towers of the city. With clearance to land
granted, the pilot levelled out and began his bumpy descent
through the cloud. On board was the usual mixture of Asian
businessmen and tourists bound for destinations in Europe
and Asia. Two of the passengers, however, Alex Carhill and
his older brother Jason, had already completed two months
travelling overland through Indonesia. They were on the first
stage of a world trip. Both planned to be away from their
home country, Australia, for at least a year, but this was
open-ended; neither had ties and both had every intention of
following whatever path materialised in front of them.

After nearly a minute of rushing cloud, the plane burst
through into the storm. Jason leaned over to the window and
watched the rain beat down on the wings of the plane. He
was the larger and more athletic of the two, with vivid blue
eyes set in a deeply tanned face. The plane banked hard
again as the pilot lined up the airport runway. Jason
scratched the stubble of blond hair on his chin and pulled out
his phone to take some photos. At first glance there seemed
little physical similarity between the brothers. Alex's eyes
were grey, not blue; his hair was brown, not blond; and he
was four centimetres shorter than Jason. He also lacked his
brother's powerful build. His arms and legs were sinewy
rather than muscular and his chest shallow rather than barrel
shaped. His mannerisms were also markedly different; while
Jason radiated confidence and ease, Alex radiated

nervousness and agitation. This was not surprising; despite being raised in the same household their upbringing was starkly different. Jason wasn't just good, he excelled at anything he applied himself to: rowing, swimming, athletics, his bedroom walls were covered with his triumphs. He had an impressive academic record, too. Anything scientific or mathematical came easily to him, culminating in the dux of the school upon graduation.

Alex, possessing only average abilities, had the unenviable task of following in the footsteps of a paragon. With only a year separating them, the inevitable comparisons did little to boost his self-esteem. But in spite of living in his brother's shadow, Alex had never resented Jason. He had elevated him almost to the position of someone God-like and unattainable, therefore not a threat. Indeed, he treasured his brother's advice, so it was natural for him to take all his problems to Jason. Too much so, for his own good, some people thought.

The plane touched down and began taxiing towards one of the many airport terminals. The brothers unclipped their belts and started collecting their belongings. As soon as they disembarked, Alex's first thought was to catch up on world events. There had not been much chance for that; travelling through the remote villages of Bali and Java the brothers had had little chance to catch up with the news. Like most people these days, Alex followed the news carefully. The warming of the earth's surface had already taken its toll on the land and the economies of many nations. Changing weather patterns and a series of calamitous floods and droughts had forced the reassessment of traditional farming practices in many countries. Deserts had been turned into huge lakes, while fertile lands had withered into arid wasteland under unseasonably hot winds and diminished rainfall. Asia had been one of the most affected areas with the failure of the monsoons in two consecutive years. This put enormous stress on the world's food resources and sent the price of cereal grains skyrocketing. New diseases had also emerged,

2

draining billions of dollars from the economies of some of the poorest nations in the world.

These problems, combined with continual high oil prices, had precipitated a world recession and heightened international tension as the nations of the world scrambled for the resources of less affected countries. Added to these tensions was the simmering unrest in the middle-east and the border tensions between Russia and the former eastern bloc countries. Russia had already swallowed up much of Ukraine and was facing off against NATO, who were backed by America. Before the brothers had left Australia there had been media revelations that America had secretly weaponised space - something strictly forbidden under the Outer Space Treaty. With tensions already running high, the increased military threat by America could not have come at a worse time.

To add to these problems, the simmering conflict in the Middle East suddenly took a turn for the worst. The Israeli parliament was bombed. Within days Israel had invaded Lebanon and the Gaza strip, sweeping away all suspected terrorist camps in a brutal ground and aerial assault. Syrian-based fundamentalist Muslim groups were enraged and threatened to attack across the Syrian border. Support, both political and military, came pouring in from other Arab nations. A resurgence in fundamental Islam had recently united parts of the Arab world. Armed with chemical and possibly nuclear weapons and sophisticated delivery systems, Israel's nuclear arsenal could now be matched with equally lethal weapons. America immediately came to Israel's aid, promising military support and arms. As the threats continued, the oil price climbed. Russia came out in support of the Arabs, matching America's offer of military support and arms. Now Russia and America had a stage for their conflict. The press were full of gloomy predictions that this could be the spark that could set the world alight.

Alex read the news reports with growing concern. To make matters worse, three days ago there had been a direct clash between NATO and Russian troops along the border of Ukraine. America was also rumoured to have sent elite troops to match a build-up of Russian troops. This news sent the price of oil and gold up and the world stock markets down. Both sides were now engaged in a dangerous game of brinkmanship - one misstep could be irreversible.

Jason, however, had no time for such stuff. 'It's mostly media propaganda,' he would announce confidently, throwing down the paper. 'Why worry?' he would continue when Alex pressed him on his apparent lack of concern. 'We can't do anything about it, anyway.'

That probably summed up Jason's view on life. He wasn't interested in things that didn't directly affect him. Whatever was going to happen would happen, and there was nothing he or anybody else could do about it.

After a few days in Singapore, they headed up the Malaysian peninsula to Bangkok, then overflew Myanmar to Kolkata. From the coast they travelled up country by train to New Delhi. Singapore to New Delhi took them just over a month. Both brothers had been sick in Bangkok with stomach pains and diarrhoea and eating in the roadside cafes in Kolkata hadn't helped matters. Jason especially had been very sick with fever, vomiting and severe stomach cramps. They had been forced to spend nearly a week in Kolkata before continuing on their way to Agra and New Delhi.

Alex found India a land of extreme contrasts. In the villages the people were poor, but not starving. They greeted the two young men warmly, without trying to prise their money away from them. In the cities, however, they were set upon by scores of beggars. Against a background of vast British built monoliths, this under class roamed the streets, while the rich patronised restaurants and cafes. Both Alex and Jason felt rather overawed with the place. Such abundance of life in all its shapes and forms, such extremes of wealth and poverty were difficult to take in all at once. On their way back to Australia they decided that they would return for a closer look. But for the moment they felt weak and drained by the experience of South East Asia. After only three weeks in India, they were glad to take the next flight to Athens, where they could eat food they would be more accustomed to and relax in the Mediterranean sun.

Alex and Jason had barely touched down in Athens, however, before they witnessed several demonstrations in the main squares. Feeling was running very high amongst the demonstrators who were calling for a jihad against the Jews; cars were overturned and the police attacked. There were other ominous signs, too. It was mid-June, the height of the tourist season, and yet there were many vacancies at the hotels. The small restaurants and cafes, usually packed to overflowing, attracted only modest crowds. The press estimated that this year only a quarter of the normal number of tourists had come to Greece because of the political crisis.

Jason and Alex spent several weeks travelling around the Greek Islands. Everywhere they went the story was the same; the beaches were almost depleted of tourists and the restaurants were half empty. Even the locals seemed more interested in listening to the latest news than catering for the tourists who, in ordinary times, were their life's blood.

Jason appeared largely unaffected by all the commotion, but Alex became increasingly more moody and distant. The excitement of travelling was beginning to wear thin. He was haunted by the possibility of war and its consequences. But Jason scoffed at his fears and reverted to his usual argument. It was only a war of propaganda. Neither Russia nor America would ever commit itself to a war in the Middle East. 'They are like two cats on a wall spitting at each other,' he would say, dismissing the bother of it from his thoughts.

It was a cause of tension, even irritation, between them. For the first time on any matter of substance, Alex considered his brother to be at fault. His eyes were opened. He grew a little older that day.

After Greece they used a two-month Eurail pass to travel through the rest of Europe. Travelling north across the top of Italy they passed through France and then continued on to Barcelona in eastern Spain. Here the sun and beaches temporarily calmed Alex's nerves, although, as with Greece, things were unusually quiet for the holiday season. The tourists who were left were mostly part of longer Trans-European tours that had started months before the political crisis had worsened. Here the Middle East crisis took a back seat to wild rumours of troop mobilisations and fevered war preparations by NATO and Russia. This type of conversation made both the brothers angry - Jason because he felt the whole thing was ridiculous anyway, Alex because it fuelled his own fertile mind and made him even more anxious.

The brothers continued on their way along the Spanish coast into Portugal, then took the train north through France to West Germany and the Scandinavian countries. Here they began to encounter pockets of bitter resentment against the cruise missile bases, which had been installed throughout Europe. Originally designed to deter a possible nuclear attack, they now seemed more likely to make them a target of one. The soothing noises of an assortment of governments were met with sarcasm and ridicule from the press. Several times Jason and Alex had to intercede in arguments between Americans and Europeans which, but for them, would have ended in blows. But this was no way to spend a holiday. Finally, feeling that enough was enough, they cut short their European trip and took a train to London.

Both Jason and Alex had lived in London during their childhood. Their parents had come originally from Southampton, but their father, who had worked for a large insurance company, had been transferred to London when Jason was seven and Alex was six. A year later he received the opportunity to head the Australian branch of the company in Sydney. It was too good a chance to miss, though they were sad to go. Alex could not remember a great deal about London, except that it was a very ancient and cold city, with huge sandstone buildings and rows of red brick houses stacked against each other in endless lines. As they approached on the train, he was pleasantly surprised to find that it was warm and not all the houses were joined together.

When they arrived at Victoria station, however, all thoughts of sightseeing were quickly driven from their thoughts. The news services carried the frightening news that America had successfully launched and tested swarms of powerful laser satellites using CubeSat technology. These satellites used new miniaturisation technology which reduced their size to less than twenty centimetres in diameter. Each CubeSat could collect, store and concentrate the sun's rays into powerful laser beams capable of destroying targets only metres across on the ground or at sea. This put all Russian ground and sea forces at risk. Russia's only option was to destroy the larger spy satellites that would provide the target information to the CubeSats. Russia responded by stating: 'Unless the Government of the United States suspends all space weapon research within the next forty-eight hours, Russia will destroy all suspected American spy satellites already deployed in space.'

The American president responded with the statement, 'Any destruction of American property or the killing of American personnel would be considered an act of war.'

The world hung on the next move in an increasingly dangerous and high-stakes chess game. As the hours ticked by, the refusal of either side to back down raised the tension to fever pitch.

In London, the news services started continued coverage of the crisis. All communication servers were overloaded as people tried to contact their friends and relatives. Airlines reported huge crowds and advised passengers not to contact them for tickets, since all flights out of London were fully booked for the next seventy-two hours. The brothers had already lost their chance to leave the country.

That afternoon a high absentee rate was reported at work as people went home at lunchtime instead of returning to their offices. All major arterial routes out of London were completely clogged with traffic by the late afternoon.

It was impossible to turn on the radio or television without being bombarded with official broadcasts urging people to remain calm and above all 'stay put'. Reinforcing your own home and stockpiling food were promoted as the most realistic and practical ways to prepare for any contingency. All major media outlets began issuing government pamphlets entitled 'Protect and Survive'. Banks reported huge monetary withdrawals, while panic buyers besieged the commercial sector. Building materials, petrol and food supplies began to run out within hours because of the unprecedented demand as people tried to follow government advice to the letter. To prevent large-scale movements of population, the broadcasts announced that most major arterials out of the city were only open to essential services and that those who abandoned their homes would face being turned back. Hospitals started to stockpile food and medical supplies; firemen, military, police and government officials throughout the country were placed on the highest alert. All demonstrations were immediately banned and their leaders detained.

The government termed these 'precautionary measures,' their effect, however, was to send the public into a frenzy. Supermarkets were besieged by panic buyers who fought each other like animals for the last scraps of food. Shops were broken into and not only for food. Gangs systematically looted whatever could be taken.

As neither power showed any sign of weakening, the first suicides were reported. Fires, accidentally or deliberately started, broke out all over the city. These often burnt unchecked as traffic tangles blocked the streets and firemen deserted their posts to join the rush for food and supplies. During the night, Harrods department store burnt to the ground, unattended by any emergency services.

The British government gagged the more sensational news outlets, tightening its grip on the media, so that only official government statements could be broadcast. The Prime Minister appeared briefly on television appealing for calm and explaining the necessity for invoking very wide powers. These included an indefinite freezing of petrol and food supplies, control of essential services including fuel depots, power stations, major industries and factories, and a temporary cut in gas and electricity, so as not to trigger any more fires.

Then, thirteen hours before the Moscow deadline, Washington issued the following statement: *'Negotiations at the highest level have been going on between Washington and Moscow since the Russian ultimatum. Both countries have agreed to suspend all space arms research in the hope of negotiating a peaceful solution to the arms race in space.'*

The news swept through the streets of London, sparking off impromptu street parties. The dancing and celebrating lasted well into the night and the next day. The power came on again and the Prime Minister went on television and announced several days' holiday and, with a broad smile, that this would mark a turning point in relations. The press, who had already dubbed it the 'Star Wars Crisis', reinforced the Prime Minister's sentiments with sparkling commentaries on the delicate behind the scenes negotiations that had achieved this success. The tabloids meanwhile focused on the suicide and crime rates. Figures were bandied about suggesting as much as a twenty-fold increase in crime and an eight-fold increase in suicides. The general feeling was that the world had been through the most critical forty-eight hours of its history. It had been brought to the brink but had drawn back in time.

Alex and Jason had spent these fraught two days in a backpacker's hostel near Victoria Station. After it had become apparent that conflict had been avoided, Alex bought several of the major newspapers and both sat down to read through them. Alex's paper had the headline: '48 HOURS OF TERROR'. After a brief article stating that the talks were making good progress it went on to focus on domestic news, recounting several family tragedies which had arisen as a result of the crisis. In one, the parents had administered lethal doses of tranquillisers to their children before dosing themselves and going to bed. Another man had shot dead his neighbour's family and stolen their food after an argument in a super-market.

In other news, control of the essential services had not been relinquished and the press still suffered censorship restrictions. The official campaign centred round the 'Protect and Survive' pamphlets, had been cancelled, but the standard warnings on protecting your home still continued to appear in the media. Re-stocking of the supermarkets had begun, but was painfully slow, and petrol supplies were still being limited.

Alex paused in his reading and looked up. Jason was deep into a dense article covering the lead up to the crisis. The writer concluded by saying that both sides would need to make significant concessions on the issue of arming space if a lasting peace was to be established. He grunted at that and glanced up.

'It seems,' he pondered, 'that there will have to be compromises by both America and Russia. They say here that this should take place over the next week.'

'Do you think they can reach an agreement?' Alex asked.

'Uh? Yes, of course they can,' the reply came back sharply.

'What I mean,' Alex continued, deciding to risk Jason's anger, 'is that neither power has made any compromises yet. They've just agreed to start talking again.'

'They've hardly had much time, have they?' Jason answered irritably. 'Arms limitation agreements can't be hammered out over lunch, you know. It could take weeks or months for them to reach common ground.'

Alex shrugged. Jason could be right. It was hardly fair to expect an agreement right away, when they had failed to reach one in over seventy years. He was probably over reacting, as he usually did. The British government was just being cautious, winding things down slowly. He stroked his chin, realising that he hadn't shaved, or had more than a few hours' sleep since the ultimatum had been announced. He now felt dirty and very tired, but his mind wouldn't let him rest. He wished he felt easier about the situation. When he had arrived, the grandeur and antiquity of London had seemed to linger in every street and building, urging him to wander endlessly, just to soak up the atmosphere. Now he felt he was living in a death trap. He knew something of the possible consequences of a nuclear exchange. If London was hit, many of its older suburbs would burn for days, incinerating tens of thousands of people. Then the lethal fallout would start. He didn't know much about the specific medical effects of radiation, but he had read enough to realise that the homeless would not survive for more than a few days out in the open.

'Why don't we start travelling around Britain now, and find a job in a couple of months?' Alex asked, on impulse.

Jason, aware of the reasons behind Alex's request, sighed deeply and put on a resigned expression before he spoke. 'If you feel safer in the country for the moment, I suppose we can go travelling for a few weeks until this whole thing blows over.'

Alex smiled back thankfully. At last, he felt he could relax a little.

Over the next few days, Alex collected piles of holiday brochures and scanned online timetables and tourist guides. Jason had stipulated that they should only be away for a month, before returning to London to look for a job. The cheapest form of travelling was coach or train, but neither of them felt like enduring the hassle of that again; besides, they had money left over from their incomplete European trip. So, after obtaining a range of car hire prices, they decided to drive.

On the morning of the fourth day after the end of the crisis, Alex and Jason took the motorway west to Devon and Cornwall. As soon as they could, they turned off and took the back lanes and secondary roads through Berkshire and

Wiltshire. They had lunch not far from Stonehenge, then travelled on to Bath that afternoon. As in Europe, accommodation was easily found, even at this time of year. After a couple of leisurely days spent sightseeing around Bath, they set out again at a lazy pace, making their way towards Cornwall. It was the seventh of July; midsummer in England, and the earth was covered in a plush carpet of green. Every plant or bush seemed to have burst out in spectacular bloom. Flowers of all shapes and sizes were in every cottage garden or window they passed. Jason was driving, while Alex had the window wound right down and the radio on. The sky was clear with only a hint of cloud on the far horizon. Alex lay back enjoying the sweet, heavy scent of flowers coming from the hedgerows along the roadside. Each time the car reached the top of a rise, the brothers could see the gently rolling hills stretching out in front of them. The occasional clusters of thatched or slate roofed villages only added to the already picturesque scene.

While driving, Jason was busily explaining some elaborate plans for hiking and fishing from one end of the country to the other. He seemed to have forgotten that there was ever a threat of war. He never spoke of it; he seemed to regard the whole episode as a closed book. Alex had not forgotten so easily but for him, too, it was like a nightmare they had put behind them.

Alex was just about to weigh in with his thoughts on the most scenic route to follow when he noticed that the radio had gone dead. Before he could reach across to fiddle with the dials, however, an official sounding baritone voice spoke.

'Attention, please! Russia has launched a large number of medium range intercontinental nuclear missiles! It is believed they will detonate over Britain in the next ten minutes. Please leave the streets immediately and seek shelter in the nearest building. If you are in a car, stop where you are and enter the nearest brick or concrete structure. The basement of any house or building is the safest. Please seek shelter immediately - this is not a hoax. Do not leave

your shelter until the authorities tell you to do so. I repeat: this is not a hoax. Seek shelter immed...'

As the broadcast continued the voice began to falter and crack. It mispronounced words and stumbled over phrases, then in mid-sentence the radio went dead. For an instant Alex saw Jason's confused features, then everything turned into a chalky brilliance, as if a dozen suns had suddenly exploded around him. He felt a blistering heat on his face and instinctively dived under the dashboard. The car crashed into the large removal van they had been following. The impact flung both brothers forward, then back as their seat belts restrained them; then forward and back again as the car behind careered into the boot. The front windscreen showered over them, then the back one immediately after. And still the heat remained. A searing heat that lasted for many seconds and forced Alex, already cut and bleeding, to squirm further under the dashboard for protection. There he waited, still held by the seat belt, but with his back exposed and burning, until his shirt felt as if it would explode into flame and shrivel him up. But, as quickly as it had come, it was gone. Alex was left severely winded, breathing painfully, covered in a lather of sweat. He gripped the dashboard and tried to pull his head up. A dreadful pain seemed to radiate from his neck, making him gasp and slump forward again. He could hear Jason's uneven, heavy breathing above the screams and shouts from outside. Finally, gaining some control over his voice, he croaked, 'JASON!'

The rhythm of his brother's breathing continued, but there was no response.

Ignoring the intense pain in his neck, Alex twisted his head around.

'JASON!' he screamed again, with rising hysteria, as he saw his huge bulk lying over the steering wheel. His head was caught awkwardly between the spokes and his arms dangled uselessly down each side of the wheel. A huge gash above his left eye almost concealed his face under a multitude of coursing red lines. Some of the blood ran off his nose, while other lines converged on his open mouth and streamed off his upper teeth and onto the spokes of the wheel. Only Jason's sharp, irregular breathing convinced Alex that his brother was still alive.

Then a shuddering, deafening roar drowned out everything. The remaining windows blew out and the car rocked violently. Alex could barely hear his own screaming above the blastwave. He put his hands over his ears, sobbing and yelling uncontrollably. When the noise finally died away and the ringing in his ears had lessened, he tried again to sit upright. Lifting his head with his right hand and levering himself up from the dashboard with his left, he slowly eased himself back. A surge of pain shot up his neck and he flinched with a sharp stabbing pain in his ribs. His breath started coming in short painful bursts and his head began to swim. He turned towards Jason and began to reach over to him with his right hand, but the effort seemed to require a strength he did not possess. His vision blurred, his hand seemed to creep forward as if time had slowed to a trickle. Then the image of his beloved brother faded into white. His head sank forward again, and he lost consciousness.

CHAPTER 2

The fusion reaction was over within a millisecond. It liberated vast quantities of radiation, heating the surrounding atmosphere to temperatures approaching the surface of the sun. This created a huge, incandescent fireball, visible a hundred kilometres away. As the fireball grew it emitted energy in the infra-red spectrum as a heat pulse, lasting over fifteen seconds. All structures in its path were vaporised up to a kilometre away. At five kilometres it charred wood and incinerated people; at ten kilometres it caused second-degree burns, igniting clothing, shrubs and trees. Its effects did not die until fifty kilometres away.

As the fireball continued to grow it touched the ground and seared out a crater thirty metres deep and three hundred metres across. Everything was turned to dust and vapour and thrown into the atmosphere in a huge mushroom cloud. After several more seconds the fireball reached its maximum diameter. The sudden heating of thousands of tonnes of air created a wall of high pressure, which travelled outward from the explosion at the speed of sound. Structures that had withstood the heat pulse, were blown apart by these over pressures and by winds which, near the centre of the blast, reached well in excess of a thousand kilometres an hour. As other blastwaves from other detonations met and collided with it, hurricane force winds ripped in one direction, only to be cancelled out within a few seconds by winds of equal strength blowing from another direction. Fires started by the heat pulse were fuelled into forest fires by the blastwave. In heavily bombed areas, cities disappeared under fire-storms. Smoke and dust quickly blotted out the sun. In the space of less than an hour, much of the greenery had been wiped from the face of Great Britain. In its place was a wasteland, ravaged by fearful winds and fires burning endlessly and out of control.

Alex had been conscious for several minutes, but had not moved from the thin, mouldy smelling mattress he had been lying on. He had drawn several deep breaths, moved his limbs around cautiously and found he was basically unhurt. His senses had cleared, too. He was acutely aware of a multitude of burned, broken bodies around him. They generated a rich, sickly smell, a combination of acrid burns, antiseptic, blood and sweat, which made him almost convulse whenever he took a deep breath. He could not believe this was happening. He found it impossible to collect his thoughts or focus on anything other than the pain and suffering that was going on around him. In one devastating blow he seemed to have been thrown into a pit of human agony. It was like waking up in hell.

He closed his eyes and concentrated hard on the events leading up to the car crash; the distraught voice of the broadcaster, the blinding flash, the heat and the thunderous roar. Then he remembered Jason's face, white, blood soaked, and he began to panic. He dragged himself upright against a sandstone wall at the head of his mattress and began searching amongst the injured. From his new position, he could see right across the room. Only it wasn't really a room, more like a large chamber, holding maybe two hundred people. And it seemed to be underground, or at least the windows were high up. In the centre a number of large columns sprang from a single base and arched towards the roof. Each column had several lanterns suspended from it, providing the only lighting. He could see at once that there was a rough approximation of order in the arrangement of the injured. Close to a large wooden door at the far end of the chamber sat a large number of people who appeared to be uninjured, except for the odd bandage or facial burn. On the far side, sitting in small groups, sometimes many to a mattress were the more serious cases, each patched up with wooden splints, slings or long jagged lengths of bandage. These people, unlike the crowd near the door, talked little; they stared dully at the boarded-up windows or appeared to be listening to the different tones of the wind, as violent gusts flung themselves against the side of the building. Finally, there were the worst cases, furthest from the door; very few of these poor souls moved at all, and if they did, they usually groaned softly to themselves. Alex searched this group carefully, looking for a figure with a heavily bandaged face, but the light was so bad he couldn't make out any detail. He was contemplating trying to climb to his feet to start his search in earnest, when he noticed a woman watching him.

'You're awake!' she exclaimed, and she began to clamber over the thick tangle of bodies separating them.

She was a very large woman in her mid-forties, with a round head and pink cheeks, which made her look as if she was permanently blushing. She reached the end of his mattress.

'How do you feel?'

Alex felt terrible, but he merely shrugged. 'A bit sore.'

She nodded. 'My name is Katie Fletcher. I was there when they pulled your friend and yourself out of that car.'

'My brother,' Alex blurted. 'What happened to him?'

'He required further medical treatment, so they've taken him to the local hospital some distance from here.'

'What kind of treatment?'

'He had lost a lot of blood and his face needed stitching.'

Alex stared at the woman for a moment longer, then finally lowered his head.

Katie had not realised they were brothers. It always seemed more tragic when families were split up. 'I'm very sorry,' she went on softly, 'but the hospital wasn't far from the scene of the accident and I'm sure they made it there safely.'

Alex nodded doubtfully. 'When do you think I can leave here?'

She lowered herself onto the mattress beside him and studied him carefully. 'I can't place your accent,' she said after a pause.

'Originally my family came from Southampton, but we left for Australia when I was young,' Alex explained.

'So your brother's the only family you have in England?'

'Yes, apart from a few cousins in Southampton.'

'I see.' She looked solemnly at him. 'And your name?'

'Alex Carhill.'

'Well, Alex, I don't think you quite realise what has been happening whilst you were unconscious. The explosion that caused your accident was the first bomb to land in this area. That's why we were able to rescue you. Any later and the fallout would have made any rescue attempt suicidal. There have been many more detonations since, especially to the east around London.' She glanced at her watch. 'It's only just past three in the afternoon, but already it's dark. Fallout has been coming down for hours. Anyone who went outside now would receive a lethal dose of radiation within minutes.'

Alex looked closely at the boarded-up windows. The wind had splintered some of the boards, but there were no shafts of light filtering through the cracks.

The woman lifted one of her fleshy arms and pushed some hair out of her eyes, following his gaze. 'Until the radiation level drops, we all have to be patient,' she said sadly. She glanced over the other side of the shelter then pulled herself to her feet wearily. 'Anything you want? Food? Drink?'

He shook his head. 'No, thanks.'

'Try and get some sleep,' she advised. 'Tomorrow things may be better. Just call if you need anything.' And with a brief smile she turned and was gone.

Alex watched her heavy frame work its way slowly over the injured until he lost her among the background of bandaged forms near the door. His eyes returned to the barricaded windows and he attuned himself to the sound of the wind as it played amongst the ruins outside. 'Tomorrow things may be better.' Her words bounced mockingly around his head. Tomorrow things would be worse, he was sure of that. And the next day, and the next week, if help didn't arrive, the situation would become horrific. As the food and water ran out there would be arguments, then fights and finally murders. He crawled back onto his mattress and pulled the blanket over his head. He thought of his parents and friends in Australia, but it was Jason who was in the forefront of his mind, and he was amazed to find himself praying for him. Not out of religious conviction, but from the sheer terror and hopelessness that comes from finding oneself in a situation over which one has no control. His prayers, however, did not ease his fears. He felt he was asking for a favour from a God he had cared little about before today. The last moments of the car crash came back and he tried hard to console himself that Jason was not seriously injured, but his body started to quiver and shake and he found he had no control over it. Only when he let his mind go blank could he wrestle the spasms into submission. Sleep when it came was total, dreamless, absolute.

Near the limits of the troposphere the millions of tonnes of soot and debris thrown up by the nuclear detonations had cooled and formed the nucleus of raindrops. As these raindrops condensed, they turned into black, billowing clouds. These clouds quickly climbed into the stratosphere and as the mushroom clouds of the holocaust dispersed, erupted in a deluge of black tarry rain. The rains fell all night, violently at first, as the winds drove them against the earth, but then with steadier insistence. The land grew cooler, but soon another wind, from the cooling land masses of Europe, was sweeping in and rising in intensity. By morning, the gentle breeze had freshened into a gale and had whipped up enormous seas in the Channel. These seas pounded the ocean retaining walls in the south east of England and flooded all the low-lying areas.

Alex, waking early, lay listening to the rain. He still felt sore, but his appetite had returned and his headache was gone. He also had a raging thirst, which the rain only made worse. He pulled off his blanket and sat up. Most people were still asleep, but the sound of coughing and someone being sick was audible across the shelter. The windows had been reinforced with plastic while he slept, but otherwise nothing had changed, except that maybe the air smelt more of sweat and antiseptic. Tucking his shirt in his trousers, he climbed to his feet and started picking his way in the direction of the door.

A short time later he found Katie in the corner of the shelter, talking with two other people.

'Feeling better, I see?' She greeted him with a warm smile.

Alex thought she looked terrible. There were deepening rings of exhaustion around her eyes and her cheeks, pinkish a day before, had drained to a pale grey.

'Would you like something to eat or drink?' she asked.

'Some water, if you have it,' he replied, still watching her closely.

She filled up a glass from a plastic water container. 'I don't blame you for not feeling much like eating,' she said, flashing him a reassuring smile. 'No one, including myself, has eaten much since this whole ghastly business started.' The smile had vanished again almost before she completed the sentence. 'I'm sorry I can't offer you more water,' she continued, watching Alex drain the glass greedily, 'but until we are more aware of the situation outside, we have to be very careful with our supplies.'

Alex nodded, for the first time noticing the men Katie had been talking to.

'Oh, I am rude,' she said. 'This is Kenneth Ward.' She gestured towards a thin, sour looking man on her right, who

20

nodded stiffly at Alex. 'And this is Jim Harrison, our local doctor.' A man, about Alex's height, and wearing a pair of steel rimmed glasses with one of the lenses cracked, shook Alex's hand.

'Kenneth is this area's civil defence organiser. He's responsible for organising emergency help and food supplies in case of a disaster,' Katie continued.

Alex detected a note of sarcasm in her voice, but Kenneth, it appeared, either didn't care or couldn't be bothered to react to the taunt. He fixed his cold gaze on Alex.

'Katie has told me you want to leave for the hospital as soon as possible.'

'As soon as the radiation count drops,' Alex corrected.

'Ah.' Kenneth looked at him thoughtfully. 'But the radiation count will not be dropping for some time, you understand?'

'How long?'

'I cannot give you a precise answer to that question,' came the reply. 'But until I say you can leave, you are not to go out of that door. Is that clear?'

Alex nodded, frowning as he did so. This man had an arrogant, rasping voice and his manner would have been offensive, under normal circumstances, but Alex sensed he was near the end of his tether.

'You see those people over there,' Kenneth continued, pointing towards a group huddled in the corner opposite them. 'Against my better judgement, we let them in late yesterday afternoon. I doubt if any of them will survive for more than a few days. They are already running high fevers and vomiting continuously.'

'But some will live,' the doctor interrupted. 'People vary immensely in their abilities to tolerate radiation. We have no idea how much these people may have absorbed, or how much the people on the other side of the door have absorbed.'

He jabbed a finger toward a large wooden door a few metres away, and Alex felt the tension between the two men suddenly rise.

'You have no right,' the doctor continued in a raised voice. 'No right at all to deny people this shelter. I have a duty…'

'Don't start talking about your duty again,' Kenneth said acidly. 'I'm not going to let people in who have absolutely no chance of survival. They'll only deprive us of valuable food and water before they die.'

'They had a chance for survival late yesterday when they first started knocking on the door. We should have let them in then. They may still have a chance now, if only you would unbolt the door.'

'It's too late!' Kenneth growled. The finality in his voice seemed temporarily to silence the doctor.

Suddenly, as if to reinforce the doctor's plea, the door shook under repeated blows as if boulders or wooden beams were being hurled against it.

Under the violence of the assault, it creaked and groaned, but the large metal latch and reinforcing sandbags showed no signs of weakening.

'What happens when they start using axes?' the doctor groaned.

'If they had axes, they would have already used them,' Kenneth replied harshly.

The group fell quiet, listening. Alex wondered how many times they had already reached this same impasse during the night. Finally, when the doctor could bear it no longer, he stormed off towards the other end of the shelter, shaking his head as he went. Soon after the pounding stopped, faint cries and sobbing could be heard next, until they too ceased and there were no more sounds.

'Let them in,' Alex pleaded with Kenneth. 'At least they will die in the warmth and not alone.'

The sour faced man glared at him, but he seemed beyond arguing the point any further. He turned and walked away without comment.

Alex was left with Katie. When she looked up at him her eyes were moist. 'Yesterday we should have let them in, that was wrong of us,' she admitted. 'But now it's too late, unless you want to watch people die slowly in front of you without being able to do a thing to help them.' Then she too, walked off abruptly.

Alex stared at the door for a long time. His conscience told him to cross the short distance towards it to draw back the bolt and fling it wide open. That would have been the humane and proper thing; but he, no more than Katie or the doctor, could do it. At length, shamefacedly, he shuffled back to his mattress and crawled in under his blanket again.

Over the next few days, the temperature over Europe began to plunge, reaching temperatures below 50 °C in the Baltic States. Only the moderating effect of the North Atlantic drift current tempered the advance of nuclear winter over Great Britain. But the temperature had still dropped far below zero by the third day, turning the intermittent rain into snow showers and blizzards.

Clothes and blankets became a much treasured and sought after commodity in the shelter. Arguments as to the ownership of these precious items began to flare; there were cases of theft and even of stand-up fights. Finally, when the temperature fell to below 15°C, Kenneth reluctantly authorised the use of several gas burners for warmth.

These were set up in the centre of the shelter, which immediately became the focal point of activity.

As the days wore on, a routine of a sort began to emerge. Twice a day a small ration of beans and rice was dished out in plastic bowls. Between mealtimes, the occupants of the shelter huddled close to the fires and would only leave to collect their ration, or to relieve themselves in the latrine, a small hole cut through the floor. Alex did the same, at the same time picking up what information he could by talking to people. This was how he learned that the chamber was actually the crypt of a fourteenth century church. While he had been unconscious the roof of the church had caved in, but the massively built crypt had escaped with no more than shattered windows and a few cracked ceiling joists. He was also delighted to find several people who had had friends or relatives taken to the same hospital as Jason. It was located twelve kilometres east, on the other side of the village. Together they all agreed to set off in that direction, as soon as it was safe to do so.

By the fifth day radiation counters poked through small holes in the boards covering the windows showed that the radioactivity had fallen to a third of its level on the night of the holocaust. When Alex asked Kenneth about leaving, however, he merely pointed, in his curt fashion, toward the group of people who had been let in on the first afternoon. 'Do you want to become like the others?' he would say, and that argument seemed unanswerable.

For, of the sixteen-people admitted on that occasion, ten were seriously ill and three had already died. Alex, like many of his companions, found himself irresistibly drawn to this wretched group. He was totally unaccustomed to death, or even serious illness. In fact, he had never even been to a funeral or suffered anything more serious than a broken bone in his life. But now, like a spectator at the scene of a grisly road accident, he watched in horror and fascination as the sickness withered and decayed their living bodies. Each individual seemed to be affected differently. The three who died in the first few days rapidly progressed through vomiting and diarrhoea, to cold sweats and severe stomach cramps, which made them clutch their stomachs and scream in agony. Katie did her best to sedate these patients with pills, but they could not keep the medication down. When the morphine ran out, their screams echoed through the shelter for days. Then, almost thankfully, they went into shock and began to twitch, their breathing became irregular and they slipped into a coma and died. But the others hung on for much longer. They reached the vomiting stage and then seemed to improve. Their fevers broke and they managed to take a little of the broth that Katie had prepared, but their bodies still continued to decay. Their hair started dropping out by the handful, purple blotches appeared all over their skin and perpetual diarrhoea withered them into skeletal forms, too weak even to move out of their own excreta. Many times their helpers tried to clean them up, but they only made more mess and contaminated valuable blankets and clothing. Finally, six days after they had been let in, their fevers returned and they quickly succumbed. After a week, eleven out of the original sixteen had died. More floorboards were torn up and their bodies were lowered in, along with any clothing they had worn.

The unfolding misery of these people had a profound and sobering effect on the rest of the shelter. Alex couldn't imagine a more painful, lingering death. The pitiful creatures they degenerated into had lost most of their resemblance to humanity. They were hairless, shrivelled, and blotched over every centimetre of their skin. Their suffering, more than anything else, made him realise the immensity of what the bombs had inflicted.

On the night of the tenth day, Kenneth was able to announce that the outside radiation level had reached a point that was tolerable. However, he warned that anyone venturing out shouldn't expose themselves to the elements for more than a few hours at a time.

The next morning, Alex and eight others, assembled in front of the door. Their leader was Hugh Trent, a local villager who had been separated from his parents in the confusion immediately following the first attack. He would guide them as far as the hospital before leaving to search for his parents. The group carried no provisions except for a medical kit, several torches and two litres of water. They were each kitted out in the shelter's limited supply of wet weather gear, leather boots and balaclavas. These had been supplied to them on condition that they scavenge for food, water and warm clothing for the shelter. Kenneth had given them a number of hessian bags and water containers, which they could fill with supplies as they passed through the centre of the village.

When all the preparations were complete, Alex and several other men removed the sandbags and unbolted the door. The assault on the door had not lasted beyond the morning of the third day. Alex had no illusions about the fate of the people outside, he only hoped they had crawled into a nearby house to die. To everyone's relief they found no bodies on the stairs. The steps were covered in half a metre of black snow and ice. Although it was nine o'clock on a summer's morning, there was hardly any light coming from the surface.

The members of the party pulled on their balaclavas and gloves and began making their way upward one at a time. All around were wooden beams used in the abortive attempt to break down the door. At the top of the stairs a small hole had been forced through the debris, but even here, there was no sign of recent footprints. They emerged and followed their leader into what had until recently been the vestry of the church. The room was now open to the sky and covered with nearly a metre of snow. A large section of the roof had collapsed over one of the standing walls, making an alcove of sorts. Hugh shone his torch in there, while the rest of the party continued on; he beckoned to Alex to join him.

As Alex had feared, Hugh had found the bodies of the people who had been locked out. Most were huddled in tight bundles at the very back of the alcove. One of the bodies was that of an elderly man. He must have died before the rest because his body had been stripped and pushed away from the others.

Another corpse was a youth about Alex's age. Most of his hair had gone, except for parts of a red beard, which still

26

clung, in ragged patches to his chin. His face was expressionless, his right fist full of hair, as though one of his last acts had been to pull all his hair from his head. Large ice crystals dangled from his nose and the remains of his beard, giving him a glassy, almost waxy appearance, like a figure in a museum. Alex couldn't tell much about the other figures, except that amongst them, there was a woman and a child, frozen together like some bizarre ice sculpture.

There were also a number of tins of food, all unopened. The large amount of human excreta and of vomit explained why they had remained untouched. Alex had expected to feel shocked, but he found he was only saddened. Already he was adjusting his pre-war concepts of normal and abnormal to fit this new reality. He realised he had expected to find them in this exact condition; no other outcome would have been possible after their exposure to such high levels of radiation. Both men returned to the party without mentioning what they had seen.

They left the church and were met at once by the full blast of an oncoming blizzard. Stinging pellets of snow, driven by the wind, slowed them down to a crawl. To Alex it felt as if he was experiencing the final burial of his world. The lush, green countryside he had marvelled at only ten days earlier had vanished under a poisonous sheet of snow. Trees, many defoliated, hung over them like giant broken skeletons in the gloom. Their branches, dangling like many broken limbs, swinging and pivoting wildly in the wind. Only the houses remained intact - lifeless, shadowy lumps of brick and wood.

Soon the party stretched out into a long line. The wind velocity increased further, forcing them to bend nearly double to make headway. Hugh forced the pace, stretching his lead over the others until he was only a faint blur against the fury of the blizzard. But the party could only travel as fast as its slowest member, and soon he had to pause to allow the others to catch up. It took nearly two hours to cover the four kilometres to the village centre, and by then many of the party were nearly spent. Several times in the last hour they had to stop to allow the stragglers to catch up. Once, a large woman in her forties collapsed and Alex and another man found themselves supporting her for the rest of the way. Only a lull in the storm and an easing off of the wind enabled them to reach the village.

Hugh finally called a halt in a former bakery shop. The rest of the party struggled in and collapsed unceremoniously on the floor. Outside, another blizzard was converging on the village. Within minutes the greyness was complete. Even the few lights coming from the second and third storey shop windows across the street had vanished. Alex took off his gloves and tried to warm his fingers by breathing on them. He had lost all feeling in his fingers and his toes about half an hour before. His face had also gone numb, making him think seriously about the possibility of getting frostbite. Having spent most of his life in Australia he had very dim memories of this type of cold. In London, as a small boy, he remembered playing in the lights of the street lamps after dark until his feet and hands had become completely numb. But then he could always run inside and warm up; now he felt he could never be warm again.

After they had rested a little, Hugh got to his feet and addressed them. 'I know it means carrying heavy packs to the hospital and back,' he said, studying their exhausted faces, 'but I think we should collect our supplies now.'

His words brought an immediate and angry protest. Most vocal was a short stout man, named Ted Richards, of whom Alex had already formed a very poor impression. For the last hour, he had been complaining bitterly, and he had flatly refused to help any of the weaker members of their group when they got into difficulties.

'Why can't we pick up the supplies on the way back?' Ted asked arrogantly.

'Because it may be several days before we can return,' Hugh replied. 'All the shops may have been ransacked by then. We must be sure of collecting the supplies we came for.'

'But no one's going to go out in this.' Ted waved his arm in the direction of the blizzard, which was now blowing directly through the broken shop window.

Hugh said quietly; 'It's been eleven days since the holocaust. If everyone has done what the government has told them and only stored two weeks of food, then their supplies will already be running low. When they realise there is no help coming, they will start to panic.' He gave Ted a frosty look. 'I'll wager a lot of the food has already been taken from these shops.'

'But the government will soon be coming to help us!' Ted stated confidently.

Hugh shook his head solemnly. 'There won't be any help around here for a long time, perhaps never,' he replied. 'Nobody would leave a cosy shelter to come out in this, the government least of all. They will wait until the worst cases have died before they attempt to feed the population. Otherwise, they would be wasting their food.'

'You're just guessing,' Ted retorted, though his voice was tinged with uncertainty for the first time. 'The government could already be on the surface trying to restore order.'

But he had already lost the argument. Hugh just shrugged. 'I'd rather be shot looting than die of starvation,' was his only comment. The others murmured their agreement and Ted, finding himself with no support, sat down suddenly and did not pursue the argument.

As there were no further objections, it was decided to spend the next couple of hours searching the shops for supplies. The general reluctance of the group was overcome when Alex suggested that only those supplies needed immediately should be taken with them. The rest could be hidden in one of the shops and picked up on the way back.

After a while, the storm passed over and the company wearily resumed their journey, this time in search of the shopping centre. Alex was given a hessian bag and assigned to a large supermarket at the end of the street. He went in through the smashed glass panels at the front, kicking away the snow piled inside and climbing over one of the checkout counters. The floor of the supermarket must have been awash before the temperature dropped below freezing, because it was now covered in a black sheet of ice. He flashed his torch down the aisles until he found the dried food section. Kenneth had given very specific instructions on the type of food to collect. Only packaged food was to be taken, preferably dried, with a high content of protein and complex carbohydrates. In places the shelves were empty and packages of food had spilled onto the floor, but it was impossible to tell whether it was looters or the holocaust which had caused the mess.

Alex opened his bag and started working his way along the shelves, reading the labels and trying to deduce the best items to take. At the end of the aisle, he came to a frozen meat section, which appeared to be largely untouched. He thought of a roast leg of lamb with fresh mint and lots of gravy and stuffing. The memory brought back the smell of the roast coming out of the oven, and a sudden sadness overwhelmed him. That would be another thing he would only ever dream of in the future. He turned away, then stopped, a small figure was huddled between some empty shelves. It was such a shock that he let out an involuntary gasp. The figure was completely motionless, and for a second Alex thought it was another frozen corpse, but as he looked closer, he saw its chest was moving. Its head was between its knees and covered by the hood of a large, bulky jacket, which also hid much of the figure's body. He took a few steps closer and shone his torch over it. The head moved sluggishly, like someone awakening from a deep sleep.

'Excuse me,' he said softly.

The head jolted back abruptly, and Alex found himself staring down at a woman around his own age. For a moment they gaped at each other, both too startled to speak. She had

30

dark hair pushed back loosely; accentuating the pallor of her face, but her eyes remained bright and intense.

'I was searching for food when I noticed you here,' Alex said awkwardly. 'I thought you might be hurt or sick.'

'I'm not hurt or sick,' retorted the women, shaking her head defiantly.

He hesitated, then suddenly realised he still had his balaclava on and hastily pulled it off. 'I'm, Alex Carhill,' he said shyly.

The women's eyes focused on the half-filled bag he was dragging behind him.

'Supplies,' he explained with a sheepish grin. 'We've stopped off briefly to get some supplies.'

'We?'

'Yes. I'm with a group of people travelling to the local hospital.'

'The hospital?' she echoed.

Alex explained about the car accident and how Jason and he had been separated. She slowly nodded as he spoke, but her face soon became dull and lifeless. Her eyes focused on a point somewhere beyond him, and he doubted if she had heard anything. His voice trailed off and ended in mid-sentence. He stared at her again, feeling uncomfortable.

'Look, I don't know what your situation is,' he said, trying another tack, 'but it seems to me that anyone sitting in a freezing supermarket in the dark must need some help. Don't you have any family, friends, anyone at all you can stay with?'

For a moment she seemed angry at his question. Her mouth tightened into a thin line and she returned his stare fiercely. 'My parents are both dead,' she said. 'The house we were staying in collapsed. I'm the only one left.'

'Oh, I'm sorry, I didn't know,' he said lamely. 'Do you know anyone in the village?'

She shook her head.

'I see...' He lowered the torch slightly, so she only appeared as a dark shape amongst the shadows of the shelves. 'So, what will you do?' he pressed softly.

'There's nothing I can do, except wait until the weather improves or help arrives.'

'But suppose there isn't anyone left to help?' he asked, lifting his torch so that he could see her face again.

'Then I will have to cope as best I can.'

Alex watched her face carefully and felt sure he could see the first signs of self-doubt and confusion flicker across her features. 'Why don't you come with us?' he asked. 'If you stay here you could freeze to death and you'll meet a lot of people scavenging for food. I'm sure they won't have any qualms about taking your food supply, if they can't find any themselves.'

She glanced around at the ice-covered floor and the scattered cans of food all around her; then she folded her arms as though suddenly feeling cold.

'There's nine of us,' Alex continued. 'I'm sure no one would object to one extra.'

'What will you do once you reach the hospital?' she asked.

He shrugged. 'I'll see what my brother wants to do.' There was a slight pause. 'We'll think of something.'

She bowed her head and stared at the ground. After a pause, she gave a brief nod and then looked up at Alex. Her face had visibly softened. 'I'd love to come along,' she said.

The party accepted the new recruit with little interest. The food was pooled and the bulk of it stored under some loose floorboards at the back of the bakery. Three days' supply was divided up between the members of the party. Although it was still snowing, Hugh was all for pressing on to the hospital where there might be some form of heating, rather than lingering near the shopping centre. So on they went.

As they walked Alex watched the woman closely. There was not much of her. She was small, with a slight, almost

32

delicate build. When she looked across at him he detected a depth of sadness in her eyes that nearly broke his heart. Almost without thinking, he reached out and put his arm around her. She smiled warmly at the gesture and Alex saw the softness in her. The suffering and loss was there, too, controlled, suppressed, but there all the same. He felt a sudden flood of feeling toward this woman, which astounded and perplexed him, so he shied away immediately. But the feeling remained, even though the moment had passed.

The women introduced herself as Tina Hartley. She had been holidaying in the area with her parents when the bombs hit. She was an only child, so the loss of her parents had hit hard. When it was clear that no help was coming, she had buried her parents amongst the ruins of the house. Since they had only a few days of food in the holiday house, after a week, she was forced to scavenge for food in the village.

After half an hour the snow had died out and the surrounding countryside became visible again. Spouting huge clouds of steam, the group had started a long ascent up a ridge. At the top, Hugh had assured them, they would see the lights of the hospital. Alex and Tina reached the top just behind Hugh. Both were out of breath. The rest of the group struggled up, one at a time, in a similar condition.

Hugh pointed to a group of lights at the bottom of the hill. 'That's it,' he announced. 'Probably no more than a kilometre away.'

It took another twenty minutes of hard walking to reach the complex, which, as they approached through defoliated trees, had a strangely forlorn appearance. Like a row of dimly lit street lamps, it stretched for several hundred metres in both directions, finally terminating in a large sprawling car park. It wasn't until they reached the perimeter of the car park that the now familiar smashed windows and blown in doors became evident.

They entered the reception area only to find it deserted. Tables and chairs had been overturned, debris lay about and patches of what looked like frozen blood stained the floor.

The party wandered around the mess in silence, hesitating in front of two large swinging doors. Beneath the doors, a shaft of neon light stretched across the floor. The signs above the doors read. 'Through to Wards 1, 2 and 3'.

Alex walked over to the reception desk. Most of the drawers had been pulled out in some previous frantic and probably quite pointless search. Its contents lay strewn around. The computer screen had also been smashed and now lay bent and twisted against a nearby wall. He picked through the rubbish with a sinking heart, then noticed a large book bearing the word 'REGISTER', written in bold black letters on the cover. With rising hope, he fumbled through the pages. It contained lists of admissions dating from the seventh of July, the day of the holocaust. He ran his fingers down one page, then another, then another until, scrawled in almost illegible handwriting he read: 'Jason Carhill, age 24, suspected fractured skull, Ward 3.' With a sigh of relief, he called the rest of the group over. Soon they were all eagerly gathered round the register. Alex pushed his way to the back and found Tina near the reception entrance.

'Is he here?' she asked anxiously.

He smiled at her. 'He's here all right, ward 3.'

Taking Tina's hand, he turned towards the swinging doors. But the distant crack of heavy boots stopped him in his tracks. The sound grew quickly, stifling even the excited sounds of the company. Suddenly the doors swung open and at least a dozen armed men, dressed in military uniform, burst in.

One of them carried a large kerosene lamp, which he placed on the floor between the two groups. The leader was not hard to distinguish; he towered over his companions, both in height and physique. His large, blunt features and flattened nose gave him the appearance of a prize-fighter, more than a soldier. His thick, meaty hands rested near the trigger of an automatic rifle. He didn't look too friendly.

Despite the warlike posture, however, Alex could hardly repress a smile; his uniform was several sizes too small for

34

him. His companions also wore dirty, ill-fitting clothes and several of them looked sick and weak.

The leader spoke in a rough, abrasive voice. 'There's no room for you here. This hospital has been taken over by the military for its own personnel.'

'We don't want medical attention,' Hugh answered. 'Over a week ago some road accident victims were admitted, we just want to visit them.'

The man shook his head. 'We don't have any road accident victims here, only military personnel.'

A voice from the group which Alex, to his dismay, recognised as that of Ted Richards, spoke up. 'So, what have you done with them?' The tone was unfortunate.

The leader of the soldiers glared at him. 'All patients who were not bedridden were asked to leave when we commandeered this hospital.'

'But these people were too sick to leave,' Ted replied.

The leader shifted his weight from one leg to another, frowning. 'When we arrived a few days ago,' he said flatly, 'there were no car accident victims here. I would advise you to leave.'

The uneasiness of his soldiers standing behind him was by now clearly evident.

'This country is under martial law, you could be shot for refusing,' he continued menacingly.

Exclamations of anger and outrage greeted this remark. Alex, knew how they felt, coming all this way, only to be threatened with death. But something told him that the slightly absurd-looking leader wasn't bluffing, and neither were his men.

Ted, however, failed to register this fact. He took another step forward. 'We know they're here; it was written in the register.'

Alex saw the leader glance at the book register, still in the hands of one of the company, then his face twisted into an ugly snarl. 'If you don't leave now, we will open fire,' he said forcibly.

Alex gripped Tina by the arm and guided her towards the back wall. He judged they would have to cover about five metres to the door if the firing started. The atmosphere had become electric. Both sides now tried silently to assess the intentions of the other. Once again it was Ted who, with monumental stupidity, broke the deadlock. Blindly, he blurted; 'And whose bloody authority gives you the right to take such murderous action?'

The answer almost tore him in two as the leader opened fire. His men responded, cutting down the screaming company in a sudden volley of lead. With the first shots Alex dived for the door, dragging Tina after him. They spilled out into the snow, clambered to their feet and ran round the side of the building towards the distant trees. Behind them others of the group had emerged and were sprinting wildly in all directions. Alex looked around and saw one figure falter, then collapse. A second weaved in and out of the cars. Several men gave chase, stopping periodically to aim their rifles. In the hospital, the last shots rang out, finally silencing their victims' hysterical screams.

Alex and Tina reached the shelter of a small wood some sixty metres from the hospital. Driven by sheer terror, neither looked back for signs of pursuit, but crashed through a tangle of fallen branches and splintered trees. Finally, Alex tripped and ended up face down in the snow. Tina followed, landing heavily on top of him. For several minutes, they lay where they had fallen, panting heavily, too scared to talk or make any noise at all. But there was no sound of pursuit, or searchlights probing the woods.

Tina was first to recover. She sat up and asked Alex if he was all right. Alex only nodded. It had all been so sudden.

Tina waited, seeming to sense what Alex was thinking, but finally even she could tolerate his silence any longer. Not knowing what to do next, she moved closer to him and put her hand on his shoulder. 'I'm so sorry,' she said softly.

Alex turned on her. 'I'm going back,' he said.

'Back where?' she asked, puzzled.

Alex climbed to his feet. 'I need to find Jason…to be sure.'

'Jason is dead, you can't change that.' Her voice climbed the scale.

But he pulled away from her. 'I'll be back,' was all he said before he ran off, leaving her floundering in the darkness behind him.

Alex was driven by emotions he never thought he possessed. Hate consumed every thought, every fibre of his body. He wanted someone to tell him that Jason was dead, then he wanted to make them suffer as he was suffering, as he would suffer in the future.

He reached the perimeter and found that the complex had two back entrances. A guard was posted at each one. Creeping closer, he noticed a place where several large oak trees overhung the roof. Quickly he retraced his steps and made his way to within twenty metres of the trees. When the guard turned his back, he sprinted across the snow, gripped a low hanging bough and hauled himself up. The darkness was almost complete above the level of the windows, but by feeling around he found a branch that seemed to lead in the direction of the roof. He started to slide along it, knocking off the snow as he climbed. After several false starts, he managed to ease himself along far enough so he could drop onto the roof. It was icy and very slippery; he almost slid straight off the edge when he landed. Eventually, however, he found himself crouched above one of the guards. The man stood perhaps two metres below him, slowly pacing the base of some stairs. He turned again, and at the same time Alex jumped, driving his feet into the man's back as he crashed down on top of him. The guard fell heavily onto the snow, then lay still, breathing in short gasps. Alex carefully rolled him over. The man's eyes widened when he saw him, but Alex had already winded him beyond any serious struggle. He picked up the man's rifle and torch from the snow and dragged him under the stairs.

The torchlight revealed a youth in his teens, with short prickly hair and an acne scarred face. Alex propped him up against the stairwell and shone the torch in his face. 'Who are you?' he growled.

The youth was reluctant to speak, but Alex placed his right hand around his throat and squeezed until he began to cough and splutter. That appeared to do the trick!

'I come from Taunton, east of here,' he croaked. 'We found a military base a few days ago with uniforms and arms. We decided that if we posed as the military, we could get food more easily.'

The words came in a quavering rush as Alex tightened his grip.

'Get food more easily,' Alex repeated slowly. 'By killing all who stood in your way, you mean.' He pushed his head against the stairwell and squeezed until the youth's face turned bright red.

'No!' he squealed. 'I haven't killed anyone. There was some shooting when we arrived, but I had no part in it.'

'Is that supposed to make me feel better?' Alex snarled.

'Look, mister,' the youth pleaded. 'There was over thirty of us, we needed food and shelter, most of us are suffering radiation sickness and the government refused to help us. I've lost my family; most of us have lost someone. In Taunton, the military are guarding all the stockpiles of food. Can't you see, we had to do something? If we had stayed out in the open for much longer, we would all have died.'

Alex stared at him for a moment, then reluctantly loosened his grip. 'Are there any patients left alive?'

The youth dumbly shook his head.

'Why did you have to kill them all?' Alex cried.

'They wouldn't let us in. Said we were too contaminated already. We had to shoot our way in and some of the guys went crazy, they shot everyone.'

Alex sat back in the snow. Tina had been right; Jason was gone and nothing he could do or say would bring him back.

The youth, who had been watching him closely, his hand feeling his bruised neck, seized this moment to spring towards the opening of the stairwell. With a howl of rage, Alex drove his fist into his jaw, smashing his head against the concrete staircase. The youth slumped to the ground, unconscious. Alex stood looking down at him for some time before collecting the torch, the revolver and rifle, and sprinting off into the approaching night.

CHAPTER 3

Tina had clawed out a hollow amongst the roots of a large, knotted oak tree and placed Alex's pack on the bottom to stop the cold seeping into her bones. The base of his torch was embedded in the snow next to her, so as to light up the tree like a homing beacon, in case Alex should come to his senses and decide to return. It was completely dark now. The temperature had dropped, and it had begun to snow again. She pulled the hood of her jacket further over her face and watched the flecks of snow drift through the light beam. It made her mad just to think of it, his running off and leaving her like that, without a word of explanation except a fleeting promise to be back later. And now she was so bitterly cold, almost frozen, and so weak that she could hardly move, all through waiting for him. As soon as the snow eased, she swore she would leave, but then she would never know what happened to him. Another shivering attack made her teeth chatter uncontrollably. She huddled closer to the tree and curled up into a tight ball.

A sudden noise made her look up. Beyond the torchlight, she caught a flash of light and heard the sound of branches being forced apart. *Someone was coming!* And it couldn't be Alex, as his torch was here. She began to panic. Wrenching her hands from around her body she lunged at the light, knocking it over in her haste, so that the beam shone momentarily in the direction of the sound. Now stricken with terror, she plunged it into the snow, finally locating the switch to turn it off. Still the light came closer, flashing through the miniature network of bracken and thistle which concealed her. Then it paused, no more than ten metres away. She crouched silent, trapped, her heart pounding.

'Tina?' A harsh whisper drifted across on the wind.

'Over here!' she hissed back, almost crying with relief.

The torch shone on her, blinding her for a second. The large shape of Alex trudged towards her and stopped a short distance away.

But once Alex was in front of her, tangible and solid, her relief turned quickly to rage. *'Get that bloody light off me,'* she fumed.

Alex obeyed immediately, fully expecting a flood of verbal abuse.

She rose to her feet, her whole body visibly shaking from the cold. Alex wanted to take her in his arms to beg her forgiveness, to physically squeeze away the cold and pain. But something in her stance told him she was too angry to be won over by such action. His hands hung by his sides. 'I'm so sorry.' He couldn't think of anything else to say.

But when she spoke, it wasn't with raging abuse, but a cold, reasoning anger that cut into him like a knife. 'What did you hope to achieve?' she asked. 'You left me here and I don't have the faintest idea where I am. You asked me to come with you and then you discarded me like a used....' She searched hopelessly for the word. 'I don't know what...like garbage you would throw in a bin.'

Alex nodded his head stupidly.

He had been imagining terrible things. She might be dead, or too frost bitten to walk, or, worse still, that she might have gone off. 'I'm so sorry,' he repeated miserably.

'I didn't even know if you were coming back!' she flared. 'So far I have been dragged who knows where, shot at and then deserted!'

She was beginning to shake so much that he could hear her teeth chattering. They stood facing each other, neither speaking nor moving. Finally, Alex took a few tentative steps towards her. When she didn't back away, he gently wrapped his arms around her. She didn't resist; instead she pushed her frozen hands under his jacket.

41

'I nearly froze to death waiting for you,' she continued, her voice losing some of its bitter edge.

She unzipped his jacket and buried herself deeper in his warmth. They held onto each other for a long time. Alex, too, had become very frightened at the thought of losing her, more than he had ever known. For he was alone now. There was no one he could turn to, no guide, no Jason... He was stranded, he knew not where, with a woman he had met only a few short hours before. He squeezed her more tightly. At that moment, he needed her more than he had ever needed anyone in his life.

When her shivering finally wore off, she asked him what had happened at the hospital, but he couldn't bring himself to explain in any detail. His only reply was that his brother was dead. 'They've killed everyone,' he said miserably.

It took them over an hour before they found a village where they could seek shelter. It was a small cluster of houses nestled along the banks of a stream. By this time both were tottering with cold and exhaustion. The snow had stopped, but the wind had increased in strength, driving against them with malevolent intent. Tina seemed to be walking in a dream, only remaining on her feet through some inborn stubbornness that refused to let her legs buckle beneath her. Alex was in better condition, but there were numb spots on his face, and he had lost feeling in his fingers and toes. His rib cage was also hurting again, making each breath sharp and painful.

They fought their way through a large, snow crusted hedge and dropped into a lane, which led down to the village, both quickening their pace at the sight of the houses.

Alex, who was slightly ahead, came to a halt outside a small stone cottage where a light was showing in a front window. He could also see smoke coming from the chimney. Tina shuffled up, no longer able to lift her feet high enough to avoid leaving a set of drag marks behind her. He helped her over the front fence and along the garden path. Then, plucking up his courage, he tapped on the door. Almost immediately there were movements inside, but no one came to answer. He knocked a second time and a man's voice rang out; *'We have no food here, please leave us alone!'*

'We're freezing to death!' Alex called. 'We just want shelter for the night!'

'Please leave us alone!' the voice repeated.

'You must help us!' Alex pleaded. 'We have been walking all day and we can't take another step!'

Another voice now joined in with the first in a muffled discussion.

'We do have some food. We'll trade it for some warmth and a place to sleep for the night!' Alex added hopefully.

The murmuring stopped and the door opened a few centimetres. A middle-aged man with greying appeared in the gap; then, seeing the rifle strapped to Alex's back, he recoiled in fear. But Alex was too quick for him. Jamming his foot in the door, he threw all his weight behind it. The door crashed into the man and sent him sprawling across the floor.

'I'm sorry, I'm sorry,' Alex said immediately, grabbing Tina's arm and pulling her inside with him. 'But I wasn't prepared to be locked out.'

The man dragged himself to his feet and stood next to a small, plump woman and a young girl. The three of them stared at Alex and Tina, their faces white.

Alex continued stumbling for words. 'We need warmth…and shelter,' he repeated. He saw that they were looking at his rifle, so he lifted the strap from his shoulder and dropped it on the floor. 'I found it. I don't even know how to use it,' he quickly explained.

Reassurance started to creep back. It was the woman who spoke first, tapping her partner on the shoulder. 'Come on, Tim, they look harmless enough. Where are your manners? Invite them in.' She turned to Alex and Tina. 'I'm sorry, but you gave us quite a turn. If you stand in the hallway a moment longer you'll catch your death. Come in and warm yourselves in front of the fire.'

Alex almost burst out laughing. He could hardly believe a place like this still existed. They were shown into a small, immaculately kept lounge, with low dark stained wooden beams and a large open-hearth fire. The newcomers wasted no time in reaching the fire and discarding their outer garments.

The woman reappeared, bringing dry clothes and offering a cup of soup from a pot that was simmering by the fire. This was greedily accepted. Both, however, found that their heads, rather than their stomachs, had done the talking, for once the cups of soup were in their hands, they were unable to eat, despite not having taken anything all day. The warmth of the fire seemed to deaden their bodies in some way, and induce in their minds a type of narcosis, so that only the pain of their thawing arms and feet appeared to be real. Looking across at Tina, Alex saw that she had already lost her struggle to stay alert. She stared into the fire, oblivious to her surroundings, swaying gently on her knees, her hands clasped firmly around her cup, like a drunk clinging to his drink at the bar.

For Alex, this was the first time he had seen Tina in anything stronger than torchlight and with more than her hood peeled away from her face. She had shed her jacket and several layers of jumpers in her haste to feel the warmth of the fire, leaving only a thin blouse, the top unbuttoned and soaked from the snow that had seeped in under her jacket. Her hair was also wet and hung in a dark tangle of springy curls around her shoulders. She raised a hand carelessly to brush it back from her face. She had small, almost delicate features, with a finely cut nose and thin eyebrows, which curved downwards slightly and gave her a brooding or thoughtful look. Her eyes, now blinking slowly with fatigue, appeared almost too large, like some creature used to the night. Her mouth was wide, but her lips were thin and stained blue with cold, so they stood out against the paleness of her face.

Noticing him watching her, she smiled, and at once her features, almost sad before, radiated such warmth and beauty that he felt like reaching across and touching her. Indeed, he would have done so if they had been alone, but the man had seated himself in a large, leather covered chair close by, and was leaning forward determinedly, studying them with a mixture of apprehension and suspicion.

He introduced himself as Tim Wane. His wife's name was Margaret, and their daughter was Anne. Alex and Tina, Alex mostly, began to tell them about themselves, until the horrified expressions on the faces of the family almost stopped him. In normal times their village had been insulated from the outside world by the surrounding hills; now, those same hills had protected them from the worst effects of the heat pulse and the blastwave. They were the first, it appeared, to have come that way so far seeking food and water; and the news they brought with them plunged the man and his wife into despair.

'I should have guessed,' Tim said, bowing his head. 'Before you came, I wanted to believe that Britain had not been seriously damaged.' He gestured to one of the windows. 'I thought this weather would only be temporary. The sun would soon return, and truck loads of food and water would be coming down the road any day. From what you tell us, that no longer seems likely. But what are we to do when the strangers start to arrive? We've only so much food. We can't afford to share it with all and sundry. I don't mean you, of course,' he went on hastily. 'It's the future we're worried about.'

'You've just got to face facts,' Tina said sharply. 'Just a few bombs didn't cause this weather. It's a major attack; maybe there's no government left to distribute food. We were at the hospital. What happened there is going to happen in every building and shelter where supplies of any sort are to be had. Your whole village should wake up to that fact now, before it's too late.'

Seeing the surprise and confusion in their faces, she frowned.

'You're agonising over the wrong question,' she continued. 'You won't have the choice whether to turn people away. They'll smash in your doors and windows; they'll tear up your floors for firewood. Your only chance lies in uniting the village into some type of fighting force to warn off the gangs that will be coming after your food.'

There was a moment's silence while her words sank in. 'I don't think you're right, you know,' Tim said defensively. 'I've already intercepted radio broadcasts, which claim the government still exists. Oh yes,' he went on, registering their startled looks, 'I have a shortwave radio set. I took the precaution of disconnecting the battery and aerial a few days before the attack. When I reconnected it, a few days after the holocaust, I found it still worked. I've been monitoring the airways ever since.'

'Go on,' Alex prodded.

'At first, I found nothing, not a whisper, despite scanning all the frequencies for several hours each day. Then I started picking up brief messages, very faint and with a lot of static, possibly from ham operators. The set has a range covering most of England, and Wales, and parts of Scotland and Ireland, so it may be that these broadcasts were a long way away.'

'What did they say?' asked Tina.

He shook his head. 'The messages kept fading in and out, so I rarely managed to get a complete sentence, but from what I could gather they were reporting on the damage in their areas and asking for help. But a couple of days ago, I suddenly received a powerful transmission, claiming to be the government broadcasting from the outskirts of Bristol.'

'Bristol?' Alex repeated, remembering what the youth at the hospital had said.

'It didn't last long, and it said nothing about how the war started or how the country as a whole fared,' Tim continued. 'But it did say they planned to start distributing food after the fourteenth day of the attack. Until then they advised everyone to remain under cover to avoid fallout. Oh, and one other thing. Tim leaned back in his chair, his eyes troubled. 'They said that at eleven o'clock tomorrow they will broadcast more information on where the food distribution points are located and the conditions under which one can obtain food, whatever that means.'

That night Alex and Tina only picked at the hot, steaming food placed in front of them. Alex hoped the radiation they had received would produce no more serious symptoms than nausea, however, while he quickly sank into an exhausted sleep, Tina's temperature began to rise. After half-an-hour she vomited up her dinner and for the rest of the night she had hot and cold flushes, diarrhoea and further vomiting. At one in the morning Alex woke up and kept watch over her till the Wanes took over. At breakfast, he was offered cereal and some fresh bread which had been baked over the flames of the fire the previous day. Although he had no appetite, he deliberately forced the food down, then tried to snatch a few more hours' sleep.

Tim woke Alex mid-morning and led him to a small room at the rear of the house. The radio occupied a large table in the centre of the room. Tim switched it on and tuned the dial. At eleven precisely, the static suddenly stopped and the following statement was issued: *This is an official broadcast by the wartime government. Great Britain has suffered a major nuclear attack. Most military installations, industrial and population centres have been hit. You are warned to remain in your homes. Large movements of people from the towns have been reported. We advise all would be refugees to turn back. Anyone committing violent acts will be shot. The government is doing its best to implement emergency measures. Food rationing centres will be established on the outskirts of cities in a few days. Country areas will have to live off their own produce until the situation improves. Food rationing will be on the basis of health and willingness to work. Fifteen hundred calories will be given to those who agree to work; non-workers will receive five hundred calories. All hospitals are severely overcrowded; resources are limited and must be directed towards those thought capable of survival. The government realises the hardship these measures will create but no good will be served in this present crisis by a failure to face the present reality. We therefore implore everyone to work together to improve conditions and reduce suffering as much as possible. A further report will be broadcast at the same time, on this frequency, tomorrow, and thereafter at times to be announced.'* The voice cut out abruptly.

'Fifteen hundred calories a day,' said Tim shaking his head, as he turned off the set. 'That's hardly enough to sustain a human, let alone keep him fit enough for a full day's work.'

Alex nodded grimly. 'And if you refuse, you starve to death on five hundred calories a day. People won't take that type of treatment, they'll riot.'

'Yes,' Tim agreed, 'they'll overrun the food stations, then head for the country to grab what food they can.'

The conversation had echoed what Tina had said earlier, Alex thought. Tim said nothing more, but Alex knew he was also mulling over Tina's comments.

After lunch Alex wandered restlessly about the house, from room to room and from window to window, peering out into the overwhelming greyness as though a different angle on it would somehow show a chink of light. But his mind was busy. He was turning over the events of the past few days, trying once more to come to terms with the disappearance of his former life, his prospects, his family and Jason. Who knew how far this contaminated wasteland stretched? Perhaps all around the world, so that there would be no escape from it. In the living room, he approached the window and rubbed some of the condensation off the panes with his sleeve. Large flakes of snow jiggled their way past and settled on the growing heap on the sill. He tapped the glass and the snow subsided, but at once more flakes settled and began to rebuild, as before.

The door opened and Tina came in, walking unsteadily. She gave him a half-hearted smile, then sank down onto a chair.

Alex thought how weak and fragile she looked; though he knew there was an enormous depth of strength within her. 'How do you feel?' he asked.

She shrugged. 'In a day or two, I'll pick up. How about you?'

Alex was silent, knowing that it wasn't his physical condition she was enquiring about.

'Are you still thinking about Jason?' she persisted.

He made a face.

'You must have been very close.'

He began to fret at this. These were his personal concerns he did not want to discuss. He hunched his shoulders and turned to stare out of the window.

'It might help if you talked about it?' she probed further.

He said sharply; 'I don't want to talk!'

She leaned back in her chair.

At that moment, he just wished she would go away. That would be the tactful thing, not to probe any further. But she remained where she was, her hand pressed lightly to her lips.

'You and I are very different,' she said, after a long period of silence. When he still didn't respond, she continued, 'you brood over the past and let it distort your reasoning.'

That was more than he could stand. He turned around sharply. 'There's nothing wrong with mourning the dead!'

'If that's all that you're doing?'

'And what is that supposed to mean?'

'You're not just feeling sorry for yourself, are you?'

Her question infuriated him. 'Aren't you upset that your parents died?' he snorted. 'Don't you care?'

'I loved them,' she said simply. 'But they're dead. There was nothing I could have done to prevent their deaths.'

'And that's it, is it?' he fumed. 'That's all you have to say?'

'Yes. Oh, don't look so superior,' she continued, seeing his disgusted expression. 'You don't hold the monopoly on feelings. I hurt just as much as you do, except I choose not to dwell on it. Nothing has ever been changed by dwelling on the past.'

Alex held her gaze for a moment longer, then sighed and turned away. 'It's not just the past,' he said in a low voice. 'It's everything past, present and future. I don't think I'm capable of surviving in this world, and I don't think I want to.'

'You mean you want to give up?' she asked. 'Lie down and let someone finish you off, like they do a lame horse? You may as well have let them shoot you at the hospital.'

'I had someone to live for at the hospital. Now I have nothing. What's the use of dragging on from day to day, week to week, just for the sake of it? Not knowing where your next meal is coming from, or if the next people you meet will try to kill you for your food? Too scared to relax for a moment and all the time slowly dying of radiation sickness?'

'Things are not that grim,' Tina said firmly. 'You're letting your imagination run away with you. It won't be like this forever. We've only seen what it's like here; this may be the worst there is.'

'No, you know that's not true. There will be much worse. The country may never recover; for all we know the whole world may be in this state.'

'If it is, we'll have to accept that. You can't give up just because the going gets tough!'

'Why not?' Alex exclaimed. 'What's the point of going on?'

50

'You can't just quit life like it was some hobby you've lost interest in.'

'No,' he agreed. 'If only it were that simple.'

There was sudden silence after these last words which made him look across to see what she was thinking. She had an almost quizzical expression on her face, as though she could not make him out at all. 'What are you trying to say, Alex,' she asked finally.

'It's just ... 'He paused with the effort to condense his thoughts into words. 'It's just that I don't want to be responsible for a person's death.'

'Life, Alex,' she corrected, 'a person's life. You have already assumed that we are going to die.'

He threw back his head, his hackles rising swiftly again. *'I don't assume we're going to die,'* he almost shouted. 'I'm just scared of someone else depending on me. I'm not a natural leader. I'll probably let you down.'

She nodded, as his meaning became clear at last. 'I'm not depending on you or anyone,' she replied firmly. 'I'll make my own decisions on my future. What happens to me will be my own doing and nobody else's.'

He shook his head. 'If we continue to travel together, then like it or not, we will be depending on each other, Tina. I'm just saying I don't know how I will react in a difficult situation. Don't you ever feel frightened? Don't you wonder whether you'll have the strength to survive?'

'Yes, but I can only do my best. If it's not enough,' she shrugged.

'The hope's there, Alex,' she continued. 'Be strong. We have only to find it. And I think we've as much chance as anybody.'

There was a ring of truth about this. The slate had been wiped clean. It was up to the survivors to inscribe it, if they had the courage. And if they had not, then they could die like the rest. Reluctantly, he turned back from the window to nod his agreement, but to his surprise the chair was empty. Tina had already left the room.

Over the next few days, he spent most of his waking hours talking to Tina. Their discussions ranged widely, and whatever the topic, he found her mind alert and her insights deep and probing. He had never met anyone like her. Before long most of the emotional barriers behind which people shield their more delicate feelings were breaking down. The speed at which their relationship progressed scared Alex. He told himself the reasons were obvious. They needed each other. Survival depended on mutual trust and commitment to each other. He wondered in normal times whether he would be this affected by her. Something told him he probably would be.

Tina began to regain her strength and their talk finally returned to their present situation. Both agreed they must leave the Wanes as soon as she was strong enough. The government broadcasts had indicated that the country areas would be receiving no help, at least for the foreseeable future. This meant that the Wanes would need every scrap of food they had stored.

Alex asked Tim for maps and they both set to work finding the places least likely to have been affected by the holocaust. Tim pointed out the location of the village. It was some thirty kilometres east of Taunton, and very nearly on the Somerset-Dorset border. To the west lay the counties of Devon and Cornwall, which had little in the way of military bases, industrial centres or large cities. Wales was in a similar position, except for its southern fringe. After a lengthy discussion, it was agreed that they would head north to the Bristol Channel and cross over into Wales. Cornwall, it was true, would be closer, but would be more likely to be inundated with refugees than north Wales. Also, the more isolated Welsh hills might not have suffered such heavy fallout as further south. Of course, all such plans could only be tentative, for no one knew what the conditions were really like; they were only formulated as a guide, to be changed as circumstances might direct.

On the fourth day after their arrival, they were ready to set out. The Wanes came to the front door to bid farewell to their visitors. Alex had managed to squeeze into a pair of old walking boots of Tim's, and Tina too had a new pair of boots belonging to Margaret, who wasn't completely satisfied until they were both covered from head to foot in thick woollen clothes. Tim had also given Alex an old cloth daypack, a compass, maps and enough food for five days. In return Alex had handed over his rifle and ammunition. He insisted that they take it, saying that it would only attract attention to themselves. The gift was gratefully accepted.

Leaving the village, they steered a course roughly northwards, skirting, with the aid of the map, the major roads or settlements where they might meet other, more desperate survivors. The weather was showing a slight improvement; the snow had stopped, and the fog had receded enough for them to distinguish the shapes of houses in the distance. Travelling was still very difficult, however, as the recently fallen snow remained soft and powdery, reaching above Tina's thighs at times in snowdrifts.

By mid-afternoon, they had descended into a large fog bank further down the valley. Alex had only very dim memories of the fogs of London. How delightful his boyhood memories seemed in retrospect, when he had played with Jason, dancing between the wisps of mist that drifted under the streetlamps. But this fog was nothing like that; it felt wrong, dirty, grey, defiled in some way. The air seemed almost liquid, a liquid that scalded the throat and burned the lungs. It reminded Alex of the old pea-souper smog's he had read about that used to choke London before they banned coal fires. And it was so unbearably cold. Soon ice started crystallising on his clothing and across his eyelashes and eyebrows. His hair became stiff and brittle, where his breath froze on it. The world had become a grey, pitiless place.

Soon the visibility dropped to less than ten metres, forcing Alex to switch on his torch. Sounds, also, were distorted in some way, so that noises that may have been hundreds of metres away were amplified and misdirected until they seemed to be coming from many directions at once. Before they had entered the fog, Alex had noted a river about two hundred metres on his right. The noise from the river now seemed closer and mixed in with it were definite sounds of people trudging through the snow. It was as though they had unwittingly stumbled across some major thoroughfare. Occasionally they could hear voices, too, raised in anger and laced with violence and fear. They quickened their pace, stumbling in their anxiety as they tried to steer a course away from the voices closing in all round them.

After nearly an hour, tired from their own exertions, they heard several shots very close by; but again the direction eluded them. Only minutes later they came across two bodies, still shedding their blood into the snow. The faces of both were bloody stumps from shotgun blasts; the clothes all but stripped from them. Two sets of footprints led off in the direction from where they had just come. The murderers must have passed within a stone's throw without knowing it. The shock of this discovery sent a fresh wave of panic through Alex and Tina. They began to imagine pairs of hands coming at them through the mist, crazed faces suddenly appearing around every hollow, every crevice.

Alex's plan had been to follow the direction of the valley northwards, but the thought of spending a night in this treacherous fog almost sent him crazy. After some discussion, they decided to abandon the valley and head eastward, hoping to strike higher ground and rise above the fog. Over the next hour, they scrambled and clawed their way up the slopes, their fear overriding their fatigue. Several more distant shots sounded, along with other indications of people passing just out of sight. Occasionally they even spotted shadowy forms, which quickly merged into the greyness again, obviously as terrified as they were of meeting a violent end. Then, as suddenly as it had appeared, the mist thinned out and was gone. They had climbed above the fogbank, they were free, somewhere on top of a snow encrusted ridge overlooking a desolate world. They hugged each other and laughed hysterically. They had woken up from a nightmare.

They found shelter for the night in a small wooden shed, filled with machinery and sacks of foul-smelling fertiliser. Amongst the sacks they discovered the bodies of a man and a woman, with a young child only a few years old. Like the outcasts who had been denied entrance to the fallout shelter, they were moulded around each other, their expressions dull, lifeless, suspended until the world thawed and the process of decay rotted them into the fertiliser they had so desperately huddled against for warmth. Alex and Tina clung together in the opposite corner of the shed, both too cold and frightened to allow themselves anything more than a fitful sleep.

When morning arrived, they rose wearily and forced down some dried fruit and cereal biscuits which Margaret had made for them the day before. Outside, the weather continued to clear, the fog of the previous day having dissipated leaving a blackened, snow-covered landscape. The light had even improved slightly, so that they could see over the countryside for several kilometres in each direction.

They made good progress northwards all that morning, only deviating from their route to avoid the patches of fog which still persisted in the valleys. By early afternoon the gently sloping land had given way to hills and large open pastures. Alex estimated they must have reached the start of the moorland, possibly only twenty kilometres from the coast. He was beginning to consider how they would cross the Channel when the sudden appearance of smoke coming from over a rise, drove all such thoughts from his mind.

They crept forward, taking advantage of the natural cover of the ground, to observe what was happening. From a hilltop, concealed among shattered birch trees, they cautiously looked down on a dozen, ragged people stoking up a large bonfire below them, while others were cutting up what looked like cattle carcasses. While they watched, a cattle grid was dragged over to the fire and mounted across two boulders. The sides of beef were then brought over and thrown on the grid. Soon the smell of roasting meat started to waft in their direction. The aroma reminded them that they hadn't eaten a decent meal since they had left the Wanes. Although they knew they couldn't risk asking for food, the smells and the sight made them linger.

'It'll be a nice, tasty roast when it's done,' a voice observed from behind them. They turned around sharply to find a short, stocky man carrying a stack of firewood under one arm.

'You two look like you're off on a couple of days leisurely hiking,' the man continued, surveying them with a faint smile.

'We're heading for the coast,' Alex explained, angry at himself for being caught off guard so easily.

'On your hands and knees, that'll take some doing, I shouldn't wonder,' the man continued with a grin.

'We were just being cautious,' Tina answered coldly. 'We've already seen a couple of murders.'

'Haven't we all, lass? But that still doesn't explain the outfits.'

'A family gave them to us a few days ago,' Alex replied defensively.

'You should've stayed with them. Around here you'll be shot and robbed if you look half decent.'

'And who are you?' asked Alex, ignoring the comment and springing to his feet.

'Me?' The man smiled. 'Shall we just say I'm a freelance poacher? We're all that these days, aren't we? How else can you survive?'

'So, you're on the run from the government?' Alex asked.

The man gave a short sarcastic laugh. 'I've got news for you, guv. We're all on the run from the government. If they catch you stealing food, they'll shoot you if you don't stop.' He paused, rubbing his bristly chin. 'Come to think of it, they'll shoot you even if you do stop sometimes. Who knows what happens to the poor bastards they take away with them?'

'So, you have had contact with the government then?' Alex asked.

'Oh, I've had contact with them all right. Six of our group were shot in a village yesterday by the military.' He nodded toward the fire. 'Take a good look at them. Six days ago, forty sick and homeless people started off from Bristol because they had no food, and the government wouldn't give them any supplies. Since then, some have died from the sickness, some have been arrested and some shot. There's only sixteen of us left now. We've lost our families, our homes, and now the government's trying to take our lives.' He took a deep breath and seemed to become calmer. 'You've been lucky, you've managed to keep out of their clutches, it seems. But watch your step from now on. And mind what I say, every man in uniform that you meet is your enemy.'

They listened to him in silence, glancing at each other.

'Come on,' he said, walking towards the fire. 'I've found some cows tied up in a barn a little way back. They were half starved, but at least they're not contaminated. In spite of your fancy clothing, you're probably as hungry as the rest of us.'

Without further comment, he strode off down the slope. After some hesitation, Alex and Tina followed.

The group at the fire eyed them with a mixture of suspicious looks and envious stares. By its light, they became fully aware of the contrast they represented to this company. Very few appeared to have escaped injury. Severely burnt arms and faces, broken limbs and festering wounds were abundant. All wore tattered or burnt clothing, often ill fitting, probably because the garments had been picked up along the way. Many had badly singed hair, or were in the process of losing it through radiation sickness. A glazed look of shock still lingered on many faces as though intelligent thought had been simultaneously burnt away with the holocaust.

'Not a pretty lot, are we? And we're the fit ones; those who were really bad we had to leave on the way,' the man commented aloud.

'Where are you all going?' asked Tina, hoping to change the subject.

'Cornwall, probably. Anywhere there might be food and no military,' the man replied, throwing the last of his wood onto the fire. 'You're welcome to join us if you like. The more able-bodied people there are, the better our chances of survival, as I see it.'

'We were thinking of trying to reach Wales,' Tina replied.

'Wales?' The man's face became thoughtful. 'Yes, North Wales is a possibility. Harder to get to than Cornwall, though, isn't it?'

'Yes, but it's even less inhabited, so we thought it's not so likely to have been a target,' Alex answered.

'True enough, but also less likely to have food, and the Welsh mightn't take too kindly to intruders. Still, it's as good a plan as any, I suppose.'

By this time the rest of the group had all but forgotten the strangers, being more intent on the progress of the cooking. When the food was declared ready, it was charred on the outside and almost raw on the inside, but it tasted wonderful! Alex and Tina tore into it eagerly. So did the others, although Alex noticed that after a few mouthfuls most of them seemed to lose their appetites.

Afterwards the man introduced himself as Cliff Benfield, a carpenter from Bristol. He hadn't been in Bristol when the bomb detonated but returned later to find his family had been killed by the blast.

'There was no warning, you see,' he continued. 'I just happened to be out of town on a job. That close to the detonation, most of the electrical systems and circuity had been fried by the blast. The population was on foot with no transport and little food. I lost my van to a mob soon after I arrived back. With no food and the government barricading the warehouses, a group of us decided to head for the country. We've been living off what we can find, and dodging patrols, ever since. The military seems to have control over the major towns, but for the moment, at least, the country is free of them.'

Well, that explained why Cliff looked in better shape than the others, Alex thought. He was just about to mention the government broadcast he had heard when the camp suddenly became flooded with light.

Everybody immediately began running in different directions. Cliff, more nimble than the rest, dived into the shadows, swearing, and Alex and Tina followed suit.

A voice from one of the surrounding slopes boomed: 'You're under arrest for looting. Anyone who tries to escape will be shot!'

Almost immediately there were gunshots and a scream of pain as someone was hit.

Alex drew his revolver and unlatched the safety catch.

Tina gripped his arm. 'Put it away,' she hissed urgently. 'If you start shooting, they'll find us in no time.'

Alex hesitated.

'Do as she says, you idiot,' Cliff growled.

Alex flicked the safety catch on and hid the revolver.

'Come on, this way!' Cliff motioned them.

The three of them struggled up the slope leaving long snaking trails in the snow. Behind, some of the group had been arrested next to the fire; others had been shot while trying to escape. Spotlights were now probing the surrounding slopes for people they had missed. Above them more beams of light appeared, making long, careful sweeps of the many leafless bushes and defoliated trees.

Cliff stopped by the base of a large tree. 'We'll have to stay here. I can't see any better cover up ahead,' he whispered.

The descending beams began to draw in towards them, accompanied by the crunch of footsteps in the snow. Below, gunfire was followed by a voice demanding surrender.

'Corporal!' a voice shouted. 'There are three trails down here leading toward you.'

'Yes, Sir,' came the reply from directly above where they lay.

'We're trapped,' Cliff groaned. 'Throw that bloody gun away.'

Before Alex could respond, however, a spotlight blinded them.

'All right, stand up, hands away from your bodies,' the corporal shouted.

More lights homed in on them as they slowly rose to their feet.

'Dawes search them!' the corporal shouted.

A blond man about Alex's height clambered down the slope and began frisking Cliff.

'He's clean, corporal,' he announced.

Stepping up to Alex he repeated the process, his grey eyes focusing suspiciously on Alex when he found the weapon.

'This man has a revolver. There's a serial number on it, could be army issue.'

The corporal came slipping and sliding down to join Dawes. 'So,' he said, eyeing Alex coldly, 'where did you get this?'

Alex hesitated. The truth sounded too incredible to be believed. 'A friend gave it to me, I don't know where he got it from,' he said weakly.

The corporal barked at once. 'Sinclair, take this man to the C.O.!'

Alex was separated from the others and taken back down to the bonfire.

The C.O., a bulky figure who sat perched on a log, warming his hands at the blaze, inspected Alex with an air of detached boredom.

The soldier saluted and repeated the charge against Alex.

Alex tried his story again, with a few embellishments.

The officer appeared equally unimpressed, his chin sinking further back into his neck as he studied Alex. 'He looks in better condition than the others,' he said finally. 'What he will be doing in the future will more than make up for his sins. Throw him in with the rest.' He dismissed Alex and his guard with a casual wave of his hand.

Alex was placed in with eight other survivors.

Tina hugged him warmly. Cliff looked surprised to see him.

'That can only mean they have something worse in store for us,' he said miserably.

Rapidly marshalled, the survivors started on a twelve-kilometre hike to the coast, more prisoners for one of the fast growing military run work camps now appearing throughout the nation.

CHAPTER 4

The loudspeakers blared.

'You have all been caught in the act of looting. As looters you have no rights under martial law. You will be required to labour ten hours a day, six days a week. Your period of internment will depend on your co-operation and what you achieve. Food will be provided according to the amount of work done. Any would be escapees will be shot on sight. You have been warned!'

The prisoners, who had so far listened in silence, now burst out angrily, expressing their outrage. They were gathered at the front gates of a large comprehensive school, hastily converted into a work camp. The march from the valley, where they had been caught, had taken four hours. No rests on the way, or stoppages of any kind, had been permitted. Those who were too sick or physically disabled to keep up had been stripped of all valuables, including food and water, and left behind. Of the original nine, only the five fittest remained. They had since been joined by other prisoners; wretched, frightened creatures who swayed on their feet and collapsed against the gates of the camp as though they had been walking solidly for many hours. Alex noticed that, despite their exhaustion, they were all in good physical shape and not one of them was older than his early thirties. Like his group, their weak and elderly probably lay strewn along their route.

Around the perimeter of the camp was a two-metre fence, with a coil of barbed wire attached to the top, so as to form a barrier nearly three metres high. Wooden watchtowers, each equipped with spotlights, were spaced along it at regular intervals. The old school fence, two metres in from the perimeter, marked the limit of the inner boundary of the camp. Between the two was the area known as no man's land, where inmates were liable to be shot if caught attempting to escape.

As the light faded, the guards started unlocking the gates. Like beggars scenting a meal, the new intake jostled forward. They could smell warmth in the waves of burnt ash wafting from the distant end of the playground, where the inmates had begun the nightly ritual of stoking up the bonfires against the freezing night. Barely waiting to hear that dinner would be at nine at the school meeting hall, they surged, Alex and Tina among them, towards the fires. Reaching the nearest one, Alex pushed through to the front impatiently, only to be driven back, so intense was the heat. At a more respectful distance, he and Tina stripped off their gloves and balaclavas and held up their frozen hands. All about them, sheets of plastic were being laid on the ground where the heat had melted the snow, and prisoners were kneeling or sitting down with blankets wrapped round their shoulders. Nobody spoke much, or moved far once they had settled themselves.

After a while, when they felt somewhat restored, Alex noticed Cliff on the other side of the fire talking to a large man in a leather jacket.

'Ah, the country hikers,' Cliff said, giving a friendly smile when he saw them. 'I've just met up with an old friend I haven't seen in years.'

He introduced Roy Flemming, also a carpenter from Bristol. Roy was a very striking figure, taller by a head than Alex. Cliff looked almost dwarfish beside him. But it wasn't only his height that was impressive; he was huge in every way. His chest was shaped like a beer barrel, his arms and shoulders were thickly muscled, so much so that they seemed to have swollen over his neck and joined directly to the sides of his head. Only his eyes were small, almost buried in his skull and covered by the thick mat of his eyebrows. He extended a massive, calloused hand.

'Roy's been telling me how he was arrested for helping an old man over a fence,' Cliff continued.

The huge man looked slightly embarrassed, smiling at this interpretation. 'Well, that's not quite true,' he said, his voice slow and good humoured. 'The man did happen to be carrying a sack full of stolen goods and I was doing a little more than just helping him over the fence.'

'How long have you been here?' asked Tina.

'A couple of days.'

'And how do they treat you?' Alex asked.

The carpenter shrugged. 'Hard work and not much food,' he commented. 'Still, in a way we're lucky. The damage around here is largely superficial, so they don't have any major rebuilding projects going on.'

'Roy thinks I'll be put to work repairing buildings the same as him,' Cliff added.

'And us?' Alex asked.

'Labouring, I expect,' Roy answered, his ruddy features becoming momentarily serious. 'That can range from anything from searching for wood, to stoking these fires, to clearing up partially collapsed buildings in town.' He turned to Tina. 'Women generally do lighter work in the kitchen,' he went on. 'But you'll find out what you'll be doing soon enough.'

Roy's words were echoed in a loudspeaker announcement later that night. New prisoners had to assemble in the schoolyard in the morning to be assigned their duties.

Dinner was in the school assembly hall. The new prisoners, now numbering over forty, were told they were part of the sixth and final meal sitting. Since the hall could only take a hundred people at any one time, and there were six hundred prisoners, feeding was a lengthy business, even with only half an hour allocated to each sitting. The meal had to be collected from huge vats at the end of the hall, eaten, and the plates washed and returned. Any slow eaters had their food confiscated and their ration reduced. By the time

Alex and Tina were served, twenty minutes of the allocated time was up. This left only ten minutes to gulp down a watery soup in a mug and eat a cold stew consisting of rice, potatoes, beans and meat. It tasted foul, but there was little waste. The new prisoners, in particular, attacked their food as though they hadn't had a square meal in days. Neither Alex nor Tina felt hungry, but both were too smart to pass up the opportunity for food.

When they had done their duty in the washing up queue, they trooped outside again where they found Cliff and Roy waiting for them. Roy had promised to show them where to find some spare mattresses and a place to sleep. He led them to a small building hidden amongst a patch of bent and broken beech trees. The sign at the front read 'ART SCHOOL'. Inside the walls were painted in a multitude of swirling primary colours, giving the place a slightly insane feeling.

'This building was only opened up yesterday,' Roy explained. 'I moved in straight away before it got too crowded.'

The room they entered was already half filled. Huddled forms under grey army issue blankets already lay along the walls. Roy fetched three reasonable looking foam mattresses and some blankets from an annex and quickly returned.

'I'm sorry I can't give you more than one mattress and two blankets each,' he apologised. 'But if the guards catch you with more than your ration, you'll lose the lot.'

He divided the blankets between them and headed for a vacant corner of the room.

'Why are there so many people already asleep?' Cliff asked.

'These people have been working all day. They're too exhausted to do anything but sleep once they have some food inside them.' He paused for a moment and looked around the room. 'You'll understand why after a few days,' he added quietly.

The air in the room was only marginally warmer than outside. There were radiators along the walls, but from the way the inmates ignored them it was obvious they were not working.

Alex asked if there was any form of heating other than the fires.

'Not for us,' Roy shook his head. 'The guards have their own generators though, which also supply power for the kitchen and the searchlights around the perimeter fence. What I do is to warm myself in front of the fire until I feel like I'm going to burn up and then quickly go to bed. That way you might fall asleep before you feel cold again.'

Alex and Tina were too weary to take Roy's advice. Tina pulled their mattresses together and cuddled up close, while the two men continued talking. Tina snuggled against Alex's chest and was asleep within minutes, too tired to discuss anything.

But Alex lay awake for a long time, listening to the sounds around him. Outside the wind had strengthened, hurling powdered snow against the boarded-up windows in fitful gusts, setting off a creaking, quivering song as the boards strained to burst the nails that held them. New prisoners came in constantly to collect their mattresses and blankets and fight for the rapidly vanishing floor space, like so many dishevelled dogs. Alex recognised many of them from the intake he had seen at the gates. Like Cliff's group they wore the same bizarre mixture of tight and loose fitting clothes. One man even had a woman's blouse on, over a tight pullover. Their varied costume probably represented the clothes of many corpses now lying stripped and frozen on the moors.

At ten o'clock the guards came to blow out the lanterns, and to order quiet. The command was almost unnecessary. Within minutes of lights out all talk had ceased and different sounds became dominant, tonal snores and the constant howling of the wind. In the total darkness, with Tina fast asleep in his arms, Alex's mind slowly relaxed into an exhausted dreamless sleep.

A high-pitched screeching burst from the loudspeaker system and tore into the bones of even the heaviest of sleepers long before light. Shortly after, their tormentors, the guards, appeared, each carrying a small wooden truncheon.

A guard leaned over Alex and poked him. 'Come on, rise and shine.'

Cliff was watching from his own mattress, close by. 'Can't you see you're disturbing his beauty sleep?'

The guard ignored him.

'The quicker you move the quicker you can have some grub!'

'And the quicker we do your dirty work,' Cliff added.

The guard glanced across at Cliff briefly but chose to ignore the comment.

'What's wrong…is it too difficult to talk and prod someone at the same time?' Cliff continued.

'I don't like this anymore than you do,' the man replied, 'but until the government can rebuild the country…'

'Rebuild the country!' scoffed Cliff. 'The military doesn't even have control of it. Last I saw of the military in Bristol the local population didn't seem too friendly to them.'

The guard's face hardened. 'If it weren't for us, you'd all be still wandering around in your shit, killing each other for scraps of food.'

'So, we should be grateful to the military for killing us instead,' Cliff responded scornfully.

The guard flushed. 'If we didn't stop the likes of you from murdering and looting, the whole country would still be in anarchy.'

'Hey, want to hear a secret?' Cliff whispered, beckoning him closer.

The guard leaned forward suspiciously.

'The whole country is still in anarchy, they just haven't told you yet.'

Several people listening to the exchange, laughed at this.

'We already have control of all the major towns in England!' the guard replied angrily.

'Oh yeah, by imprisoning the population in forced labour camps. And if anyone objects, that's fine, you just shoot them. After all, anything is justified under martial law.'

The guard glared at Cliff. The anger was vivid on his face, but he seemed at a loss to know how to reply.

'You have five minutes to get down to the mess hall,' he said finally before striding off down the room.

By this time, Alex and Tina were awake. Cliff caught them watching him.

He shrugged. 'I'm not the subtlest of buggers, I know,' he said dryly, 'but prancing down the room waking everyone like we were in some type of holiday camp.' He shook his head in disgust. 'It made my stomach turn.'

Breakfast was lukewarm oatmeal porridge with sugar, no milk and a weak mug of tea. The shivering inmates consumed it in silence; the line of whom stretched the length and breadth of the mess hall. It was six in the morning. Above the freezing mists and endless cloud banks that clogged the earth, the sun was just clearing the horizon. But at ground level the temperature was minus twelve, the wind was freshening, and more light snow was falling. The prisoners clutched their mugs and drained them before the tea lost all its warmth.

Tina was beside Alex, her arms tightly wedged between him and another inmate. She finished the porridge, licked the spoon, then wiped the bowl with her fingers and licked off every morsel, until it looked as if she had washed it up as well. In contrast, Alex ate his breakfast slowly and deliberately, his mind elsewhere. She nudged him, impatient to reach the warmth of the bonfires for half an hour before the work parade at seven. Alex came to with a start and stared at her as if he did not recognise her, but before a word was spoken, Cliff and Roy sat down at the two vacant seats opposite.

'Sleep well?' Cliff asked with a grin, which Alex and Tina were fast learning meant he wasn't just inquiring after their health.

'Very well,' Tina replied.

Alex nodded agreement.

'Good, because I want you both to be as alert as possible, so that you can absorb every detail about this camp.'

It came as no surprise that this suggestion should emanate from Cliff and they didn't need to be told what was behind it. Cliff seemed to have an innate hatred of authority. The idea of passively accepting imprisonment had probably never entered his head.

'What are you planning?' Alex asked.

Cliff leant closer. 'At the moment, nothing definite, but from what Roy's been telling me it's nearly impossible to escape from the camp once the gates have been locked for the night. During the day, however, work parties are constantly being sent out to projects all over the place.'

'What type of work?'

'Digging, repairing,' he shrugged. 'The point is, it's a golden opportunity to find out how the military operates. What their weaknesses might be. Maybe we can even smuggle some weapons we find back into the camp.'

Alex and Tina nodded politely, neither willing to commit themselves until they had had more time to think.

Cliff studied their faces for a moment, then leaned back with a disappointed expression. 'We can't stay here and let these bastards work us to death,' he exclaimed. 'Surely you must agree that escape is our only chance.'

'Hey!' a guard called out. 'Move along, this isn't a place for a social chat.'

Looking around, Alex noticed the place was almost empty.

'We'll talk more later, when you've had time to chew it over,' Cliff smiled, the confidence returning to his voice as they dutifully joined the now rapidly diminishing washing up queue.

At seven, Alex and Tina assembled for the work parade with the other new arrivals, as instructed. A sergeant ordered them into three ragged lines. When assembled, a tall, hawkish man in his early fifties came out to address them.

'I'm Major Hayes,' he announced, starting to wander slowly along the first rank. 'I'm in charge here. I think you know the ground rules already. If you do as you're told, you'll be fairly treated, if not, the penalty will be death.' He paused to let this statement sink in. 'Now, I know that for many of you caught looting, the choice was simple: steal or starve. Most of you are perfectly respectable citizens who have lost everything, your homes and your livelihoods. You are not common criminals, and you won't be treated as such. That is why we don't segregate men and women or make you obey rigid rules outside working hours. This is a camp that allows the homeless to work for the food they need instead of stealing it. This gives the government the manpower for recovery and stops homeless people roaming the countryside. However, in order to maintain an efficient camp a minimum of rules have to be obeyed. Every day, except Sunday, you will be woken at five thirty in the morning. At seven you will be assembled ready for work. By seven thirty you should have reached your respective workplace where you will continue to labour until twelve thirty. Half an hour will be allowed for lunch; the afternoon shift continues until six. Any person claiming exemption through illness must report to the sick bay to obtain written permission excusing them from work. Extra clothing can be obtained at the office if you need it. You will now be sorted into work details according to the skills you possess. If you settle in well, you have nothing to fear. Sergeant!'

He turned on his heel and strode off.

The sergeant now came forward, strutting and arrogant. 'You heard the Major, you're going to be here till you rot and it's my job to keep you in line.' He walked along the first row of prisoners, hands behind his back, inspecting them as though they were on parade. Reaching Alex, he looked him up and down slowly. He had a pallid, almost sickly complexion, with tiny features, which looked as if they had been squeezed into the centre of his face, leaving vast expanses of white cheek and forehead. He stared at Alex for some seconds, his face very close and intimidating. Then he moved on, repeating the same display as though deliberately trying to frighten the prisoners. 'A' EASE!' he yelled. The prisoners responded sluggishly. 'ANY TRICKS AND ONE DAY YOU MAY BE DIGGING YOUR OWN GRAVES, IS THAT UNDERSTOOD!' he bellowed.

He ordered his men to write down the pre-war occupations of each prisoner. Within fifteen minutes everyone had been assigned his or her new tasks. Cliff was taken off to join a building repair detail as Roy had predicted. Tina was sent to the kitchens and Alex was given a shovel and marched through the gates, along with about twenty other men.

The leader of the party, Alex noted with some regret, was the sergeant. He kept them moving at a brisk pace until they reached the outskirts of town. There the party was ordered to a halt while the escort took up defensive positions on their flanks and behind.

Alex soon understood why the guards were being so cautious. The military had lost control of this area. Gangs of youths and packs of starving dogs roamed the streets at will. The locals watched the work party in silence, neither screaming abuse nor shying away. Alex sensed an air of confusion amongst these people. It was as though they hadn't yet decided whether the military presence was a sign of an end to the chaos, or just another threat to their lives.

'This is your work assignment for the next few weeks,' the sergeant grunted, halting the prisoners in front of a huge pile of twisted rubble caked with thick ice and snow. From the remaining walls, Alex judged, it had once been an office block. 'Sift through the rubble for bodies, and we'll bury them by the roadside,' he ordered.

The job was hard and gruesome. The block must have been full when it collapsed without warning, for the rubble held many bodies, mostly crushed and mangled beyond recognition. The sergeant drove on the work with abuse and threats all day. By five, the workers could hardly stand; two had actually fallen and lay exhausted where they were, the sergeant not bothering them when it was obvious, they would not work again.

Finally, as the light began to fade, the party dragged themselves back to the camp. At the gate, each man was searched for concealed weapons before being dismissed by the sergeant with a few sarcastic comments.

After dinner Alex collected his ration of blankets from the Art School and joined the others sitting by the fire. Tina had spent the day preparing food and Cliff and Roy had been repairing buildings for the military's use near the centre of town. Alex recounted his day, feeling equally as despondent as the others.

'Your sergeant sounds like he needs a lesson in manners,' Cliff said.

Alex frowned. 'I wouldn't want an escape to misfire with that bastard in charge.'

'Hmm,' Cliff wrapped his blankets around himself more closely. His expression was troubled for the first time, as though the day's work had tempered his spirit somewhat.

'One thing that today has taught me,' Alex continued, 'is that with guards like the sergeant, any attempted breakout must be a planned, precise exercise. If they catch you, you'll not get a second chance.'

'I agree,' Roy said. 'The day before you arrived the Major showed us the bodies of three men who were shot trying to scale the perimeter fence at night. The fourth member of the escape party was executed in front of the whole camp while we assembled for morning parade.'

'All right, so we bide our time and plan an escape that can't fail,' put in Cliff, after a moment's thought. 'But we can't afford to wait too long, otherwise, none of us will have the strength left.'

He got up and wandered back toward the Art School, watched by the others. Patience was not Cliff's strong point.

In the days that followed, both the health and morale of the camp took a steep dive. The rations seemed barely enough to sustain life in the face of such heavy workloads. Many prisoners, already weakened by radiation sickness and physical injuries, could drive themselves no further. The small sick bay could do little except administer basic first aid and hand out its small supply of antibiotics. By the fifth day even this store had dried up and diseases quickly spread. Septicaemia became a problem and dysentery swept through the camp until stricter washing precautions were taken in the kitchen. There were darker rumours, too, of a fatal disease, which were fuelled when the sick bay commandeered a nearby storeroom for its patients.

Tina, however, was able to slip the men some rations she had taken from the kitchen. After assuring Alex that she wasn't putting herself in any danger, he took his share gratefully. Each day she managed to skim off enough rations to ease their hunger and sustain them while others succumbed.

Alex witnessed several ill planned escape attempts over the next few weeks. Usually they occurred late at night, and the inevitable sequel was a neat line of corpses laid in front of the camp, like prizes from a turkey shoot. These failures simply hardened the resolve of the group to plan their escape carefully.

Alex's work detail was down to half strength after three weeks. The sergeant seemed to take a sinister delight in this fact. Unlike the three guards who stood their distance, the sergeant liked to move amongst the workers, prodding and goading them, driving them to the limits of their endurance in a sadistic game to see who would collapse first.

Alex's face had become gaunt, his bony shoulders supporting his clothes like a coat hanger, but hardship had strengthened his will. The battle to survive was fought again on each succeeding day.

'Come here, Carlson!' the sergeant shouted. He had been terrorising this small, balding man since he had joined the detail a week ago. His chosen victim dropped the shovel on which he had been leaning and slowly trudged nearer.

'Feeling a little weak, are we?' the sergeant asked.

Carlson didn't answer. He never did, being totally submissive. It was precisely this type of creature that the sergeant enjoyed bullying most. The weaker and more defenceless the prey, the more he relished it.

'Well, Carlson, what do you say?'

'I feel sick and exhausted,' came the reply, mumbled miserably.

'What's that, Carlson? Come closer, I can't hear you.'

The man hesitated. Everyone avoided getting too close to the sergeant.

'Well, come on.'

He shuffled into the target area.

'Now then,' said the sergeant soothingly. 'What seems to be the trouble?'

'I feel sick and exhausted,' Carlson repeated.

'Ah, so we want to go back to camp and lie down, do we?' the sergeant mocked.

'I feel terrible. If I could just rest for a while…just a few minutes.' The man's pleading was pitiful to watch.

The sergeant's face became hard; his mouth vanished into a cruel line. Suddenly reaching out he gripped Carlson by the collar and started shaking him. 'You'll rest when I tell you to rest, understand?'

The man struggled weakly to free himself.

'Answer me!' roared the sergeant.

74

'Go to hell!' Carlson murmured under his breath, turning his face away.

This was the response that the sergeant was hoping for. He laughed loudly, then his knee jerked up into the little man's groin, sending him reeling to the ground in agony.

A shockwave of revulsion swept through the watching workers. Several men dropped their spades and stepped forward; their advance only checked when the guards levelled their rifles.

'You sadistic shit!' one shouted. 'Bastards like you should be cleaning the latrines, not us!'

This man's name was Anthony Dougan. He was the only one in the party who had repeatedly stood up to the sergeant, and he suffered daily because of it. He had been forced to work harder and longer than the rest; he had been hit frequently and even his lunch ration had been taken away. In spite of this, Dougan's spirit had not been broken. On the contrary, he seemed to grow stronger and more determined with each new cruelty. To plan the sergeant's death was all he ever talked about, the only thing that seemed to keep him going.

The sergeant moved towards Dougan menacingly, picking up a lump of wood as he advanced.

The man backed off, raising his spade for protection, his eyes locked against the sergeants' defiantly. The guards kept their rifles trained on the other prisoners, knowing full well what the outcome would be. The sergeant was a self defence expert. He handled the wood like it was part of him. Dougan was knocked senseless into the snow without landing a blow.

The sergeant dropped the wood and dusted off his hands. 'If anyone else gives me trouble, I will personally march them over to those holes you have dug and shoot them. Is that clear?'

In the silence that followed, he smiled broadly, well pleased with the fear he read in their faces.

A few days later, Alex met Tina, Cliff and Roy in a small, seemingly forgotten storage room, tucked away on the second floor of the Science block. It was Sunday, kept as a day of rest, and the inmates were allowed free run of the camp. However, the guards roamed around constantly, so it became imperative to find a quiet spot where they could not be overheard.

Tina lit a kerosene lamp that she had taken from the kitchen and placed it on the table before them.

'It's been over three weeks and we still haven't come to any final decisions,' Cliff said, reversing a chair and sitting on it backwards.

'We can't delay any further,' Alex agreed.

'Have you discussed all the details of our plan with your work party?' Cliff went on.

'Yes, I have. All that is needed is the word from me.'

'And they have all agreed to the plan?'

Alex paused before answering. He was thinking of what had happened the previous day. The sergeant had ordered Carson into some ruins that had become unstable, as soon as he started to dig, part of the wall had fallen on top of him, crushing him to death. The sergeant had just laughed.

'Oh yeah,' Alex said aloud, 'They agreed alright.'

'What diversion have you worked out?' Tina asked.

'When we pass through the outer suburbs the guards always take up defensive positions around us, so as not to offer easy targets for any possible mobs. One man falls in on each side of the prisoners and a third is close behind. They are never more than a couple of metres from the group. The sergeant, though, is usually way ahead trying to force us to keep up with him. On the way back to the camp they are less wary, knowing that we are tired and hungry, and therefore unlikely to try anything.' Alex paused for a moment. 'On my signal, Dougan, one of the workers the sergeant bullied the most, will start lagging behind. If the sergeant runs true to form, he will drop back and start harassing him. When I give the signal, the others will pounce and take out all four of them.'

The others nodded grimly.

76

'You know where to find the Land Rover?' Roy asked.

'Yes, it's down one of the streets we walk by, on the way back from work.'

'The military have hotwired it, since we stole the keys a few days ago,' Cliff said. 'All you have to do is jump in and connect the wires under the dashboard.'

'Are you sure it'll be there?'

Cliff and Roy glanced at each other. 'We hope so,' Cliff continued. 'While we were working on a building in the area, a Colonel Kirton used to park it there about six in the afternoon, every Monday and Tuesday, while he attended some type of area coordination meeting with other high-ranking military brass. We think the meeting must go on for some time, although we've no way of knowing for sure.'

Alex nodded. 'Alright, so I'll just have to reach it as quickly as possible.'

Tina handed him a packet. 'Here's a razor and some soap to shave with,' she said. 'I found the razor in the toilets yesterday. Don't slit your throat now,' she smiled.

Alex managed a small grin as he pocketed the precious items. 'It should take me about fifteen minutes to shave and put on the uniform. Maybe another twenty minutes to find the Land Rover and start back towards the camp. Will there be any guards near the vehicle?'

'No, but a patrol passes by every quarter of an hour. Wait for one to pass before you attempt anything,' Cliff replied.

'When you reach the gate,' Roy continued, 'you must say you have a dispatch from Colonel Bradshaw of the Bristol prison camp. This Colonel Bradshaw seems to send dispatches regularly to the camp. We saw a dispatch driver arrive this morning. He only said a few words at the gate and showed no identification. As long as you look the part, they don't seem to worry about confirming your identity.'

'I'll get as much food as I can from the kitchen and meet Cliff and Roy near the front gate,' Tina said.

'I have one last comment,' Alex put in. 'As soon as you see me drive through the gate, start running. I won't have time to stop. I must get up enough speed to smash through the gate and get away before they have time to shoot at us. If I manage to seize a rifle, someone can use it to cover our rear as we escape.'

'I'll do that,' Roy volunteered.

'Good,' said Cliff. 'Now all we need to do is set the day.'

Alex leaned back in his chair and studied each of their faces. There were deepening shadows of exhaustion around their eyes, a tightening of the skin around their cheekbones and a paleness that made their features look almost ghostly in the lantern light. They were all much weaker than when they arrived, and every day that they remained, they risked exposure to one of the many fast spreading diseases that afflicted the camp. 'Tomorrow,' he said firmly.

That night there were fresh rumours of an epidemic and talk of more than forty deaths in the past three days. The next morning the weather closed in, bringing strong winds and blizzard conditions. The Major called a rest day, promising extra rations and medical supplies and denying the wilder stories. The parade broke up with audible sighs of relief.

Alex wandered round the camp grounds in a tense mood. The more he thought about it, the more flaws he detected in the plan. What if the Land Rover wasn't there, or they couldn't overpower the guards? Before the war, only five short weeks ago, he would never have dreamed of taking a risk like this. The whole idea was more suited to Jason's swashbuckling style.

His wandering eventually led him to the sick bay where he watched a burial detail, harnessed like pack animals, pulling a cart loaded with bodies towards the camp entrance. Apparently, the number of men employed full time to haul and bury the bodies had risen to eight. It was considered the most hazardous job in the camp, with a life expectancy of only a few weeks. The sick bay, he noticed, had overflowed again. An adjoining classroom had now been taken over, as well as the storeroom. The symptoms he had heard mentioned suggested an influenza epidemic. Quite possibly a resurgence of covid-19, or some other new strain, he thought grimly. He had once taken a course at university on contagious diseases. Influenza had rated as one of the most infectious and lethal killers, especially in crowded conditions. It had killed millions in World War 1. The previous night people coughing and sneezing had kept him and Tina awake. There had also been many complaints of sore throats and headaches; all possible symptoms of influenza. Time could well be running out, he thought, as he turned sharply around and started walking back to the fire for some warmth.

To his right he passed the military quarters, a long drab sandstone structure which had served as the staff recreation block before the war. A place where battle fatigued teachers in the old days could retreat to enjoy lunch or tea without hordes of kids pestering them. A large wooden sign outside the front entrance read: *'Students are strictly forbidden in this area without the permission of a teacher.'*

As Alex strolled past, a door opened and a small figure laden with packages staggered out. Alex's heart missed a beat. The figure, hurrying and kicking up flurries of snow, as it went, was unmistakable.

'Tina!' he shouted.

The figure didn't respond at first; rather, it quickened its pace, only turning around when he trotted up behind.

'Hello,' she said, 'I didn't expect to see you here.'

Her face he thought looked flushed.

'I was just taking a walk to clear my head,' he explained.

'I'm running an errand for one of the guards in the kitchen,' she said quickly, as though to forestall some question of his. 'Often they tell you to get something they have forgotten.'

Alex noticed that the food packets she was carrying were the same type she had said she had taken from the kitchen. At that moment, the door she had emerged from suddenly opened and a man came out, tucking in his shirt tails and doing up his trousers. Alex turned sharply back to Tina. She glanced up at him guiltily, then strode forward again so that he had to exert himself to keep up with her.

'Tina, how have you been getting your food?' he demanded.

She gave him a fierce look. 'You know,' she said, pushing past him.

He caught up with her again and gripped her tightly by the arm, spinning her round, sending the food packets flying. 'Sleeping with the guards, eh?' he accused, totally incensed and only half believing what he saw.

She met his gaze squarely, the picture of stubborn defiance.

'Answer me!' he almost screamed at her. 'Have you been sleeping with the guards?'

'What I have been doing is no business of yours,' she blurted, her face now showing just as much anger as his.

'You bloody whore!' He felt the sudden urge to slap her face. 'Haven't you any sense of morality?'

'Morality,' she echoed mockingly. 'Now there's an obsolete word. Haven't you noticed there's no such thing anymore? Survival is the only reality now and survive is what I intend to do, no matter what it takes.'

Alex shook his head in disbelief. 'You sell your body like a piece of meat for extra morsels of food. Don't you have any respect for yourself as a person?'

'Look around you, Alex,' she said bitterly. 'People's hair dropping out, their faces scarred from burns and ulcers, their skin blotched, their bodies withering in front of their very eyes. The mirrors in the toilets were smashed long ago because people couldn't bear to see what they were becoming. We all look like hideous monsters, that's the reality. The only advantage I have is that my hair hasn't fallen out yet and my skin and face aren't scarred yet. If I can use that to help me survive, then I will.'

Alex's expression had not changed. His fists were still clenched at his sides, his eyes still glared wildly at her.

But Tina had grown frighteningly calm. 'Tell me,' she said, 'are you going to stop eating my rations because you found out how I got them?'

He ignored that thrust. *'You're not doing this again!'* he bellowed.

'Don't order me around! I'll do exactly what I want to do! Besides, if we break out tomorrow, I won't have to,' she added. She paused and her expression softened. 'Oh, Alex,' she went on, 'do you think I like doing it? A number of us were propositioned. If I hadn't done it someone else would have, then I wouldn't have been able to get this food. If it keeps us alive, then nothing else matters.'

But it did matter to Alex, it hurt him deeply. He felt betrayed. What she had done would have been unthinkable to him. He was looking at a person he thought he knew, but he had been wrong.

'I won't do it again,' she said, seeing the struggle going on within him. She took a step towards him and tried to put her arm around him.

Alex stepped back quickly. 'You can't dismiss what's happened, as if I had caught you stealing a bag of sweets,' he spat.

'I did it for you, Alex. I did it because I wanted you to survive!'

He opened his mouth to speak, then changed his mind. Turning away abruptly, he marched off, leaving her staring after him in the snow.

Alex slept only fitfully that night, his mind jerking forward constantly to the demands of the coming day, when so much would depend on his judgement and courage. Much of what he was thinking he normally would have discussed with Tina, and he knew she was awake hoping he would talk to her, but a gulf existed between them now. They had lost their intimacy. Their whole relationship had been corrupted, bruised, stained by what had happened.

He dressed early, even before the screeching alarm had gone off. Tina pretended to be asleep beside him.

'I'll see you at the gate tonight,' he whispered.

But he was gone before she could raise her head to answer him.

Alex found most of the work party round the fires after breakfast. He went over the details of the escape with them, making sure that everyone knew exactly what was happening. Then they shuffled off to assemble for parade. The previous day's snow had been replaced by a thick, choking smog, which reduced visibility to less than thirty metres; if this persisted, Alex thought, it could be useful.

The sergeant greeted them with his usual smirk, crunching around the detail like a growling wolf around a pack of sheep. 'Well, after your little holiday I expect you all to work extra hard!' he shouted. 'And if any of you thieving bastards gives me any trouble I'll have him doing burial detail after dinner at the sick bay. You'd enjoy that, wouldn't you? Now, left turn! By the left, hup, two, three, four; hup, two, three, four.'

They reached the ruins where they had been working before, and the sergeant announced that it would be their last day on that site. Nearly a metre of fresh snow had fallen, choking what they had cleared before, and adding to the burden of their labours.

At lunch, Alex sat next to Dougan, whose once powerful frame had wasted under the demands of the heavy work, leaving only the framework, the skeletal shell of the former man. A black swollen bruise still scarred one side of his face from the beating he had received a few days previously. One black eye, half closed and bloodshot, winked unnervingly at Alex while he talked.

'Are you clear on everything?' Alex asked.

Dougan nodded grimly. 'I can't wait,' he said.

'Remember,' Alex warned, 'only attack when I give the word. If we bungle this, we'll be slaughtered.'

'I'll remember.'

'Where are you planning to go afterwards?' Alex asked, deciding to change the subject.

The man shrugged. 'West probably. Yes...that's what I'll do. How about you?'

Alex hesitated. He had not told Dougan about the Land Rover and he didn't intend to now, in case he might want to come with him. 'I'll try and reach Wales somehow,' he said.

'Wales!' Dougan looked surprised. 'How are you going to get across the water?'

'I'll find a boat, hopefully.'

Dougan pulled a face. 'Seems like a lot of effort to me, when you can head west on foot.'

'What about the others?' Alex asked.

'Pretty much scattering in all directions, from what I gather. Some are for going east, hoping that the government is handing out food, but most are heading west. Maybe one or two will try for Wales.'

'Lunch is over!' the sergeant suddenly bellowed. 'Let's get cracking. Remember, I want this site cleared today.'

Dougan gave Alex a quick smile before collecting his shovel and resuming work.

At six the long march back to the camp started. As the detail proceeded through the centre of town, Alex peered down the street where he had previously seen the Land Rover. It was there! He breathed a sigh of relief so far, so good.

When the first houses started appearing the guards took up their usual positions. With the sergeant striding well ahead of the rest, Alex had positioned himself at the back of the two columns of men, and Dougan was third from the front. As soon as they had got clear of the last military patrol, Dougan started limping and the detail slowed down to keep pace with him. The sergeant dropped back and drew alongside Dougan.

'Sore leg, is it, Dougan?'

'No, I always walk with a limp.'

'Any cheek from you and I'll halve your dinner rations,' the sergeant replied coldly.

'Yeah, that's exactly what I'd expect from a piece of shit like you.'

The sergeant looked genuinely shocked. 'What did you just call me?' he asked, daring Dougan to repeat his words.

'Piece ... of ... shit!' Dougan mouthed the words slowly and clearly, so there could be no doubt as to what he had said.

'You'll live to regret those words, Dougan!' the sergeant scowled, his face twisting in a nasty snarl.

'Why, are you going to murder me like you did Carlson?' Dougan asked. 'Or maybe you'd like the personal touch, like smashing me over the head with a shovel...'

Alex watched the performance, full of admiration for Dougan's courage. Looking left and right, he was glad to see that the guards had closed in on the column and were listening to the argument. The guard behind, Alex judged, was about two metres away. He could see the other prisoners snatching quick glances back at him.

The moment had come.

Alex readied himself to pounce.

'NOW!' he screamed.

He sprang backwards off his haunches into the guard. The man went down with Alex on top of him. Quickly Alex rolled over and tried to pin him to the ground until the others reached him, but the guard was much stronger and broke Alex's grip, pushing him off. Fortunately, a second prisoner landed on the guard and began showering him with wild punches. A third man also joined in, kicking and punching. Alex pushed the rifle away and looked around.

The column had scattered into a mass of struggling forms. The sergeant had attracted the most attention and was now lost somewhere under a pile of thrashing bodies. One guard lay motionless in the snow, and a second was being badly beaten by four of the workers. The guard behind Alex was still fighting back. He rose to his feet, shaking off his weakened attackers, and Alex went for him again, pushing his face deep into the snow. But he twisted away and lashed out; a knee jerk into the groin made Alex dizzy with pain, but now he had his hands around the man's throat. Steadily he tightened his grip until the guard's eyes bulged, his hands fluttering desperately, trying to loosen the vice of the closing fingers. Once again, the two prisoners weighed in, and one of them, retrieving the guard's rifle, bashed away with the butt until he didn't move again.

All the guards were now overpowered. As for the sergeant, six men, including Dougan, were standing over him. Dougan had the sergeant's knife in his hand, and from the savage wounds plastered all over his body, it was clear that he had taken his revenge. Blood still oozed into the snow in every direction. Alex, sickened by the sight, turned away, leaving Dougan still staring wildly down at the dead man.

Already the group was beginning to break up, warning each other as they scattered of the dangers of meeting a military patrol. Alex grabbed the sergeant's rifle and ammunition and disappeared into the shadows to shave, hoping that when the men from the work party had disappeared, he could strip down one of the guards before a patrol arrived. He climbed a fence into someone's front garden and knelt by the light of one of the windows. The razor was awkward to handle with his gloves on, so once he had splashed his face with snow and lathered it with soap, he took them off.

It was slow, painful work, scraping off a centimetre of thick growth that had accumulated since the holocaust. Frequently the razor became clogged, and he had to rub it in the snow to clean it. At best he knew it was going to be a rough job, with no mirror to work by, but as Tina had said, appearances were not what they had been, these days, even the soldiers looked scruffy and unkempt. He doubted his appearance would attract much attention.

When he looked around again the street was empty except for the bodies of the guards. Alex stripped one about the same height as himself. The man was unconscious but breathing steadily. He dragged him to some shelter and dressed him in his own clothes so he wouldn't freeze, then set off towards the town centre.

Flickers of light were beginning to appear in the houses as night started to close in. Alex hurried on his way, staying close to the huge ridges which the snowploughs, in their repeated passages, had piled up on either side of the road. Each time he heard a vehicle approaching, he threw himself over this ridge and waited until it had passed. After half a kilometre, the two storey, grey brick terraces and closely packed shops of the town centre replaced the cottages of the suburbs. He moved more cautiously now, glad of the fading light. Finally, he reached the road junction where he had seen the Land Rover. When he turned the corner, he found the whole military base and its surrounds lit up by powerful floodlights, and directly below one of these lights stood the Land Rover. Alex swore under his breath. He thought his luck was too good to last. Everyone in the street would be able to see him steal the vehicle.

Despairingly, he crept as close as he dared and waited. After a while, a patrol appeared and flashed its way into the darkness again. There was nothing for it but to take a gamble, he decided. Plucking up his courage, he tucked his ragged hair under his beret, straightened his uniform and slung his rifle over his shoulder. He strode out to the vehicle with as much authority as he could muster. The tyres had chains on them, which explained how the Land Rover could still negotiate the icy streets. However, it also meant it couldn't reach high speed without ripping the tyres apart. He opened the door and found the wires under the dashboard. When he touched them together the engine ticked over. That was a relief, anyway; he threw the gear lever in first and eased up on the clutch.

A face with a handlebar moustache, and with an officer's tabs visible, appeared at the window. Alex's heart pounded. Another military patrol was approaching down the road. He wound down the window and saluted.

'What are you doing with this vehicle, soldier?'

Alex thought fast. 'Colonel Kirton ordered me to park it in the garage, sir.'

'There is no garage, that's why he parks it here.' The officer's eyes narrowed as he watched Alex's face.

Alex swallowed. 'Not this building, Sir. The one two doors along, with the driveway.' Alex pointed to the driveway he had just been hiding in.

'That's a residential house,' the officer said, frowning.

'That's right. Colonel Kirton doesn't think the Land Rover is safe here, since he lost his keys. The owner of the house has offered him the use of his garage.'

The officer scratched his jaw thoughtfully. 'I see.' His eyes returned to Alex's face. 'Why haven't I seen you here before?'

'I just arrived today with Colonel Kirton, Sir,' said Alex smartly.

The officer nodded slowly, then stood back, satisfied for the moment at least. 'Very good, soldier, carry on.'

Alex figured he would be confirming his identity with Colonel Kirton at the first opportunity, but he would be long gone by then.

'Sir,' Alex saluted. He put the vehicle into gear and drove slowly to the driveway. There he parked it and pretended to fiddle with the garage door. A second patrol crunched past while the officer watched him, before finally disappearing into the building. Alex immediately jumped into the vehicle, reversed up the drive and drove off as fast as the chains on his wheels would allow.

Ten minutes later, the gates of the camp came in sight. Alex, calming his nerves, mentally rehearsed his story, trying hard to reason out all the possible questions he could be asked. The gates opened and a young blond soldier with sunken eyes and a drawn face waved him down.

'I have a dispatch from Colonel Bradshaw from the Bristol camp,' Alex recited.

The man looked puzzled. 'We had a dispatch two days ago,' he said.

'This is a special dispatch, marked urgent,' Alex replied, trying to sound full of authority.

The guard walked round the back of the vehicle, then returned to Alex. 'Why isn't the usual dispatch driver here?'

'He was taken sick this morning,' Alex replied promptly. 'In fact,' he went on, confidentially, 'I think my camp's coming down with the flu. That may be what this urgent dispatch is about.'

The guard registered alarm at the very mention of flu. He leant closer to Alex, 'There's a strong rumour here also, about a flu epidemic. Many of the inmates have already died and a number of the guards are becoming sick, some very seriously. They say there's no cure.'

Alex nodded. 'Don't tell anyone,' he said, 'but I think Colonel Bradshaw is thinking of abandoning the camp because the epidemic is out of control. We hardly have any medical supplies left. He may be instructing Major Hayes to do the same.'

The soldier grew wide eyed. 'No, that's impossible!'

'I don't know for sure,' Alex said. 'But in these conditions flu spreads like wild fire. The Spanish flu killed fifteen million in World War I, you know. Well,' he continued, tapping significantly on a folder he had found under the front seat, 'I'd better get this dispatch to the Major.'

'Oh yes,' said the guard. 'By God, abandoning the camp, is he? It must be bad.' He signalled the guard towers and waved him through.

Alex smiled, feeling pleased with his performance. When he was sure he was out of sight of the gate, he switched off his lights and waited for the others. He didn't have to wait long; Tina, Cliff and Roy bundled into the back almost immediately.

'Congratulations, guv. Any trouble?' Cliff asked.

'I'll tell you later,' Alex said. 'Keep down low, I've decided to try and bluff my way out?'

'Is that wise?'

'I've no choice. This Land Rover's got chains on it; if I try to reach high speed, I'll only tear up the tyres. Besides, I doubt whether I could control it in the attempt. The guard expects me back about now, anyway, so I can at least approach the gate without being shot at. We're quite chatty. There's an outside chance we might get clean away.'

'What if he looks in the back?' Tina asked.

'That's a chance we'll have to take,' Alex replied. 'If the worst comes to the worst, I'll ram the gates. Get down, now.'

The blond guard saw him coming and waved him down again.

'I just want to ask you,' he said. 'Did you see a group of workers marching here on your way in?'

'No, I can't say I did,' Alex replied, trying to sound casual.

'That's funny. They were due back over an hour ago. The sergeant who's in charge of them is a stickler for time. Something bad must have happened.'

Alex shrugged sympathetically. 'Hmm, I don't like the sound of it. Well, I'll keep my eyes open. If I see any sign of them, I'll let you know.'

The guard seemed satisfied with Alex's offer. 'Okay,' he said, slapping the roof. 'I won't keep...' He stopped in mid-sentence and leaned through Alex's open window into the back. Alex knew then that the game was up. With his right hand, he gripped the guard around the neck, while he threw the Land Rover in to gear with his left. The wheels spun, then gripped the road, making the vehicle lunge forward. The guard struggled violently, forcing Alex's head over the back of the seat. Roy suddenly appeared and Alex heard his fist crash into the guard's face. The force of it catapulted the guard out of the window. The gate sprang back on impact as Alex jammed his foot down on the accelerator.

Shouts of alarm and curses sounded through the darkness as the huge searchlights were swung round a hundred and eighty degrees and brought to bear. But a full thirty seconds had elapsed before the guards could open fire on the receding vehicle. Although some shots came close, the Land Rover was already a distant shape, well out of effective range, tearing along the road.

CHAPTER 5

Alex brought the Land Rover to a halt by the side of the road. Beyond, the land fell away steeply into the Bristol Channel. He switched off the engine and headlights and turned on the cabin light. Earlier, he had found a number of maps in the glove compartment, one of them showing the county in some detail. He unfolded this on his lap and scratched his cheek thoughtfully. By his estimation, he had driven about thirty kilometres north-west of the camp. Wales was twenty kilometres further north, across freezing, ice laden waters.

Since escaping from the camp events had taken a distinct turn for the worse. Even with chains, the Land Rover had proved very difficult to manoeuvre above forty kilometres an hour. Twice they had rammed the snowbanks piled along the sides of the road, and although there had been no damage, it spelt out just how impossible it would be to leave the cleared tracks and strike across the country by themselves. And by following the roads, they were inevitably going to come across a military checkpoint at some stage. At night they had proceeded without incident, unchallenged by the army vehicles they had passed. But in daylight, when the military reasserted their dominance over the land, they would be required to identify themselves. With only one rifle between them, they were hardly equipped to shoot their way out. So, it became clear that comfortable and reassuring as the Land Rover was, they could not stick with it for very much longer. It would be madness to do, yet difficult to give it up.

'Where are we?' Tina was looking across at him from the passenger seat. Those were the first words she had spoken to him since they had left the camp.

Alex sensed that she wanted to repair the bridges between them but had not found a way to do it. A problem he had also been struggling with. He pointed to the map. 'Somewhere near Minehead would be my guess.'

Cliff craned over from the back seat to see. 'How far west do you intend going?' he asked.

Alex had been waiting for that question ever since the escape. He had been turning over the options in his mind and more and more the decision to head north seemed the only sensible one. 'I want to try and cross over into Wales,' he said.

Cliff took the news without any noticeable emotion. 'I guessed as much,' he said mildly.

'It's the natural place for people to go,' Alex continued, warming to his theme. 'Very little industry, population thinly spread, no obvious military targets.'

'The same could be said for Devon and Cornwall, of course,' Cliff replied. 'A community could be forming there right now.'

'But everyone will be going there,' Alex argued. 'It's so accessible, that's half the problem. And if the refugees have taken the epidemic with them, as they're likely to have done, that doesn't make it a very inviting prospect.'

'I think Alex is right,' Tina weighed in enthusiastically. 'There are bound to be thousands of people heading west and probably very little food for them when they get there. I can't help feeling that Devon and Cornwall wouldn't be able to cope with the numbers.'

Roy, who had been studying a map of Wales in his quiet, methodical way, broke in at this point. 'Blaenau Ffestiniog,' he said, indicating the place to Alex and stumbling over the strange Welsh words. 'I know the government has a huge underground storage facility there somewhere.'

92

'Storage facility?' Alex queried. 'What do you mean?'

'I read somewhere...' Roy sat back in his seat; his large broad features creased in thought. 'Yes, I'm sure.' He leaned forward again and drew an imaginary circle around the area of the town with his finger. 'There's a large disused slate mine, it's government property. They took it over for storage space in case of war.'

'What do they store?' Alex asked.

Roy shrugged. 'In the last war, it was British art treasures, but I assume it could be almost anything. Apparently, the mine is huge.'

'If the government foresaw what was coming,' Tina picked up the thread of the argument, 'they'd have had time to fill it with stores and supplies. There could be tonnes of food there, just waiting to be discovered.'

'It won't have been a very well-kept secret if they did,' Alex said sourly. 'I'm sure the local population would know about it and the government would be bound to post a guard.'

'But they might be rationing it out to the survivors,' Tina persisted.

'Hmm.' Alex nodded his head slowly. 'It's certainly a possibility. Anyway, I think there's more hope for us in Wales than further west.'

'So how do we get across?' Cliff asked.

'I wish I knew,' said Alex. 'Maybe we could find a small boat. Or, if it comes to that, I suppose we could build a raft.'

Cliff sat back. 'Do you reckon?' he said. 'Oh, don't misunderstand me, guv,' he went on. 'It's fine if it can be done, but those are treacherous waters, and with the weather the way it is, well...'

Alex took the point. Although they had not seen the Channel by daylight, they had been driving along its shores and the sheets of floating ice had shown up in the beams of their headlights. In some places, the ice sheet had appeared complete, solid and glistening as far as they could see.

'But what chance do we have on land?' Alex turned back to Cliff, his need to reach Wales suddenly becoming paramount. 'We can't drive on roads which have not first been cleared by the military, and by daybreak it will become obvious that we are not an official patrol. They may have even radioed our description ahead, so they'll be looking out for us, which makes the Land Rover a liability. And without it, on foot…we have to go somewhere we're not known, and where no one else is willing to go.'

The argument for abandoning the Land Rover had obviously not occurred to anyone else, and it met with a number of heated objections, but the logic behind it remained sound. If they wanted to avoid being a sitting target, they had to find some other way. Crossing the Channel, despite its hazards, seemed to offer a real possibility of deliverance. This was the position finally reached; it was agreed they would leave the vehicle in the morning and travel along the coast until they found a crossing point. If necessary, they would venture into the coastal villages to find a suitable craft.

The discussion ended on a dejected note, exhaustion and depression finally silencing the company. The remainder of the night they spent huddled up against each other for warmth. Without any invitation, Tina curled up in Alex's arms and immediately dozed off. The simplicity of her actions amazed Alex. With one act, she had invalidated the barriers that had built up between them. How could he continue to rage at someone who wrapped her arms around him in such a fashion? She nuzzled up closer to his chest and he found himself watching the gentle lines of her face as she slept. They had taken on a curiously serene appearance, as though her mind was completely at ease. This ability of hers to accept and to go with the flow was a tremendous gift, he thought. She appeared to suffer none of the inner turmoil he always endured. For him, the events of the past twenty-four hours were like splinters of horror that jagged at him through the darkness; the white, terrified faces of the soldiers as they

94

tried to fight off the work party, Dougan with his bloody knife and mad eyes, the corpse of the sergeant, punctured and bleeding. Even on the edge of sleep, another fearful image would leap out at him and jerk him back to consciousness, so that he dozed only in snatches.

He awoke properly as the shadows drained from the soupy smog, heralding another day. Tina still lay, as she had done for hours, half on his lap with her arms around his waist. He could hear Cliff and Roy conferring quietly, rummaging through the supplies for something suitable for breakfast. He gently eased Tina to one side and climbed outside. More snow had fallen during the night, giving the Land Rover a fresh dusting of powder. Inside again, he exchanged a few words of greeting, but nobody felt much like talking. Tina awoke a few minutes later and they dutifully forced down a breakfast of salted meat and soya beans. Then the remaining food and water was divided amongst the party in makeshift blanket bags, which they slung over their shoulders before they set off.

A chilling wind had begun to blow from the east. The smog rolled up and fled before it, leaving behind a vista of a shallow, dipping plains, rising to blunted peaks in the distance. Soon the wind brought more snowflakes in its wake, which turned to pellets that stung the exposed skin, forcing the party to avert their faces.

They began their journey in a westerly direction, hugging the coast, searching each bay and inlet for boats as they went. By mid-morning they had covered nearly five kilometres. By now they were strung out with Alex leading, then Tina, and Roy and Cliff bringing up the rear. All except Alex had their heads tucked into their overcoats for protection against the cold, so it was Alex who first spotted the lines of people. They stood out as black dots, moving against the snow, all in formation like ants on the march. The appearance of order, at a distance, made him think it must be the military abandoning the camps en masse and moving further westward. But a closer view soon revealed that, unwittingly, they had stumbled on one of the main arterial routes westward. These unhappy pilgrims were what were left of the survivors from south eastern England. Not the indirect victims of the bombs, like Alex and the others, but people who had seen and experienced a nuclear explosion at close range. These were the walking dead, hairless, pitiful creatures, covered in heat blisters and lesions. Many nursed blackened limbs bent and twisted into impossible positions. Alex felt his own flesh creep as he watched them pass. By rights most of them should have died weeks ago. Only the numbing effect of the extreme cold had kept the wounds from festering, and the pain from killing them.

They stopped at the edge of the road and watched. Their presence was ignored. No one paused to ask who they were, or even noticed them, it seemed. The procession of ragged forms just continued unbroken, appearing through the driving snow a hundred metres to the east, and fading back into it a hundred metres to the west.

Alex grabbed the shoulder of a short, hunched figure who came trudging past. A finely built man, still dressed in the remains of a dark business suit, looked up. His young face was skeletal and the eyes unfocused and dull, as though the passing world had ceased to register on his mind.

'Where are you going?' Alex asked.

The man's blank expression didn't alter.

Alex clung on to him. 'Did the military tell you there was food and shelter further westward?'

The man blinked, then moved his head vigorously, as though trying to shake out an answer. 'No,' he frowned. 'Yes, I mean, someone said there was food and shelter in Cornwall.'

'Who said?'

'I don't know, I don't know.' The voice faded into a mumble as Alex released him. The man re-joined the flow and shuffled on as if the conversation had never taken place.

Cliff and Roy were getting a slightly better response a few paces away. They had stopped a young couple whose

96

injuries were not so serious. They had come from a small village north of Southampton and had spent the past two weeks slowly working westward. As one food station had become too crowded, they had moved onto the next, hoping eventually to reach a place where the government had complete control and the food and shelter were plentiful. But they had no positive reason for believing that conditions would improve further west; it was just that it could not be as bad as what they had left behind. Several other people said more or less the same thing. No one really knew where they were going, and no one really cared.

After they had watched them for a while, Tina put one hand in Alex's pocket. 'We may as well follow them,' she said gloomily.

That was the last thing Alex wanted to do, but the road having been cleared of snow, it was likely to be the quickest route westward. He finally nodded and they reluctantly joined the ranks of the survivors.

By the afternoon, the snow had eased. The land reappeared, its summer beauty irrevocably broken. Every house they passed had its doors kicked in, the windows smashed and its curtains missing; every last item of warmth was gone. Not a single tree had escaped damage, much of it from the burden of the snow snapping the boughs under its weight. Their upper branches, which still clawed the sky, whistled in the wind like a multitude of tuning forks. This sad music, which rose and fell as the wind strengthened or died, seemed somehow appropriate to Alex, like a mournful serenade of the doomed. It would be the last sound that many of the walkers would hear as their strength failed them and they fell over for the last time.

But Alex did see one hopeful sign in all this destruction. The snow was losing its smoky grey colouring. In places, where the crust had fallen, the different layers stood out like strata, almost black at the bottom, like slate, then merging into a dirty white. Presently the road broadened and dipped through a forest of broken saplings and spiky heath; then, after passing through an open meadow, it brought them to the outskirts of a town. The town was on the water's edge and from the number of wharves and jetties Alex imagined it was a fishing or trading port of some kind. However, he could see no sign of any boats. The main street was lit with rows of roughly slung lights. The road snaked down into this area and its human freight formed ragged black lines, which trailed off into the town centre. The heavily cloaked figures of the military could be discerned, moving alongside them, like dogs patrolling a flock of sheep.

They reached the town half-an-hour later and joined the end of one of the long queues. Alex hadn't spoken a word since they had first sighted the military, for a plan was forming in his head. He still had on his military uniform and rifle, concealed under a blanket so as not to tempt the anger of the crowd. Now, it seemed to him, was the time to be a soldier again. All he needed was the nerve to sustain the part.

After rehearsing his plan several times in his head, he flung off his blanket and turned to Tina. 'I'm going to find out what this is all about,' he said. 'I'll be back as soon as possible.'

Tina would have objected, but he was gone before she had a chance to do so.

Alex walked briskly and purposefully towards the centre of town. He was wound up tighter than a spring, firing possible questions at himself and quickly thinking up the answers. He knew that to hesitate, or to sound uncertain in any way, would spell disaster. Many inconsistencies could be concealed by a forcible, authoritarian tone.

As he advanced, he noticed how the condition of the survivors seemed to deteriorate steadily. A great many had died while queuing for food. The bodies of these had been dragged aside and gathered into neatly stacked piles. Burial details could be seen here and there, covering these mounds.

Further on, Alex came across a large detention camp. Its inmates were the human work horses the military used to haul away the dead. When Alex saw them he felt like

98

weeping. They were worse than caged animals because they were quite clearly starving to death. All hope was gone for them. They would work on until they too fell into the snow, to be added to the cartloads of corpses they had just been dragging. He was thinking this when a horrible choking smell came drifting across from the camp, a foul miasma of unwashed bodies and disease, which affected even the queuing survivors with looks of fear and dread. The stench could mean only one thing; the epidemic was here before them, scything down the weakened and the hopeless. Their suffering would soon be at an end.

But it made Alex quicken his pace, the need for information becoming even more imperative.

The food distribution point, when he finally reached it, proved to be only a small makeshift canvas shelter. Four fires were burning with cooking pots simmering on each. Large surly looking men stood behind each pot, ladling out half cupful portions of lumpy fluid. Hardly enough to keep a small child alive, let alone an adult, Alex thought bitterly. He turned back to the lines of survivors and approached one of the patrolling soldiers, a sharp eyed, sharp nosed little man.

'Hello,' Alex called. 'Am I glad to see you! My vehicle was ambushed some distance back and my C.O. was killed. I've been on foot ever since.'

The soldier surveyed him suspiciously and did not reply.

'We were driving down from our headquarters, near Bristol, when we got bogged. The survivors converged on us like vultures, I was the only one who escaped,' Alex continued.

'GET BACK IN THE QUEUE!' the soldier, yelled at a woman who had fallen in the snow. 'YOU!' he shouted at a tall, still fleshy man standing behind her. 'HELP HER UP!'

The man obeyed grudgingly.

'You'd better report to Captain Shaw,' he said to Alex in a more listless tone. 'Don't ask me where he is, though. I haven't seen any officers for over two days.'

'Why's that?' Alex asked, trying to sound concerned.

'Why? Why do you think? The place is falling apart. We've barely enough men to control the crowds.'

An old man nearby, who had been supporting himself on a roughly cut stave, suddenly collapsed into the snow. The soldier crossed over to him and rolled him onto his back. The elderly face was disfigured with purple blotches, the eyes glazing over, and with each breath he let out a raucous whining sound like an asthmatic wheeze.

The soldier gave a satisfied grunt. 'He's finished,' he concluded. 'You and you,' he pointed towards a man wearing a balaclava and a youth no older than twenty. 'Drag him over to the side of the road.'

The dying man was unceremoniously hauled over to a group of bodies and dumped on top. While he lay there, still rasping for breath, the two detailed to remove him proceeded to strip him of his clothes.

Alex was appalled. In a couple of strides, he was beside the man with the balaclava, grabbing him by the collar and throwing him back across the snow. 'At least wait for him to die!' he shouted.

The youth, seeing him coming, ducked out of the way and meekly re-joined the queue.

'What did you do that for? He was virtually dead, anyway,' the soldier asked.

'Aren't you supposed to be setting an example?' Alex retorted, stalking over to him and stopping in front of him, deliberately using his height to intimidate the man. If you let them behave like animals,' he continued forcibly, 'you'll lose what little control you have. They won't think twice about doing the same thing to you.'

The soldier seemed momentarily taken aback by this show of anger, and hesitated before he replied. 'Ah, and how would you know?' he said finally. 'Animals are what they are. The only way to control them is to give in to them occasionally.'

The fact that the soldier had not seen through Alex's façade spurred him on. He decided to continue his attack.

'We have exactly the same problems as you, ye know,' he stormed. 'We control them by discipline. Once that goes, so will you.'

'Well, you've probably got better conditions than us,' the soldier replied defensively, waving his hand toward the lines of people.

'Our work camps are collapsing, our food is almost gone,' Alex lied. 'That's why my C.O. was coming here personally. He wanted to assess how bad the conditions were. I'm sure if he had seen all this,' Alex gestured vaguely, 'he would have ordered the abandonment of this distribution station immediately.'

This last statement had its desired effect. The soldier's eyes narrowed, and a look of pure astonishment swept over his face. 'You mean your C.O. was coming here to tell us to clear out?'

'More than likely.'

'And he's dead?'

'I told you. I barely escaped with my own life. There was no time to think about him.'

'Shit!' the soldier hissed, something close to a snarl appearing on his face. 'It's useless hanging on here as it is. We'll be out of food in a day or so, anyway, and rumour has it there's a flu epidemic.'

Alex nodded. 'That's right. Over half the inmates in the camp I come from have gone down with the flu.'

'Yeah, I hear a lot of the camps east of here are pretty bad. This lot are carrying it west with them.' The soldier unslung his rifle and leaned closer to Alex, lowering his voice. 'In my opinion we have to abandon this whole food campaign,' he muttered. 'Just guard the food stocks instead.'

'What? And let the population starve?'

'They're dying anyway, what's the use of a few more days of life to them? With the weather the way it is there won't be any food grown for a long time. The remaining stocks will have to last for years.'

Alex opened his mouth to speak but then shut it again. The man was talking sense, in a way. The weather hadn't altered appreciably since the holocaust, and even if it cleared overnight the land had suffered enormous volumes of fallout. It would be madness, from the military point of view, to waste their food supplies on people who couldn't possibly last the first winter. He frowned and decided to change the conversation.

'Have you heard anything about the conditions in the south east?' he asked. 'It must be pretty dire.'

The soldier nodded gravely. 'I've heard a few things from some of the refugees. Apparently, London was hit many times. Some said as many as five. Not much was left standing. The fallout was enormous over the whole sector. There's nothing doing there. People were too badly contaminated to live for long. I understand the nearest distribution point was forty kilometres out.'

Alex shook his head in disbelief.

'And that's not the worst of it,' the soldier continued. 'All transport was knocked out, along with everything else of any use. All the survivors were on foot. Within days of setting up food distribution points they were overrun. We had to pull out and re-establish them further and further west. But that was in the first days; we're down to this trickle now, and they won't last much longer. This is the third distribution point I've been posted to and we're receiving very few people from around London anymore.'

'How about further west?' Alex asked.

'Na, we're one of the last. This lot aren't going anywhere.'

Alex's eyes went from the soldier to the lines of the starving people, shuffling forward. The will to help them was almost gone. Soon the military would be withdrawing and then even this nightmare would grow horribly worse. The thought made him suddenly feel very cold and frightened.

'Thanks,' he said. 'You've told me all I need to know.' He turned and strode off.

102

'Hey, where are you going?' the soldier called after him.

'Wales,' Alex shouted back without turning his head.

'So, there's no choice but to cross the Channel,' Cliff concluded, after Alex had related his grim tale.

'None,' Alex replied. 'Otherwise, we'll be caught in the carnage that is sure to follow once the survivors realise there's no more food.'

'But are we likely to find a suitable boat to take us? Anything that can float will surely have been taken by now,' Tina added. 'I suggest we should consider building one of our own.'

'We've certainly got the skills,' Cliff said, 'but it wouldn't be easy, just the same. Not only would such a craft have to carry us all, it would need to have enough clearance to stop the waves lapping over the top in a storm. In this weather, adrift for seven or eight hours or more, it could be fatal if we became soaked with water.'

'Nevertheless,' Alex put in, 'that's what we'll have to do unless we can find something we can use soon.'

The discussion continued, with Cliff and Roy remaining unconvinced of the need for urgency. They both felt that any trouble which might flare up would be directed at the military, rather than toward other survivors. Alex, however, did not share their optimism.

After pushing their way out of the queue, they set off at a brisk pace towards the shore. The lanes, as they left the centre of the town, showed little sign of life. But if the streets were empty, lanterns and shadowy forms at the windows indicated that many of the houses were still inhabited, whether or not by their original occupants, they could not be sure. On the water's edge, however, away from the distribution point, the empty derelict properties seemed to increase.

Roy and Cliff forced their way into one, a large brick house with a garage and adjoining workshop attached. Alex and Tina took over its exploration as soon as it became clear that the house was empty. Meanwhile Roy and Cliff scoured the shoreline for materials for the raft. Alex wanted to find some clothes to replace his military uniform and, though the house had been ransacked, it appeared that the looters had only been after food, as the upstairs rooms were untouched.

Alex took several woollen jumpers, a down jacket and a woollen based pair of trousers from a wardrobe in one of the bedrooms. Tina, meanwhile, went to the dressing table and stared at her reflection in the mirror. Her actions were so deliberate that Alex could not help watching her. She licked her fingers and gently wiped away the smudges of dirt from her cheeks, carefully examining her skin for purple blotches - the tell-tale signs of radiation sickness. Then she tugged gently on her hair. A large clump came out in her hand. She let the strands of hair fall through her fingers onto the dressing table and stood staring blankly at them.

Alex stopped what he was doing and went straight to her. She remained motionless, staring down at the table. He placed his arm around her shoulder. 'Mine's the same,' he said softly. He pulled hard at his hair and emptied a handful of it over the table. The strands drifted down and settled amongst Tina's hair.

'We're turning into monsters,' she said sadly. 'Like those poor creatures back at the work camp. Hideous, hairless monsters.'

'Just because we have lost some hair,' Alex said firmly, 'doesn't mean we're going to die.'

'I don't feel well,' she said flatly, and suddenly her eyes were soft and moist. 'It's more than just nausea. I have stomach cramps and I get so weak and tired. I just want to lie down and not get up, ever.'

He put a hand over her forehead. She felt hot, not burning up, but she definitely had a temperature. His heart began to pound at once. *'How long has this been going on?'* he demanded. *'And why didn't you tell me earlier?'*

'I'm not about to drop dead,' she said quietly. 'I just don't feel very well.'

Her voice was sad, filled with a weariness he had never heard before. She walked past him and sat on the bed. Alex followed, and took both her hands in his. They were freezing.

'Are you getting worse?'

'No…not really. Just very tired.'

He switched on his torch and examined her more closely. Her face was deathly pale, the lines of exhaustion etched under her eyes. She looked dreadful.

'Lie down,' he ordered. 'I noticed some medicines in the bathroom.' He darted out and returned a few minutes later with some tablets and a flask full of water from their supplies. Tina had climbed under the blankets and was curled up into a tight ball. The fact that she had obeyed him so meekly sent a new wave of unease through him. He gave her two aspirins, then sat on the bed beside her, watching her anxiously.

'I'm really okay,' she said, trying to sit up and smiling at his mournful expression. 'I probably got a bit of a high dose. And all this walking hasn't helped,' she added unconvincingly.

Alex's alarm was deepening rapidly into misery and torment. 'You must sleep,' he pleaded. 'Sleep will make you strong again. You just need to sleep.'

But she shook her head. 'There's no time for that. Once we're in Wales, we can start to think about relaxing.'

'You sleep,' he said sternly. 'Leave us to sort out where we go from here.'

They stared at each other and for a moment their wills clashed, but now his strength easily matched hers. After a moment, she leant back on the pillows.

'Events have rather swept us along, don't you think?' she said quietly, a clear note of surrender entering her voice.

Alex nodded.

'You know, I had a lovely life planned before the war.' She was gazing directly ahead now, at no place in particular. 'I was going to be a photographer. Travel the world taking marvellous pictures.' She turned to look at Alex. 'Funny, isn't it? In one fell swoop, everyone's dreams and aspirations have been wiped away. They all seem rather silly and self-centred now.'

'Yes, we've all suddenly been brought to the same level,' Alex agreed. 'There's no rich or poor, or talented or beautiful anymore. We're even beginning to look the same.'

At this last comment, Tina lowered her eyes and pursed her lips with such a lamentable expression that it made Alex ache. He felt as if he was made of glass and inwardly, he was shattering. 'Things always seem worse than they are, Tina,' he added. And he kissed her lightly on the forehead.

She reached up and wrapped her hands around him, holding him tight. 'I don't feel so strong anymore,' she whispered. 'Suddenly I seem to go to jelly. I want to be well, I want to cross the Channel, but my body continues to grow weak and decay.'

He disentangled himself from her arms in horror and disbelief. 'What are you trying to say?' he gasped.

'Only that I feel as if my strength is leaking away, and I'm very scared.' She looked into his eyes with a mournful, hopeless expression that made Alex's heart ache. 'I've never felt like this before. If something happens to me...'

'Nothing's going...'

'If it does,' she persisted, tears swelling in her eyes and beginning to tumble down her cheeks, 'promise me that you'll not leave me to die by myself.'

Alex's immediate impulse was to dismiss her words as an over-reaction, but he knew Tina well enough to be sure she would not say something without good cause. And the pleading look in her eyes was not one of self-pity. He could not speak.

'I don't mind dying, I just couldn't bear the thought of dying alone,' she continued miserably.

He reached out and gently stroked her forehead. 'I won't leave you; you know that.'

'Yes, yes,' she said more calmly, 'I think I do. I didn't want to upset you, Alex,' she went on. 'I just thought you ought to know. I remember reading somewhere that we all have different levels of tolerance to radiation. Well, I think I must be near the limits of mine.'

'But you've been eating.'

'No, 1 haven't, not really. I have been trying to force food down, but I have been vomiting it up again an hour later. I also have had diarrhoea for over a week now.'

'But we all have diarrhoea to some degree.'

'I'm passing blood,' she said bluntly, 'and it's getting worse.'

Alex covered his eyes with his hand, rubbing his forehead as if he suddenly had a headache. He felt he would lose all grip on reality if something happened to Tina. 'When we reach Wales,' he said, almost on the verge of tears, 'I'll find a shelter for you and we'll stay there until you're better again.'

She leaned over and put her arms around him, gently drawing him back to her. Alex climbed in under the covers and took her in his arms. She was icy cold. Desperately he wrapped himself around her, trying physically to smother her in his own warmth, until finally, like a little bird cradled in a nest, she closed her eyes.

For a long time, Alex lay beside her, waiting for the deep rhythmic breathing of sleep to descend on her. When he was satisfied she was asleep, he gently disentangled himself and changed into the clothes he had previously laid out on the bed. He had heard some explosions earlier and when he looked out of the window of the bedroom, he saw the cause of them. The food distribution point must already have collapsed. Huge fires were engulfing the town higher up. Angry voices sounded in the street. He ran down the stairs and met some passers-by. These people told stories of mayhem and slaughter, as the refugees took revenge on anyone who resembled authority. The closing of the distribution point had worked them all up into a kind of frenzy. They now knew, or guessed, that no more help would be forthcoming, and survival would depend on their own resources.

Some, of course, had Alex's idea and contemplated escape across the water northwards to Wales. These survivors poured onto the shore in search of any craft that could take them across the Channel. In their search for materials to build craft, they took anything that would float, couches and tables among them, and quickly swamped the more promising vessels by crowding aboard in the shallows. Shouting and flashing knives, they would let no one else depart this way, if they could not go themselves. The sick were trampled underfoot; it was a vision of hell, made the more persuasive by the sudden breaking out of fires.

Alex found Cliff and Roy in the garage. Their search along the shore had not been fruitless. They had collected a number of large oil drums from a nearby service station, along with several large rolls of plastic. They had not dared to take any more for fear of attracting attention to themselves. With Alex's help, they now began tearing up the floorboards, ripping doors off their hinges, breaking up cupboards and chairs and dragging the whole lot down to the garage. When Alex told them about Tina, they both looked shocked, neither having suspected that anything was amiss. But this bad news only served as further incentive to escape.

After five hours of work, the raft was finished that same night. It was a large, awkward looking craft, held together by nails, wire and odds and ends of rope. Five drums served as buoyancy tanks, with a deck above them, made of doors and wooden beams, lashed and nailed together. Metre high planks rimmed the front and sides to give some protection in choppy seas. Roy had cut holes in these, through which could be slotted four oars to row them when the raft was safely at sea. Thick sheets of plastic stretched over a wooden beam, which ran along the centre of the raft, and served as the spine of a ridged canopy for warmth and protection. A rudder, crudely made, with a tiller attached, meant that the raft could be comfortably steered without leaving the shelter.

Alex inspected the result critically. The raft was certainly large enough and would apparently be stable so long as the sea remained calm. But its size made it too heavy to carry. They would have the advantage of darkness, and the water was not more than eighty metres away but dragging it over that distance they would be frighteningly vulnerable to attack. It only needed someone to come along with a lantern or torch and discover them and they would be fighting for their lives.

While Roy and Cliff equipped the raft, Alex went upstairs to wake Tina. He found her still curled up tightly against the pillow in the same position as he had left her. At his approach, she stirred lazily, stretching her tiny limbs down the bed before turning toward him. He sat down beside her and asked how she was feeling. Her eyes rested on him contentedly, a slow, full gaze that filled him with a curious sense of excitement. A feeling of strength and self-importance.

'I had a wonderful sleep,' she said blissfully. She lifted his hand to her forehead. 'I think my temperature has gone.'

It was true. Her forehead was noticeably cooler. 'Yes,' he agreed.

Reaching up impulsively, she ran her hand down the side of his face. 'Oh, Alex, despite the fact that you drive me crazy sometimes...' Her voice tapered off. She smiled warmly, but the smile could not wipe away the depth of sadness behind.

He leant across and kissed her softly. 'I understand,' he said quietly.

'Yes,' she said, 'I think you do.'

Gently he brushed away some of the hair from her face.

'It's ready, isn't it?' she asked.

He nodded.

She gave him one final, emotional hug, but the next moment she was out of bed and quickly throwing on clothes from the wardrobe. The tenderness she had shown a minute earlier had vanished. Already she was bracing herself for the coming ordeal.

They reached the garage to find that Cliff and Roy had completed their final checks of the raft. They had also attached two ropes to the front to help drag it to the shore. After a rapid discussion on tactics, they switched off their torches. Alex strapped his rifle to his back and Cliff and Roy swung back the garage doors. In silence, they took up their positions on the ropes and pulled the raft out into the freezing night air.

The day, towards its close, had been violent and bloody, but the evil seemed to have worked itself out for now, and sleep had overtaken aggressor and potential victim alike. The raft glided noiselessly through this artificial calm, centimetre by centimetre, metre by metre, across the snow. When five minutes had passed, Alex estimated there was still another thirty metres to go, most of it on the road before they hit the shallow incline of the beach. Then there would be a further ten metres of ice encrusted gravel before they reached the water. Roy and Tina were pulling at one rope, Alex and Cliff at the other. In front was total darkness, with only the sound of small waves breaking on the ice bound shore to guide them. Alex couldn't remember being more frightened. It would only take one torchlight trained on the raft for a few seconds and everyone within hundreds of metres would know what was afoot. They had already agreed what to do if that happened. Only if they were overrun by an armed mob would they desert the raft. Anything less and they were all prepared to fight. After the events of the past afternoon, no one was going to give up the chance to leave these shores without a struggle.

The road surface was safely traversed, and the powdery snow gave way to ice as they reached the shallow descent to the water. After a few more metres, Alex's feet struck gravel. Cliff slipped and went down, recovering himself with a volley of curses.

'Shut up!' Alex hissed.

Still there was no answering light from the shore, although here and there, far off, a shout or a scream was occasionally heard. Then, further on, the inevitable happened. The raft struck a patch of gravel where the tide had eroded away the ice, and the tin drums produced a rasping sound, which made Alex's hair stand on end. They stopped pulling at once and looked around anxiously. All was quiet. The raft was too heavy to lift, so there was no other choice but to continue. They all strained again at the ropes. The scraping echoed and resonated along the shore, stirring up the tranquil night. Squares of windows were suddenly illuminated only fifty metres away. Then a large spotlight found them. Voices rang out in anger and footsteps could be heard pounding in their direction.

Alex looked around; the sea was no more than five metres away. 'PULL! PULL!' he screamed.

The raft lunged forward again. Beads of sweat were pouring off his face. The shouts were much nearer now. The raft gained momentum down the shallow incline to the sea. Three or four smaller lights came bobbing up, held by running figures, waving clubs and yelling as they closed. Alex's feet struck water. His chest was heaving. Cliff fell again, but dragged himself upright quickly. Alex's own feet struck floating ice, which brought him to his knees. The grating stopped as the raft hit water, but the mob was almost on them. With his heart pounding he fumbled for the strap of his rifle and turned to face them.

The leaders were several large youths brandishing what appeared to be carving knives. Alex fired directly over their heads, then dived to the back of the raft to join the others who were already frantically pushing it out to sea. The leaders faltered for a moment, but only to give the rest of the gang time to catch them up. Then they surged forward again, wild, merciless faces in the torchlight.

Alex hesitated for a second, vaguely aware of the shouts of the others behind him imploring him to shoot. Then the rifle came up and he was shooting like a madman, bullets tearing into flesh, bodies jerking backwards, again and again. He saw predation turn to terror as the impetus of the mob was broken. His own body seemed to be on automatic, functioning without his mind's permission. Then there was nothing, his ammunition was spent. He was in total darkness again and the screams of revenge were all about him. Mechanically he dropped back to the others who were still pushing the raft through the knee deep water. A single torchlight, probing the dark, touched his face. The mob sensed that his rifle was empty and renewed their attack. Cliff and Roy turned together at his side, each with a knife in one hand and a lump of wood in the other. Tina had jumped up on the raft and was impotently trying to paddle with one of the oars. The water was now up to their thighs.

A youth about the same height as Alex tried to split his head open with an iron bar. Alex blocked the stroke with his rifle, then rammed the butt into the youth's face. He went down, but two more immediately took his place. Then the dancing torchlight slipped from someone's grasp, and again the mob was thrown into confusion. Arms threshed about in the darkness, people fell, screams and shrieks rang out all around Alex. He weaved to the right and struck into the darkness where he had last seen one of his adversaries. His rifle only found empty space. Lunging back to where he supposed the raft to be, he found nothing. A wave of panic almost paralysed him, then he heard Tina's frantic voice rising above the turmoil. The raft must have been more than five metres away. He dived back further, pushing his way between members of the gang that had surged past him. Something heavy crashed into his shoulder. Swinging round with all his strength, he brought his rifle to bear, this time, with better effect, judging by the thud and cry of pain. Then he discarded the weapon and dived. The freezing sea struck his face and robbed his lungs of air. After a few strokes he was forced to surface. He could hear the waves lapping against the raft and the splashes and agonised screams of a

112

struggle only metres away. Gasping for air, he swam on, dimly registering the frantic voices of his friends. He felt for the corner of the raft, found it and hung on, too exhausted even to cry out. Beside the raft, the battle still raged. The other three were mounting guard, desperately calling to each other, as the mob tried to scramble aboard.

Directly above him he heard Tina scream, then there was an enormous splash as something fell off into the water. To Alex's horror, in the flash of a torchlight, he saw Tina surface next to him, spluttering and screaming hoarsely as though some dead weight were dragging her down. Then her voice vanished completely. Alex nearly went berserk. He felt the head and shoulders of someone, and his feet touched another body, Tina's, being held beneath the waves. He gripped the head of the man who was holding her under and dragged him down. Tina surfaced again, gasping and spluttering, but her agony only reinforced his rage. He dived deep, dragging the struggling man down after him. There in the depths, he put his knee in the man's back and pulled his head back with all his strength.

Nearly a minute later he broke the surface once more and cried for help. Cliff and Roy responded immediately. After a last desperate lunge toward their voices Alex was pulled on board. Tina lay severely winded and exhausted beside him. The last of the attackers had been repelled; the paddles were in the rowlocks, and they were rowing for their lives.

CHAPTER 6

Eleven hours had passed since the battle on the Somerset shore. The raft now lay close to the coast of Wales. There was no wind; it had died with the coming of day, leaving a lumpy, agitated sea, which periodically flung ice onto the deck. Roy, Cliff and Alex were at the oars, stroking mechanically. They had discarded their wet clothing in preference for layers of plastic sheeting, in which, swathed from head to foot, they looked like three monstrous grubs emerging from cocoons. Tina had on the few items of clothing that had not been soaked in the struggle. To these, Alex had added what remained of the sheeting. In spite of this, however, she continued to shiver uncontrollably, and her teeth chattered like castanets. Every so often the noise would drive him to her side, where he would wrap himself around her till the shivering eased. But he knew she was growing weaker by the hour, and the urgency to reach Wales and find a place for her to rest soon forced him back to the oars. Each time he returned he would row like a madman till his arms ached and he heaved for breath. Then, exhausted, he would pause momentarily, and begin again in a listless, sullen fashion, silently caught up in his own torturous thoughts.

But now, with the shore so close, their strength seemed to return. The raft was crashing through sloppy seas toward a long spit of land less than two hundred metres away. Fifty metres short of land the front timber stuck a solid sheet of ice and stuck fast. Alex jumped out immediately and tested the strength of the ice. When he found it would bear his weight, he wasted no time in lifting Tina out of the raft and carrying her towards the beach. Roy and Cliff were left to pack up the supplies and hurry after him.

They had gone only a short distance when Tina started to complain. She was not an invalid, she protested, she still had legs and he had no right to assume she had forgotten how to walk. He dumped her so fast that she landed on her backside, where she sat quivering slightly; Alex wasn't sure whether it was from rage or the cold. But she didn't get angry, instead she rose to her feet, brushed away some of the snow and strode on gamely.

Alex hovered round her, noticing the rigid way she held herself, straining for each step. He blamed himself for letting her stay for too long in wet clothes at the beginning of the crossing. They had all been too busy to notice the state she was in. Her clothes had seemed to draw all the heat and strength from her. It was only when she started to shiver violently that he realised that something was wrong. At once he had ordered her to strip and put on the remaining dry clothes from the supplies. He had then cut up the roll of plastic and layered it over her. At Cliff's suggestion, she had tried rowing for a while to warm herself up, but it was agony to watch her, so Alex had been reduced to periodically holding her tight. It was like trying to warm a sheet of ice. At times during the night, he almost felt she was slipping away. Worst of all had been the moment a few hours' past dawn, when she suddenly stopped shivering. He rushed over, rubbed her hands, talked to her and slapped her gently on the face to force her to respond. Finally, she did so; and later she began to shiver again. To see her now, actually walking, stubbornly resisting his attempts at assistance, made him feel very proud. But he knew that this effort must have drawn on her last reserves of strength.

He drew alongside her. 'We'll stop at the first house we reach.'

She nodded. 'You know what I was dreaming about on the raft?' she said, her voice taking on a whimsical quality. 'I was dreaming of falling asleep in front of an excruciatingly hot fire, after consuming a dozen cups of steaming soup and feeling the warmth seep right down to my toes.'

'That shouldn't be too difficult to arrange,' Alex said brightly. 'Even if we have to sacrifice the furniture, we'll build a roaring fire just for you. And I'm sure we can cook up something resembling soup from the supplies.'

She managed a faint smile, which slowly faded. 'Was it you who pulled that brute off me when I fell off the raft?' she asked suddenly.

'Yes, it was.' What had happened afterwards was something he didn't care to dwell on.

'I thought so. I heard you groan, you see…when I surfaced, I mean. I heard you groan, then jump on top of that animal. I've really been getting my money's worth out of you recently, haven't I? It seems to be a full-time job just keeping me alive.'

The plaintive note made Alex put his arm around her shoulder and draw her reassuringly close. 'You'll be doing the same for me one of these days, I've no doubt.'

'Yeah,' she said mournfully, and the single word was so barren of conviction that he knew his attempt at comforting her had failed.

The shore, to which chance had brought them, seemed sparsely inhabited. Houses stood here and there, but with no lights on, and they met no one in the narrow lanes they travelled along. Finally, they selected a two storey place a short distance from the shore. It was a red brick house with a slate roof and beautiful wooden trimmed bay windows. The front door, as expected, and some of the windows, had been kicked in and the place had been ransacked. But the lounge was still intact and it had a large, ornamental fireplace, complete with an intricately woven hearthrug.

They searched the rooms briefly to be sure they would not have company, then the men set about lighting the fire, while Tina rested on one of the lounge chairs. There was no firewood in the house, so Alex poked around picking up anything that looked as if it would burn. The place was

116

bursting with antiques and silverware. The owners seemed to have had very good taste. Ornate cups and candlestick holders, seventeenth and eighteenth century paintings and beautifully carved wooden statuettes adorned every shelf or cabinet space. Alex collected them by the armful and carted them off to the fire. This would surely rank as the most expensive and sacrilegious fire he had ever made, he thought wickedly, but this was no time to be reverential. Roy found some matches and with the aid of some old newspapers, and a generous number of eighteenth-century oil paintings, Cliff was soon nursing a few tentative flames. The carvings, which were tinder dry, and a few antique chair legs, quickly built it into a blaze.

Tina discarded her plastic sheeting and curled up on the hearthrug with only her jumper and jeans on. Cliff and Roy wrung out and aired the rest of the clothing, while Alex rummaged through the packs for something to eat. They had run through most of their water, but at Cliff's suggestion he found an uncontaminated supply in the hot water tank in the roof. There was no food at all in the cupboards, but all the culinary equipment that a master chef could require. He mixed flour and water, grated cheese over it, and tipped the concoction into a shallow baking dish. With cans of beans and a packet of noodles, he made a passable soup, which he spiced up with beef stock cubes. Everyone commented on what an excellent meal he had cooked.

Afterwards, when the warmth of the fire had penetrated every bone, with their bellies full and out of any immediate danger, they one and all fell fast asleep. They didn't wake up till the morning of the following day.

Several more days were spent at the house regaining their strength. The men recovered quickly, but Tina seemed barely to be holding her own. Although she had partaken of the meal with the others, when they first arrived, she could not be persuaded subsequently to eat much. Her nausea attacks continued and generally culminated in a dry retching that

117

seemed to tear at her insides. She also developed a cough and a sore throat, symptoms not usually associated with radiation sickness.

Alex worried about these most of all because it was obvious that her weakened immune system was allowing secondary infections, which could easily kill her in her enfeebled state.

As her illness continued, he went to extreme lengths in his attempts to try and shield her from any possible source of stress or exertion. He not only searched the house thoroughly, but he persuaded Cliff and Roy to help him rummage through the medical cupboards of the nearby houses for any drugs which might help her.

Their endeavours brought them, time and again, to scenes of tragedy and despair. More than once, in some deserted property, they found the badly hacked corpses of the previous occupants lying in the kitchen or dumped across the entrance to a ransacked larder, their blood frozen in black puddles around them. But at length, in a dusty bathroom cabinet in a partly burnt-out cottage, Roy came upon some broad-spectrum antibiotics and Panadol tablets, which made the search worthwhile.

Alex immediately gave them to Tina. He fussed over her at night too, bullying her to take her pills, or to go to bed, or to eat all the food he had piled on her plate. By the end of the fourth day his efforts were rewarded. Her fever had subsided, her sore throat had gone and her diarrhoea had eased. Only then did Alex finally listen to the pleas of Cliff and Roy that they resume their journey north. Cliff had estimated that it would take them well over a week to reach North Wales. The food they had with them would be exhausted before then if they did not start soon.

They set out the following day. The war damage was less than in England, although most houses appeared to have been vandalised in some way. The snow also had the same gradation of greys. But this landscape had an altogether different feel; one of desolation, vacancy, abandonment. One had the impression that nothing living, man or beast, existed for hundreds of kilometres.

They also stumbled on scenes of recent conflict; and there were some sights to which they could never be inured. In one place, the surface of the snow was interrupted by large numbers of mounds. When they started to walk across these areas their feet struck many bulky objects under the snow. Cliff and Roy, kicking with their heels, found that the snow was stained with blood. The hard objects were bodies, hacked, shot, even blown apart with missing limbs. One such battleground stayed with them in their minds. The mounds here were scattered over some distance. At their centre a large building had once stood, now reduced to a few charred walls. Surrounding its entrance were an array of military trucks, vehicles with machine gun mounts and armoured cars. All these vehicles had been gutted by fire or turned over on their sides. The bodies of soldiers still hung from the windows and doors, the snow heaping on them indifferently.

Alex could not suppress a brutal satisfaction at seeing the military, here at least, overrun. It seemed only right that after all the suffering they had inflicted in other places that somewhere, at least, the tables had been turned. But how costly this victory must have been, that men should be prepared to fight against machine guns and mortars! Surely the building must have been the main food store for this region, and starvation must have driven the people to such desperate courage. Where were they now, the survivors of this carnage, and would they turn their wrath on a group such as themselves? Though the battle was clearly some weeks old, they moved cautiously for several kilometres, determined at the very least to sell their lives dearly, if need be. But houses and streets and roads were as desolate as before; they did not meet a living soul.

Early in the afternoon they came across a sign which read AMMANFORD. This meant they had travelled about twenty kilometres inland from the coast. The huge dark forms rising into the clouds on their right were the foothills of the Welsh hills. Ahead, the first ridges of Black Mountain formed a long tapering wall, like the back of some huge prehistoric monster. Tina was looking very tired and beginning to lag behind, but Cliff and Roy wanted to push ahead until Alex put his foot down and refused to drag her any further. She had not complained, but Alex knew she was walking way beyond her strength.

They took shelter for the night in a small hamlet, close to a river. Tina fell asleep straight after dinner in front of the fire, leaving the men to discuss the best route north. Eventually they decided to avoid the interior of Wales and travel along the coast. This would mean a detour, but it would at least lead them through some of the more populated areas. If some type of organised community had drawn in the population from the south, they would most likely find it on the coast, since that region possessed no obvious military target. If nothing else, it would make easier going than the mountainous interior.

The next day they started out at first light. Snow had fallen during the night, but the increase in temperature it brought more than compensated for the heavier going. They made excellent progress all that morning. Tina seemed to be back to her old self; enthusiastic, talkative, even jovial at times, but by early afternoon she was beginning to lag behind again. By mid-afternoon she was all in and they had to stop for the day. Alex felt that she was growing weaker again and he urged her to take some dinner. Eventually she ate half of her meal, but unlike the previous night she slept only fitfully. Alex lay beside her, also not sleeping, waking every time she moved and watching her uneasily.

The following day Tina seemed exhausted from the very outset. She dropped back and began complaining of dizziness and fatigue. By early afternoon they had barely covered five kilometres. Again, Alex called a halt. They had reached a small coastal village. After a brief inspection, they plumped for a small brick house with a large chimney stack and a steeply sloping slate roof. They chose it because it was completely intact, as though its occupants had just walked out and left it. Many of the houses they had passed that day were in a similar condition. Blast effects in this area appeared to be minimal. The inhabitants, it would seem, had moved away more from lack of food, than threat of attack from other survivors.

Alex led Tina straight to one of the bedrooms and made her lie down. Feeling her forehead a little earlier, he had found she had a fever again. She also now admitted to having a sore throat and a feeling of giddiness. He put her to bed almost in a rage, frustrated beyond words at her for not confiding her symptoms to him.

Tina watched his stiff, angry movements with a hint of amusement, as he rummaged through the cupboards and threw piles of blankets on the bed for her. 'Oh Alex, don't be ridiculous,' she said finally, when she could take no more of it.

He stopped sorting out the pile of blankets and glared fretfully at her. 'Why is it,' he said, 'that I can never strike any sort of harmonious relationship with you? You either make me feel wonderful, or throw me into a rage with your behaviour.'

'I think you're a very sensitive person, Alex,' she said softly. 'You read meanings into my actions that are not there.'

'But I expect you to tell me when you're sick! I thought that at least we had that much understanding.'

She pursed her lips and gazed thoughtfully at him. 'I think we have a lot of understanding,' she said. 'Much more than is ever spoken between us. But there can't be plain sailing all the time in any relationship, especially if the people are deeply involved with one another.'

It was the first time either of them had actually put their feelings for each other into words, and Alex was deeply moved. He came over and sat beside her. 'I just can't lose you,' he said sadly. 'Not now, not ever. I couldn't even begin to imagine going through all this,' he gestured toward the window, 'without you.'

Tina saw the agony in his face and she reached out and pulled him towards her.

He kissed her, then climbed into bed.

'We've got to get to a working community soon,' she said softly. 'Otherwise, our food will be gone and we'll all be stranded. So, you see I have to push myself.'

'But to the point of your own death?' Alex pleaded.

She was quiet for a moment. 'I should have told you sooner,' she conceded grimly.

The next day, Cliff found Alex alone sitting dejectedly on a bed in one of the spare rooms. He was staring through the window and didn't move, nor altered his expression, when he entered. The older man knew the cause of his distraction. Poor Tina had had a terrible night. The sickness had swept in upon her almost without warning; severe headache, fever, aching muscles and glands that had swollen to the size of small grapes on the sides of her throat. Alex had gone almost crazy with worry. He had pumped all his remaining antibiotics and Panadol into her and rushed around the house searching for more pills, in vain.

By early morning, when the medication had worn off, she was visibly worse. The search for more medicines had been renewed and he and Roy had joined in, but all to no avail. The people who lived here must have had plenty of time to collect their belongings, before leaving. He doubted there was any medication within kilometres. Now all anyone could do was to wait and hope. But it seemed that there could not be much hope left. With every hour her condition deteriorated. There were a number of secondary infections; acute diarrhoea, vomiting, pains in her abdomen and a rash no one could identify, as though every disease in the country had suddenly decided to take up residence within her. They had all seen similar versions of her symptoms back in the work camp.

122

Cliff knew attempting to console Alex with words would be useless; indeed, they had far too much respect for each other for such foolish talk. But an idea had occurred to him, and it was significant enough to be worth breaking in on his pain. So, he walked round in front of Alex, blocking his view of the window. 'How is she?'

Alex shook his head mournfully. 'No better, but at least she's sleeping now. That may help, a little.'

Cliff nodded. 'Did she sleep at all last night?'

A slow shaking of the young man's head was his only answer.

'Look guv,' Cliff went on, 'it seems to me that Tina is getting worse. She needs a lot more help than we can give her.'

Alex shifted his gaze to Cliff's face.

'Now, I'm not trying to be funny,' Cliff put in quickly. 'But we have been looking at the map and think we can reach the Blaenau mine in three days and be back in under a week. If there's a community up there, then maybe we'll be able to get some medicines. If not,' he shrugged, 'well, at least we saved Tina the trip. And we can always look for medicines on the way there and back.'

Alex sighed deeply and slumped back on the bed. 'Why didn't I think of that?' he mumbled, half to himself.

Cliff suddenly became serious and intense. 'You didn't think of it because you're too involved, Alex. You can't think or act objectively anymore. Your mind's blinded by your feelings.'

Alex frowned, as if he failed to gather the import of this.

'She's bloody contagious, Alex,' Cliff blurted. 'If you get too close you'll end up the same as her.'

'What are you trying to say?' Alex's tone was suddenly sharp and resentful.

'Just don't get too close.'

'I don't care…I don't care,' Alex repeated, and he sounded as if he meant it.

'Well, you should. The last thing Tina wants is for you to give up. You're no good to anyone if you're as sick as she is.'

'Don't tell me what Tina wants!' Alex suddenly exploded. 'Don't you think I know better than anybody what she wants?'

'Then you'll know I'm right,' Cliff retorted. 'She's concerned about you. She wants you to live.'

Alex was too choked to respond to this, so he said nothing.

'I just don't want you coming down with the flu, that's all,' Cliff persisted more softly.

'You don't expect her to recover, do you?' Alex asked, throwing it down like a challenge.

But Cliff said simply; 'She's a fighter. If anyone will pull through this, it'll be Tina.'

And with this he turned and left the room.

When he was gone, Alex turned back to the window. The grief rose within him like physical pain, tears welled at his eyes and dropped onto his shirt.

Cliff and Roy left later that morning, carrying only four days' supply between them. This was partly to enable them to move more quickly, but their main reason was because they felt that Tina would need the remaining food if she was to have any chance of surviving. As it was, they were both reasonably fit and healthy and could take advantage of any opportunities that came their way. Alex, on the other hand, would be too tied up caring for Tina to scavenge for food. He would have to survive exclusively on the supplies they had left him.

From the start they set a rapid pace. By mid-afternoon they were already moving up the Dovey Valley. They found their first signs of recent human activity in this valley, with many sets of footprints in the snow, and they heard the occasional distant shout, too. Once they even saw a house burning and many figures silhouetted in its flames, watching it burn. As the day wore on, they passed the blackened, shells of more houses, as though the demoralised population had taken to burning them down just for warmth. These were not encouraging signs. Here, too, it seemed, the mob ruled. By nightfall, their worst fears were confirmed by the discovery of two massacres. These were not old battles, like those they had stumbled on earlier. No snow lay on these bodies, the skin was still elastic and supple.

They spent the night in a small cottage somewhere along the banks of the Dovey. They had covered an enormous distance in only eight hours, and both were very near exhaustion. Roy started a small fire and they heated up beans and ate them with some of the unleavened bread that Alex had baked a few days previously. They spoke little while they ate, each content to review in his own mind the meaning of what they had seen that day. Roy, with his large, coarse features, chewed away with that massive deliberation so characteristic of him, as if all night would not be long enough for the task he had on hand. Cliff, in contrast, picked at his food nervously, his face constantly registering his thoughts in a series of curious grimaces and deepening frowns. When the meal was over, he boiled some water and they added one or two stock cubes for flavour.

'I hope we've done the right thing,' he ventured finally, sipping cautiously at his drink.

Roy glanced over at him. 'Seems logical to me.'

'Logical, yes,' Cliff agreed. 'But suppose Tina dies while we're away? Alex is very involved so he could easily do something stupid.'

'You think she's going to die?'

Cliff looked across at Roy, realising this was not an option that the big man had previously considered. 'Can you remember any people in the camp who recovered from the flu?' he asked.

'Can't say I can, off hand,' he responded in his slow deliberate way. 'But they were all taken to the sick bay before they got too sick.'

125

'I visited people who were taken ill a few days after we arrived. They were all dead within two or three days.'

'But they were already weak,' Roy replied.

'Not before they were taken ill, they weren't. Anyway, none of us are in particularly good shape.'

'But not all Tina's symptoms are the same as the ones we saw back at the camp,' argued Roy.

'It's the flu all right,' Cliff replied flatly. 'Her other symptoms just indicate that she has a secondary infection of some kind as well as radiation poisoning.'

Roy's mouth opened slightly, and his eyebrows knitted together into a single line across his forehead, but he said nothing. He seemed to be digesting this new information with all the caution and patience he had shown in eating his food. He sipped his drink briefly, then turned back to the fire. But Cliff knew his old friend; he did not need to be told what he was thinking. That added pinch of sadness in his expression, that forlornness that wasn't there before, said it all.

By first light they were moving north again, Roy striding ahead with a pace which ate up the kilometres. By mid-afternoon they had climbed through most of the pass separating the mountains of Cader Idris and Dinas Mawddwy. Although they had come on the occasional corpse, the mountains seemed devoid of human life. But when they descended into the next valley it was quite a different story. Some enormous battle seemed to have been staged there. Villages were burnt out, bridges torn up and thrown into the gullies they had once spanned. And worst of all, they found evidence of another massacre: bodies, thousands of them, strewn along the ground, as though the whole Welsh population had travelled north to perish in this exact location.

Their first thought was to turn back, and find another way around the area, but the questions posed by this scene seemed to draw them on relentlessly. They reached the valley floor and Cliff dug through the snow and exhumed a number of corpses. Although some had been beaten or knifed, most bore shrapnel or bullet wounds. But there were no military personnel amongst the dead. The story told of a complete slaughter. These civilians appeared not to have been able to kill any of their attackers. Cliff swore wildly when he realised this fact, while Roy just shook his head in disbelief.

They walked on cautiously and found the remains of more recent massacres. But here, a new element seemed to have entered, and a very sinister one! The sheer barbarity and sadism of these later acts left both men shaken. At first Cliff had thought that the mutilations of these bodies must have been caused by packs of wild dogs, until they came on the corpses of about a dozen victims no more than a few hours old. The men had been physically beaten until their whole bodies were smashed to pulp, every bone broken, every bit of flesh bruised, their faces featureless, as if the attackers had set about them in an uncontrollable frenzy. The women, before death, old and young alike, had been stripped and raped. Some many times from the amount of blood lost from their groins. But several human torsos in this ghastly scene, both young males and young females, had had their arms and legs roughly hacked off for a different purpose. The realisation of what they were looking at horrified both men. Neither had any doubt that these were the victims of human cannibalism.

They immediately retreated into the shadows of the closest houses, where they debated their options heatedly. After nearly turning around again, they finally decided to press on; hoping the mountains which lay directly to the north would be as deserted as the ones they had just left. They could not help being frightened; reacting to even the smallest sound, for it had become obvious that regardless of what had happened in the valley before, it was now ruled entirely by mobs in the lowest state of degeneracy, who preyed on each other for food.

All that afternoon, they narrowly avoided contact with large gangs. The individuals they glimpsed were heavily armed with an assortment of kitchen knives and crudely carved spears, but they were also marked with what looked like white paint across their foreheads. Many of the bodies they came across later also had this same curious symbol on their foreheads.

By dark they had climbed the steep, winding road out of the valley and had penetrated several kilometres into the mountains. Happily, they had met with no more gangs, and the smooth surface of the snow bore no human footprints. They continued their ascent till it was completely dark, when they stumbled into a house by the roadside. It seemed too risky to light a fire, so they ate the remaining supply of bread and then curled up to sleep for the night.

The next day they pushed on as soon as it was light. The mine lay only a dozen kilometres to the north and, providing there were no more surprises, they expected to reach it by late afternoon. They travelled all that morning through a narrow, U shaped valley, which, even before the war, must have been a very barren and formidable place. For there were no trees, not even the shattered stumps of them, and no houses. Only the wind seemed to frequent this valley, where it howled and shrieked like some caged predator, bouncing off the sheer cliffs and whipping up powerful eddies which at times engulfed them in whirlpools of biting snow. Along the top of the cliffs huge ice fields hung, and now and then they would fall with thunderous detonations to the valley floor below. The fine, powdery snow from these avalanches swept right across the valley in a fine particle mist, creating white out conditions where they could see no more than a few metres in front of them for many minutes at a time.

By late morning they had traversed the most dangerous section and the cliffs had fallen back and dwindled. But now, if anything, the scenery took on an even more savage appearance as they moved deeper into the rich slate mining area of Northern Wales. The high content of slate in the rock had reduced the cliffs to blackened scree slopes, which climbed into the clouds like huge rock piles, broken and shattered as though thrown up by chain gangs of giants.

Further up, the valley broadened and left space for an iced-up lake to form, with a number of houses clustered by its shore. As they approached these houses they became aware that the settlement was occupied, and that their progress was being carefully watched. Soon they could see men at the windows with rifles apparently trained on them, but by this time it was too late to turn back. Other signs of habitation, smoke rising from a chimney, a four-wheel drive obviously still in use, at least consoled them that they weren't dealing with the mindless, butchering mobs who lorded it over the valley. There was a measured caution about this group, a sense of purpose and calculation in the way they waited. But Cliff and Roy were not about to offer themselves up at point blank range. A short distance from the nearest house, they drew to a halt and prepared to await developments.

Presently the door of the house opened, and two men came out. Both were dressed similarly in grey, wet weather gear and large leather boots, which reached up to their shins. They were unarmed, but other men in the house covered their every step. They approached to within a few metres of Cliff and Roy, then stopped and looked them up and down. One of the men had a large, bristly beard and ruddy, inflamed features as though he had been standing in front of a fire for most of the day. His companion was rather smaller, more refined and delicate in appearance with a pointed face and a pair of steel rimmed spectacles resting on his nose.

'And where would you be going?' the bearded man opened the conversation.

'We're travelling north,' said Cliff, shrugging his shoulders. 'Looking for some type of settlement we can join.'

The man smiled wryly at this. 'Where have you come from?'

'Bristol.'

'All the way from Bristol,' the man echoed, more thoughtfully. 'What makes you think there's a community you can join here?'

'It was a long shot,' Cliff admitted. 'But we know there's a mine here which the government took over in the last war. We thought they may have stored food up here.'

The man nodded. 'We've heard that story before,' he said. 'But you're the first for nearly a week now. The last people through here said anyone without the mark was being killed.'

Cliff frowned. 'I don't understand,' he said finally. 'What mark are you talking about?'

'Have you had any problems over the past few days?' This was from the man with the spectacles, who had not previously spoken. He seemed to be examining their faces with a good deal of interest.

'None to speak of,' Cliff replied cautiously. 'Although the last valley we travelled through looked like a huge graveyard.'

'Graveyard?'

'Bodies everywhere. There were gangs of survivors, too, still roaming around killing each other.'

'But you managed to avoid them?'

'We made sure we did,' Cliff answered. 'And we sighted no one once we reached the mountains.'

'These gangs you mentioned,' the bearded man continued. 'Did you notice anything peculiar about them?'

The question seemed to carry some weight or significance, which escaped Cliff. He thought back. 'They looked thin and sick,' he said slowly. Then he remembered. 'Ah, the paint! They had what looked like dabs of white paint on their foreheads.'

'And you have no idea why they had this paint on their foreheads?' the man with the spectacles asked, in his rather irritating pedantic way.

130

'No, none.' Both Roy and Cliff answered almost together.

The two strangers glanced at each other quickly before continuing. 'We marked their foreheads,' the bearded man said bluntly. 'They had been rejected from our community on health grounds. To stop them from re-applying, we painted their foreheads with a special paint which cannot be removed by solvents.'

'Won't they just rub it off anyway?' Roy asked.

'Eventually, yes, so we also branded the right hand of each one before we released them.'

Cliff resisted the urge instinctively to look down at his own hand, feeling that any such action might be misinterpreted.

The smaller man pushed his spectacles back up his nose. 'The bottom line, gentlemen, is that if you wish to join our community, you have first to prove to us that you have not already been rejected.'

Cliff's gaze went from them to the riflemen mounting guard at the windows beyond, and back again. He shrugged and stretched out his arm. 'The right hand, did you say?' he said in his best sarcastic voice.

After Cliff and Roy had shown that their hands were unmarked the atmosphere changed entirely. Their questioners became pleasant and congenial, even friendly. It was the first time since the holocaust that anyone had treated them with any degree of warmth. They were taken into the house and placed in front of a large fire and given cups of coffee. When Cliff and Roy explained that they had been carpenters before the war, they were even more pleased. The community, it seemed, had any number of building projects they were contemplating, but starting was hampered by the scarcity of trained craftsmen. They had a glut of office workers, whose skills were no longer valuable, and who they had been obliged to retrain as tradesmen and the like.

Cliff took full advantage of their hospitality to fire off a lot of questions. The mine, it appeared, did exist and was indeed full of food and equipment. In fact, there were enough supplies to feed and clothe a population of fifty thousand for up to a year. The military seemed to have been caught by surprise when the war broke out so suddenly, as they only had a company of men guarding the mine. In the immediate aftermath, the locals, who were well aware of the location and purpose of the mine, had crowded up to it asking for food. All their pleas, however, had been to no avail. Soon, refugees from much further afield, began arriving till thousands upon thousands of starving people were clamouring at their doors, but still they were not helped or admitted. The mine was too well defended to fall to an unarmed mob and the military couldn't be starved out, so it was a stalemate. Then the survivors heard rumours of several battalions of soldiers slowly butchering their way north towards the mine. The valley that Cliff and Roy had crossed the previous day had been where these reinforcements had fought their last battle. The disappointed survivors were roused to fury by the thought of these newcomers turning the mine into a fortress and they had attacked the column relentlessly, moving in human waves over their own dead. Eventually, after a terrible slaughter, the spirit of the soldiers had been broken. Rather than continue a useless struggle, they had capitulated and agreed to lead an assault on the mine themselves. With their weapons and leadership, and the weight of so many survivors, the balance of power was altered and the three hundred men guarding the mine gave in after the entrance was blown.

The survivors could hardly believe their good fortune; the place was like a small city. The workings themselves spanned twenty-six levels and over sixty kilometres of tunnels. In the few years since the military had taken control, the top four of these levels had been completely remodelled. Fluorescent globes lined the tunnels, the walls had been reinforced with concrete, large conference rooms, offices and spacious dormitories had been carved out, complete with panelled walls and superior furnishings. Five thousand people could be fed and accommodated with ease. The whole place had power and heating, supplied by three huge generators deep within the interior of the mine. Every conceivable item to sustain a colony was also there from tea and coffee to agricultural equipment and vehicles. This final assault and occupation had taken place only three weeks previously, but already the mine had a membership of eleven thousand survivors.

When Cliff and Roy finished their coffee, they were driven to the mine. Both felt rather overwhelmed by all this, as though they had suddenly stepped back from chaos into civilisation. Cliff, however, had not forgotten their reason for coming all this way and he wasted no time in telling them about Alex and Tina. Their talk of returning into the wilderness caused some raised eyebrows as it was considered an impracticable idea. Nevertheless, since they persisted in it, they were advised to seek permission from a man called Marcus Higgins. He had been a Major in the army until three weeks before when he had persuaded his men to stop the killing and join with the survivors against the mine. He was now in charge of maintaining security, and he supervised the screening of new community members.

The mine was situated at the bottom of a narrow valley, closed in on both sides by towering mountains. The driver shifted into second gear and started a steep ascent. But after only a few minutes he turned off to the left along a narrow gravel road. The road ended in a large man-made plateau carved directly out of the side of the mountain. Here, over two hundred people were busily at work, erecting buildings, repairing cars, and cooking food in huge, charred pots over blazing fires, while further off, small squads of survivors were being trained in the use of rifles.

They drove further on and stopped at what must once have been the entrance to the mine. Now only a gaping hole remained with a narrow yellow glow in its centre, where the new entrance had been constructed. The driver hopped out here and went in search of the Major. A few minutes later he returned, accompanied by a large, powerfully built man with cropped grey hair and the beginnings of a thick, almost white beard. He must have been in his early fifties, Cliff estimated, which by post war standards, was extremely old.

He came up and shook hands with them both enthusiastically. 'So, already you gentlemen want to leave us when you've only just arrived.' He spoke in a good humoured, faintly amused manner.

'We don't really want to leave,' Roy said very seriously. 'But we can't just abandon our friends.'

'Hmm. And you want to take some of our medicines with you, I understand? Just how seriously ill are these friends of yours?'

'Ah…it's only the girl that's sick,' Cliff said quickly, afraid Roy would say something that would reveal the hopelessness of Tina's case. 'And she's more weak from lack of food, than anything else. But she does have a terrible cough and a sore throat. If you could see your way to letting us have some antibiotics and something to lower her temperature, we would be very grateful.'

Cliff felt Marcus's keen gaze fixed upon him as he said this, and he had the impression that he didn't believe a word of it. But nothing was said, and he turned his attention to Roy, whom he scrutinised in the same sceptical, analytical manner.

'Of course, you do realise, don't you, that your friends and yourselves have to undergo a very rigorous screening procedure before you can be permitted to enter this community. Anyone suffering from a communicable disease, or so ill that they cannot recover, will not be admitted. Still,' he continued more thoughtfully, 'you both look healthy enough. After your examination, we shall be in a better position to consider your request.'

'Can we have this examination today?' Cliff asked.

There was a slight pause at this. 'Very well,' Marcus said at length. 'I imagine that could be arranged. But

134

whatever the outcome, I still haven't decided whether I'll let you have any drugs.'

'But we'll be back in a few days,' Cliff protested.

'Oh, I'm sure that would be your intention, but that's not the problem,' Marcus replied scratching his beard reflectively. 'The problem is that it's open season down south, especially on anyone who hasn't been exiled from the community. You're both very lucky to be alive, but I doubt you will have the same luck twice.'

'Why not mark our foreheads, the same as you do the other exiles?' Cliff asked.

'Yes, that might be an idea,' Marcus said, suddenly becoming thoughtful. 'And there's something else we could do.' He mumbled something to the driver, who immediately disappeared and came back with a map of Wales.

'Now, show us exactly where your friends are,' Marcus said.

Cliff indicated the place.

'Ah!' Marcus leaned over the map. 'I think you might be in luck,' he said at length, looking up. 'We actually control a lot more of the mountainous interior of Wales than we do the coast. Not because we have taken it by force, but because no one can live there anyway. We can probably drop you here.' He pointed to a place inland and considerably further south than where Cliff and Roy had first encountered the community. 'This would be less than two days' walk from where your friends are, and you could avoid travelling along the coast.'

'Then you will let us have the supplies?' Cliff asked eagerly.

'If you pass your medical and you are both carpenters, as you say you are, then I'll consider it.' He gave a brief smile and turned back towards the mine.

'When will you let us know?' Cliff called after him.

'If your medical report is good, you'll hear by tomorrow morning,' he called back before disappearing from view.

The medical lasted for nearly two hours. Both men had to strip off and submit to scrupulous external examinations. Every bruise, abrasion or lump of any kind was carefully recorded. Samples of their blood, their faeces and their urine were taken away for analysis, and their throats were swabbed. While the results of these tests were being assessed, they were asked about their movements since the holocaust. How close had they been to a bomb zone? How long did they stay under cover? Were they ever sick? What did they eat? Where did they find their food? The questions flowed past them in an endless stream, and when they were complete, they were required to sign their names to their statements.

Then, at last, they were free to go and were led to a large kitchen on the second floor of the mine where they were invited to eat as much as they liked. In front of them were pots of steaming noodles, mixed with canned meat and vegetables, freshly baked bread, thick vegetable broth and a pot of hot coffee. The sight of so much food was enough to make them giddy, but they did not constrain themselves. Finally, almost dead on their feet, their bellies full and bloated, they were conducted to the dormitories and given beds for the night. Despite their precarious circumstances, neither man could remember even laying his head on the pillow.

Early the next morning a tall, smiling youth woke them and introduced himself, in a pronounced cockney accent, as Rashi. He had a note for them from Marcus, which read:

Congratulations, you have both passed your medicals with flying colours. The arrangements for your trip have been made. Rashi will issue you with all the medical supplies you will need and drive you as far south as is safe to do so.

Best wishes and a safe journey,

Marcus.

Rashi had already organised a week's supply of food for them, and enough medical supplies to cover just about any contingency. He marked both their foreheads with white paint and gave them special passes to show to the border guards on their return, and an extra two for Tina and Alex.

Driving south, by late morning they had reached the most southerly point of the community, a small outpost manned by half a dozen men. Neither Cliff nor Roy had said much during the trip. The indulgences of the night before were already forgotten under the urgency they both felt. In the car they had spoken of trying to reach Alex and Tina by late the next day. Rashi had doubted this was possible, but even one night's delay seemed criminal when they had the medicines to cure Tina's sickness in their hands. Leaving Rashi and the men at the outpost, after a brief farewell, they set off almost at a jog.

Three days later, exhausted and desperate after spending a day and a night lost amongst the hills, they burst into the house. There was no one there and no explanation as to why not. Ten minutes later, while searching the surroundings, Roy came on a wooden cross planted over a freshly dug mound of earth. The words scratched on the wood read:

TINA HARTLEY
20 years
a brave soul
much loved and missed

They widened their search at once, and after several hours they found Alex perched on a boulder overlooking a frozen stream. His jumper and his gloves were missing, his hands soiled, his nails split and bloody. In spite of repeated attempts to make him talk, he did not respond. Finally, Roy took off his jumper and they wrapped him in it and urged him back to the house.

The following day, Cliff and Roy led the forlorn and silent figure of Alex back towards the mine.

Three years later

CHAPTER 7

Since its inception, the community had grown enormously.
As the word spread, refugees had flooded in from all corners
of England and Wales. By the end of the first year its
numbers had swelled to nearly twenty thousand; by the
second year they had reached thirty thousand, until by the
end of the third year there were over thirty-five thousand
members. At the same time its influence had extended to the
east and south, until it controlled territory from Porthmadog
on the coast, across the Welsh highlands as far as the Welsh
border and north to Colwyn Bay. All the land to the west,
including the island of Anglesey, was under its command.

But for each new member who was accepted, many
more were rejected and expelled into the wilderness. These
exiles formed roaming bands on the borders of the
community who constantly threatened the security of its
inhabitants. Therefore, new members were required to
undertake defence training. This included military drill, hand
to hand combat and small arms practice for all ages, except
the very young. Children were given basic schooling and
adults received lessons in farming and building skills. When
this stage was complete, the peacetime occupation of each
person was examined and he or she was placed in the
position which would be most beneficial to the community.
Free choice, personal fulfilment, democracy, in fact all the
terms and phrases held dear before the war, meant nothing
here. In the eyes of the community, the individual no longer
existed, except as one more cog or workhorse to be used
creatively for the general good. The colonists were told when
they could sleep, when they could eat, what job they could

140

do, where they could do it and for how long. No facet of one's life was left open for individual decision.

Laws were formulated and passed by a committee of twelve men and women. Their authority was absolute and the principle on which they worked was that the well-being of the community overrode all other considerations. If someone was pronounced diseased, or was insubordinate, or refused to work, he or she was given a week's supply of food and expelled. Only exceptionally gifted or invaluable members such as doctors, nurses, engineers or agricultural advisers could hope for a reprieve. Even in their cases, however, they were certain to be removed as soon as a suitable replacement could be found. Such a person didn't last long in the wild, the food they carried being more attractive to the other exiles than any skills they might happen to possess.

But the harsh laws of the community had paid off. There had never been a significant outbreak of disease, their external defences had not been seriously breached, and vast agricultural and building projects were constantly pushing the frontier eastward through the Welsh highlands. As a matter of policy, all arable land had been converted to agriculture and the hills to the rough grazing of sheep and cattle. Extensive chicken farms had been set up in the lowlands and the seas were being harvested again. With these successes, the community's own produce now accounted for over eighty percent of the total food consumption. Dried foods, such as fruit and cereal, were still being supplied from the dwindling reserves of the mine.

However, the future of the community remained uncertain. After the war, the land had changed from a dark smoky wasteland, tortured by snow storms and gale force winds to the climate of a savannah. Midday temperatures often climbed into the high thirties, little rain fell and winds constantly ripped through the land.

The first harvest had been an unqualified disaster. Radiation and freezing conditions had laid a poisonous frozen crust on the ground, which had to be peeled off and taken away by hand before any crops could be planted. Even then, each fall of rain or snow brought down more radiation. The new crops germinated and withered under the poor half-light of the sun. The poor harvest was then attacked by an insect plague from the east and their ravages had scarcely ceased when a rat plague followed, devouring the insects and anything else in their path. Even tethered cattle were attacked. The rats tore at the legs of these beasts until they collapsed, kicking and grunting, under a tide of gnashing teeth and ripping claws. Then they in turn starved and disappeared from the land.

The next harvest was better. This time the improved weather conditions had allowed most of the crops to germinate and start shooting. The insects appeared again, but now the colonists were ready for them with pesticides drawn from the store in the mine. Very slowly the crops struggled towards the sun. As the rain was more infrequent, huge irrigation channels were dug and water pumped by hand from pre-war reservoirs near Mount Snowdon. The whole community held its breath while the crops grew, but as harvesting day approached it became evident that the cereals had not swelled in the ear, and the vegetables, small and parched above the ground, were withered in their roots.

Fortunately, there were a number of environmental and agricultural experts among the survivors in the community. They explained how the drastically altered climatic conditions were affecting the whole cycle of nature. Apart from smoke, the incineration of the world's forests and cities had also released billions of tonnes of nitrogen. This nitrogen combined with oxygen to form nitric oxides, which in turn produced ozone on the earth's surface. In the stratosphere, however, the formation of these nitric oxides actually had the reverse effect and destroyed the ozone layer. Previously, by converting ultra violet light to heat, the ozone had formed a warm, protective envelope around the earth's surface. Now that the ozone was on the planet's surface and not in the stratosphere, UV light penetrated to the surface and heated it, creating a greenhouse effect. Apart from raising the surface temperatures both the UV light and ozone also affected plant growth by destroying vulnerable shoot tips.

To add to these problems, the mine was critically short of fertilisers and farming implements. Without fertilisers, the type of intensive agriculture that had evolved in Great Britain before the holocaust was not possible. Although the machinery for such farming still existed and could be repaired, the fuel to power it was not available. The supplies the mine possessed had to be used on essential services, like the transport of materials and on generators for the production of light and heat. The farmers amongst the community were forced to revert to skills they had discarded as old fashioned, and in which they had no experience.

These difficulties were debated in committee for weeks before a new farming strategy emerged. In broad terms, this entailed protecting the crops in every conceivable way; nothing was left to chance. Vast glass houses were to be constructed covering many hectares of land. The glass would exclude UV light, radioactive fallout and any sudden insect plaques, and at the same time provide a safe working environment. All water to be used in irrigation was first to be sand filtered in huge tanks, under the force of gravity, to remove any radioactive particles. Large amounts of decomposing vegetable matter were also scavenged from the surrounding countryside and placed in these glass houses to provide the carbon dioxide vital for plant growth. Limited hydroponic greenhouses were also constructed for more intensive agriculture with crops such as tomatoes, cucumbers, peppers and lettuces powered by a limited supply of solar panels scavenged from nearby towns. These changes, once introduced, were soon rewarded with results.

Although the number of crops grown was relatively small because of the labour involved and the difficulty in finding materials to build the glass houses, the potatoes flourished, and the fruit and cereal crops grew high. The community had achieved its first major success.

The rearing of farm animals, however, presented an entirely different set of problems, which were not so happily solved. Finding sufficient feed was easy enough since grass was one of the most resistant forms of plant life. The surrounding hills and plains had quickly become blanketed with a flowing mat of green, but heavy fallout limited their apparent usefulness. When cattle and sheep grazed in the open, they concentrated certain long life isotopes, such as caesium 137 in their tissues, and iodine 131 and Strontium 90 in their milk. Only by cultivating grass especially for feed could this drawback be overcome, and there just was not the manpower or the glass covering available to do this. So, if meat and dairy products were to be consumed, a proportion of radioactivity had to be tolerated in the diet. Specialist teams were formed to investigate the problem. A partial solution was found by converting all milk into hard products such as cheese, where the radioactive mineral content had been reduced. But for this generation at least, a complete alteration of diet was deemed essential, and was introduced. Cereals such as barley, oats, maize, rye and oilseed rape, which before the war had been used largely for animal feed, now had to be made palatable for human consumption. Meats and fresh eggs were to be taken only in small quantities, so as not to exceed the radiation tolerance level of the body. In effect, the community became almost vegetarian, eating mostly cereals, breads, cheeses, fruits and small amounts of salted meats.

Long before Alex drew near in his Land Rover, his presence had been detected by sentries in a series of black slate turrets and radioed back to the mine. With the manpower at their command, the community had been able to deploy a force of over four thousand men and women in turrets like these, along the whole length of the border. Like the threads of a spider's web, the slightest twitch or disturbance in the surrounding countryside could bring reinforcements scurrying to the scene.

Alex passed through without incident and was driving for another hour before he reached the nerve centre of the mine. He parked the Land Rover in the service and maintenance area, where it would receive a thorough overhaul after each mission and climbed out and stretched his limbs.

Three years had wrought its changes in Alex. He was barely twenty-five, but he looked ten years older. Like most survivors all fleshiness had disappeared from his face. His skin now clung in a taut, lined mask to his bones, giving him an almost haunted look. The wasting of his face had also enlarged his eyes, making them more intense and sadder somehow, as though he was keeping some enormous flood of emotion bottled up there.

Alex walked round to the front of the Land Rover and began slowly packing various papers into a small leather satchel on the front seat. He had just completed this task when Cliff suddenly appeared from behind one of the vehicles. The sight of him both delighted and perturbed Alex. The little carpenter had become his closest and most treasured companion. Cliff possessed a rare quality of total, incorruptible honesty. His opinions were his own and he stated them with a bluntness which most people found upsetting, but which Alex never failed to admire. Their discussions had no hidden undertones; each man spoke out and respected the opinion of the other. Together they shared a strange type of alliance against the community, Cliff because of his natural hatred of rules and regulations, Alex because he hated everything the community stood for. He loathed its harshness, its inhumanity. The system was working; they were winning against the elements but at what cost? The day of human individuality was gone forever.

And it saddened Alex to see how sick Cliff looked. Much of his hair had dropped out and refused to grow again. A skin cancer was starting to swell on his face, and his arms and legs had withered, as though some malign thing was eating away at him from the inside. It was sickening to watch and always became more noticeable after long trips away.

The carpenter stood up and embraced him. 'It's great to see you,' he grinned, barely able to contain his own relief. 'Everyone's been concerned, you're two weeks overdue. What the hell was so bloody interesting?'

The intensity of Cliff's greeting surprised Alex. 'Things just took longer than I anticipated,' he answered mildly.

Cliff shook his head. After each mission Alex seemed to come back more withdrawn into himself than ever. 'I thought you were finished this time. I prayed you weren't, but by God I was worried. Give it up, guv, you've already run more missions than anyone still alive. Stop before you get yourself killed.'

Alex raised his eyebrows but did not speak.

They had been over this ground before. Cliff was aware of Alex's suicidal tendencies and had done his best to snap him out of them, but Alex had so little desire for life left.

Cliff sighed deeply but decided not to pursue the matter for the moment. 'What did you find in London?'

'Just more unsolved mysteries, I'm afraid.'

Cliff frowned. 'So, London is the same as the other cities?'

'Worse in some respects. There seem to be pockets of radiation all over the city.'

'The committee isn't going to be pleased.'

Alex nodded slightly. In his opinion, the committee would have every right to feel concerned. He walked around to the front of the Land Rover and stared out at the sunset. 'That's eight cities that have registered high radiation counts,' he said, more to himself than to Cliff. 'It's not right. If this was fallout, it would be all over the place. There wouldn't be intense patches everywhere.'

'So, you don't think your readings are from fallout?'

'I don't know what to think.'

'Maybe the committee will come up with the answer.'

'Maybe.'

146

Cliff watched the exhausted silhouette of his friend. He knew that something else was troubling him, but Alex rarely revealed what he was thinking these days. Although he was open enough about minor problems, it always seemed to Cliff that he had permanently closed off that part of him that Tina had once shared. He drew nearer to him, studying his face and trying to assess his mood. 'Did you run into any problems on the trip?'

'No... no the trip was fine.' He fell silent, as though reliving his experiences in his mind. 'It was like walking back in time and seeing it all over again,' he said after a pause. 'No one has been there since the holocaust. Skeletons all over the place, very little plant life and the rats, and flies...' He shook his head. 'So many rats! And they were so hungry they started to tear into my clothing. I had to continually kick them away.'

'Not nice, eh?' Cliff agreed. 'But there's no point in dwelling on the past, is there? You've always been one for that.'

'Yes,' Alex said distantly.

'We can't dwell on the past, we have to look to the future,' Cliff persisted as though trying to reinforce his point.

'What future, Cliff?' Alex suddenly blurted out. 'Don't you see? I don't pity these skeletons, I envy them. They suffered for a few minutes, maybe a few hours or days, but then they were free. And us? We are still here, still struggling, and for what? A few more years of life scratched out of a wasteland until our own deaths?'

'You always were a pessimist, Alex. I agree the world will never be the same, but the land will regenerate. The animals and plant life will slowly start to return.'

'It won't always be like this,' Cliff argued, determined not to be beaten. 'The radiation levels will drop, and the animals will start to multiply again.'

Alex took a deep breath, and then looked back at the sunset. As the sun approached the horizon, the huge dust burdens in the stratosphere magnified it to many times its normal size. Like some grotesque, flaming fireball, it stained the sky in rainbows of deep purples and crimsons, and the land in the colour of blood. The irony of that never failed to make him smile. 'I don't know,' he said finally. 'Does fertility return just because the radiation level drops? Or is the damage permanent?'

Cliff knew without asking what was being referred to here. Over the past three years there had been just over twelve hundred births in the community, and over half of these had had to be terminated because of physical or mental defects. There would be precious few children to inherit this mess.

'Even if most of the survivors remain sterile, their children won't,' Cliff said.

'How can you say that? It may take generations before the population becomes fertile again. Our children's children will still be eating contaminated food before some of the longer life isotopes have fully decayed.'

Cliff shook his head slowly. At times like these, there was little point in trying to reason with Alex. He would pick holes in any argument, however convincingly put. In truth, the root cause was Alex's emotional state. He was a brooder, he worried about things that he couldn't change. He had lost all that was most dear to him, and he dwelt on that, almost to the exclusion of hope.

The two friends parted, Alex to get something to eat, Cliff to return to work. Alex knew he had put a damper on Cliff's cheerfulness and that he seemed to be doing it constantly these days. But he could draw on experiences of which the little carpenter had no inkling. Cliff had not seen what lay beyond the frontiers of the community. He was buoyed up by his own driving optimism, like a swimmer in an enclosed pool who has never had to face the waves. The land wasn't regenerating; it was rotting under the blazing sun, ravaged by cycles of plague, growth and more plague. And Cliff couldn't see himself, how aged and physically how much weaker he had become in the brief month that Alex had been away. It would only be a matter of time before someone in authority noticed as well. He was slowing up, sinking visibly before the onset of disease. As long as his work didn't suffer and he wasn't contagious he would be ignored, but one day some jumped up bureaucrat would force him to attend a medical and the truth would be out. He would be placed on the short list of the sick, and one fine day he would be given his week's rations and told to leave, the payment for all the work he had done.

Alex strolled to the open-air eating area, hugging these unhappy thoughts. All around him people were busy preparing the evening meal. Huge pots were gently simmering over log fires. The cooks were adding the final touches and the kitchen staff were preparing the necessary plates and cutlery for the three hundred odd residents of the mine. Now that the community had pushed its boundaries further eastward, the underground population had steeply declined, and only administration staff still lived there.

After a few minutes, he was joined at his fire by Terry Aldiss, the mine's chief motor mechanic, a very tall, ungainly looking man with skinny limbs and an expressionless face, which always gave the impression of boredom. He rested his elbows on his knees and studied Alex without speaking. Alex made no move to greet or acknowledge him in any way but continued raising his cup of herbal tea to his mouth.

'It's a good thing you can't see yourself in a mirror,' Terry said, after he had finished his inspection. 'You look like death warmed up.'

Alex ran his fingers through his hair, opened his mouth to speak and then decided it wasn't worth it. He went on sipping his tea.

Terry smiled briefly at this deliberate slight. 'I can understand if you don't want to talk,' he said. 'I'm probably not your idea of a welcome home party.'

'You're the last person I want to speak to,' Alex said coldly.

This response drew a loud burst of laughter from Terry.

Fuming Alex rose to his feet, tossed the dregs into the fire and strode off without another word.

The next morning, Alex reported formally to the full meeting of the committee in the main conference room. Eight men and four women faced him around a large, oval shaped table. Each member was responsible for a facet of community life, rather like the minister in the cabinet of the old government, except that here there was no election and no House of Representatives. Most of these eminent citizens had been with the community since its inception; only three were not from Wales.

A man with greying hair and dark, bristly eyebrows stood up and announced the topics for the day's discussion. Alex's trip was first on the agenda. Alex delivered his conclusions from the data he had recovered at length, including the high incidence of radiation in the cities. The committee listened quietly, some frowning, others expressing surprise. When he finished he remained standing for questions.

'This confirms our suspicions,' Marcus summed up. 'The eight largest cities in England and Wales still have areas of severe contamination.'

Everyone's eyes turned to a short, lean man in his mid-forties with a pair of reading glasses resting on the bridge of his nose. His name was Arthur Kenwell a Londoner who had formerly worked in a nuclear power plant near Bristol, and never allowed anyone to forget that fact. Arthur's imperious glance took in the circle of expectant faces before he wriggled into a more upright position in his chair and started talking.

'Ah well,' he clasped his hands together in front of him. 'As you all know, before the war I was engaged in researching more efficient ways of deriving non-destructive forms of energy from nuclear power.' He paused to clear his throat. 'In retrospect, it proved rather an inconsequential exercise. However, I did gain some expertise with radiation

150

and a rough knowledge of the type of nuclear warheads in each superpower's arsenal. From what Alex has been telling us, the radiation is intense and localised. This can only mean the Russians used what are commonly termed 'dirty bombs' on all the major cities. These bombs are designed specifically to leave behind long life isotopes such as radium 226, strontium 90 and caesium 137, which not only remain dangerous for years, but also become incorporated in the tissues or the bones and cause cancers.'

'But what would be the point of such bombs,' a ginger-haired man asked. 'Surely the immediate effects of their bombs, and the subsequent radiation would be enough to ensure almost total death in the cities.'

'Why, my dear chap,' said Arthur, taking off his glasses and setting them down neatly in front of him. 'At first glance, I would agree, it may seem like an overkill situation. But if one thinks about it, it's not such a ridiculous idea, in fact it's rather ingenious. After all, the sooner a nation can reoccupy its industrial areas and start manufacturing goods; the sooner it will recover. By contaminating the cities for as long as possible, the aggressor can ensure that he gives himself a head start in the post war race for domination.'

'But surely the radiation would be everywhere and not just localised?' Alex asked.

'I think what you have been seeing is drainage effects,' he answered confidently. 'Several years have now passed since the holocaust, during this time most of the radiation will have been washed into underground streams or reservoirs or concentrated in gullies and minor depressions. This would give rise to discrete pockets of radiation all over the city. I'm sure if you had had more time and taken more readings, you would have discovered this effect yourself.'

Alex, who couldn't recall whether he had been walking over depressions or gullies when he registered these high counts, sank back in his chair and kept quiet.

'Well as always, Arthur has given us much food for thought,' commented Marcus, falling into the now customary

151

role of filling in the awkward moments when discussions had gone flat. 'In your opinion, Arthur, when do you think the radiation will be sufficiently low enough to allow people to re-occupy the cities?'

The great man shrugged, then threw himself back in his chair in an exaggerated gesture. 'It is too difficult to estimate,' he said, rubbing his chin as though he was performing some complicated calculation in his head. 'Unless a very exhaustive study of each city is taken, we will have no way of knowing what type of isotopes have been left behind.'

'But the radiation levels Alex obtained were so high,' another man interrupted. 'Surely these long-life isotopes you're talking about won't be present in sufficient amounts to cause such high readings?'

Arthur met this new challenge head on. 'You still don't understand, do you? Strontium has a half-life of twenty-nine years, Caesium two years; both are specific decay products of fission bombs. If the Russians had wanted to, they could have designed bombs capable of producing long-life fission products which could contaminate a city for centuries.'

His persuasive manner and the depressing scenario plunged them into silence once again.

'All right then, if we can't repopulate the cities in the foreseeable future, do you think scavenging parties could collect material from them without running a serious health risk?' Marcus asked.

'If the area was monitored beforehand and they had adequate protective clothing, I see no problem,' Arthur replied.

'We're running low on fuel and building materials,' Marcus continued. 'I suggest, therefore, that a party should be outfitted and sent to either Liverpool or possibly Birmingham as soon as possible.'

The motion was passed unanimously, and the committee moved on to discuss the types of materials needed and the easiest city to reach. After some further debate, Liverpool was chosen, and the size and date of the scavenging party was fixed.

Alex listened to the debate politely and offered his opinion when called upon to do so, but to his surprise he was not asked to participate in the expedition. He was just collecting his notes before leaving when Marcus motioned him to stay.

'Mr. Rawling,' Marcus cut through the general chatter that had broken out, 'may I ask, have you intercepted any further radio messages from other countries?'

A short, squat man with a broad face and flat, ugly features looked up. 'Yes, several in fact from various parts of Europe; and, of course, from Ireland, which having received only a few bombs, has been broadcasting continuously. However, it's obvious they consider Britain beyond help. They refer to us as a nuclear wasteland, would you believe.'

'What about the ones from Europe?' Marcus urged, bringing him back to the point.

'Rather weak signals on the whole. They seem to be attempts by the remaining factions of governments to calm the survivors. One mentioned that several cities are to be abandoned because of an epidemic. I suspect they may be in an even worse state than us.'

'Nothing from further afield?'

'None we could pick up with our receivers.'

'I see.' Marcus leaned forward on his elbows and began tapping with the base of his pen on the tabletop. 'Ladies and gentlemen,' he continued, 'the world picture is naturally very hazy, but I think we have to assume international devastation, and possibly a world-wide nuclear winter causing massive crop failures. If every industrialised country has suffered equally like us, it follows that our main priorities must be to increase our own strength and concentrate on finding any other sizeable communities which may be able to help us.' He switched his attention to Alex. 'You have not, I believe, encountered any signs of organised military force on any of your trips?'

'Other than a few ragged bands of men dressed in military uniform, I've seen no evidence of any military activity for over two-and-a half years now,' Alex replied.

'Extraordinary,' a well-spoken man beside Alex said. 'Tell me, do you have any explanation as to where they could have gone?'

'It's puzzling,' Alex admitted. 'Some may have deserted. But I suspect many more must have died in the flu epidemic. Their work camps were a perfect breeding ground for the virus.'

'And no drivers have found any organised communities?'

'None larger than a few hundred people.'

'But no drivers ever came back from Scotland,' Marcus broke in.

Alex nodded his agreement. 'We've lost six drivers in five months. It's possible some group there is capturing or killing them, or, more likely, they have been caught by exiles.'

'Would you be willing to find out for us?' Marcus asked.

The question startled Alex and he stared at Marcus with his mouth open, then looking around at the other members of the committee, he suddenly realised what the previous discussion had been leading up to.

'I suppose you have thought all this out beforehand?' It annoyed Alex that he should be asked to go out again so soon.

'Yes, we discussed it before you arrived,' Marcus replied. 'We'd not be sending you out on your own,' he added quickly, seeing Alex's grim expression. 'You would have at least three or four of our best men with you and extra guns and ammunition. It is essential that we know what is going on up there as soon as possible. If there is another community of comparable size to our own, we need to find how advanced they are and whether they are friendly. If they are not, we may have to divert more of our resources to

154

defence. They may already know about us from the drivers who have disappeared.'

Alex nodded slowly. He could see the logic of it. All the drivers had gone missing in the same general area of north England. Parts of Scotland, even more than Wales, were likely to have escaped direct bombardment, and it was quite possible that a large community could be extending its influence there.

'Why not send a large armed force up there instead of me?' he asked.

Marcus frowned at that. 'How do you think they'd react if they saw a small army marching towards them? We want their friendship, Alex, not another war on our doorstep. We've discussed this matter at length and decided that with six successful missions under your belt you have the necessary expertise and good judgement we need for such an assignment.'

That endorsement, Alex well knew, left him with no escape route. 'When would you want me to start?' he asked wearily.

'Within a week.'

'A week!'

'We've already delayed this trip till your return,' Marcus replied. 'We can't afford to set it back any further.'

Alex leaned back, closing his eyes briefly. If he didn't agree, he would be sent under orders anyway, and that way he would lose any leverage he might have had. Besides, he had known some of the missing drivers personally. Their disappearance, coupled with what he already knew about the area, left an intriguing puzzle. Something very strange was happening in Northern England. 'All right, I'll take the job,' he said, 'but only under certain conditions. Firstly, I want to pick all the food and supplies myself.'

Marcus nodded.

'I want the use of that new long base Land Rover you have recently repaired, and I want to choose my own team.'

'Marcus looked as if he was going to challenge this last demand, but then seemed to change his mind. 'Okay,' he said, 'as long as I have the final say on whom you select.'

Alex shook his head. 'I want total charge of this one. You said just now that you trusted my judgement. It's important to me, Marcus.'

'Very well, you win,' Marcus agreed reluctantly. 'Choose who you want, but if they don't want to come with you, I won't have them forced. If they drop out, you'll go with the men of my choice. '

Alex finally agreed to this arrangement.

The engine of the Land Rover was still rough idling. Terry figured it was the spark plugs misfiring. After scavenging another set of spark plugs from a second Land Rover that was now used for spare parts, the engine idled much more evenly.

Terry had only recently been placed in charge of the mine's workshop facilities. He was now responsible for the service and maintenance of the mine's fleet of transport vehicles, a job he did well and enjoyed immensely. This was a man who, on the surface, struck most people as hard working and intelligent with more than his fair share of initiative and ambition. Just the type of person the community was crying out for. But underneath the ostentatious goodwill and community spirit, there lurked a darker side. He came from a depressed area of London and from his school days onwards he had been a natural rebel.

His father was a mechanic, who stimulated his son's interest in cars from an early age. By the time Terry was thirteen, he was already a practised craftsman. By fourteen he was dodging school to steal parts off cars to fence. By eighteen, by which time he had taken an electronics course, his talents extended to burglar alarms and home wall safes. But Terry was too smart to continue stealing and he set himself up as a fence and made a comfortable living for several years. At the age of twenty-three, however, his

156

chequered past had caught up with him and he was jailed for three years for burglary, car stealing and receiving stolen goods. But with the holocaust, the slate had been wiped clean. Terry and a group of inmates had struck out for the west in the immediate aftermath, but by the time he had reached northern Wales all the members of the gang had either died or disappeared. He had stumbled across the community by himself. With his knowledge of electronics and mechanics he had been eagerly accepted.

'Hey, Terry!' one of the mechanics called. 'I've bypassed the ignition, but this truck still doesn't start.'

It was that idiot Jefferson, a former salesclerk who was all at sea in this field. 'Just a minute!' Terry finished wiping his hands, then walked over. He was now in charge of eleven somewhat dubiously qualified mechanics. Although he could have occupied himself entirely with administration work, he liked to get involved.

The man removed his head from under the dashboard of a Toyota truck as Terry came up and gave Terry a cheery grin. Terry did not respond in kind.

'Have you checked the battery?'

'No,' said the other man sheepishly.

'Then don't bother me until you've checked everything,' Terry said angrily.

The man gave another stupid grin and quickly shuffled out of sight around the front of the vehicle. Terry returned in disgust to completing his checks on the Land Rover. He was no longer the wild youth he had been before the war. He had learned how to conceal his impulses and channel negative feelings to more useful ends. His reward had been the responsibility for this workshop. He was making himself indispensable to the community now; one day, he reckoned, he would be almost immune from its laws. He would control and rule, rather than be controlled and ruled. This power over people, he found exciting and he wanted it more than anything. Only individuals like Alex fathomed his true nature, and not always consciously. In Alex's case, it manifested itself as a clash of character, Alex's painfully honest, uncompromising approach to life, against Terry's subtle scheming. They saw in each other everything they inwardly loathed; everything that was at variance with what they were. Two such opposites could never be friends. The peace between them often bordered on open conflict.

In the afternoon of the following day, Alex persuaded Cliff to accompany him to Anglesey where he hoped to find Roy and another man called Wayne Fletcher. Cliff adopted his usual wry expression when Alex said he would explain matters when they were all together. Roy had been living on the island for nearly a year now and had recently been placed in charge of a large wheat crop. He had been brought up on a farm and liked the idea of combining his building work with farming. Wayne had been a farm labourer before the war and was now Roy's right-hand man.

It was close to sunset when they reached the island, and they passed hundreds of hooded figures plodding back to the settlements after spending all day in the green-houses. An alarming increase in skin cancer had made such garments essential for all outdoor workers. Probably there had not been such a concentration of hoods on the island since the Druids lived here, a couple of civilisations before, Alex mused.

Alex shifted into second gear and drove through the outskirts of a recently completed village. Only four months before it had been deserted land now it was filled with rows of clay brick houses. According to Roy, each of these buildings had been designed to have one large dormitory containing twenty beds, a communal living room with a log fire and a communal bathroom. The larger and longer buildings were the kitchens and mess halls where food was rationed out three times a day.

This village was typical of a new breed of settlement under construction by the committee, part of its master plan to enshrine its socialist based system in bricks and mortar.

158

No favouritism, no luxuries, everyone working the same hours for the same food and shelter; the only concession was that families with children were placed on a short list for a separate room. Another of this world's ironies, Alex thought. A war against such a system had created the perfect conditions for its implementation.

Roy and Wayne were living in one of the few pre-war houses near the centre of the settlement, along with eighteen other men and women. Cliff knocked on the door and a small West Indian girl let them in. The two men were in the living room talking to several members of the household. They sprang up with delight when they saw Cliff and Alex. Roy hadn't changed, unless perhaps he was even stronger and larger than when Alex had seen him last. His thick, brown beard and brawny arms gave the impression more of a bear than a human. Wayne was quite different; small and wiry, with a wispy beard and matted brown hair that had probably not seen a comb since the war. Always gaunt in appearance, with a triangular shaped face that tapered to a cleft jaw, his appearance was almost sinister, yet he possessed a warm nature, and his mind was quick and sharp.

After a few minutes of discussing pleasantries, they all trooped upstairs to a small bedroom overlooking the street where they could be alone. Wayne stepped up to a small, highly polished cabinet and produced four glasses and an old wine bottle filled with a clear liquid.

'Freshly distilled potato wine,' he announced, proudly waving the bottle in front of them. 'A bit rough, but the best our local stills have been able to produce.'

He filled each glass half-full and handed them around.

The wine turned out to be considerably worse than anyone had anticipated. Coughing and a burning sensation right down to the stomach seemed to be the usual result of taking a medium sip. In spite of this, however, no one's thirst seemed to be impaired.

With the opening of the bottle a more light-hearted mood descended on the company, diverting them from

Alex's request for a serious talk. Cliff embarked on his favourite pastime of running down the committee; acting out, with some exaggeration, the mannerisms of the various members as they went about making their decisions. Wayne joined in with his own sharp wit, spicing the absurdity of the situations Cliff conjured before them. The men laughed long and hard as all the strain and frustration of their lives seeped then blasted forth in unrestrained laughter. The pompous, the petty minded, the bureaucrats were all ridiculed in turn, the laughter acting like some huge emotional sink. Before the war Alex would have frowned on such a scene and thought it bordered on hysteria, but most social gatherings these days had this slightly frantic air about them. When criticism could earn expulsion, laughter behind closed doors was the only outlet for freedom left.

Finally, when they had settled down a little and Wayne was searching for a second bottle, Cliff introduced a graver note.

'Well, guv,' he said softly, 'you still haven't mentioned anything about your trip yet, or why it was you wanted to come down here all of a sudden.'

'No, I haven't.' Alex smiled thinly, and the light-hearted mood of his companions suddenly dissipated. 'Perhaps I'd better start by going back a bit,' he went on, when he saw he had their attention. 'About eighteen months ago, I was asked by the committee to do a survey of the radiation levels in Newcastle. So off I went, taking the old M6, when I began to notice a large number of corpses, none of them more than a few weeks old, extending in what seemed to be a continuous trail towards the north. On my return from Newcastle, curiosity got the better of me and I decided to follow the trail.' He took another sip of wine. 'At the time I kept expecting it just to peter out or end in some vast community like our own, but it never did. I stopped at some towns along the way and found they also were littered with bodies about the same age as the ones on the motorway. But the towns themselves were largely intact, with very little blast damage and numerous signs of recent occupation. Not a soul about, however. It looked as though this whole region had supported a large population and that something had driven them northwards only a few weeks before I found them.' He paused and glanced at the faces of the others. 'I never found the end of the trail,' he said, shaking his head solemnly. 'My fuel reserves were running low and I was forced to turn back.'

'How far north did you go?' asked Wayne.

'Oh… a fair way, within twenty kilometres of Glasgow and Edinburgh.'

'And you've never reported this to anyone?' Cliff asked.

'You're the first.'

'But why us? Why not the committee?'

'I didn't report it to the committee because I know how they'd react; they'd have banned me from taking part in any further missions on the grounds that I was taking unnecessary risks. Besides, at the time I only had large numbers of badly decomposed bodies and a series of deserted towns to report, nothing more substantial. I wasn't going to put my whole future in jeopardy for a little thing like that.'

Cliff nodded. 'So, why are you telling us now?'

'The one thing I did notice in these towns was rats,' Alex continued. 'Quite a lot of them, in fact.'

'So, you think that the population was trying to escape some disease carried by rats? Something like bubonic plague?' Cliff suggested.

'Or typhus,' Alex added grimly. 'Either way it set me thinking that perhaps that large scale movement of population had been driven by fear of a contagious disease. If so, the key to whether any of them survived lies at the end of that trail of bodies I was following.'

'So, you think there could be another community in Scotland?' Wayne asked quietly.

'Yes, I do,' Alex replied firmly, 'and so does the committee. We've lost six drivers in the last few months near the Scottish border. The committee is of the opinion that they could have been kidnapped or killed by this community. And they've asked me to lead a small party of men up there to try and find some answers. And in case you're wondering, the group is to be small because, in the words of Marcus: 'We want their friendship not another war on our hands.' This is purely a peaceful mission aimed at making contact and establishing friendly relations with any sizeable community we find. It is therefore important that we start off on the right foot.'

'So, it will be you and a few others,' Cliff replied.

'Myself and three others to be precise.' Alex looked slowly around the faces of his companions to make sure there was no doubt in their minds as to his meaning.

'Not us?' Cliff asked, his face showing surprise and alarm in about equal proportions.

'I wouldn't ask you if I didn't think it was absolutely necessary,' Alex said quickly. 'All our best drivers have been killed. The men Marcus could have offered me would have been untrained recruits, who have never been through the type of situations we have. We can have the best Land Rover the community has and all the arms and supplies we need. Northern England and Scotland were deserted when I was there, so I don't anticipate any trouble.' He appealed to them more directly. 'I need men I can trust,' he added, feeling like a cheap sales commercial.

In the silence that followed, Wayne was the first to speak. 'I don't know,' he said. 'I mean, it's so dangerous. Even if we do find another community, who's to say how they'll treat us? They could be diseased or intent on killing any intruders.'

'I know I'm asking you to take a risk,' Alex said. 'But there's another way of looking at it. Each of us has been ill from time to time, but none of us has reported sick, and for good reason, we're scared of being pushed out. That's the whole basis of this society that we're all expendable, and for each of us, sooner or later, our time must come. But this other community might have more medical supplies, better care or not operate such a harsh system. Maybe that's why the other drivers never returned. They may have decided to stay where they would be better off. It wouldn't mean that you had to give up anything,' he went on, pleading with them. 'I only want you for this one trip. In a few weeks, we should know what's going on, one way or another.'

It was at this point that numerous questions began to be fired. Alex did his best to reassure them that travelling beyond the community's boundaries was not what it had been. He described what he had seen on his last few trips and how much the land had changed from when they had travelled through it three years before. As the debate continued, he sensed an easing in their resistance. Cliff actually came out in defence of Alex several times. In the end their consent came, if not easily, then at least with a quiet conviction.

Alex was deeply moved; toasts were drunk, Wayne even scrambling in search of a third bottle, but the mood never reached the spirited heights it had before. There was good will, but no sense of exhilaration at the prospect of a dangerous job.

Early the next day Alex and Cliff drove back to the mine. Cliff reported for work on a new administrative block that was under construction, while Alex went in search of Marcus.

He found him hunched over some notes in his small, dimly lit office on the second level. Alex told him the good news at once.

'Who have you chosen?' asked Marcus.

Alex reeled off the names and received his approving nod. He realised that Marcus had guessed all along whom he would pick.

'Now, let's get down to business.' Marcus opened the top drawer of his desk and produced a sheet of typed paper. 'The committee have drafted a list of instructions for you. I hope we've covered all the contingencies you may face.'

Alex skimmed through the list.

'Any questions?'

'Why are we taking ten kilos of tea and coffee?'

'Like beads and mirrors in the old days, the committee thought it would be useful for breaking the ice so to speak. A gesture to demonstrate our good intentions.'

'Does that mean hands off?'

'We've already gift wrapped it, but I'm sure it would be possible to manage some extra for such an important mission.'

Alex raised his eyebrows; this indulgence was an indication of just how eager the committee was to please him. 'In that case,' he continued, studying the list again, 'I want one hundred and fifty litres of extra fuel, not a hundred; two months' supply of food instead of one month and I'm picking my own guns and ammunition.'

'Hmm. The committee were a bit dubious about giving you so much authority, Alex, but since I sign the requisition forms, I see no problem in obtaining the extra. There, then.' Marcus took the list from Alex and amended the figures. 'Which brings me to a rather important point,' he continued, returning the corrected list across the desk. 'The number one priority of the committee is to establish relations with any community as soon as possible. In the event of such a meeting taking place, it may be that one of your party will have to stay behind with them in exchange for one of their representatives. Now, the feeling was that a committee member should accompany the expedition to do any negotiating. However,' he added quickly when he saw Alex was about to object. 'I managed to talk them out of the idea, providing you volunteer to stay behind and handle the diplomatic side of things.'

Alex weighed this up, but not for long. It was not a development he had foreseen, but on reflection, staying as the guest of another community might be quite interesting.

'We urgently need a breakthrough here,' Marcus continued. 'If both communities are allowed to become too

164

autonomous, it will make co-operation between them that much harder.'

'Okay,' Alex agreed. 'If it comes to that, I'm prepared to trade places with someone, at least until a more suitable candidate can be found.'

'Good.'

Marcus gave a satisfied nod. 'And I must add that if you don't return within the time allowed, we will assume that you have been killed and act accordingly.'

'In what way?'

'Prepare for an attack, Alex.'

'You'd send an armed force up there?'

'We would seriously consider it. Just to find out once and for all what's going on.'

'So, I'd better get back in time to stop you from starting World War Four.'

Marcus grinned. 'Something like that.' He leaned back in his chair again. 'So, when do you think you'll be ready?'

'If the Land Rover is operational, I propose the day after tomorrow.'

'Excellent. I'll see to it personally.' Marcus stood up in his place and extended a hand. 'Good luck, Alex.'

Roy and Wayne arrived from Anglesey the following morning. Together, having collected the Land Rover from the workshop, they began loading the supplies. They spent their last night in the community in the dormitories and rose well before dawn to run a final check. Then, as the horizon began to turn into shades of purples and reds, they scrambled aboard and, Alex driving, started on their long trek north.

CHAPTER 8

For the rest of that day, they made slow, careful progress eastwards. The roads leading out of the community were often watched by exiles, so Alex had fallen into the habit of leaving the track as soon as possible and continuing across country. Since much of the country was now quite dry and covered by grasslands, cross country driving usually proved only marginally more uncomfortable than the cracked and overgrown roads from the pre-holocaust era.

By dusk they had spotted a number of small communities centred around petrol driven generators and rows of solar panels. These communities, like the Welsh community, were sealed off behind wire fences and guard posts. The people, however, kept to themselves, showing no interest in the noise of a passing vehicle. An attitude, Alex reflected, that had become increasingly more common over the past year as self-reliant groups had started replacing the starving and frenzied mobs.

It was nearly two years now since Alex and his co-driver, whilst returning from a mission, had been ambushed by such a mob. This had been in northern England, in hilly country. The road had been dipping and climbing for ages as it etched its way south from Sheffield. Alex had been driving, his companion dozing beside him. The Land Rover had just crossed a shallow trough between two hills and was descending into a valley when a large fallen tree blocked its path. This was not an unusual sight. Many trees had died in the first winter after the holocaust, and when the sap dried in the roots, the trees easily fell victim to high winds. Alex had assumed as much in this case and was about to climb down to see what could be done when he noticed several sharp cuts around the base of the trunk. He remembered the sudden alarm that had swept through him, his quick, frightened glances at the hill above. The tree lay directly around a sharp bend in the road so that anyone approaching would be nearly on top of it before they realised it was there. The slopes were steep and craggy, a perfect place for an ambush. In a wild panic, he had thrown the Land Rover in reverse and slammed his foot down on the accelerator. Immediately, arrows, spears, rocks and a series of huge boulders burst from the crags above.

His co-driver had woken with a start and began demanding to know what was happening. Even now Alex could remember the man's clumsy attempts to shoot back at the attackers while screaming in fear as more boulders landed on the cabin roof. Then the whole vehicle shook and the screeching sound of tearing metal tore at their ears. Huge steel rods, sharpened at one end, crashed through the roof. Alex knew that one of these rods had impaled his co-driver, but he could do nothing to help him. He barely managed to weave his way through the mounting boulders still tumbling all about him. Finally, he found a place wide enough to turn around, several hundred metres further up the road. By that time his co- driver's twitching and squirming on the end of the rod had ceased. He hung suspended from the roof, the rod driven through his abdomen and into the seat. His head rested on the dashboard as though he had gone to sleep rather than died.

Something in Alex had snapped after that incident. He was no longer scared of running missions for the committee. In fact, he even volunteered for more, but he always laid down one condition - the committee wouldn't make him take on an inexperienced replacement. This went against their policy of always sending out drivers in pairs for protection; but since volunteers for such missions were next to impossible to find, they had been obliged to accede to Alex's demands. The last two missions he had completed by himself.

'We'll stop here for the night,' Alex announced.

They had reached a group of cottages nestled along one side of a broad, grassy valley. A stream was tumbling and bubbling past, dropping noisily from cleft to cleft before disappearing round a sharp bend. Alex stopped the vehicle, and a rapid but cautious search of the area was carried out. As he had suspected, the picturesque cottages were nothing more than shells. They had all been stripped long ago, so that only the stone walls were left.

They laid out their beds inside one of them and cooked dinner. By the time they were finished the last of the twilight was gone.

Alex set six-hour watches and placed himself on the first one, until midnight. Not so much to set an example to the others, but to avoid sleep for a few hours. He always had nightmares the first day out on a mission. Only when he was completely exhausted would he submit to lying down, knowing that then his rest would be deep and peaceful, and not haunted by bad dreams.

Some of these dreams went back to before the war. Snippets of boyhood memories flashed before him, always of times when he had been afraid, bullied perhaps by older boys, but with the reassuring presence of his brother in the background. But sometimes the images were far more frightening and vivid. They would trouble his thoughts for days. Often an enemy he couldn't see or hear was chasing him through a forest at night. He only felt him drawing closer, a presence that filled him with such terror that he threw himself over ledges and into raging torrents to escape. There was no brother to protect him, no comforting presence of Tina. And he would wake up terrified, drained, screaming, soaked in sweat. For hours after he would still be shaking. He used to climb into the Land Rover and lock all the doors like a little boy scared of the night. Then the sun would rise and the day would pass, maybe without incident, and gradually he would forget. Somehow, he always found the strength to continue, throwing himself into scenes of danger,

168

fearless of what became of him. It was only in the night-time that he was afraid.

The next morning, they steered a course between the ravaged cities of Manchester and Leeds, hoping to link up with the M6 motorway heading north.

By the morning of the third day, they had reached the M6. The fourth day brought them to Carlisle. Alex had travelled through this town on his previous trip north and had no wish to repeat the experience. At that time, the streets had been littered with bodies and grey rats, some the size of small cats. Thousands of them were picking the last remnants of flesh from the corpses. He remembered cruising the streets in a sort of dazed horror, the loathsome creatures clambering over his Land Rover and across his windscreen as he drove. Some type of rioting or power struggle had clearly taken place only weeks before. Every shop window was smashed, cars were overturned and a whole row of terraces was burnt out. In some streets, the corpses lay too thick to count. The smell had made him vomit. He could only think the military had something to do with a massacre on this scale. Maybe some renegade company of soldiers had attacked the town for their food, then moved on to avoid the disease that this number of bodies would attract. Whatever the cause, he had wasted no time in looking for survivors. He couldn't remember wanting to leave any place so badly.

He parked the Land Rover on a vantage point overlooking the town. To the right, the motorway continued on its way in a wide, skirting loop.

'I've been down there before,' Alex said, watching the others peering through the windows. 'Most of the population were out on the streets at the time,' and he went on to explain what he had seen, leaving out none of the horror.

'And you saw nothing living?' Roy asked.

'Only rats. The survivors from here headed north. I tracked the ones that didn't make it for another seventy kilometres. They ended up as a long trail of festering corpses lying by the roadside.'

169

While he was talking, Wayne had been searching the town through a pair of binoculars. He finally climbed out of the Land Rover and pointed to a spot a few kilometres out from the centre of town. 'There's a fire burning. I can see people gathered around it,' he announced, handing the binoculars to Alex.

Alex could see four figures tending what looked to be a cooking pot.

'It's a perfect opportunity to know once and for all what went on here,' Cliff said, after taking a turn at the binoculars.

Alex disagreed. 'What would be the point? We already know the direction in which the population chose to go. I'm not for running risks unnecessarily. Besides,' he continued stubbornly, 'these people probably know the streets as well as the rats do. We wouldn't get within a kilometre of them before they disappeared.'

But Cliff and Wayne argued forcibly that these survivors might be able to tell them whether a large community in Scotland did exist. Even Roy, who rarely offered an opinion, came in on the side of Cliff and Wayne, suggesting that if they were fully armed such a small group would not present any real threat. In the end Alex was overruled, but he insisted they all take revolvers and automatic rifles, and retreat at the first sign of trouble without offering a fight.

An hour later, Alex squatted down next to the dying flames of the fire and picked up one of the many discarded cans lying amongst the coals. They had left the Land Rover several blocks away and travelled on foot, cautiously picking their way between the buildings, never exposing themselves for more than a few seconds in the streets, communicating by signs, but all to no avail. The people had gone and so had the pot, only the lingering smell of cooking remained. Alex nervously glanced around him. The fire had been built on the edge of a small suburban park, surrounded on all sides by shabby terraced houses. They had already searched the area and found nothing, although he was convinced the survivors were not far off. He suddenly found that thought rather disturbing, so he quickly went to join the others who had entered a large stone house on the far side of the park.

He reached the house and gently pushed open the front door. Inside, it was surprisingly dark and cool. The curtains, he noticed, had been drawn. He called out softly, his voice echoing around the Spartan furnishings. No one answered so he tried again. They must be at the back of the house, he told himself reassuringly. If they had run into trouble, he would have heard something, shots, some kind of a struggle. He drew his revolver and flicked the safety catch off with his thumb. He had entered a long narrow hallway, lined with dusty paintings and antique side tables. The house was much larger than it looked from the front. It seemed to extend backwards in a series of spacious, but mould blackened and musty rooms. The last one was blacker still, although some light filtered round the rim of a door opposite. He paused, waiting for his eyes to adjust, then strode forward. Suddenly there was sound and movement behind him, but his reflexes were too slow. He heard the thud on his skull and felt his knees buckle underneath him. By the time he hit the floor he was unconscious...

Alex was aware of arms gently lifting him onto a chair against a wall. A woman's face came into focus, anxious, concerned, framed by a tangled mop of blonde hair. He reached up and touched a large painful bump near the base of his skull, and when he looked at his hand it was covered in blood.

The woman grimaced when she saw it. 'They hit you too hard,' she apologised. 'They were only meant to disarm you, not knock you unconscious.' She lifted a glass of water to his lips and he took a careful sip.

Alex studied the woman more closely while he drank. She was younger than himself and tall, with thin arms and legs, deeply tanned, as though she spent much of her time outdoors. Her face had small delicate features, which were set in determined lines. In the first rush of returning consciousness, he had dreaded death, but her presence comforted him somewhat.

When he turned his head, he could see that he was in a very large room filled with desks, cupboards and filing cabinets stuffed with books and folders. There were no windows, and the ceiling was criss-crossed with wooden beams. The smell of damp and mould was so strong that he had the impression he was below ground. He remembered seeing a wooden flight of stairs curling downwards when he was in the hallway and guessed that they were probably in the basement.

His companions were sitting dejectedly along the wall a little further off, with their hands tied behind their backs. All were looking anxiously towards him. Three ragged men and a second woman were also watching him intently.

'Still a bit dizzy, I shouldn't wonder,' came a voice from the other side of the room. The owner of that voice, a man in his mid to late fifties crossed over to where he sat. 'Shame about the head,' he continued, in a rather offhand tone. 'We got a bit nervous when you took off the safety catch on your revolver. We thought it would be safer to knock you out than risk confronting you like we did the others.'

Alex stared up at this tall, remarkably elegant man. He had cropped hair touched with white and a neatly trimmed beard and was formally dressed in a pair of grey trousers and a pink shirt. The shirt even looked clean and ironed. Alex was struck by the contrast of his appearance to that of the rest of their captors. The men had ragged beards and the two women long matted hair, and they all wore torn and patched clothes.

'I'm Samuel Dunham,' the man continued in a pompous tone, which Alex did not much care for. 'This is Elaine,' he gestured toward the woman who had given him the water, 'and Cathy, Alan, Ted and Jeremy. Our little band' he smiled briefly. 'Well, young man your friends have already told me much of what I want to know. You come from Wales, I understand, and are looking for a Scottish community. Is that right?'

Alex nodded his head painfully.

Samuel stared at him briefly, then turned and, with hands clasped behind his back, slowly walked toward the others. 'And what will you do when you find this Scottish community?'

'It does exist, then?' Alex asked hopefully.

'Oh yes,' Samuel replied, turning on his heels and striding back. 'Certainly. It's quite sizeable, I believe. It comprises all the remnants of the towns down here.' He crouched down next to Alex. 'Most of the people who once lived here are now in Scotland. They decided to flee north ahead of a typhus outbreak brought on by a rat plague. Terrible business that was, thousands must have died, possibly millions by the time it had run its course.' He made an embracing gesture. 'Those you see here, and a few others, who at this moment are tending crops on the outskirts of town, are all that is left of Carlisle.'

'Why did you stay?' Wayne asked.

Samuel glanced round at him. 'This is our home,' he said flatly. 'The others hoped to outrun the plague by heading north.' He shrugged. 'We chose to stay.'

Alex thought he was beginning to get an inkling of this man's character. He was dogmatic and complacent at the same time, and he had the preacher's trick of projecting words and emphasising them by subtle changes in tone and inflection. His movements, too, seemed too exaggerated, part of a deliberate performance.

'But not all the dead in the streets died as a result of the plague,' Alex spoke up.

Samuel turned his head and compressed his lips, almost in a pout. 'What makes you say that?'

'I was here over a year ago,' Alex explained. 'I saw scores of corpses in the streets. They hadn't died of typhus; they had been shot.'

'Ah! We are referring to, are we not, to some bodies in front of a tall, white office block with tinted windows?'

Alex had some vague recollection of an office block, but he couldn't remember what the windows looked like. 'Possibly,' he said after a pause.

'Most likely you saw the results of a massacre, then,' Samuel continued solemnly. 'Thirteen months ago?' He turned toward Elaine, who was leaning against the wall next to Alex.

'More like fifteen,' she corrected.

'Indeed.' He shook his head ruefully and walked back to Alex. 'Fifteen months ago, a dreadful battle took place between the remaining population of Carlisle and the people who lived in the basement of that office block.' He paused, ensuring he had the attention of everyone. 'It was the nuclear winter after the holocaust' he continued thoughtfully. 'Terrible weather that, really shocking. There were so many of us, you see and so few resources. We had no direct bombardment, you understand. Only minor damage here and there, you know; doors blown off, one or two fires, a collapsed roof or so.' He paused, clasping his hand behind him again, in oratorical pose. 'For a week or two things were not so bad. All of us being shell shocked, as it were, we failed to appreciate the gravity of the situation. But then people began to think what would happen to them. No communications, not even with the next town. Appalling weather, contamination raining from the sky, no food or water and worst of all, not a sign of any help from the government.' He shrugged. 'That was the end of civilisation as we knew it. People had to go out into the contaminated streets in search of food. The shops were cleaned out in the first week. Fights to the death occurred over scraps of food. Neighbour rose against neighbour. And then there was the flu epidemic. They died in their thousands. By the end of the nuclear winter only twenty or thirty thousand people were left. We were down to eating rats and wild dogs to survive.'

'And the military didn't try to establish food distribution centres?' Roy asked.

Samuel shook his head. 'Survivors fleeing from the south made mention of food rationing stations outside London. Some even went that way to try and find them, but no military ever reached this far north.'

Samuel had by this time stopped pacing back and forth and was leaning on a heavily cluttered table in the centre of the room. After a pause he continued. 'Inside this white office block there was a large metal door. Thinking it was some dusty old vault full of papers or useless money, it was ignored. But then a series of air vents on the surface were discovered. These vents were traced back to a large area behind the door. Several attempts were made to force the door, but as it was steel, embedded in a metre-thick concrete wall, these efforts met with little success. We then tried to break in through the ventilating system, but found that it, too, was encased in concrete and protected by a thick steel grid. As we listened on the surface we could hear the sound of generators and even of voices coming up the ventilating shafts. Gradually we realised that we were not dealing here with a few ragged survivors who had happened to stumble across some nice cosy place to weather out the nuclear winter. This was a large, well-constructed fallout shelter encased in concrete, fitted with its own generators and air filtering systems.

'In a funny sort of way,' Samuel continued, 'the more impregnable that shelter seemed, the more it seemed to unite the people on the surface. Finally, they had something to focus their hate on. It became an obsession, a lock to pick as it were, no matter what the cost. For two months, we struggled to break through the door, but it was proof even against oxy- acetylene equipment; or at least we could make little impression. Then someone suggested that we seal all the ventilation shafts to deprive them of air. It took another few days before they were forced to come out.'

He paused reflectively, his fingers clawing through the strands of his beard. 'They must have decided that throwing themselves on our mercy would be to no avail,' he continued softly. 'They burst out of that door armed with machine pistols and explosives. Everyone standing near was killed. Then they ran onto the streets and massacred a large group of people cooking their evening meal. Those were the bodies you saw, young man, when you were here last,' he said, looking across at Alex. 'They were still in uniform.' He shook his head slowly. 'Maybe they thought that that would intimidate us, or perhaps they had no civilian clothes down there. In any case, there was no reasoning with them; they were out of their minds with terror. They ran through the streets shooting at anything that moved. We hunted them down, singly and in packs, and killed every last one. We were not afraid. By mid-morning the next day they lay dead, fifty-five men and twelve women.'

The recital seemed to end here on an almost triumphant note. Alex, looking sideways, noticed the looks of mild boredom on the faces of Elaine and the other members of her group and supposed that this was not the first time they had been obliged to listen to this talk.

Cliff asked the inevitable question. 'What was down there?'

Samuel appeared to have been waiting for this.

'We were amazed and shocked at what we found. It contained a mass of computer terminals, communication equipment and defence systems. The piles of papers you see all around you,' he gestured toward the cabinets overflowing with papers, 'I have collected them from there in order to try and piece together what happened before the holocaust.' He had begun his pacing again. 'The people who were in that shelter were members of a military elite called 'the HUD'. That stands for 'Holocaust Underground Defence.' They were all specialists in one form of high technology or another, and the shelter they occupied was called a 'Citadel'. There were at least thirty of these citadels throughout Great

176

Britain before the war. They were linked together by fibre optic cables and connected to early warning systems, spy satellites and radar networks to all the nuclear weapons of Great Britain. In other words, the idea of these Citadels was to continue a nuclear attack effectively even after the surface had been reduced to a mass of cinders and nuclear potholes. It's quite likely that the military personnel in that Citadel were responsible for conducting the final stages of the war.'

He paused and scanned them for a reaction. When it failed to come, he frowned.

'None of you seem particularly startled by what I have just said,' he continued with a slightly raised eyebrow.

'Well, I'm not, if that's what you mean,' Alex spoke up. 'Cliff, Roy and I,' he nodded towards the others, 'survived a military labour camp soon after the holocaust. We're all aware of what the military is capable of.'

'I see.' Samuel seemed temporarily thrown off his stroke. 'You think you know what the military is capable of, do you?'

Alex's head was aching. At least the bump on his head was real, he thought sourly. He could not vouch for anything else he had heard since waking up. His friends, it appeared, were in a similar plight. Samuel continued to stand over them, as if waiting for some expression of astonishment.

'So, you're saying that the military continued firing nuclear missiles even after the holocaust had happened?' Roy asked, frowning as he tried to concentrate.

'Exactly.'

'But for what possible purpose?' Alex queried.

'The purpose?' Samuel raised his eyebrows as though the question was almost too silly to bother answering. 'Man's history,' he began in a condescending voice, like a lecturer about to deliver a well-rehearsed talk on a pet subject, 'is riddled with violent acts of murder, rape and torture. Such elements, indeed, seem to be bound up with his essential nature. It was factors like these, which he harnessed to help him build the technological world that existed before the war. But was his aggression really tamed?' Samuel looked around at the blank faces. 'Of course not, it was just repressed, waiting for an outlet, a way to express itself. Then the arms race started. Bigger, better, more devastating weapons.' He threw his hands up in the air. 'It was inevitable really. He could channel all his creative energy and intelligence, while serving his primitive urges for violence and destruction. And for a time, it fulfilled its function admirably. Only, of course, complex technology and primitive urges are not really compatible. If either gets the upper hand, the world falls victim and is destroyed.'

He was standing, towering over them, chest puffed out, his eyes alight with his own cleverness and discerning. Once again, he seemed annoyed by their blank looks.

'I didn't really expect you to understand,' he went on at length, dismissing them with a wave of his hand. 'You are too tied to the present, you can't look forward or back. How to fill your bellies, how to get through today, tomorrow, next week, next month; that is all you are concerned about. You are like the masses before the war that obeyed blindly, the human fodder of the holocaust. And you, their leader.' He was at Alex's side now, a certain wild gleam in his eyes. 'Do you ever question or think? Are you ever responsible for your actions? Why, in your opinion, did your superiors send you on this absurd mission?'

Alex was alarmed how quickly Samuel could change the conversation, but he met his eyes firmly. 'The purpose of our mission is simple enough. We have been ordered to establish friendly relations with any community we might find in Scotland.'

'You're the first flush of a new poison,' Samuel scoffed. 'What are these 'friendly relations', except trying to rebuild the Old World system out of the ashes of the nuclear wasteland! Nothing has changed. Indeed, no change is possible while the agents of the old order think and scheme and act according to its laws. We have suffered; we have seen our planet plunged into darkness through the folly of planners more powerful than your masters. And now that the light is beginning to return, do you think we will permit the same mistakes to be made again? An opportunity has been given to the few, the men of vision, to shape a more beautiful world. No empire builders, no emissaries of petty kingdoms struggling for dominance can be allowed to corrupt the little glimmer of hope, the purifying flame we hold cupped in our hands.'

He rose to his full height.

'You're wrong about us,' Alex cried. 'Things are not like that anymore. We come to establish…'

'You come in peace and are armed for war,' Samuel retorted coldly. 'You are not the first young man who has pleaded before me for his life. Do you think the good gardener lets the nettles grow because the weeds are innocent? The taint has to be cut off at the root!'

Alex glanced towards Elaine and the rest. He knew now why she looked so agitated. This scene had been enacted before. It was at Samuel's hands that the drivers from Wales had been killed. First, he lectured them, and then he slaughtered them. He caught Elaine's eye and knew that in her answering gaze he had an ally. But even he was astonished by her next move. Instantly she was on her feet and had taken Samuel's arm.

'Not this time,' she said loudly. 'Not these, Samuel.'

He turned his head very slowly towards her. 'My dear…the disease needs to be cut out?'

'Let them go, Samuel!' she ordered.

He smiled. 'You think we should?'

'Ted!' She turned towards a tall, olive skinned man with long, greasy black hair, who was helping to guard the others. 'Don't let this happen again!'

The man swallowed, raising his rifle defensively over his chest. 'Killing these men won't help,' he said unconvincingly, to no one in particular.

'Cathy! Alan!' She implored the couple standing across from Alex. 'You know this is madness. Samuel is no longer rational.'

'Samuel knows what he's doing,' Alan answered coldly.

The word 'rational' seemed to have snapped something in Samuel. His face flushed up, his composure was forgotten. He was actually shaking with fury. He took a step towards Elaine and Alex felt sure that he was going to strike her.

'You're mad, Samuel, quite crazy!' she goaded, her eyes darting around the room for somewhere to run.

Alan and Cathy moved forward, sensing a crisis was near. Elaine continued to move back, still glaring defiantly at her leader. 'You're a crazy, senile old bastard!' she screamed at the top of her voice. 'You can no longer reason, you're a maniac!'

Samuel pounced. 'Stop it, stop it!' he yelled, reaching for her neck.

Ted stepped between them, rifle up to fend him away. For an instant, the opening was there. Alex was forgotten. He sprang to his feet and in one movement ripped the rifle from Cathy, sending her sprawling across the floor. Before Alan could respond he found himself staring down the barrel of Alex's rifle. Immediately Ted and Jeremy turned their weapons on Alex's companions. Everyone in the room stood suspended, frozen at the moment before carnage.

Samuel took a deep breath and smiled. He was back in control. 'This is foolish,' he said smoothly in his normal voice. 'Put down your rifle before someone gets hurt.'

Alex watched this transformation in amazement. How could someone change that quickly, from murderous rage to calm reassurance?

'We have no intention of harming you,' his voice went on. 'This is all completely unnecessary.'

Alex looked past Samuel at the two rifles levelled at his friends. Ted was hesitant and unsure; Jeremy was impassive, watchful; ready to carry out any order from Samuel.

'Ted!' Elaine called frantically. *'Put the rifle down!'*

180

Alex could see that Ted was faltering, his eyes shifting swiftly between Elaine and Samuel. He made his decision, lowering his rifle towards the floor.

Jeremy gave him a murderous glare.

'Drop your rifle!' Alex screamed at Alan.

Alan stared at him and slowly he, too, began lowering his rifle.

Immediately Samuel placed his hand over Alan's arm.

'NO!' he roared. That same insane glint of rage was back. All Alex's uncertainty was swept away at that moment. He slipped his finger onto the trigger of his rifle. With one sustained burst, he cut down Alan and Samuel. At such close range, the force flung them backwards. Alex saw the flash in indignance on Samuel's face as he fell back against the wall and slowly slid to the floor.

On the other side of the room, Jeremy had turned and shot Ted. Then he turned wildly and began spraying the room, vainly searching for Alex. Someone pushed him from behind and he slipped. Falling, he swung to fire on his attacker. Alex saw Wayne dance briefly, then crumple, leaving the wall spattered with blood.

Coldly, dispassionately, Alex lined Jeremy up in his sights and fired. His chest exploded, his arms flew up in the air and he fell back on the body of Wayne. Blood quickly pooled on the floor from the gaping holes of the wounded. None lived more than a few seconds.

Alex suddenly felt very dizzy. The floor quickly became covered in blood from the gaping wounds of the dead. He fell forward onto the floor, then lapsed back into unconsciousness.

CHAPTER 9

Alex woke up hours later. It was dark and he was in the back of the Land Rover, which was in motion, his head resting on Elaine's lap. As soon as she saw his eyes open, she lifted him into a sitting position.

'It seemed the best way to stop your head from bumping around,' she said shyly, pushing away some hair from her eyes.

Roy was at the wheel, with Cliff beside him. They were driving fast along a two-lane highway between sparsely tufted slopes with just the occasional stunted tree or bush to vary the landscape.

Wayne was not with them and Alex suddenly remembered why. His thoughts all ran together in his head. A confused tangle of quick desperate movements, strange expressions, frightened and confused faces. But the last few seconds before the killings were crystal clear. Not the events so much as the face of Samuel, his look of total self-righteousness, the cold, widening intensity of his eyes. Then blood, shots, flesh, screams and silence. He couldn't remember how he had ended up in the Land Rover.

'How's your head?' Elaine bent closer.

'A lot better, I think,' Alex answered, raising his hand to the bump and finding a wad of bandage there.

'I thought a bandage might stop any infection from getting in,' she explained.

Alex watched her thoughtfully, for the first time really taking note of her appearance. She was more attractive than he had realized with high cheek bones and a full mouth. In the shadows of the Land Rover, he could also see the soft curves of her body.

182

Cliff turned in his seat. 'I wish we'd taken your advice, guv.'

Alex nodded, but found nothing comforting to say.

'We had to leave your dead companion in the cellar with the others,' Elaine said. 'There are other members of my group who would have heard the shots and come to investigate. If they had caught us...' She shook her head, leaving the sentence unfinished.

'And the other woman, Cathy?' Alex asked.

'She didn't want to come,' Elaine replied. 'She and Alan, you know...' She shrugged.

Alex curled up in his seat and stared out the window. He had a bad headache and felt dizzy, but that wasn't what was troubling him. He had killed again. Something that he had managed to avoid since the death of Tina. He re-played the final moments of the scene in his head before he began shooting, trying to convince himself that he had no other choice. But there were always other choices. He was guilty of murder again and no rational argument could relieve him of that fact.

Several hours of driving later, Roy pulled off the road in front of a pub in a small, deserted village. They were somewhere north of Dunfries. It didn't seem to matter where exactly. Roy and Cliff carried out a brief search, then helped Elaine unload the stores for the night.

Still feeling sick, Alex said he needed to lie down, so he collected a lantern from the Land Rover, and gingerly made his way up to one of the bedrooms on the second floor. The room was rather large and drab, with the familiar smell of rotting wood and damp. Two single beds stood under a window on the far wall. They were dusty and had been stripped of sheeting and blankets, but he found a pillow in a cupboard and an old bedspread. Quickly stripping down to his underwear, he wrapped himself up in the bedspread and climbed into one of them.

Below he could hear the sounds of a fire being lit and food prepared. He was not tired, just filled with emptiness.

He leaned over and blew out the light. He thought of Wayne, a bundle of nervous life, lying dead in a cellar. It was hard to lose a friend; it would be harder for Roy, though the big man would never show what that death had meant to him. But he and Wayne had complimented each other perfectly; each contributing what was missing in the other's personality. Now Roy would regress into his old state; reclusive, silent, confiding in no one. It was so terrible to lose a good man, and Wayne would still be alive if he hadn't persuaded him to come on this trip.

He rolled onto his side and stared dully into the comforting blankness of the night, but his mind remained active, ploughing through the memories. Soon all track of time was lost. Wayne suddenly appeared on the doorstep of the pub, Roy and Cliff greeting him excitedly, but he was furious, having walked most of the night to try and catch up with the Land Rover. He had three bullet holes cut diagonally across his shirt, blood completely saturating his shirt and trousers, but he didn't seem at all concerned about his injuries. He just kept accusing Roy and Cliff of leaving him to die in the cellar. Then he noticed Alex in the background and he began screaming a horrible frenzied scream, full of hate and impotent rage. His eyes burned like Samuels. Terrified, Alex backed away. But Wayne came after him, babbling wildly and accusing Alex of trying to murder him. There was a sound at the door. Samuel appeared ... Alex woke up suddenly in a cold sweat. Someone was tapping on the door.

'Hello, Alex.' The door opened tentatively, and Elaine's tall figure stood there. 'I'm sorry to wake you,' she said gently, 'but I thought you might be cold so I brought you up some blankets.'

She came forward, closing the door behind her. She was carrying a lantern in one hand and a large bundle of sheets and blankets in the other. Alex noticed she had washed and changed. She looked fresh and revived, as though the events of the day had already been washed off and discarded with her clothes. She had on a large woollen jumper and a pair of baggy jeans several sizes too large for her, which were held up with a cord tied in a bow around her waist. She looked formless and comical, like a little girl who had dressed up in her father's clothes.

'I found them in one of the other rooms,' she said, looking down rather self-consciously. 'Not much of a fit, I'm afraid.' She deposited the blankets and the lamp and came to sit on the end of the bed.

'Are you hot,' she asked, frowning at him.

'I had a bad dream,' Alex explained, looking at the bedspread he had thrown on the floor.

'Oh! Were you having the dream when I knocked on the door?'

'For a moment, I thought you were Samuel,' Alex said, smiling briefly.

'Samuel?'

'Just a silly dream,' Alex shrugged.

They stared at each other uncomfortably for a moment, then she lowered her eyes pretending to examine her fingernails.

'No one felt like eating much. Still a bit shocked, I suppose.' She flicked some of her hair away from her face as she raised her head to look at him, in what Alex was beginning to realise was a nervous gesture.

He nodded. 'Yes, I imagine they were.'

Again, the conversation petered out. 'Well, maybe I'd better leave.' She began to get to her feet.

'NO! ... I mean, don't go,' Alex said quickly. 'I'm sorry. Please!'

She hesitated, then sat down again. Watching him, she asked; 'Did you know Wayne well?'

'No, not really, he was Roy's friend.' Alex sighed and pulled himself up to a sitting position. 'And you...did you know Samuel and those others very well?'

'I thought I did,' she said softly. 'I lost most of my friends and family in the plague. Samuel and his followers were all that was left.'

'Why didn't you go north with the rest of them?'

'I...' she began. 'It just didn't work out like that,' giving up on an explanation.

'Do you want to talk about it?'

Her head went down, and he thought he had trespassed too far, when out of the silence she began to speak.

'I worked in the pathology lab before the war. I was actually in the lab when the first shock waves hit the town. I remember it all so clearly, the shaking, the noise, glassware and chemicals crashing down all around me. I didn't think of the bombs at first, I imagined it must be an earthquake of some sort. Then it passed and everything went so quiet, not a murmur. I thought, vaguely, I must be the only one left alive, but of course it was just shock,' she said with a grim smile. 'The hospital basement was several stories underground so as we realised what had happened all the staff went straight down. Over a hundred-people crammed into three poky rooms. No one could sleep; there was no proper sanitation provided and no food and water. After the second day, I left and went home. My mother and brother were still there, my father had been, but he had gone out the previous day after food and not returned. My brother was killed the same way a month later, in a fight over food.' She paused reflectively. 'So, my mother and I were left alone. Things were pretty desperate, I can tell you. Almost nothing to eat. We had to chop up the furniture to keep a fire alight.'

'Is that when Samuel appeared?'

She nodded. 'It was marvellous what he did. In those early days he was the one person who seemed to be in control. He organised scavenging parties, pooled resources. Cared for the sick. He was like a father to us. He took us under his wing, not only my mother and me, I mean everybody who was lost and frightened. And that was just about the whole population at that time. Of course, he also had his own elite followers, his right arm so to speak, who enforced the law. Somebody had to do it, there were such brutes of men, you wouldn't credit it, men who thought nothing of raping and killing. Somebody had to take charge.'

'You admired him for it,' Alex said simply.

Elaine raised her head sharply and searched his face, as though trying to fathom if this were meant as an accusation. 'Yes, I did,' she said softly. 'Truly, I believed in him. He seemed to know exactly what was best for us. We were carried along by him, by his vision. He gave us hope for the future, purpose where none had been.' She paused. 'You would have had to live through those times.' She sighed. 'But then things started to go wrong. People started dying of typhus. Samuel was at the height of his powers and making some of his most inspired speeches. He talked of the plague as a test of our commitment to staying, as a trial sent down from heaven. He even quoted verses from the Book of Revelation about terrible plagues and famines. He said he was building a new society, where love and respect would be all that would count, not like in the old days of greed and selfishness. He dreamed such wonderful dreams, and he said he wanted us to share in them. We were going to start again, he said. And who knows what he might have achieved, only the times were against him.'

'Why, what do you mean?'

She frowned, turning over painful thoughts. 'He should not have insisted that we stay during the plague. It obsessed him. He called the survivors who stayed the 'chosen', and insisted that they wouldn't get sick, but thousands did, and no amount of lies could hide that fact.'

Alex nodded. They had been driving amongst their skeletons on the motorway all the afternoon.

'I stayed because my mother would not leave Samuel. She trusted him and nothing would shake her devotion to him.'

Alex sensed from her hesitancy that there was more to follow.

'Mother died from typhus about a month later,' she continued after a pause. 'Since then I have watched Samuel deteriorate into a babbling, irrational fool, striking out left and right, and ordering executions for even the slightest disloyalty, as he called it. He killed foreigners, too, you know.' She looked up at Alex. 'Six men from your community.'

Alex nodded his head slowly. 'I thought as much,' he said.

'I should have stopped him when he killed those drivers,' she went on bitterly. 'I shouldn't have waited all this time, but it's hard to break away from someone you've believed and trusted in, knowing the world has nothing else to offer. I was weak, I saw through him, but I didn't do anything about it.'

Alex, seeing her close to tears, reached across and took both her hands in his. 'You've done nothing wrong,' he said, almost in a whisper. 'You are like everyone else. You've been swept along by events you could not hope to control. Each of us does what he can. That's all anyone can ask.'

Suddenly, for no reason, he had an image of Tina, and he nearly groaned out loud. But instead, he squeezed Elaine's hands more tightly for comfort and he could see some of the sadness lift from her face. He shook his head, scattering his guilty thoughts.

'And you,' Elaine said, more warmly. 'You know everything about me, but I know nothing about you.' She tilted her head to one side, inquisitive, half-smiling.

Alex leaned back against the rail of the bed head and studied her thoughtfully. He took in all the curves of her body, the way her hair hung in loose tangled spirals over her face and the lovely formation of her eyes, nose and lips. He imagined how he would have responded to that invitation in the old days; the careless, flirting talk, the dinner date at his favourite restaurant, watching the late movie together, chance meetings, renewed affection, laughter and happiness; it all seemed so far away now. Today, every conversation

188

was serious and tinged with sadness, and carefree smiles were only on the faces of madmen.

'My story may take some time and it's equally as miserable as yours,' he replied.

'Whose isn't?' She dropped her legs to the floor, stood up and walked over to the other bed and pushed it next to his. 'You don't mind if I listen in bed? I'm freezing.'

'Please do,' Alex smiled.

She took some sheets from under the pile of blankets she had brought in and quickly made the bed, giving one of the blankets to Alex. 'I couldn't have spent the night alone,' she said earnestly. 'Not after what happened today.' She dragged off her jumper and jeans and clambered between the sheets, rolling over to bring her face near to his.

Alex started recounting the events of the war. He talked mainly about the first weeks of the holocaust, the death of his brother, and how he had met Tina, Cliff and Roy, the labour camp and the crossing of the Bristol Channel with that terrible battle in the shallows. By the time he had finished Elaine was curled up, fast asleep in his arms. He gently lifted the rest of her body across to his bed, pulled the bed covers over them both and wrapped his arms around her. His last thoughts before he drifted into sleep were how nice it was to feel a woman's body again.

The next day they set off early, eager to reach their destination. Cliff was at the wheel and Roy sat by his side, directing him by reference to a huge, tattered map of Scotland. Although neither had said anything, Alex sensed that they were aware that Elaine and he had spent the night together. There was an understanding between Elaine and him also, though he found it hard to put his finger on it. Some type of security or companionship that Cliff and Roy couldn't fail to miss. He looked out of the window at the passing sights. It was close to midday and they were passing the ruins of Glasgow. The ruins looked painfully familiar. Nottingham, Birmingham, Liverpool, London, Alex had had his full share of ruined cities, but he could see the macabre fascination they must exercise on the less experienced. It was obvious to him that this one had suffered several direct strikes. No buildings as far as he could see were intact, though the jagged and burnt-out shells of many buildings rose above the stunted vegetation. Occasional howls from roaming packs of dogs testified to what was probably the only life still left in the city.

'Grim,' Roy said, shaking his huge head slowly.

'It's strange, though,' Cliff mused, peering over the steering wheel at the road. 'This close to the blast you'd expect to find a lot of debris on the road, but over the past few kilometres it's been completely clear.'

Alex was annoyed with himself for not noticing this. Cars and Lorries, which at one time had evidently obstructed the highway at the places where their owners had died, had been pushed unceremoniously to one side. Travel became easy, though as yet there was no sign of who had organised these deliberate clearances.

Soon they came to a rugged landscape, deeply indented with lochs, and chiselled mountains that climbed into the clouds above. A mist came down as they began to climb, the road surface became slippery and visibility dropped down to less than fifty metres. Alex warned everyone to stay alert, as the road began snaking and twisting on itself in and out of valleys. If it had been thought worthwhile to clear tracks as far south as Glasgow, they could not be far off their intended goal.

Indeed, only a few minutes later, they heard the first signs of the Scottish community in the clear sound of heavy machinery being operated somewhere ahead. Cliff pulled the Land Rover to the side of the road. The noise grew quickly, and soon they could hear the gear changes as the machines negotiated the slight grade leading up to them.

'They're behind us as well,' Alex said, opening the door and climbing out.

190

They were on a sharp bend, with the mist closing in. On their left the valley wall fell almost sheer. On their right, boggy land, deeply eroded, and waved over with bog Cotton. They had been very cleverly trapped. He told Roy and Elaine to remain in the Land Rover and beckoned Cliff to join him. He unslung his holster and placed it on the bonnet, telling Cliff to do the same. 'You'll have to cover us if there's any trouble,' he shouted to the others. The drone of the powerful engines now completely filled the air.

The next minute a huge bulldozer rounded the bend ahead with five men clinging precariously to the driver's cabin. It stopped a short distance away and crashed its shovel onto the road. Seconds later its companion appeared from behind and halted with similar menace. The men on both machines trained an assortment of shotguns and automatic weapons on them, while a large figure with a long, ragged beard came towards them from the bulldozer in front.

Alex began; 'we come from a community in northern Wales I...'

'Tell your friends in there to throw out their weapons and come out,' the man said in a thick Scottish accent, waving his rifle in the direction of the Land Rover.

Alex hesitated only for a second. He gave the signal and one by one they stepped down.

'Good,' the man said more pleasantly when they were all assembled before him. 'From Wales, you say? And what brings you all the way up here, I wonder?'

'We represent a large community in North Wales,' Alex repeated. 'We are here to try and establish friendly relations.'

The man looked them up and down critically. 'You don't look like any delegation to me.'

'And what's a delegation supposed to look like?' demanded the irrepressible Cliff. 'Sorry if our appearance offends you, but our pressed suits are still at the dry cleaners.'

Alex cringed, he would not have ventured such a jibe at this stage, but fortunately the man had a sense of humour.

His face softened into a mild grin. 'Well, you're certainly the cockiest intruders we've had so far.'

'We've been through a lot to get here,' Alex explained quickly. 'One of our group was killed yesterday, so we're a bit on edge.'

The Scotsman nodded but did not seem altogether convinced. 'I'd have thought that a delegation all the way from Wales would have brought more reinforcements for protection,' he said suspiciously.

'That was an option we considered before we started,' Alex replied. 'But we reckoned a small armed force could be open to misinterpretation, so we decided not to bring them.'

'Hmm...' The man scratched his head as if he didn't know what to believe. 'Well, it's not up to me to decide what to do with you,' he said finally. 'That's for the authorities back on the island.'

The Land Rover was searched, and all firearms removed before they were allowed to continue on with an escort. Three hours later they crossed over to the Isle of Skye.

CHAPTER 10

It was dark when they reached their destination. For the
nerve centre of the community, it seemed strangely modest -
an old pub, no less, wedged into a row of drab two storey
shops in the centre of an island town. They were directed
upstairs into a large, ornately decorated room where a man in
his late forties, with weathered features and a hard,
expressionless face was sitting at a leather panelled desk.
Their guide went forward.

'These are the people I radioed in about earlier,' he said.

The man at the desk looked them up and down, before
getting to his feet and slowly coming forward. 'Wales,' he
muttered to himself, while shaking their hands. 'I've lived
half my life in Wales, near Cardiff. I don't suppose you know
whether it was destroyed or not?'

'We come from the north-east,' Alex spoke up.

'But someone in your community must know?'

Alex glanced quickly at the others. He realised that this
was some sort of test and that their integrity was already
under fire. 'I believe it had a direct hit. We have very few
survivors from Cardiff.' he responded coldly.

"Huh...shame.' The man stepped up to Alex. 'Do I
gather that you are the spokesman for the group?'

'I'm in charge, if that's what you mean.'

'Well, then,' he said briskly, 'you're the person who can
tell me what this is all about.'

'We've come to offer our friendship and maybe
establish some kind of trading links,' Alex replied.

'Friendship? Trading links?' the man permitted himself
a smile. 'And what is it you want to trade?'

'Simply anything and everything.'

Still smiling, as though he found the whole concept faintly ridiculous, their interviewer resumed his seat. 'Nothing in this world is ever simple, my friend,' he said. 'What gives you the idea that we even want to trade with you in the first place?'

'I think you've misunderstood our intentions,' Alex said firmly. 'We've been sent here as a gesture of friendship and goodwill. We've even brought gifts; ten kilos of tea and coffee.'

The man did not seem to welcome this gesture. 'We have difficulty in feeding ourselves, so we certainly have no food to trade with you, or give you for that matter, for your precious tea and coffee.'

'We don't want your food,' Alex said. 'We have more than enough. We are here primarily to promote friendly relations between our community and your own. I advise you not to treat us with such contempt.' He did not hide his anger and frustration at the way this meeting was going, and this seemed to produce an effect.

'You don't want any food from us?' The man sounded a trifle perplexed for the first time.

'We produce a surplus as it is,' Alex said more calmly. 'We certainly don't need to add to it.'

'So, if it's not food, then what is it that you do want?' The conversation seemed to be going full circle.

'We can trade food with you if you like.' Alex was being as patient as he knew how, sensing that the penny had dropped at last.

'How much food?'

'Well, at the moment our community numbers around thirty-five thousand members,' Alex replied. 'The harvest looks good, so we expect to produce well in excess of our needs.'

The man looked rather shell-shocked. He stared at Alex for a moment, grunted to himself, then lowered his head, shaking it ruefully. 'Do me the courtesy to show me exactly where your community is located on the map, will you?' he said at length, producing a battered school atlas and opening it at the appropriate page.

The others gathered round as Alex marked the boundaries in with a pencil. He also explained about the mine, its location, and some of the farming techniques and the type of produce the community would most likely want to trade.

The mood after this changed dramatically. The man, who introduced himself as Peter McCaffrey, apologised for seeming abrupt, and explained that they were often being pestered by small Scottish communities for quantities of stores and provisions. In the case of Alex's community, the boot was clearly on the other foot.

Now chairs were brought in, and the visitors were seated in them and served presently with steaming herbal tea, brought in by a smiling woman. Alex sniffed at its aroma but failed to identify the brew.

'Ah, we don't have any tea or coffee left,' Peter explained. 'So, this is our own concoction, the staple drink of the community, and not bad at that.' He poured a green coloured fluid into the cups and passed them around. Alex sipped his cautiously, then nodded his approval, making a mental note that it tasted remarkably like the herbal tea back home in Wales, which goes to prove, he thought ironically, that the same wild herbs have survived in both places.

'I don't know how your community has fared, but we have lived through some shocking times. Beyond imagination some of the things that have happened.' He leaned across and looked hard into their faces. 'I've often wondered what happened to the government. You know, all during that first year after the holocaust, I was expecting them to march up here and start issuing food rations and organise rebuilding programmes.' He sighed. 'All our arrangements were only temporary then, in the nature of a stopgap until help arrived. But slowly it dawned on us that this was an illusion; there would never be any help. We were all there was. Quite a traumatic moment that. I don't hold such fantasies now,' he went on coldly. 'Until just now I fully believed that we were the only sizeable group left in Great Britain, maybe even the world. But your arrival, bringing news of a community actually larger than ours and willing to trade its surplus food...'

He shrugged, his eyes never leaving Alex's face. 'Well,' he said at last, 'you will understand if I find it difficult to get used to the idea.'

Alex understood perfectly, he had made a claim to represent a huge and successful community in Wales. Now he had to justify that claim. As accurately and methodically as possible he launched into a detailed history of the Welsh community. He explained, with help from Roy and Cliff, how it was established, its struggles, political structure, rules, farming techniques and even its future plans for expansion. Alex decided that if his story was going to sound convincing, he could not afford to suppress any aspect of it.

At first it was clear that Peter was trying to find inconsistencies in their stories. But his questions soon lost their suspicious overtone as Alex continued to pour out the complex social and political structures and the philosophy of the Welsh community.

When this process of verification was complete, to the satisfaction of both sides, Peter drained the last dregs from his third cup. 'Your community seems extremely well organised and considerably better off than ours. Our efforts have been hampered by not being able to build up a stockpile. Just after the war, we had to cannibalise whole towns for medical supplies and food to stay alive.'

Alex pointed out that they were not just interested in trading links. The point of the visit, he insisted once again, was to open channels of friendly communication.

'And how are you proposing to do that?' Peter asked.

'A representative from our group will stay here as a token of our friendship,' Alex said promptly. 'In exchange, you may send one, or as many representatives as you like, from your own community, back to Wales with us to talk with our committee.'

'Yes, good, good,' Peter enthused. He explained that he and two others ruled their community with dictatorial powers. 'I will have to talk it over with my associates, of course, but I'm sure there wouldn't be any problems. Despite our poor agricultural situation, we have considerable electrical and mechanical equipment still intact and other items you may be interested in, which we would certainly be willing to exchange for your surplus food.'

Alex assured him that the Welsh community would be more than willing to trade, and having again offered the tea and coffee, which this time was more graciously received, the meeting broke up on a very open and optimistic note. Peter shook hands all round and they were shown to well-appointed rooms at the back of the pub. Bathing facilities were attached and they were assured that hot water flowed through the taps.

That night Alex and Elaine shared one of the bedrooms. An initial awkwardness was soon overcome, and they talked for hours about their past lives, jobs and families, both being anxious to learn as much about the other as possible. Then, tired out with talking, they pushed the beds together and got between the sheets. They kissed lightly and then with more urgency, Alex began to explore every curve and crevice of her body. She sighed and responded with soft warm kisses that soon turned to passion, unrestrained and uninhibited. For the first time since the war, Alex found he could look into the future and not feel a pit in his stomach.

Over the next few days, they were treated like royalty. Nothing was too good for them, or too much trouble. The following day they were introduced to the two other members of the junta, Dimitri Antoni and Matthew Langley, both sad faced, tired looking men. Elaine found their coldness unnerving, but the more Alex learned about the community the more he thought he could understand them. Peter turned out to be the most affable of the three and he put himself out to show them around, pointing out new building projects and agricultural ventures. But the people on the whole looked far from healthy, with many instances of skin cancer, tumours and coughing fits. When Alex asked about this, Peter just shrugged.

'We've all been affected by the radiation to some degree,' he said. 'We have only one rule: if you can work you can stay.'

'And if you can't?'

'Same as you, in theory, at least. But in practice our people choose another way out. Our chemists have formulated a drink, very pleasant to take and rapid in its effect and it kills within minutes.'

'And how many take this option?'

'Everyone,' Peter told him. 'Since exile often means a cruel and lingering death, or being torn apart by wild dogs, this drink is by far the most humane way to die.'

Alex didn't ask any more questions. He was fast learning of the savage history of this community. Originally there had been nearly a quarter of a million survivors. They had fought each other until less than sixty thousand remained. The plague had halved that number. Of the two thousand men and women who had left Carlisle, less than five hundred had got this far. Truly the twenty thousand survivors that now made up their number were very tough individuals. The decision to take a poison would be nothing more than common sense to these people.

After a week of discussions, it was agreed that Dimitri should lead a twelve-man delegation to Wales. Cliff and Roy would go with them to act as guides and to introduce them to the committee. As Alex had promised, he and Elaine would remain behind. He found himself looking forward to the prospect, and indeed their status as honoured guests continued. Not only were they allowed a free run of the place, but Peter insisted that they be present at the policy meetings between himself and Matthew. Alex was never able to warm to the latter. He never smiled or joked but seemed

198

determined always to put the worst interpretation on events. Peter laughingly called him the devil's advocate of the junta, but Alex found his brand of depressive realism almost morbid. He could appreciate, however, how the different personalities of the junta made it work. Peter, he quickly realised, was the eternal optimist. He treated Alex and Elaine as royalty because he thought the Welsh community was the answer to all their problems. Dimitri gave the impression of practical common sense. All shades from light to dark were represented here.

But since Dimitri was absent, Alex increasingly found himself called upon to occupy his place and mediate in the frequently heated exchanges between Peter and Matthew. That so much passion was generated was understandable, given the difficulties that the community still faced. Like their Welsh contemporaries they had experimented with cultivation under huge greenhouses, but they seemed to lack the technical expertise that had made the Welsh harvests so successful. As a result, their crop yields were still very poor. The previous year no less than five hundred of the weakest members of the community had taken the 'suicide drink'. This year the crop had not been much better and unless a huge injection of food was found from somewhere, more survivors would have to die. Both Peter and Matthew emphasised this point to Alex more than once. He did his best to suggest ways of improving their techniques, but he wasn't a farmer and he found himself floundering when they asked for specific details on his recommendations. In fact, their agricultural problems were so great that Alex even began to wonder if the Welsh community had enough surplus food to make up the shortfall.

He was discussing this with Elaine one night in their room when she suddenly became very thoughtful. It wasn't like her to be silent, and Alex asked her what the matter was. For an answer she brought an atlas of the country from a bookshelf and laid it open on a desk. Alex joined her as she found what she was looking for.

'Yes, that's it,' she said. 'Box. I thought I remembered the name.'

She had her finger on a small village about ten kilometres north-east of Bath.

'Samuel was always quoting from those papers and maps he found in the citadel,' she explained. 'Some of them alluded to other citadels and to storage places like your mine in Wales. There was a huge repository near the village of Box.'

Alex remembered that much of the sandstone used around Bath had come from quarries in that region. 'The Corsham quarries,' he said, looking across at Elaine for confirmation.

'That's right. There had been a lot of mining in that area for centuries before the war. The quarries were enormous. Samuel said they had been under military control for some time and had been completed re-fitted and upgraded with new equipment.'

'And the entrance to these quarries is near Box?'

'Yes, but there were no details as to where exactly.'

'I see.' Alex began to pace the room. In the chaos of the holocaust, it was just possible that such a food dump could have been overlooked. 'Did Samuel ever mention how many bombs had been dropped in that area?'

'Hmm,' Elaine frowned, trying hard to remember. 'He did show us a map once,' she said slowly. 'As I recall, several bombs landed north of Bristol and a few to the east on Greenham Common. Box, I think, would have escaped. Why, do you think it's worth a look?'

Alex leaned over and studied the map further. 'Yes, I do, very much so. And that may not be the only food dump in Great Britain. If the military lost its grip at an early stage, as we now believe, there could be thousands of tonnes of food just waiting to be found.'

'Wouldn't it have gone off by now?'

'Not necessarily. The Welsh mine had its own generators and enormous freezing and refrigerator capacity. I imagine that if the government had upgraded these quarries, as you say, they would have been bound to install similar facilities there. Besides, a lot of the food would be dried. Providing it's kept in a cool place it should last for years.'

The more Alex thought about it, the more he became determined to travel to Box and spent the following days debating with himself what his next move ought to be. His first reaction was to inform Peter and get him to send a convoy down to investigate. But he abandoned the idea as too risky given the tenuous nature of the links with the Scottish community. If something were to go wrong, if say the convoy failed to return, the relationship between the two communities would be seriously strained at a time when it had barely begun. He also could not imagine the Welsh committee, on his return there, sanctioning a mission of its own to Box on such flimsy evidence. More than likely they would refuse him. And if he were to go against their ruling, he risked being banished; others before him had been expelled for less. No, his only option was to investigate Box himself. He could join the next convoy heading south and leave it at the Welsh border. The whole trip would take less than two weeks. Given the impending success of the Scottish mission, he felt the committee would be more amenable to an unsanctioned side trip.

When he confided his decision to Elaine, she naturally insisted on accompanying him. He had not even considered her up to that point and at first resisted strongly, but she made so much fuss that he eventually gave in.

After a month, the delegation returned with three of the Welsh committee in tow. The Scots had been delighted with everything they had seen and delivered glowing reports on the friendliness and co-operation of the Welsh community. Without exception they raved about its efficiency and its numerous agricultural advances, which could be directly applied to their own agricultural problems. Alex noticed several agricultural advisors amongst the Welsh delegation. They were to remain in the north until the reforms they suggested could be implemented. In exchange, the Scottish community would send mechanical parts and machinery to Wales. They also had access to a huge range of weaponry and fuel reserves left behind by the military, which they were willing to ship south in exchange for surplus food.

The committee members made an enormous fuss over Alex when they saw him. They relayed the thanks and gratitude of Marcus and his associates and made him an honorary committee member. They even suggested that he could become a permanent member of the committee if he wanted. Alex was flattered but was less inclined to accept when he learned that his old adversary Terry had also been nominated for a post.

For Alex this was both a sad and a happy time. During their stay, he and Elaine had grown very close, spending nearly all their spare time together. It was not, nor could it hope to be, given Elaine's temperament, a tranquil relationship. She was too intelligent, and at times too bloody minded, to knuckle under to him. She had an enormous capacity for ideas and defended them against Alex's attempts to reason with a ferociousness that sometimes brought him close to screaming point. They would talk and argue till the early morning, completely losing track of time. She verbally poked and prodded him until he was forced to defend even his most innocuous thoughts and assumptions. However, such a lively companion did something for him that Cliff had failed to do. She made Alex re-assess and even amend his sullen view of life. In one short month she had re-moulded him and most importantly become an intimate companion.

Meanwhile, preparations had been continuing for the first shipment of fuel and machinery to leave for Wales. Alex broke the news of his little side trip to the visiting committee members. At first, they had flatly refused, thinking he was asking their permission. But when they realised that he was going regardless of their objections, they softened their attitude and allowed him to load up with supplies, unhindered.

The day of their departure dawned, cold and misty. Alex and Elaine took their leave of Peter with their grateful thanks and climbed into their Land Rover. On a signal from the leading vehicle the convoy of armoured cars, lorries and trucks moved slowly on their way bound for Wales. Alex and Elaine would travel with the convoy past Manchester. When the convoy turned westward along the M56, Alex would strike out south and continue past Birmingham and Bristol, then on to Box.

CHAPTER 11

They reached the small village of Box on the morning of the fourth day after leaving the convoy. Thus far the trip had been without incident. The land was quiet, menaced only by clouds of insects and lean packs of dogs. Even the open wounds of cities were slowly healing as the march of vegetation overgrew them.

Alex shifted into second gear and cruised through the streets of the village, watchful and uneasy. They had stopped and searched several houses since their arrival and found not the slightest sign of looting and this struck a decidedly false note. He imagined every house in Great Britain must have been looted by now. When they made this discovery, he had immediately begun monitoring the area for radiation, supposing that locally high levels may have had a deterrent effect. But their counters had not registered anything above background levels. And another aberrant factor gave cause for alarm. For the last ten kilometres, the usual smattering of communities had been completely missing from the landscape. It was as though this whole central region of England had been swept clean. For some reason no one had survived the holocaust and no survivors had ventured back into the area to re-colonise it.

He pulled the Land Rover over to the side of the road and switched off the engine. They had reached the outskirts of the village for the fifth time. Despite searching every street, they had found no sign of a tunnel entrance. If access to the underground store, supposing that such a place really existed, was this well-hidden it might be impossible to locate.

204

'Are you sure you can't remember any detail as to the whereabouts of this store?' he asked Elaine, who had a detailed map of the area spread over her knees.

She shook her head irritably, without looking up. He had asked her the same question many times in the last half-hour.

He sighed. 'Well, at least we know it's not in the immediate area of Box, so we'll just have to widen our search.'

These words were hardly out of his mouth when Elaine's head came up sharply.

'Can you hear something?' she asked.

Alex craned his head out of the window. There was a low rumbling noise that he identified immediately as coming from another car engine, and not far off. They stared at each other in shock, for it was already too late for them to drive off without being heard. Urgently, they checked their handguns and waited for the vehicle to come into view. But the sound stopped directly behind a grassy hill to their right. When they heard the doors of the other vehicle open, they quickly climbed out of the Land Rover and crept up the other side of the hill.

A khaki-coloured van had stopped in the middle of a field beside what looked like a large funnel. As they watched, two men came around the back of the van carrying tool kits. To Alex's amazement both were dressed in military uniform, and not the tattered rags Alex had seen on gangs in the months after the holocaust, these uniforms looked clean, uncreased, and their owners well-fed with short hair and clean-shaven chins. The men dismantled the top of the funnel, changed what appeared to be a filter, then re-assembled it. Within a few minutes, they had finished their work and climbed back into the van. They drove off in the direction they had come, leaving a clear set of tyre prints in the tall grass of the field.

Alex and Elaine watched and waited for a few minutes after the sound of the engine had died away, then climbed down and walked over to the funnel. It was a solid structure, flaring outwards from a square concrete slab and rising to about a metre before it bent horizontally, terminating in a fine wire grid. Alex walked around it, tapping it critically.

'Must lead to some type of underground chamber,' he speculated.

Elaine didn't answer. She had her ear pressed firmly against the wire mesh. 'I can hear a faint hum,' she announced.

'Maybe an underground generator, like we have at the mine,' Alex suggested.

'We found funnels of this type in Carlisle,' Elaine said thoughtfully. 'They turned out to be the ventilation shafts leading to the underground citadel. Those men, who do you think they are? Did you see the uniforms on them?'

'Yeah.' Alex couldn't understand it. If this was a citadel, why should they still be living underground? The land was not cultivated in any direction, so he had to assume that they were sustaining themselves from a huge food store that should rightfully belong to the survivors. The thought, and their well-fed appearance, enraged him. 'We'd better follow them,' he said coldly. 'I think we might find our food store after all.'

After some discussion, it was decided to go forward on foot. They couldn't risk the noise of the Land Rover giving warning of their approach. Besides, if they were standing on top of the citadel the entrance couldn't be far away.

They hid the Land Rover in a nearby garage. Alex put together enough food and water for the day in a pack, along with a map, binoculars and a compass. They took a handgun each and several clips of ammunition.

The tyre tracks went on considerably further than they had anticipated and soon they began to regret their decision.

In some places the grass reached past their thighs, concealing the uneven ground and making the going difficult. It was the hottest part of the day, too, with the temperature climbing into the high thirties. Soon they were exhausted and dripping with sweat. After well over an hour, they sighted some spirals of black smoke. The tyre tracks tended in that direction, but another hour passed before they approached the source.

After climbing out of a steep gully, they found the grassy track merging with a broad, immaculately maintained bitumen road. It ran on straight for several hundred metres on a spur of land, before dipping into the valley beyond. Ready to spring for cover at the smallest sound or disturbance, Alex and Elaine cautiously climbed to the top of the last ridge.

Less than a kilometre away, in a valley, stood four chimney stacks, two of which were belching out smoke. Below these chimneys and close to a tunnel entrance, people, like ants, swarmed in their hundreds. Alex hadn't seen such a sight since before the war. The prevailing costume was either khaki, like that of the two maintenance men, or a kind of grey flannelette suit, which covered the whole body. But what amazed the watchers more than anything was the carefree behaviour of this vast crowd. They seemed to be strolling about, enjoying the outdoors, talking, reading, laughing and none of them looked skinny or half starved. Many were overweight, bouncing around playing volleyball or soccer, or even picnicking as if they hadn't a care in the world.

Alex felt totally bewildered by all this, and not a little angry. He felt like storming down there and demanding an explanation, screaming and ranting at them until they justified their extravagance. But instead, both he and Elaine sunk into a nearby rock outcrop and lapsed into silence. Neither spoke nor even moved for a long time. They sat amongst the rocks whilst these cheerful people consumed meat, vegetables, bread, salads, fruit, and cheeses, throwing the scraps carelessly away. Precious water was tipped onto the ground. Such behaviour was deemed criminal in the Welsh community and was punished by expulsion.

The light had faded before the celebrations died down. Then the crowd slowly filtered back into the tunnel.

Alex had hardly said a word as they watched. Certain things, though, had become clear in his mind. The indulgence they had been witnessing pointed to a huge food supply and from the amount of fresh meat and vegetables being consumed it was obvious that they must have access to farm animals and were growing crops somewhere. Possibly this place was similar to the Welsh community. A large supply of stored food had provided the nucleus for a thriving community, which must have overcome, like them, the problems of soil contamination and poor crop yield. Yet everything here was on a much grander scale. All the people they had seen had been exceptionally well clothed and their bodies were soft and fleshy. They lacked the sinewy, slightly emaciated look he had come to expect from survivors. The whole atmosphere told of an easy lifestyle. Only the men dressed in military uniforms had any strength or leanness to their bodies, but even they were a far cry from the ragged, dishevelled soldiers who guarded the borders of the Welsh community.

'I've been watching those buildings over there,' Elaine said, pointing to a cluster of houses scattered to the left of the entrance of the tunnel. 'People have been entering them, but not coming out again.'

Alex focused his binoculars on the same place and saw a constant stream of people disappearing into a small red brick building.

The last of the military entered the tunnel at dusk. A huge metal door was then drawn across the entrance. By the time night fell nothing stirred on the surface not even a solitary light betrayed what had gone on here during the day.

Alex and Elaine crept down and inspected the tunnel entrance and peered through the windows of the buildings. Their torch beams revealed nothing but empty rooms with dusty tables and chairs. When they came to the small red brick building, the door was ajar and the windows open.

208

They ventured in and found themselves in a narrow corridor, which led into a large vinyl tiled room and two thickly carpeted offices. They began looking carefully for any concealed trapdoors, but they uncovered nothing more dramatic than scraps of food and empty drink containers. The walls appeared to be brick and the floors solid concrete. Alex was just contemplating tearing up the carpet in one of the offices when he heard a loud grating sound, like heavy slabs of rock moving past each other.

Elaine came hurtling through the door and pushed Alex against the wall.

'Keep very quiet,' she hissed.

The sound had stopped, and they were aware of a white glow.

'What is it?' Alex whispered.

'The floor,' she breathed. 'I was tapping it when suddenly a whole section started sliding apart.'

Alex could hear the hollow crack of leather boots, as though someone was emerging from a long tunnel. The sounds came closer and soon they could make out voices. Two men could be heard laughing and joking with each other. The footsteps stopped only metres away from where Alex and Elaine were hiding. Then the grating sound started again and the light began to fade. When all the noise had ceased, the footsteps began to recede towards the front of the building. Alex drew his revolver and pushed past Elaine.

He shone his torch at the soldiers just as they were approaching the front door.

'Back here!' he yelled, waving his revolver in their startled faces. 'Hurry!' he continued, as they appeared to hesitate. The threat was enough to make them scurry back into the room.

He told them to throw down their weapons, which they did. When they were fully disarmed, he drew nearer and shone his torch in their faces. Both had short haircuts and were clean shaven.

'What's down there?' He gestured toward the floor from where they had emerged.

There was a pause. 'It's an underground complex,' the blond one said at length.

'A citadel?'

'Yes, that's right, a citadel.'

Alex nodded slowly, surprised at their cowed looks. He would have expected more spirit from the military. It seemed that just the appearance of Elaine and him had taken the fight out of them. 'Who are you?' he asked.

The dark-haired man tried to shrug the question off. 'We're the same as you.'

'You are obviously not the same as us,' Alex responded sarcastically. 'You are both dressed in military uniforms and you're very well fed. We witnessed your little party this afternoon.'

'We weren't involved in that,' the other quickly replied. 'We're just soldiers going out on guard duty.'

'But whose soldiers are you? Who commands you?'

'Are you members of the HUD?' Elaine broke in, walking up beside Alex. 'That stands for 'Home Underground Defence',' she added, seeing their obvious confusion.

They shook their heads.

'Don't move!' a voice, shouted from the windows directly behind them.

They turned to see two rifles pointing at them.

The dark-haired soldier retrieved his rifle and handed the other to his companion, then gave a low whistle. 'Phew! Are we glad to see you two. You took your time.'

'Dirty mutants!' sneered the other, quickly recovering his nerve in the face of two more reinforcements. 'Not saying a great deal now, are you?' He poked Alex in the ribs with his own revolver. 'You really don't know what's down there, do you?' he went on, pointing towards the floor. 'Well, soon all your questions will be answered.'

210

They held a brief discussion amongst themselves, then made Alex and Elaine empty their pockets and searched their pack. After a short discussion, the two soldiers Alex had surprised took their leave, and one of the other soldiers pulled out a remote-control device and pushed a button. At once, two floor panels began to grind apart.

'Where are you taking us?' Elaine asked.

'You'll see,' the man replied coldly.

Alex and Elaine were led down a concrete staircase, then along a lighted tunnel in which a faint rumbling could be heard. Their eyes widened, as with a tremendous noise and a sudden gust of wind, a tube train drew up beside them when they reached a platform. The air compressed doors hissed open as hundreds of people from the sixteenth sector caught the tube to the central shopping complex some four kilometres away, under the small village of Box.

The soldier grinned as he saw Alex's incredulous expression. 'Everything here is linked by train,' he said mildly. 'It's like the London underground before the war, except the city is underground as well.'

But the train was not for them. At the end of the platform, the soldier pushed a button to summon a lift. The doors slid back and they were pushed in. They descended nine floors in a matter of seconds, emerging into a chilly environment of shiny corridors. The two soldiers kept back beyond arms' length, perhaps, Alex thought, to prevent being surprised, but perhaps simply to avoid contact with the 'dirty mutants', as they persisted in calling them. Certainly, with their creaking, mirror like boots, their bright brass buckles and clean-cut looks, they looked a world apart from Alex and Elaine. Even the tone of their voices conveyed a sense of unabashed superiority.

At length, they came to a halt outside a large, iron-ribbed door, bearing the inscription 'Security Section 16G'. The leading soldier identified himself by means of an intercom and a lock snapped open. Alex and Elaine were gestured into a stark, cream coloured office.

211

'Major Collins, Sir.' The soldier saluted a thin, grey haired man sitting at a desk. 'We caught these mutants holding two of our men at gunpoint at the entrance to quadrant sixteen.'

The Major examined the two prisoners without much interest. 'And why have you brought them here?'

'Standing orders, Sir. Any mutants found within a kilometre radius of any main entrance are to be interrogated.'

The Major's gaze returned to Alex and Elaine. His eyes were deep-set and cold. 'Why were you holding my men at gunpoint?'

'We were trying to find out what was down here,' Alex replied.

'You don't know what's down here?'

Alex shrugged. 'Should I?'

'From what we overheard,' the soldier interrupted, 'he hadn't a clue we even existed.'

The Major nodded. 'Where are you from?' he asked abruptly.

'Oh, around here,' Alex replied, making a vague gesture.

The man smiled thinly. 'That's not possible. You see, the few mutants that still remain in this area wouldn't dare come within ten kilometres of here. They know we exist and they have better sense than to try and bail any of us up at gunpoint.'

'And who is 'us'?' Alex asked.

This question was ignored. The Major turned his attention to Elaine. 'And where do you come from?'

'North of here,' she replied.

'How far north?'

'Ten kilometres,' Alex cut in.

The man looked back at Alex briefly. 'Don't cling to a statement we've already established can't be true.'

'We come from Wales?' said Elaine.

'Wales?' An eyebrow went up at that. 'What part of Wales?'

212

'The south.'

He frowned and tapped on the desk. 'Soldier, have you checked through their belongings?'

'Yes, Sir.'

'What did you find?'

'Ammunition, food, clothing.' The soldier paused. 'And a map, Sir.'

'Map? Anything written on it?'

'I didn't check Sir.'

The Major spread the map on the desk and studied it for a few seconds, then let out a short grunt of satisfaction. 'You've stumbled over a couple of prize fish here, soldier!' he smiled. 'All right, take them to the detention room and lock them in. I'll be along in a few minutes.'

They were led through the office into a narrow corridor flanked by numbered steel doors. As they reached door eleven, the soldiers stopped, drew back the bolt and pushed Alex and Elaine inside.

It was a large, bare chamber, the only furniture being a small, metal legged desk cluttered with papers in the centre of the room, with three wooden chairs clustered untidily around it. Directly above the desk, a fluorescent globe hung from an uneven sandstone roof. The walls were a shiny white.

'He knows about the mine, doesn't he?' Elaine asked.

Alex nodded. 'Don't you remember? I circled it when I was showing you where I came from.'

She sighed, then walked over and sat on the desk. 'But who are they? And why do they call us mutants? What does that word mean, mutants?'

Alex tried to smile back reassuringly, but only managed a grimace. The implication of any survivor calling another survivor a mutant was that the name caller had been living below ground at the time of the holocaust. This whole complex must have predated the holocaust, probably by years. These healthy, effortlessly superior people, incredible as it might seem, had perhaps never been exposed to radiation, perhaps had not even heard the bombs falling. They had lived underground while the surface was incinerated.

The door clicked open and Major Collins came in carrying Alex's backpack, followed by a thick set man, with brawny arms and a bulldog face.

'Corporal Rowell, one of our most experienced interrogators,' the Major said casually.

The corporal closed the door and took up position close to it, standing with legs slightly apart and his arms clasped behind his back, waiting to be called upon.

Major Collins crossed over to the desk and pulled out a pen and pad from one of the drawers. 'It was extraordinary luck you appearing on our doorstep, so to speak,' he said in quite an amiable voice. 'We've known of the existence of your colony for nearly two years now, however until now we have lacked any information about you.'

'Why are you so interested in us?' Elaine asked.

'Purely academic,' the Major smiled. 'We're naturally concerned with anything that's happening on the surface. How the survivors are coping, the difficulties they face…that sort of thing.' He straightened the paper and wrote rapidly across the top.

'We still don't know who you are?' Alex said forcibly.

'Yes, yes,' the Major nodded, 'I imagine this whole thing has come as a rather nasty shock. It's not every day you find an underground city, especially after spending three years believing you were the only large-sized colony left in Britain.' He clasped his hands together and leaned forward, confidently. 'Well, as you must have gathered, even from your brief time here, our city is very large and technically advanced. Such an achievement you would expect to take years of planning and building. In fact, it took fifteen years to construct from its inception. It was designed as the last refuge for the government, a place of safety where our leaders could withdraw to wait out a nuclear holocaust. It was built as a precaution in the nineteen-eighties.'

214

'Rather an excessive precaution.'

The Major shrugged. 'Obviously, these things don't come cheap.'

'So, you are what is left of the government?' Alex asked.

'Exactly. This city is the kernel, if you will, the embodiment of our civilisation. And now that the radiation has dropped to acceptable levels, we have decided to re-populate the surface. This is why we seek information on colonies such as yours, so as to be able to render assistance, and indeed to learn from you.'

Alex frowned. 'I'm not sure that I believe you,' he answered.

'Really,' the Major raised an eyebrow. 'Then what do you believe?'

'None of this makes any sense,' Alex admitted. 'But if you are the government, then you've already deserted the population once. I'm not giving you the chance to do any more harm.'

The Major sighed and leaned back in his chair. 'We had to abandon the population. They were out of control, overrunning ration stations, killing anyone who stood in their path. All our attempts to establish some sort of discipline were thrown out of gear by the survivors themselves.'

Alex shook his head. 'You were slaughtering anyone who opposed you. Your soldiers collected the healthiest people and put them into work camps where they laboured until they dropped or died of disease.'

'We were trying to rebuild the country.'

'You weren't doing anything of the sort. All you were interested in was keeping the food supplies from the survivors so you could hoard it all down here and let the 'mutants', as you call us, die in our millions on the surface.'

The Major's face hardened considerably at these words. 'Of course, you have every right to be upset. I couldn't begin to imagine what it must have been like. No food, contaminated water, snowstorms, hardly any difference between night and day.' He looked from Alex to Elaine sympathetically. 'In a way it's amazing anyone could have survived those conditions. That's why our soldiers have rather indelicately referred to you as 'mutants'. You represent something that is totally foreign to us. You have endured so much and you look so different it becomes difficult to…' He paused, searching for words.

'To think of us as human?' Alex broke in.

'I was going to say that it becomes difficult to relate to you,' the Major replied coldly.

'Difficult to relate,' Alex repeated. 'Yes, I would agree with that. I certainly found it difficult to relate to that feast we observed out there this afternoon.'

'Ahh,' the Major nodded. 'Now I see what the problem is. And you have a valid point, I admit. We do have an excess of food.'

'Then why didn't you give it to us?' Alex cried. 'The people on the surface have been starving for three years!'

There was a long pause as the Major seemed to brood over this question. Alex and Elaine waited patiently. At length he looked up. 'This is a tough one,' he said, 'but you have to try to imagine what effect an offer of food would have had on the survivors. At no point had we enough food to feed everyone. We would have been swamped with demands, overrun with people fighting, squabbling, killing. It would have been a repeat of the holocaust. Riots would have broken out; the city itself would have been attacked. We would have been forced to kill survivors in our own defence.'

'But if you had only shared some of your technology!' Elaine put in. 'Told us how to deal with the radiation! How we could solve our farming problems!'

The Major shrugged. 'One thing leads to another,' he said. 'And that's precisely what we're offering now.'

'But you wanted the dirty, contaminated rabble out of the way first, is that it?' Alex said. 'You let them die in their

216

millions, and then you emerge like some fairy godmother waving your wand to put it all right again?'

'You're talking about strategy here,' the Major replied in a weary tone, as if the conversation had exhausted his interest. 'The point is, we are willing to help you now. We have tremendous resources which we would gladly make available.'

Alex shook his head. 'I don't believe a word of it. If your motives were sincere, you'd have helped us long ago.'

'Don't try my patience,' the Major warned. 'Ingratitude is an evil under any circumstances.' He gestured for the corporal to move closer. 'I want a little information from you, and I am prepared to go to some pains to obtain it. Do I make myself clear?'

Alex didn't answer. The corporal stood at ease, staring at the wall impassively. Neither Alex nor Elaine doubted for a moment that he would carry out the Major's orders, whatever they might be.

The salutary effect of the corporal's presence seemed to please the Major. 'Well now,' he said more calmly, 'how many people are there in your colony?'

'Ten thousand,' Alex lied.

The Major heaved a sigh. 'Young man, you're being very foolish. We know there are at least twenty thousand, if not more.' He put down his pen and nodded. 'Corporal!'

The corporal moved forward slowly. Alex nervously backed away; his arms raised defensively. The corporal closed his fists. Then, in a sudden fury, he struck Alex first in the stomach and then in the face.

Elaine screamed and rushed at the corporal, only to be flung across the room, landing heavily on her back.

Alex straightened, gasping for breath. Another blow struck him in the midriff, winding him. He was aware of blood pouring from his nose and his cut mouth. His chest stung, he gasped and coughed, trying to support himself on his hands, waiting for the next sickening blow. Instead, he was grabbed by his clothes and dragged across and dumped on a chair.

'You see, it's useless to lie to me,' the Major said, examining a tiny spot of blood, which had appeared in front of him. 'We know certain facts about your colony already. There's no point in trying to deceive us. The truth is so much cleaner somehow, I always think.'

Alex turned his head and saw Elaine rise shakily to her feet. The corporal had resumed his place like a shadow, just behind.

'Now, let's try again. How many people in your colony?'

'Twenty thousand,' Alex groaned.

'And what type of military hardware have you got?'

'Not a great deal.'

'Not a great deal?' The Major tapped his pen on the desk. 'You'll have to be more specific than that. What type of military…'

'I don't know!' Alex pleaded. 'I'm not in charge of defence! I only work in…' Another blow sent him sprawling across the floor.

He rose slowly to his knees. His head was spinning and his right ear was numb from where the corporal had struck him.

'It's true!' Elaine shouted. 'He doesn't know. He works in the fields, the same as me. We found a report mentioning a village called Box and we thought there might be some food down here. That's why we came.'

'How did you get here?'

'We stole a Land Rover.'

There was a moment's silence as the Major considered Elaine's explanation. 'A large amount of ammunition, a couple of revolvers, packaged food, maps and a Land Rover. No, it won't do young lady. This trip was planned with the knowledge of your superiors. You'll have to do better than that.'

The corporal grabbed Alex by the collar and lifted him onto the chair. The Major's calm, faintly amused face appeared again.

'Each of us has his line of work, you know, and the corporal here is no exception. He's very very good at this,' the Major said dryly. 'He knows how to prolong pain, what the body can bear and what it cannot. Now, before he starts bending and breaking things, I want to give you another chance. I need your help, you see. I want as much detailed information as possible on the size of your forces, the amount of weaponry and ammunition you have, how well the colony is defended and so on. The precise location of those defences will also be very helpful.'

'Why? Why do you want such detailed information?' Alex asked, hoping to stall so that he could have time to think.

The Major flicked his eyes up at the corporal and a pair of muscular hands closed round Alex's throat. As the pressure increased, his face turned red and his nose erupted in a fresh stream of blood.

'Just answer my questions, young man,' the Major growled.

Alex tried in vain to loosen the hands around his throat, vaguely aware that Elaine was digging her fingernails into the corporal's face. The pressure eased for a second. Alex broke free and dived across the desk at the Major, his right fist smacking into the Major's face, knocking him onto the floor with Alex on top of him. Dizzy and gasping for breath, Alex fought to pull himself to his knees. He turned, only to find the shiny black barrel of a revolver hovering centimetres from his head. The Major's flushed and enraged face glared from behind it, a trickle of blood ebbing down his chin from a split lip.

'Get up!' he snarled. 'Get up before I kill you!'

Alex rose slowly to his feet. Major Collins rammed the revolver into his nose, making him wince in pain.

'Corporal, bring the girl here!' he yelled.

The Major's face was so close that Alex could feel his breath. 'That's the very last trick you'll ever play on me, mutant!' he growled.

Two figures edged into Alex's view. The corporal, dragging Elaine, forced her onto the chair Alex had been sitting in. His face had deep bloody scratch marks stretching diagonally from his right forehead to his left cheek. He pulled Elaine's head back as if to display what he had done to her in return. Alex drew a sharp breath when he saw her. The right side of her face was already black and swollen; the corporal must have struck her there repeatedly. Blood was still pouring freely from her nose and cut lips and her cheek had swollen till her eye was no larger than a slit.

The Major grinned when he saw the horrified look on Alex's face. 'No one does that to the corporal and gets away with it.' He jerked the gun further into Alex's nose. 'Now, corporal, I want you to continue working on the girl.'

The corporal started twisting Elaine's arm around her back. She began to cry out, a horrible, high pitched scream that only stopped long enough for her to fill her lungs again.

'Stop it!' Alex screamed. 'It's not necessary! I'll talk!'

The Major signalled to the corporal and the terrible screaming stopped.

'Now, I want some answers,' the Major said coldly.

'Just one lie, one mistake, one answer that doesn't tally with what we already know, and your girlfriend pays for it. Do you understand?'

Alex nodded obediently.

Over the next few minutes Alex spilled out everything he could remember about the mine's defences, armaments and military strength, only marginally understating the true figures - the fear of seeing Elaine torn apart foremost in his mind.

The Major sat at his desk, taking detailed notes. Indeed, he continued writing long after Alex had finished. When he finally looked up, his face had resumed that earlier mask of calm. He told Alex to sit down next to Elaine and began reading through his notes.

Elaine sobbed in Alex's arms like a child, her battered face turning more bulbous and deformed by the minute. The corporal stood by, at ease.

'Well,' said the Major, walking around to sit on the desk in front of Alex. 'All things considered, this has been a very successful session, although a bit more traumatic than I had anticipated.' He pulled out a handkerchief and dabbed at his chin.

Alex didn't take his eyes off him.

The Major seemed to take a sadistic delight in the hate in Alex's eyes. 'You asked before why we wanted information on your colony's defences,' he continued. 'If you haven't already guessed, we want to destroy you, as well as the Scottish colony and any other minor ones that may exist in Great Britain. No one is to be left. The cleaning will be thorough, the extermination complete. The land will be set free, ready for our people to stream forth upon it. All the disease and sickness left by the bomb will be wiped out when the last mutant dies.'

He stared triumphantly at Alex.

Elaine had stopped sobbing and was listening intently.

'You must be wondering who we are,' the Major went on in an almost jocular tone, as he savoured the moment to the full. 'I may have deceived you when I told you that we were the government. The government ceased to exist on the first day of the war when a ground burst detonated directly on top of the Whitehall complex. So much for central planning.' The Major paused, a faint smile lifting the corners of his mouth. 'We're the military, my dear young friends. You don't seem particularly surprised?' he added, when he saw no reaction from them.

Alex was not surprised at all. Only a totalitarian force like the military could attempt something this monstrous. 'Is the whole city full of troops?' he asked.

'We have an armed force of twenty-five thousand soldiers, and a civilian population of sixty thousand men, women and children.'

'And do they approve of the slaughter of all life on the surface?'

'They are prepared to be guided by wiser counsels than their own.'

'How diplomatic!' Alex spat. 'In other words, they either don't approve, or they don't know.'

'What an angry young man you are. Surely you must have learnt these are not times for qualms or moral judgements about right or wrong,' the Major replied.

'But why?' Elaine interrupted. 'I don't understand. Why do you have to wipe out all the survivors?'

The Major's face softened slightly. 'To turn the argument on its head, young lady, why not? Look at you both; skinny, diseased, your bones probably laden with radioactive strontium, and your tissues filled with radioactive caesium. Anyone who lived through the first year of the war must have accumulated lethal doses of these isotopes. I guarantee that not one survivor in the whole of Great Britain wouldn't have developed some radiation-related sickness within the next ten to twenty years. You're riddled with it. All that awaits you is a painful, lingering death.'

'After all that we have suffered,' Alex cried.

'Oh, don't get so self-righteous,' the Major scoffed. 'You're infinitely expendable.' He waved his revolver in a dismissive gesture. 'What can't be cured must be killed. You have no place in the world we are going to create.'

'We fought to survive in a world you have destroyed. You've no right to say that we have no place! YOU HAVE NO PLACE!' Alex was screaming now. He tried to rise from his seat, but the corporal slammed him back down. 'YOU CAUSED THE WAR!' he ranted. 'YOU SHOULD BE HELPING US, NOT TRYING TO DESTROY US!'

'Tut, tut, tut,' the Major shook his head. 'Losing your temper isn't going to get you anywhere. 'Actually,' he

222

grinned as though about to relay a particularly amusing story, 'to address your last comment. We did not cause the war. From what our intelligence can gather it was a computer malfunction. 'Yes,' he continued in a whimsical, faintly amused fashion. 'You see after the end of the cold war all those computer-based early warning systems in Europe were just left decaying. No money to maintain them you see. Well, it was inevitable really. One of the computers must have malfunctioned, someone panicked, maybe a computer accidentally sent off a few nuclear missiles. Who knows? The rest, as they say, is history. Once the first real nuclear missile was launched, the cascade affect must have been amazing. All the countries that had nuclear arsenals just started popping them off until the planet was thick with flying missiles and mushroom plumes'

Alex glared at him for some time before lowering his head. Somehow this revelation made the holocaust even more hideous. He shook his head. The whole human race annihilating itself accidentally.

When Alex spoke again his voice was subdued, but it had lost none of its underlying intensity. 'What will be so different about the world you will create?' he asked. 'You'll still have to face the same problems, and you'll have to adopt some of the same solutions if you want to survive.'

The Major shook his head. 'That's where you're wrong. There is a fundamental difference. You mutants are now at subsistence level, barely producing enough food to fill your own stomachs. You exist from day to day, totally dependent on the elements for survival. The few pieces of machinery you have salvaged will be of no more use when the parts wear out or the fuel dries up. And when the last survivors die from cancer, the land will be inherited by your noxious, ignorant children. Civilisation will be thrown back thousands of years. Man will have to begin again, think of that! Having to relive all his mistakes! Disease will be rampant, war, famine, fire, flood. Civilisation put back in the nursery and having to crawl and drag itself up to maturity.'

223

He paused, but as Alex said nothing, he resumed.

'We don't want to have to go through all that. Down here we have some of the best minds in Britain; doctors, surgeons, lawyers, administrators, scientists, have been down here for years. And knowledge is not only banked in the human brain, we have marvellous libraries and huge computer databases on virtually everything. We have been patient, and now we are ready to start afresh. There will be no more bombs in the new world, none of the vices that ruined the old; no social problems; every man will have his own piece of land and we'll create a golden age once again.'

Alex continued to glare at him but said nothing.

'You find my arguments unanswerable, don't you?' he went on with a smile. 'You're thinking how logical your eradication sounds. As indeed it is. In six weeks, our forces will surface and advance in all directions, wiping out all degenerate human life in their path. The operation will be completed within six months and sweetness and light shall reign.'

'Aren't you forgetting the rest of the world in your calculations?' Alex said. 'What happens when other nations start arriving here? When your crime is made known they will destroy you utterly.'

The Major shrugged. 'You obviously have no knowledge of the extent of the war. There are no countries left. It's no use you looking out there for your protection. We shall have a free hand, never fear. And if there should be other civilisations like us that have survived, I cannot imagine that they would condemn our actions.'

'What about the radiation in the cities?' Alex suddenly remembered. 'We've tested it and the levels are so high they're uninhabitable.'

'Oh, but we know all about that. We contaminated the cities ourselves by spraying them every six months with radioactive isotopes.'

'You?' Alex stared at him dumbly. 'You contaminated them? Why?'

224

'Because we didn't want any large colonies of survivors living in the cities. We don't want to have to level whole blocks or put industrial complexes to the torch to drive out the mutants. We prefer them out in the open where we can keep an eye on them.'

'But you're making your own cities uninhabitable?'

'No, we're not, the half-lives of the isotopes we use are very short. That's why we have to keep on spraying. By the time we want to inhabit these cities again the radiation will be minimal.'

'You bastard!' Elaine could bear no more of it. 'You want us herded into the country like cattle so that you can slaughter us.'

'These things just evolved like that, it wasn't planned exactly,' he said almost casually. 'The surface was supposed to be cleared of people well over a year ago, but we under-estimated the resourcefulness of the survivors. We thought that by initiating the typhus plague we'd have swept the place clean.'

'You did that?' Alex rose to his feet beside Elaine, causing the corporal to move a pace nearer.

Major Collins paused, watching their faces with obvious enjoyment.

'As I recall,' he continued, 'the land was almost overrun with rats at that time. We felt sure that if we contaminated some rats and released them in populated areas, they would spread the disease pretty well everywhere. But we underestimated the lengths to which the survivors would go to escape the rats, and the natural resistance of the population. Still, we did manage to wipe out many of you...'

His words were cut short by an ear-splitting scream from Elaine as she flung herself at the corporal. He knocked her away with one long powerful sweep of his arm, but the distraction was enough. The corporal's attention had faltered. Alex sprang past him at the Major, grabbing his gun hand and throwing him onto the floor. But the corporal was only moments behind. A split second before he arrived, Alex

225

jumped onto the desk and leapt high, smashing the fluorescent globe with his fist. At the same instant he took one last look around the room. Elaine was crumpled up in the corner where the corporal had thrown her. The Major was on his back on the floor and the corporal was lunging at his feet.

Alex landed back on the desk, springing away again as massive hands groped for him in the dark. He dropped lightly near the door, rolled over and avoided the desk as it was thrown after him across the room. The corporal's footsteps moved towards him, kicking and scraping the floor in a futile search for him.

'Corporal, have you found him?' The Major's voice allowed Alex to get a fix on him.

'No, he's moved. He must be over the other side of the room!' the corporal shouted.

The Major began shooting wildly into the dark. Alex crept up behind.

'Hey, what's going on in there?' came a faint voice from outside.

'Open the bloody…'

Alex pounced in the direction of the Major's voice and brought his left arm up under the Major's throat and gripped his revolver with his right hand.

'Corporal, he's here!' the Major croaked.

With a strength born out of desperation, Alex tightened his grip on the revolver and aimed it at the rapidly advancing footsteps.

Two shots rang out.

A short distance away the corporal gasped in pain as the bullets tore through his chest. He staggered for a second and then collapsed onto the floor.

Alex tightened his hold on the Major's throat, completely blocking his windpipe. The revolver clattered to the floor as the Major tried to loosen Alex's grip. The next moment the door suddenly burst open and the silhouette of the guard appeared in the gap. The revolver was close by but out of reach. Alex knew he only had seconds. Flinging the

Major away, he scrambled across the floor, grabbed the revolver and pointed it at the guard who had now shouldered his arms. Two shots sent him sprawling backward into the corridor.

When he turned back, the Major had nearly reached Elaine. Alex shot him in the side as Elaine attacked him from the front. The Major dropped forward, gasping. Alex grabbed him by the collar and dragged him toward the light from the door.

'Pull that guard out of the corridor and keep watch,' he hissed at Elaine.

He pushed his face next to the Major's and rammed the revolver up his nose. The entire colour had fled from the sadist's face.

'Now,' Alex snarled, 'I want you to tell me exactly what the strength of your military forces are, and don't leave out any details.'

CHAPTER 12

A bullet through the head ended the Major's ignominious career. Seconds later, Alex and Elaine burst out of room eleven, and were running down the corridor. Alex had the Major's revolver and ammunition belt strapped around his waist, and his note pad, papers and maps stuffed in his backpack. Elaine had the guard's automatic rifle and a pocket full of ammunition. At each corner, they halted and went on cautiously, but they didn't come across any military until they reached the front office. Alex waved several startled staff into a room and locked them in with their own keys. A man and a woman were taken as hostages.

Alex ordered the woman to run in front and the man behind to act as body shields. After a few minutes, they had reached the lift. Alex's ribs ached from the beating he had received, and his nose throbbed painfully, but he still felt strong and alert. Elaine, however, was near the end of her strength. She ran the last fifty metres at a stagger and then immediately collapsed against the wall, next to the lift.

The lift arrived and Alex bundled the hostages in, then helped Elaine. Once in the lift, he examined her more closely. Blood was still pouring from her shattered mouth and her eye was now almost completely closed. Tearing off part of his shirt he tried to wipe her face. The hostages, clear white skinned and flabby-cheeked, looked on in horror from the corner of the lift where they huddled together.

Alex only felt contempt for them and a deepening resolve not to let such people wipe the survivors from the face of the land.

'We don't have those remotes they used to activate the trapdoor.' Elaine's voice was distorted as she tried to speak through the pool of blood that was gathering in her mouth.

Alex stared at her for a moment then turned to the hostages. 'Is there any other way to open the trapdoor?' he asked harshly.

'No, you need the remotes,' the woman replied, shrinking back.

"Shit...where does the train go?' he demanded.

'Either to the suburbs or the city centre. There's one every fifteen minutes,' the man explained obediently.

Alex ordered the man to press the button for the level the train line was on. When the lift doors opened, he pushed them out. The platform was empty, although he knew it wouldn't be long before it was swarming with patrols. Removing his belt, he wedged it in the doors, jamming the lift. The platform had two train tracks, one either side. At the centre of the platform was a large digital clock which read 20.06. Directly beneath it, an illuminated sign showed how the train route linked the twenty-three residential sectors of the city. The exit to the right was for the train travelling to the central business area and it was from there that the growing roar was coming. Alex directed the hostages toward the train. A large crowd was already gathered, waiting for the train to stop and the air pressure doors to hiss open. No one noticed the strange appearance of Alex and Elaine in the crush to get a seat. The hostages, however, used the opportunity to lose themselves in the crowd. The doors had closed and the train was already moving forward when Alex realised that neither of the hostages were aboard.

Elaine clung to him, burying her head in his chest. For the first time since their escape Alex had a moment to take stock. The hostages even now could be warning the authorities, and soon the train would be pinpointed and stopped. They had to exit quickly and disappear into one of the sectors.

The people in the carriage were beginning to wake up to the presence of strangers in their midst. As each in turn noticed them, or was alerted, conversation died. Alex became aware of their many startled, gaping faces. People like this would have been two a penny on any train or bus before the war; now he found their smooth faces and neat clothes almost as repulsive as they must have found him. Most were casually dressed, some had suits and others wore the same hooded tracksuits he had seen on the surface. Even the children, chubby and unblemished, stared open-mouthed as they clung close to their parents. Nothing much was said, and nobody seemed to know quite what to do.

Alex felt a fresh trickle of blood seep down from his nose and he cuffed it away with his sleeve. The sudden movement riveted all eyes on him. Then the train slowed bringing them to a station, and several people near the door shuffled out quickly. The incoming passengers turned around to look at Alex and Elaine in astonishment.

The train lurched forward again.

'ATTENTION, PLEASE, THIS IS AN OFFICIAL ANNOUNCEMENT,' the speaker system on the train blurted. 'TWO MUTANTS HAVE ESCAPED FROM THE SECURITY SECTION. THEY ARE ARMED AND VERY DANGEROUS. DO NOT, I REPEAT, DO NOT APPROACH, BUT REPORT ANY SIGHTINGS IMMEDIATELY TO THE NEAREST MILITARY POST.'

The atmosphere in the carriage became electric. Some people screamed, while others started a mad push to distance themselves from the pair. Several of the men stood up and began moving menacingly forward. Alex instantly drew his revolver and stopped the advance.

'Now listen, all of you!' he yelled. *'We won't harm you if you don't cause any trouble!'* His voice came across as a raucous, half hysterical scream that pierced every corner of the carriage.

Elaine unslung her rifle and levelled it in one quick movement. The sudden exposure of her battered face sent a wave of gasps around the carriage.

Alex ordered two of the passengers who were wearing loose fitting hooded pullovers to strip, and, as the train pulled into another station he and Elaine clambered into the clothes and pulled the hoods over their heads.

While they waited for the doors to open, Alex took one last look around the carriage. No one had moved a muscle since they had seen Elaine. The same horrified but vaguely fascinated expression was on all their faces at this revelation of a world beyond their own. The doors opened and Alex and Elaine pushed out through a surge of impatient people. Moments later the station was emptied, and the train sped on its way.

They began walking quickly through the corridors of the fourteenth sector, soon becoming lost in a maze of glossy tiled tunnels. After a few minutes, they reached quieter corridors with brick walls and coarse grey carpets. The walls were punctuated at regular intervals with wooden doors, inscribed with family names. Elaine was starting to flag again. Alex put his arm around her and propped her up, examining her face hurriedly. She was coughing up so much blood that he couldn't tell whether it was coming from her lungs or her mouth. Gently he eased her arms away from her chest and unbuttoned her shirt. Her ribs were badly bruised; that could explain why her breathing was so shallow.

The plate on the nearest door read 'Dr F. Harris'. He knocked hard and impatiently, but there was no answer. Hurrying to the next, he tried again, without result. But the third door, labelled 'Dr M. Crean', suddenly opened at his knock and a tall, dark haired woman came forward inquiringly. She stopped short when she saw Alex, first astonished, then shocked, then horrified by this apparition. She tried to retreat, but Alex jammed his foot in the door and quickly dragged Elaine inside.

He laid her on a large sofa, near at hand, ignoring the woman who had rushed to scoop up a little girl, about three or four years old, sitting at the kitchen table. Mother and daughter backed away as Alex looked up.

'Are you alone?'

She nodded, looking very frightened.

'My friend here is badly hurt. Do you know first aid?'

Elaine had rolled over on her side and was choking and spitting out more blood.

'Please!' he appealed to the woman, who still hung back. 'She could be bleeding internally.'

The woman put the child down and came over. Alex knelt down beside Elaine and examined her.

'There doesn't seem to be anything broken,' the woman said after a quick inspection. 'The blood she is coughing up has probably run down from her mouth.'

'Are you sure?'

The woman looked up. 'I'm not a doctor, but I've done nursing,' she said, 'and I don't think there's anything worse than severe bruising.'

'If you're not a doctor, then who is Dr Crean?'

'My husband. He has a PhD in Biochemistry.'

'And where is he?'

'Still at work.'

The clock at the train station had shown 20.06, Alex recalled. 'He's a bit late, isn't he?'

She shook her head firmly. 'He works late most nights. He'll be home around nine o'clock.'

Now that they were talking, the woman seemed to have lost her immediate fear of him, although much unease still remained. But he detected no trace of disgust and contempt, which had been so prevalent among the guards.

'The military will probably be searching this area very shortly. Do you have a place we can hide?'

She stared at him for a moment, evidently not expecting this. 'Yes,' she said at length, seeming as though she had come to a decision. 'There's a ventilation shaft in the hallway that leads to part of the old tunnel system. If you took that grid off, you might be able to squeeze through. I'll show you.'

She led the way into a corridor at the back of her flat. A large fly wire grid, blasting out warm air, covered part of the ceiling. The woman found a stool and a screwdriver and Alex quickly unscrewed the grid.

'It leads to a large shaft,' the woman explained. 'There are manholes along the shaft which open out into the tunnels.'

'And where do the tunnels lead to?'

She shrugged. 'Everywhere. The whole region is honey-combed with them. The guards would never find you once you reached the tunnels.'

He looked down at her anxious face and knew she hoped that they would reach the tunnels and keep on going. He couldn't blame her. Then she would be able to tell the soldiers where they had gone with a clear conscience without further danger to her family or herself. But Elaine was in no condition to run anywhere. She needed food and rest.

There was only one way to ensure that the woman wouldn't inform on them. Alex jumped off the stool and crossed to the living room where he had left Elaine. She was sitting up, the girl watching her wide eyed at a distance. Without warning, he strode over to the child and grabbed her arm. The woman gave a scream and rushed forward, but he drew his revolver and barred the way. 'You're coming into the ventilation shaft with us,' he said flatly.

The woman suddenly lost all control, wailing, imploring, beseeching; it wrung Alex's heart. Seeing her mother in such distress the girl also began to cry. Alex assured the woman that they would not be hurt. However, it was Elaine who finally managed to calm her down reasoning with her that they couldn't risk being betrayed. It wasn't until the woman's husband arrived home a few minutes later that the situation was finally resolved. Alex explained the situation and the husband agreed to answer the door while they hid in the vent.

It wasn't long afterwards that the security guards burst in. Alex heard the man denying seeing or hearing anything strange as the rooms were hurriedly searched.

When the security guards had left and all was quiet again, the husband unscrewed the grid and they slid out.

He was a small, balding man, with blunt, ruddy features and a curiously pointed nose. His eyes widened when he saw the condition that Alex and Elaine were in. Alex drew his revolver and handed it to Elaine, then lifted the daughter down. She ran to her father, who swept her up protectively and hugged her to his chest.

'Did security do that to you?' the husband asked.

'Yes,' Alex said coldly. 'Routine procedure, I understand. All mutants receive a good, thorough interrogation.'

The bitterness in his voice drew the couple closer together.

'Now look here,' said the man in a trembling voice. 'Don't think we have anything to do with the military.'

'We,' snorted Alex. 'Who's we?'

'The scientists. This whole sector houses the scientific community of the city. We are a completely independent entity and have no say over the military's policies or actions.'

'And I suppose you'll tell me that they have no control over you?' Alex asked sarcastically.

The man ran his fingers through his thinning hair. 'No, not exactly. What I mean is that they run the city and leave us to our own research without any interference.'

'So, you have no idea what the plans of the military are?'

He shook his head.

Alex glanced at Elaine.

'I'm not lying,' he continued. 'They administer the city and also act as security police. I'm sorry they've been so rough with you.'

'Who directs your research projects?' Alex asked.

'All the work we are currently engaged upon was already well under way before the war.'

'Here?' Alex stabbed his finger towards the floor. 'You worked down here before the war?'

'The research was with secret government funded projects on the surface,' he said defensively. 'We were invited down here before the holocaust.'

'And you have no inkling of what happened on the surface once the bombs started falling?'

'We were told that it was total devastation, a nuclear wasteland,' the woman interrupted. 'The radiation was so bad that no significant numbers of survivors were left after a few months.'

'And you swallowed that without question?'

'A sector of the city caved in and over five thousand people were killed. We had no reason to doubt them.'

Alex could see they were telling the truth as they saw it, but the thought of their living at ease in their plush flats, while the world died overhead grated badly.

'Don't you care what has happened to the rest of humanity?' he asked bitterly. 'What about all your relatives and friends who were not fortunate enough to be picked for this underground city? Has it never occurred to you to go up on the surface and look for yourselves? You've been three years down here, staying put because the military says so. Not very scientific, is it?'

The couple looked perplexed at Alex's harsh words. 'The authorities have always told us that the few survivors that remained had reverted to total savagery. They said they were diseased and too badly contaminated for medical help,' the husband said.

'Do we look like we're too badly contaminated for medical help?' Alex asked scathingly. 'Are we your idea of savages? You just don't care, do you?' he replied angrily, taking a step forward. He could see they were frightened but was too worked up to care. 'You've no idea what it was like to survive the holocaust. To watch tens of thousands of people die...'

'Stop it, Alex!' Elaine cried from behind him, labouring to form the words between her puffed lips. 'You're no better than they are if you take your anger out on them.'

He turned round sharply.

'Don't you see?' she continued. 'They're just pawns in a game, the same as us. They're just as much victims as we are.'

'Oh yes,' Alex went on wildly. 'It's very convenient, isn't it, to live in comfort and let the lies of the military lap over you? The meek shall inherit the earth, they say. By God, it makes me sick. And don't try to tell me you were forced into submission,' he continued, turning back sharply to the couple. 'We've seen your little party on the surface. For all we know you could even have dreamed up the slaughter of all the remaining survivors yourselves.'

He began advancing again; the two fell back, almost tripping over the furniture in their haste.

'Stop it!' Elaine cried. *'Can't you see that they don't even know what you are talking about anymore!'*

That hoarse plea came from the heart and stopped Alex in his tracks.

'You're behaving exactly how the military has told them you would behave,' she went on thickly, seeing she had gained his attention. 'What do you want to do here, kill innocent people like a wild animal? They aren't your enemies. Their only crime was to obey an authority they had no good reason to doubt.'

Alex closed his eyes and drew a deep breath. He knew Elaine was right. The daughter had started to cry. The father was bouncing her in his arms, shielding his wife from a possible onslaught. They clung together, supporting and comforting each other, suddenly he saw they were just frightened and confused people. He sighed and nodded agreement.

236

He saw the renewed hope and relief come flooding back into their eyes.

'What are your names?' he asked in a more subdued tone.

'I'm Martin Crean,' the man replied. 'And this is my wife Debbie and my daughter Louise.'

A groan from behind turned Alex's head. The crisis seemed to have exhausted the last of Elaine's strength. She tottered and only by moving fast was he able to catch her as she collapsed in his arms. Everybody helped to carry her to a bedroom and lay her down. Bandages and ointments were brought to dress her wounds.

Later, as she lay sleeping, Alex sat with the couple and told them about himself, and what had brought them to Box. He spared them the details of their treatment at the hands of the military, but he dwelt on the plans for the future that Major Collins had revealed at their interrogation. The Creans seemed genuinely shocked by it all and repeated that the scientists had never been privy to any of this scheming.

'Scientific parties did go up to the surface about a year back,' Martin said. 'They reported that the radiation levels were still extremely high, especially in the cities. They mentioned nothing about large numbers of survivors.'

'But some of the scientific community at least must be aware of what's going on,' Alex said. 'Those parties you mentioned probably engineered the typhus plague. Do you remember any of the names of the men involved?'

Martin left the room and came back with a thin, glossy covered magazine. 'This is the monthly edition of the 'Science Bulletin',' he said. 'It reports all the latest scientific discoveries and local news in the colony.'

On the cover was an aerial shot of London in ruins. The place where the Houses of Parliament had once stood was shown as a huge frozen lake, which must have measured half a kilometre across. All around the lake the surface was levelled except for the distant jagged outline of suburbs. It was head-lined: 'The Death of Great Britain'. A footnote at the bottom of the page read: 'Full details on page four'. Alex opened the magazine at the article. The pages were liberally splashed with more pictures of London and other major cities. Selective radiation counts, records of vegetation re-growth and animal life were given for eight other cities. There was no mention of survivors, only graphic details of the numbers of dead and speculation on the possible diseases which would have wiped out the remainder of the population. The whole tone of the article left the reader with the impression that nothing could have survived the holocaust and remained human.

Alex looked up frowning. 'And everybody believes this?'

'Yes,' Martin replied.

'Well, they have been misinformed. We have no intention of standing by and letting the military pursue their final solution.'

'What will you do?'

It was easier to put the question than to form an effective answer to it. 'I'll warn the communities,' Alex said vaguely.

'And what will they do?'

'I don't know,' he admitted, 'but together we should be able to work out some strategy to stop them.'

'Do you have any idea,' Martin went on, 'of the scale of the military arsenal in this city?'

Alex nodded grimly. The Major had spilled out the frightening details in the moments before he had shot him.

'You can't hope to win against such a force. Nevertheless,' Martin continued, 'we scientists are not without influence. I'm a member of a committee, which reviews the progress of all the research projects in the city. My fellow members hold powerful positions within the main frame of the government. I'm sure that if they were told of the attack they would take steps to stop it.'

Alex was caught flat footed by the offer. It was more than he could have dared hope for and, glancing at Martin's face, he could see he was being sincere. It was an open face, guileless, a little naive, like his own used to be. The face of one who, still in spite of everything, believed in heroic values. Or, to put it another way and less kindly, a dangerous innocent.

'You realise what the military will do to you if they catch you interfering with their plans, don't you? Elaine and I got away but if they caught you, they would tear you apart.'

Martin winced and glanced quickly across at his wife. 'I'm aware of the risk,' he said. 'But in spite of your poor opinion of me, I do care about what happens to the survivors. We can't just stand by and let this happen, no more than you can.'

Alex nodded. He was growing to like the good doctor and he was sure he could trust him. It was, in any case, no time for looking on the dark side. He walked over to his backpack and pulled out a wad of papers that he had taken from the Major's desk. 'You'll be interested in these. They confirm everything I've told you. I got them from Major Collin. There are personal communications between him and the Commander-in Chief, setting out the attack strategy; with detailed requirements of military vehicles, personnel and objectives…it's all there.'

'May I see?' Martin examined the papers carefully, turning over page after page. When he looked up again, his eyes were wide with excitement. 'This is dynamite,' he said. 'Will you allow me to take copies? The copier is just down the hall. Wait till I show these to the committee!'

'Sure, copy them if you like,' Alex said. 'But how can you be sure that the members of the committee aren't in league with the military?'

'I can't,' Martin admitted. 'I can only speak for them as colleagues, and to my mind, decent ones at that. I happen to know the scientists who were involved with that article, and none of them are on the committee.'

The next day Alex slept in, and when he awoke, at ten o'clock, he could not for a moment imagine where he was.

Then Debbie Crean came in bringing a hot drink and the news that the military had scaled down their search; no doubt they assumed that the two intruders had already got away. Martin had gone off to work and Elaine had had a peaceful night, although she was stiff and sore from the ill treatment she had received.

It was a touching moment for Alex when he realised how easily the Creans could have betrayed them while they slept. Fate had thrown them in with people who were not, like Major Collins, scalped of all human decency. It gave him hope, despite the ominous signs, that a genuinely free society could one day be built.

Martin came in later with news that he had managed to convene an emergency meeting of the science committee for nine o'clock the following morning. He had kept his reasons for making this unusual request deliberately vague, saying only that he had discovered something the military had done that would affect the whole city.

Alex was very pleased and suggested that to increase the impact, he and Elaine should be present at the meeting to be able to amplify and verify statements as required. Martin, to his surprise, absolutely condemned the idea.

'The evidence should speak for itself,' he said firmly. 'It would be better to say that you had escaped to the surface. Then, if anything goes wrong, at least they won't come looking for you. It will also allow me time to assess their reaction. If it's favourable, I can produce you later to back up my claims.'

This was the first clear evidence Alex had that Martin doubted the loyalties of some of the committee members, in which case his caution was fully justified.

Martin left for the meeting early the next morning, and in good spirits, promising to return as soon as he could to bring them the results. But when he did come back, it was with such a trailing step and sorrowful face that Alex knew at once the news was bad. He sat thoughtfully in a chair and for a moment, saying nothing. 'I'm convinced that most of them knew about the plans before I told them,' he finally lamented.

'What happened?' Alex asked.

'Oh, they were very clever. They pretended to be astonished, but it wasn't long before they were reasoning away everything I could put before them. It's a game we play in academic circles, only this time it was no game. They questioned my sanity, they threw in charges of forgery, they disputed the figures, hinted that it would be dangerous to upset the 'delicate balance of our relationship with the military, as they put it, by publishing such a vicious slander, and so on, and so on.' Martin shook his head wearily. 'In the end, all I could do was gather up my papers and come home.'

'I'm so sorry,' Alex sighed. 'How will this affect your position now?'

'Oh, I'm sure they will be engineering my removal from the committee as I speak. But that's not the point, and I'm not finished yet,' Martin said, pulling out his mobile phone. 'We've started something now that we couldn't possibly stop, even if we wanted to,' he continued. 'It was clear that I was treading on some pretty important toes in that meeting. The military will be hearing from them very soon. I've no doubt about that. The only way we can stop them now is if we can get your story in a newspaper. Get it out in the open where the authorities can't stop it.'

Martin found the number he wanted. 'I'm going to ask to see the editor of 'The Chronicle' this afternoon. It's the most popular civilian run newspaper in the city,' he explained. 'Until we can get this story onto the streets, none of us will be safe.'

He began talking into his phone, giving his name and speaking in a sharp, authoritative tone to a number of people.

'They'll see us at three this afternoon,' he said after the call. 'When this gets out the military will find that they don't have the final say on everything.'

Alex and Elaine nodded, however neither felt terribly convinced.

CHAPTER 13

It was obvious that the apartment was no longer a secure refuge for any of them. Mrs Crean and her daughter were therefore packed off at once to stay with friends in another sector, while Martin, Alex and Elaine collected their belongings and prepared to leave for the meeting. It was still some hours before the appointed time but mingling with the crowds seemed to them a less vulnerable option than hanging around the flat, waiting any moment for the doorbell to ring.

As they had time to kill, Martin, having conducted them to the central business area, suggested that he show them around. Since their battered faces would have immediately drawn attention, Elaine and Alex opted for the hooded garments they had taken from the train passengers a few days earlier.

The central business district was vast, a technical and engineering marvel which couldn't fail to impress. Above them, over one hundred metres high, the roof converged into a glistening dome. At its apex, an intense shaft of light from the surface diffused through a series of huge, transparent filters, bathing everything in a soft golden light. Directly beneath the dome was an expanse of greenery which Alex estimated could not have been less than half a kilometre across. Like another Garden of Eden, it was filled with every conceivable type of flora, from large oaks and beech trees, down to the smallest daisy and buttercup, a reserve or ark of natural life, which was both a solace to the spirit and the seedbed of a regenerated world. Eight floors of tiled walkways, tinted glass and colourful shop displays surrounded this garden. Balconies protruded from these tiled walkways filled with tables and chairs, where people sat sipping drinks and eating meals. The murmur of their voices on so many levels reminded Alex of a vast indoor shopping in pre-holocaust times.

Like children let loose in paradise, Alex and Elaine dived into the wonderful world wandering amongst the huge variety of trees and shrubs, sniffing the sweet scent of the flowers that had long since vanished from the face of the land, and feeling the texture of healthy trees again. Finally, when they had trodden every pathway they could find, Martin led them to one of the balcony cafes several floors above. There they sat and sipped coffee and ate cakes.

Martin was delighted with Alex and Elaine's reaction. Their excitement had lifted his mood and he began to talk more freely about the city. He spoke of its vast scientific laboratories, its advanced horticultural gardens where hydroponic techniques were used to produce a rich diversity of fruits and vegetables capable of tolerance to high radiation levels. And all the time, scientists were improving crop yields with genetically engineered hybrid plants. Advanced gene splitting techniques based on CRISPR technology had already produced leaner cows, with more meat per kilo. They were even well advanced in producing synthetic meat which looked and tasted like the real thing and could be manufactured from amino acid mixtures. Trout and salmon had been bred to the size of small sharks; sheep had coats which grew continuously so their wool could be sheared three or four times a year. The list was so long and impressive that Alex could not keep track of it all. For the first time he understood something of the deep pride these people took in their city. He even began to share it. In such a place it would be easy to forget the flickering dismal light of the outside world.

The head office of the newspaper was on the sixth floor of the complex. Martin guided them into a small, tastefully decorated office with oak panelled walls and a thick piled carpet. A woman sat typing in front of a large computer screen, occasionally stopping every now and then to put her finger on a page of hand-written text. She smiled briefly when she noticed them. 'Oh, I'm sorry. It's always murder trying to type other people's handwriting.' She resembled a porcelain doll, not that she looked particularly fragile, or beautiful. But her lavish use of makeup made her appear so. Every feature was emphasised, the thick glossy lips, cheeks heightened by a dab of rouge, large innocent eyes with immaculate eye shadow. Alex couldn't help staring.

'Can I help you?' she asked.

'We have an appointment with the editor,' Martin replied.

'May I have your name?'

'Dr Crean.'

She wriggled out of her chair. 'I'll see if Mr. Casey is free.' In a few moments, she returned. 'This way please.'

They followed her past several large, noisy offices until she stopped at a door marked 'Chief Editor'.

She knocked and put her head around the door. 'They're here, Mr. Casey.'

They were ushered into another, much larger office. A man with greying temples and thinning hair was leaning over a desk at the far end, studying what looked to be the layout of a newspaper. He came forward.

'Good afternoon,' he said. With a gesture, he included a small, middle aged woman sitting at the desk. 'This is Denise Boswell, my assistant editor, and I'm William Casey.'

He stepped forward and shook Martin's hand. Martin then introduced Alex and Elaine. Both were wearing the tracksuits they had taken from the people on the train. Elaine had kept on her hood as they entered the office, so when he looked closely at her, he got rather a shock.

'We're what your military would term 'mutants',' Alex said bluntly, watching his reaction. 'They did that to Elaine when they questioned us.'

The editor gave him a startled look, as if unsure whether to listen any further or to yell for help. 'Are you the two that escaped?' he asked.

244

Alex nodded.

'We have a story that we want you to print,' Martin said. 'It concerns military plans to wipe out tens of thousands of survivors on the surface.'

'But there's nobody left on the surface.'

Alex smiled. 'There are over sixty thousand people in two large, well established communities, with many more in smaller ones.'

The editor frowned and turned to his assistant as if for her support, but she just shrugged.

'Do you have proof of what you say?' he asked at length.

Martin held up his briefcase. 'Proof of the military's plans to clear the surface of mutants in official documents, specific down to the smallest details.'

He drew out the papers and handed them a copy each. While they read, Alex went on to describe the condition of the communities, how Elaine and he had been interrogated in security section 16G and what the Major had told them. It was plain from their faces that he was laying before them facts and circumstances of which they had no conception.

Martin took over next, to unfold what had happened at the Science Committee meeting, their apathy, and why it was so urgent that this whole matter be brought to the public's attention. It was gratifying to him to find in the editor, and his assistant, a much more attentive and responsive audience.

'Well, that's quite a frightening scenario all in all,' the editor concluded, after looking through several pages of notes he had taken during the course of the questioning. 'The authorities certainly seem to be up to something.'

'I think that's an understatement,' Martin said sternly, 'considering what we have told you, it's quite clear they don't deserve our trust. Not only are they cold bloodedly planning this massacre, they have also been lying to us all this time.'

'Yes, yes, I appreciate that,' the editor said quickly. 'But what I mean is this is going to be no ordinary story. Your story has massive consequences and I hardly need to add that they will include the future of this newspaper, if we get it wrong.' He shuffled some of the documents again and then cleared his throat. 'The key issue, really,' he went on after a moment, fixing his eyes firmly on Alex, 'is how many survivors still remain. These documents are not specific on numbers. The military will simply argue that the numbers are all exaggerated and this attack is merely a mopping up operation to remove dangerous mobs.'

'But look at the amount of weaponry and the numbers of troops involved,' Alex pointed out. 'And why, if it's little more than a policing exercise, should they plan to devote six months to the sweep? You can't tell me that's just to dispose of a few ragged bands of survivors.'

The editor nodded. 'Yes, that's a good point. We can definitely build on that. But to revert to what I said earlier when I mentioned the closing down of this newspaper. If these people really are as ruthless as you say, they're not going to be satisfied with that. All our lives could well be in danger.'

'So, you aren't going to publish this?' Alex asked.

'I didn't say that,' the editor replied firmly. 'I think it would be criminal not to publish, but we must face the consequences squarely. After all, the people of this city owe their lives to the military for inviting them down here in the first place. There may be strains in the military civilian relationship, but there's also a substantial sense of loyalty.'

'You think the people won't believe it?'

'I think there's a strong possibility that we could be accused of grotesque exaggeration. If there's even a hint of that, we'll be laughed out of court. The whole thing will likely blow up in our faces.'

'Then we'll have to present the evidence in such a way that the public are compelled to see the gravity of the situation.' This was the assistant editor's first substantial contribution to the discussion. 'If we are going to expose the military, we may as well clean the cupboard right out and use all the disappearances, falsified scientific reports and so forth to build up a concrete case against them.'

'Yes,' the editor looked thoughtful, 'what is the position of the scientific community?' he asked Martin. 'Where do they stand? And is it correct that certain of your colleagues are publishing statements at variance with the true substance of their work? These are very damaging rumours, if true.'

'Not in my department,' Martin said firmly, 'I'm glad to say. But yes, it is possible that work in certain fields has been pushed beyond what they are willing to admit to.'

'From what Alex has told us it's clear that the military engineered the typhus plague and were responsible for contaminating the cities after the holocaust,' the editor concluded. 'They couldn't have done either of these things without the help of scientists. So, some scientists at least are in league with the military.'

'If this is happening, wouldn't someone have said something. Complained to the authorities?' Alex asked.

'Some may have already done so.' The editor opened a filing cabinet behind the desk and pulled out a manila folder. 'This is a recent request from friends and relatives to publish a description of a missing scientist.' He pushed an A4 sheet of paper in front of them. 'The military, of course, washed their hands of any responsibility for his disappearance. They say he probably wandered off when he was on the surface and got killed by mutants, but it's more likely he found out something the military didn't want him to or objected too strongly to a particular line of research.'

He pulled out another folder. 'There are three years of disappearances catalogued here, over one hundred missing persons.' He slapped the folder on the desk. 'To date, five have turned out to be murders, the rest remain unsolved.'

'Your achievement,' Miss Boswell said, turning to Alex and Elaine, 'is to have provided us, at last, with the hard evidence we need to present a strong case against the military. They must be stopped, and by devoting the whole paper to them, we might even stir up public opinion and begin the process of bringing them back within the law. I can't see why this could not be done.'

Alex looked at their determined faces and knew that the publication was now unstoppable. But in his excitement, he did not lose sight of the time factor. 'Don't forget, the military's plan is to be activated in a little over a month,' he reminded them.

'Things move fast when there's enough public pressure,' Miss Boswell told him confidently. 'If we can really make it buzz, we might be able to stop them inside a week. I propose that we print our allegations in the day after tomorrow's issue. That gives us one clear day to collect the evidence and present our arguments as clearly and convincingly as possible.'

With the agreement of everyone present, the setting up of the special edition began at once. Tables were cleared, the various documents were spread out, food and drink were brought in to sustain them in their labours. The editor and Miss Boswell undertook to do all the writing themselves, as even their key reporters were not to be trusted with so delicate an assignment. No detail was to be left out, and the perspective was widened to include a critique of the military from the first days of the holocaust. The brutality of the work camps was vividly described, and the unimaginable horrors of the engineered plagues. The same thread was tightly woven into each article: the calculated murder of the survivors by whatever means possible. All disappearances in the city since the holocaust were re-examined in the light of the new theory, and in most cases there were links or reasons, especially dissident activity, to suggest that the military may have been involved. Lastly the fragile trust between the scientists and the general population was shattered by allegations levelled at the scientific community as a whole. How the atrocities committed on the surface must have been supported by elements of the scientific community.

As a final support to all these claims, the documents that Alex had recovered were published, along with Major Collin's own notes of his interrogation.

Late the next day Alex, Elaine and Martin, having spent the night on makeshift beds of cushions in the office, held a final conference and the editor read them his concluding paragraph. In this he called for immediate demonstrations, stop work meetings and a general boycott of all food and materials produced by the civilian population until the military came up with adequate explanations for their activities. He explained that as the paper hit the streets, he and Miss Boswell would be ringing all the people who held positions of influence in the civilian government to demand that something be done immediately about the situation.

When Elaine enquired what Alex and she should do, he became very serious.

'I want you both to stay in hiding,' he said. 'Only if events begin to move our way, as I trust they will, are you to emerge.'

When they questioned him further he said that the response of the military was likely to be severe. Everything would depend on how the public would react. He then went on to outline several possible routes of escape if things didn't work out. He also gave them maps of the city, showing the military's storage facilities, their fuel dumps, armaments stores; in fact, everything which an aggressor, contemplating an attack on the city, could possibly need. There was no doubt in Alex's mind as to why he had given them this information. As far as the editor was concerned, the publishing of these articles was an act of war. If they failed below ground, it was up to Alex to continue the fight from the surface.

When the final editing was finished, they were all invited to the editor's office to review the articles. They were excellent. The first issues would be out in a matter of hours. The editor opened a bottle of French wine and they toasted the success of their efforts, all feeling like saboteurs about to embark on a dangerous mission. Alex put his arms around Elaine and they laughed and joked. Even the grim-faced Miss Boswell seemed to relax slightly.

But just before three in the morning a young man with a white and very worried face rushed into the office. He whispered something to the editor and immediately the mood changed. Mr. Casey stood up unsteadily. Alex hurried over.

'I don't know how, but the military have found out about our plans,' he said urgently. They could be here at any minute. You must go now.'

'What about you?' Alex asked, suddenly feeling ill.

'I shall make those phone calls at once and send out the articles.'

Alex was struck by the bravery of his words, but he could see how frightened he looked. 'Are you sure you won't come with us?'

Mr Casey shook his head firmly. 'Please go. You have little enough time as it is.'

Alex turned sharply to Martin, who also shook his head.

'I have to find my wife and daughter before the military does and you must get back to your community with this information as quickly as possible.'

Alex stared at him, lost for words. The swing from triumph to abject failure was too sudden for any of them to take in at once. 'I'm so sorry,' he said uselessly.

Martin shook away his words. 'Go before you lose your chance to escape.' Then abruptly, as though gripped by panic he could no longer control; he turned and ran from the office. Alex gathered the plans the editor had given him, gripped Elaine's arm and they fled after him.

As before, the quickest way out of the city was through the ventilation system. The main ventilation shaft terminated in a duct embedded in the pavement in a nearby walkway. Alex and Elaine unscrewed the grid and climbed in, drawing it back after them.

Once inside they had to contend with a steady blast of warm air. The duct ran under the pavement until it reached

250

the corner of the building, then climbed steeply and disappeared into the roof. Soon they became saturated with sweat as they slowly elbowed their way upward. Reaching the top, they began to cross the newspaper building. Down shafts opened up at close intervals to ventilate the various offices of 'The Chronicle' below. The escapers traversed this section with extreme care, as each shaft brought its own tale of screams, harsh orders and shouts as the raid beneath them got under way. At one vent the voice of the editor could be heard demanding an explanation for the invasion in ringing tones. They stopped to listen, their hearts gripped with fear and sadness for him. Tables and chairs were being overturned and glass was being smashed.

'You're too late!' they heard the editor say confidently.

'No, I don't think so,' retorted a calm, self-possessed voice. 'We've already cut all communications from your office. Nothing got out.'

There was a pause.

'I've been in touch with several people in the government and told them everything,' the editor said.

'They won't do anything,' the voice replied casually.

Again, there was a pause.

'You don't have that much power.' But this time, they noticed, the statement was more in the nature of a question.

'Anyone in the government with any influence answers directly to us,' the voice replied. 'I'm afraid you have made some serious miscalculations.'

'I don't believe you,' the editor replied.

'You must think we are very naïve, Mr. Casey. You made three phone calls in four minutes. The first was to Anthony Thorn, deputy leader of Food Resources; the second to Mark Langley, minister for Health and Safety; and the third to Brian Garrett, leader of the civilian government. We routinely monitor all your newspaper's calls. They would have been foolish indeed not to have reported your conversations to us.'

This time the silence stretched for several seconds. Then, very slowly, in almost a resigned voice, the editor asked, 'You're saying you control the whole civilian government?'

'Always have,' the other voice responded in a condescending tone. 'One city cannot have two masters. We built it and we control it, as always.'

'Then why?' the editor cried. 'Why the charade? Why not just order us to obey you, instead of this elaborate invention?'

'You can't master a wild beast by continually beating it over the head with a stick,' the voice continued. 'You will only ruin its character. It will brood over its ill-treatment and wait for its moment of revenge. A civilian population is like that. But if you pamper it, if you coat its chain with sugar and change its straw frequently, it will soon forget any other way of life. It will even lick poison from your hand.'

'But we rebelled,' the editor interrupted.

'Not on your own initiative. Without the missing pieces supplied by those two mutants, you would never have worked out what was really happening.'

'But you couldn't honestly expect to keep the truth from us for ever. If the survivors from the surface hadn't contacted us, something else would have given you away. Once the colonisation of the surface began, it would have become obvious that you weren't telling the truth.'

'Not so, not so.' The voice sounded completely at ease. 'Without those two mutants, you would have remained submissive and contented, happily swallowing all the information we fed you. By the time, you were allowed on the surface it would be exactly as we have described it. Our misinformation, as you term it, would have become literal truth.'

'But it's not the truth,' the editor protested, 'it's lies.'

There was another pause. Alex could just hear the sound of army boots pacing the floor. 'You talk of truth as though it's some absolute, some ultimate goal that everyone must strive for,' the voice went on. 'But it's not; like morality, it changes from generation to generation and from one section of society to another. Before the war, for instance, if you can cast your mind back that far, do you imagine that truth for the masses was the same as truth for the politicians? Of course not,' the voice continued, answering its own question. 'The politicians distorted the truth to suit their own purposes, just as you or I, in private life, might lie to cover up some indiscretion. Politics is not a doctrine of truth; it's a means of persuasion. Truth is what you believe, nothing more. And by raising the threshold of comfort, we can lower the resistance to manipulation.'

'And what of the two mutants? Aren't you afraid they might spread the real truth about your activities? You can't control them at least.'

'They are of no consequence. Without your support no one would listen to them. Besides, I'm sure they're well on their way out of here by now.'

'And you're not going to try and catch them?'

'There's no point. They can't do anything to stop us. They've already done the worst they're capable of.'

'And us?'

The voice replied chillingly; 'The frankness of our conversation, which I must say I have enjoyed, precludes your entry into society, I fear. My superiors must decide your ultimate fate. Guard, take him away.'

Alex and Elaine climbed out of the tunnel system several hours later. There had been no sign of pursuit and there were no military patrols on the surface. They reached Box late that morning and found the Land Rover where they had left it. Exhausted and deeply depressed, they started on their journey back to Wales.

CHAPTER 14

It took them six weary days to reach the community again. Elaine eyes were so swollen that she had difficulty focusing. This meant she could not drive for long periods. Although Alex had tried to compensate for this by increasing his spells at the wheel, the after effects of their experience in the city, and the need to keep a sharp look out, drained his strength. So, the journey was a long one, with frequent stops though they begrudged every hour that passed.

As soon as they arrived Alex went straight to Marcus's office and blurted out the whole story. An emergency meeting of the committee was convened at once. They were both required to attend, but a few minutes were allowed for them to wash and change into the grey shirt and baggy trousers, standard issue of the community's clothing section. Elaine's eye was properly bandaged for the first time, but the rest of her face had lost little of its grotesque appearance.

Alex was immediately called upon to relay every detail of his trip. He hung up a large map of England and indicated the location and the extent of the underground city. With Elaine's help he recalled everything that could be relevant, backing up each statement with documents. Particularly useful for the tacticians were the ground plans of the city, which the editor had given him.

To say that the committee was flabbergasted would be no exaggeration. To learn of the existence of a sophisticated underground city and to be told simultaneously of its well advanced plans for your extermination was no small thing.

Marcus led off with the first question. 'In your opinion, Alex, do you think there's any chance of the military being persuaded to stop the attack?'

'No,' Alex replied firmly. 'None at all. They have every intention of carrying out their plans and nothing will make them deviate from that.'

The decisive tone of these words drew a wave of muttering from the committee.

'But as I understand it, the civilian population still doesn't know we exist. I mean, surely they'd make a stand if they were informed of exactly what their military were up to.'

This was from Arthur Renwall, the self-important, self-satisfied nuclear expert, now peering at Alex like an over-excited schoolboy.

'I agree,' Stephen Perez added, an excellent organiser but fatally short-sighted beyond the field of his own routines and timetables. 'We must send a delegation to them immediately to sort this whole thing out.'

'It's just not that simple,' Alex retorted impatiently. 'The military would prefer to kill any delegation than talk to them.'

'They will have to use the tunnel entrance that you came out of then, and bypass the military to reach the civilian population,' Stephen continued.

'It's only logical,' Arthur chipped in. 'This whole business could be solved by exposing the nature of the attack and letting the other members of the city deal with the military.'

'I thought I'd explained how we've already tried that, working from the inside.' Now Alex was angry. 'A very brave newspaper editor has died, and probably others, too. You don't seem to appreciate the enemy we are up against. These people have already abandoned us once; they've tried to wipe us out with a typhus plague and their poison sprays have kept the radiation in the cities high. And you're saying the strength of public opinion is going to make them change their minds!'

'Gentlemen, gentlemen!' Marcus rose to his feet and motioned with his hands for quiet. 'Let us keep our minds on

255

our immediate objective. We are not here to pick holes in what Alex has to say. The evidence he has presented us with is substantial, detailed, widely based and, I believe, authentic. From what he tells us, we have just over four weeks to plan a strategy to defend ourselves against attack. I suggest we set about that task immediately, without wasting any more time.'

'I'm not suggesting that sending a delegation is the only thing we can do,' Arthur said defensively. 'Obviously, we have to prepare for every contingency. But we cannot pass up the opportunity to settle this matter peacefully.'

Alex drew a deep breath. 'After all I've told you, I'm surprised that you think the civilian population would respond positively to the leadership of a band of mutants or heed their advice. As we overheard, they have been taught to follow the military's lead. Even if we could contact the city again, we would be handed over directly to the authorities.'

Arthur frowned at this and seemed at a loss as to how to reply. He took off his glasses and rubbed his lenses thoughtfully. 'Well, we must try something,' he said at length.

'Of course, we must, but not that,' said Alex.

'There is one way to make them listen,' another voice called.

Alex had wondered how long it would be before they heard from his old friend Terry Aldiss.

'It's clear that the civilian population is not strong enough to oppose the military. So, to make the military listen to us, rather than destroy us out of hand, we need a bargaining chip.' Terry rose and came forward. Alex's plan of the city was still pinned up on the front blackboard and he studied it carefully for a moment. 'Yes, their ammunition supplies are located largely in one area, sector seventeen.' He picked up the pointer Alex had been using and tapped the plan. 'There are ventilation shafts either side of this sector, here and here. All that is needed, therefore, is an armed force to descend by these shafts and seal off this section with

256

explosives. There would be enough ammunition here to blow up half the city. This would be carrying the war right into their own camp; if, after that, they did not come to terms, they'd risk their total destruction.'

In spite of his dislike for Terry, Alex had to admit that his plan was very good. Marcus, too, from the look of him, was giving it very serious consideration.

'One of the most ridiculous suggestions I ever heard,' Arthur piped up. 'Any number of things could go wrong with it. What if the armed force failed? The military would be on the surface in a flash, after the rest of us. Then there'd be no reasoning with them.'

Alex and Marcus's eyes met across the room and for a moment, in the older man's eyes, Alex glimpsed the strain of the responsibility that was weighing him down.

Raising his hands to silence the babble of voices which had joined in denouncing Terry's plan, Marcus once more called for quiet. He stood and surveyed the gathered company until all was quiet. 'This business has come rushing upon us,' he began, so softly that they had to be completely silent to hear him. 'As in the time of the first bombs falling that destroyed the world we knew and loved, we are unprepared. But in that dreadful time we were individuals, citizens without a voice, suddenly overthrown in the ruin of our country. Today it is not quite like that. This is our home now, a home we have built up and moulded with conscious purpose. It is the work of our own hands, and we have justifiable pride in what our own labours have achieved. Let us therefore stand to arm and ready ourselves to defend it and all those who have entrusted themselves to our care. I call for volunteers from both the Scottish and Welsh communities. Together we shall raise an army and march to the underground city and, if necessary, be ready to attack it if it threatens to destroy us.'

Arthur Kenwall was still persistent in his dissent. 'Are you saying that we should attack the city without first trying to negotiate with them?' he interrupted.

Marcus waved his objection aside. 'I approve the pre-emptive strike that Terry has suggested. The aggressive intentions of the military are beyond reasonable doubt. Whatever the outcome of that strike, it follows that we also need the immediate threat of an army to add weight to our claims to destroy the city, or to launch an immediate assault if the sabotage fails.'

'But we don't have the arms to supply an army of any size,' Arthur persisted.

'Sir, you are mistaken.'

Alex recognised Dimitri Antoni, one of the three-man junta of the Scottish community. Tall and with a hawkish face, he stared Arthur down relentlessly.

'Scotland is well provided with arms and ammunition,' he continued, seeing that he now held the floor. 'It is the one surplus we can call upon. We place them unreservedly at the disposal of our Welsh friends, whose fight is ours.'

'That is most generous, Dimitri,' said Marcus. 'What volume of armaments and what time scale are we talking about?'

Dimitri shrugged. 'Enough to equip a force thirty thousand strong. We can contribute ten thousand of our own men. They could be on their way within a fortnight.'

'And your colleagues on the junta? Would they be likely to raise any objections?'

'I speak for them. I repeat; your fight is our fight. Alex's arguments and evidence are unanswerable.'

This sudden pledge of arms and men did much to stir the committee into action. The general principle of Terry's plan was adopted and several leading men from the community's armed forces were called in to examine the logistics of it. Dimitri, meanwhile, discussed with Marcus how best to combine the Scottish and Welsh armies and organise the support facilities in the few weeks that remained. Marcus eventually agreed to supply all the food and trucks, if the Scots could take care of most of the arms. If everything went according to plan, the two armies would merge in three weeks' time on the outskirts of Stoke on Trent and advance south together to the city. Dimitri would leave for Scotland at first light the next day, by sea, on a Welsh trawler, as it was expected that this would more than halve the travelling time.

The committee meeting was adjourned in the early hours, with an agreement to meet again in several days to review progress.

Alex and Elaine, feeling more dead than alive, slipped away quietly to catch up on some sleep. They did not wake until late the next day.

Alex found Elaine sitting at a table by herself, staring distantly at her food. He crossed over to her, not expecting an enthusiastic greeting and not getting one. She turned and smiled briefly, more out of politeness than pleasure.

'Your face looks a lot better,' he said awkwardly, when she did not speak. 'I mean a lot better than it did a few days ago,' he added quickly, as her hand went instinctively to the swollen purple area.

She withdrew it and nodded, but still she did not reply.

They had had a blazing row the day before. He had never seen anyone quite so angry. The whole argument had come as rather a shock. She had asked him if he would be joining the forces to fight the military, if it came to a battle. He had shrugged and said he supposed he would, not really giving the matter a second thought. She had then started asking him a whole series of awkward questions. Why did he want to fight? Hadn't he already done enough? Did he really want to be involved in another war? This negative response had irritated him; it was his duty, he had said. Immediately she had flown off the handle. What was the matter with him? Did he take some morbid delight in war? When he had attempted to defend himself, she had simply raised her voice and finally had stormed off. Neither of them had said a word to each other for the rest of the day. It was now dinner time on the day after and still they had not spoken to each other.

'The funny thing about this,' she began suddenly, returning effortlessly to the theme of the argument, 'is that I don't even think you believe we can win a battle against the military, anyway.'

He opened his mouth to speak but found that she was largely right. 'If we attack while they're still underground, I think we have a good chance of beating them,' he corrected her.

'And if they manage to reach the surface?'

'That will be more difficult,' he agreed.

She continued to watch him, her face a mixture of anger and misery. 'You'll, be glad to know I've decided to join one of the assault units myself.'

Alex frowned. 'And they have accepted you?'

'They have.'

'I wish you wouldn't.'

She laughed bitterly. 'I can do exactly what I like.'

'Why don't you join one of the supply units at the rear of the column?'

She shook her head. 'Promise you won't fight at the front, and I'll promise to join one of the supply units.'

For one long sad moment they stared at each other, Alex thought of Cliff and Roy and all they had been through together. It would almost amount to an act of desertion not to be with them when they faced the military. He didn't have to answer. She read his decision in his face and turned away in disgust, and he failed to find the right words to soothe her. Every time they tried to discuss the matter further they just got tangled up in each other's emotions. She wanted a commitment he couldn't give, and he wanted her safe, which she wouldn't allow. In the end he left her. Being together at this moment only made things worse.

Marcus was standing now, hands firmly planted on the desk as he leaned across at Terry. 'I think you know my position, Terry. But if you want me to spell it out, I shall do so. I will not be putting your name forward to lead this assault.'

'Why not?'

Marcus leaned forward till their faces were level. 'Because I can't trust you. You're a manipulator and a schemer. I couldn't give you specific instructions and expect them to be carried out. You would always work a situation to your own advantage.'

Terry's face hardened with anger.

'Besides you have no experience of planning or executing such a raid,' Marcus continued as an afterthought.

'Neither has anyone else!'

'That's true, but there are people a lot better qualified for the job than you, who will also carry out the orders I give them, without question.'

'I have a good deal of support in the committee, you know,' Terry said defiantly. 'I will get them to vouch for me.'

'You can do what you like,' Marcus replied mildly.

Terry grunted, then turned away abruptly and stormed out of the office.

With a sigh, Marcus sat down and drained his tea to the dregs, then, reached for a notepad from under a pile of loose papers on his desk, he frowned, poised his pen and began to write steadily, filling the page.

Three hours later, at the committee meeting, things went pretty much how Marcus had anticipated. Terry had been busy lobbying for support and had several members arguing heatedly for his cause. He had also drawn up a very comprehensive plan for the assault, which he made a great show of explaining to the committee. Indeed, the plan was excellent. He had divided the assault party into two groups. Both groups would enter sector seventeen via two large ventilation shafts on the surface. While one would concentrate on reaching the armament stores and wiping out any military, the second group would mine the tunnels that connected that sector to the rest of the city.

The debate was long and arduous, but at its conclusion Marcus had succeeded in placing Jeff Barrett in command of the operation. He had been a police officer before the war and had extensive training in tactical response work and anti-terrorist activities. From all accounts, he had strong leadership qualities and a cool head if the situation became difficult. Terry was placed second in command. The assault team would be composed of two hundred men. Jeff would lead the attack on sector seventeen, while Terry would be in charge of sealing off the sector. The strike would begin soon after the army had taken up position outside the city. At first, scouting parties would be sent out at night to verify the positions of the ventilation vents. All being well, the saboteurs would descend into the complex a few hours before dawn on the following day. Just as dawn was breaking, they would detonate all the explosives, effectively sealing off sector seventeen. On the surface, all entrances would be simultaneously closed. The army would then swarm over the whole area, picking off any military soldiers who attempted to escape. In this way, the military should be cut off from their tanks and armaments and marooned underground. Radio contact would then be made with the city and the demands of the survivors put forward. If the military still didn't agree to abort their plans, the ammunition dumps in sector seventeen would be blown up, probably taking the whole city with them.

After the meeting Marcus returned to his office, well satisfied. The task of organising and leading the community's army had fallen on him, as he knew it would. He had already completed most of the requisitioning of supplies. Contingency plans remained to be considered. If, for some reason, the battle turned into a long, drawn out siege, the supplying of the army would create enormous problems. Since the surface was still largely a wasteland, all food would have to be drawn from the Welsh community's stocks. By his calculations, based on current estimates, the war had to be decided one way or another in three weeks. At a pinch,

262

the food stocks could be stretched to five weeks, but the physical condition of the army would suffer.

The kettle boiled and he made himself a fresh pot of tea. Tea, he always found, helped to clear his thoughts. And it would work for him again, far into the night.

CHAPTER 15

Dawn, and the land was in twilight, barely visible as a murky, red stained surface, rising through a soup of mist. To the east, purples, magentas and reds, the many auras of the sun, pushed upward through the thick atmosphere of the horizon. Then, like an incandescent fireball, the sun detached itself, climbed higher and shrunk through reds and oranges to its normal size. The warmth of its rays, laden with ultraviolet, could be felt at once, dissipating the night dews and stirring up wind eddies. Within an hour strong winds had swept the last of the mist from the valleys. The land had been laid bare for another day, the cities ghastly in decay, and the lacework of motorways remaining as the only testament to man. In the savannah of dried grassland, the howls from packs of dogs and insect hazes rose to greet the sun.

Yet this morning there was an additional sound. Along one of the motorways an active line, like a monstrous column of ants, snaked its way slowly south. Its front roared, as walls of bulldozers cut a path through rusted cars and rag covered skeletons. Behind them came tanks, rocket launchers, mounted artillery and supply vehicles. To either side of them, stony faced men and women marched along. A vanguard over twenty-five thousand strong had been armed with modern weapons. Another fifteen thousand carried spears fashioned from iron railings, axes, sharpened picks and an assortment of implements of home manufacture, including bows and arrows. An imposing force, but it represented the total strength in arms of the two communities. The decision had been made to throw everything into this assault. There would be no second wave. Victory or defeat would be decided at the city.

264

Riding in a large, armour plated van near the front of the column was Marcus. With him were Dimitri Antoni and Peter McCaffrey from the Scottish community. Since the meeting of the two armies several days previously, the three of them had been engaged in long discussions. Neither Dimitri nor Peter had raised any serious objections to the assault plans Marcus had proposed, and in the disposition of forces they deferred to him.

By the evening, if all went according to plan, the army would be less than twenty kilometres from the city. Somewhere in between, scouting parties were already fanning out, searching the land for any sign of the military. So far nothing had been seen and, as Alex had reported, the whole sector appeared devoid of human life. Only the constant howls from packs of wild dogs accompanied the column as they pushed forward. No intelligence was available within a ten-kilometre radius of the underground city. These areas would not be explored until darkness fell and the army had taken up its position.

Marcus, seated by one of the windows, stared out dejectedly at the passing countryside. They were traversing the once beautiful valley of the River Severn. He remembered many trips into this area in the back of his father's old Vauxhall. Mother and Father had sat up in front and his elder sister had teased him continually when their backs were turned. With the windows wound down, the scent of flowers in the spring had been intoxicating; in autumn, the woods had flamed with colour. And years later, when he was posted to Birmingham, he had travelled the back roads and lanes through this region on his way to see his girlfriend in Cardiff. Along the banks of the Severn were some of their favourite picnic spots. Now that landscape, the creation of a thousand years, was gone. The river, even its most secluded reaches, was poisoned, the flowers no longer bloomed, the population was dead. He closed his eyes and let his mind drift back through the years. All the work, the excitement, the tardy reward of promotion, the endless drill, the passion

for order which eventually consumed his whole life - that
had been his world. There, insulated from reality, men had
planned imaginary manoeuvres to counter imaginary threats.
When war was talked about it was with a certain glint in the
eye, as though this was what all their training had been
preparing them for, the ultimate accolade. Somewhere in that
kaleidoscope of fractured impressions he had become lost.
Or, maybe, he had finally found himself. He had discovered
the meaning of it all: that there was no meaning. The rot set
in at that point. His realisation brought with it a restlessness
and a horrible sense of waste. His whole life was a useless
nightmare. Better not to think those thoughts. Better to bury
oneself in the war games and the routine, reassured in the
stumbling faith that you were preparing your country in case
the unthinkable happened. But the unthinkable was not
assessable to reason, that was the problem. Irrational
weapons to fight an unthinkable war. That way madness lies.
In the finish you end up staring down each other's cannons
and the sequel was as inevitable as the dawning day.

Marcus opened his eyes again and continued watching
the passing countryside. And now like the re-run of an old,
tacky movie they were back at the beginning. We would
make the first strike to avoid being struck.

These past few weeks of tension had been a very difficult
time for Alex. He and Elaine had not been getting on well. In
fact, they had been fighting like cats since their arrival back
at the community. Both were now utterly polarised in their
views. She had thrown up the threat to join one of the
forward units. But it had failed to dissuade Alex from doing
so; now she was flatly refusing to have anything to do with
the fighting and had attached herself to a supply unit in the
rear. If the army was defeated, she would be one of the first
back into Wales. The combined fleets of the two
communities waited at anchor off Holyhead, ready to ferry
the survivors to Ireland, if necessary. Elaine had wanted
Alex to agree to flee with her if the military broke through,

266

but he had refused. This was the fruitful cause of fresh arguments. She wanted him retreating safely with her; he wanted to fight till there was no chance of winning. He couldn't help thinking of Tina after these arguments. She was not like Elaine in that sense. The battle with Tina would be to stop her fighting alongside him to the very end. Elaine's choice was better in that sense. Knowing she would be safe was a great comfort, but he couldn't forget all that had happened, and he couldn't wash his hands of this last great struggle. He was constrained by too many painful memories. He would be fighting for the people who were already lost: for Martin, Debbie and their daughter, for all the people at 'The Chronicle', for Jason, Tina and Wayne. Thinking of them alone forced him into the front line for one final, terrible confrontation. Roy, Cliff and he would vent their rage together. He wanted his revenge.

The column didn't stop moving until well after midnight. Alex had left Roy and Cliff soon after dark and had driven to the rear of the column, where a large proportion of the Welsh community's supply vehicles were camped. This would be his last chance to see Elaine. Once the army reached their positions outside the city, there would be no more opportunities. The attack could come at any time.

And yet, once he had found her, he had no idea what he was going to say. Really nothing had changed; he was still as determined as ever to fight. But he felt somehow, things had been left unfinished. He couldn't bear the thought of going to meet the enemy with the knowledge that the last words he had said to her had been angry ones. Their relationship deserved a better ending. No, he thought savagely, not 'ending'; that was too negative. This was not the end; it was just a temporary lull, a passing phase. When the military was defeated he looked forward to a long and happy life with Elaine. For when all was said and done, their dispute basically boiled down to her concern for his safety. If more tranquil times were coming, they would never need to argue.

At the rear of the column, he asked for the location of supply unit 12, Elaine's unit. Eventually, his searching brought him to a small circle of campfires surrounded by over a dozen supply trucks. A group of about forty people were gathered there. In the light of the fires, Alex could see that most of them were either women or older men, some with physical disabilities that would have prevented them from fighting. They had just finished dinner and several pots of water were gurgling away among the flames. As with nearly all the camp sites he had visited so far, the survivors were talking amongst themselves happily, no doubt excited at meeting members of the Scottish community and at the same time being given a chance to escape the tedium of hard work. He doubted the rank and file had any idea of the seriousness of the situation. Not even the officers could guess what they would be up against. This had been done deliberately by Marcus and his Scottish counterparts in case the military agreed to a climb down. To tell the truth about them would be to risk the possibility of a bloodbath. So, the army had simply been told that an underground city had been found full of food and sophisticated technology. This show of force was intended to let its occupants know that the survivors meant to have their share of its wealth.

Elaine was not among the group at the fires. But further off he spotted her, a tall, slim figure standing slightly apart from the others. He drew a deep breath as he remembered their last torrid meeting.

As he approached, she moved towards one of the fires to warm her hands. Alex paused for a moment and watched. Like everyone else, she was wearing a grey shirt and pants. Her clothes, however, were too large for her, giving her body no definite shape, except where the black belt clung tightly around her waist. From what he could see of her face the bruising had gone, although several curls of her hair were draped across it, obscuring his full view. He came forward into the light and waited for her to look up. At first, she didn't notice him, but kept her head bowed staring distantly into the flames. Then, as though conscious of being watched, she raised her head and looked straight at him. For a moment longer her eyes remained hazy, unfocused. Then she realised and her face lit up.

'Alex!' she squealed with delight.

She danced round the fire and threw herself into his arms. There they clung tightly, she to him and he to her, neither wanting to let go. For long moments they continued their embrace. When they finally released each other, he noticed that her eyes were moist. She was smiling at him with the kind of warmth that made his resolve to fight wither within him. He kissed her gently on the lips and she responded with unexpected feeling. Her arms slid up his back and pressed his face into hers, burying him in a mass of blonde curls. Then, as suddenly as she had started, she stopped and drew away. Alex felt as if a door had been opened, then slammed in his face. A harsh, resentful expression had appeared on her face.

'I just wanted you to know,' she said, 'what you are missing and that you mean more to me than any of this.' She flung her arms open wide to indicate the scatter of armoured trucks and troop carriers around them. 'I only want a chance for us both to start again.'

'I know, I know,' he said soothingly. 'When this is all over…'

'What will you do if they break through your lines at the city?' she interrupted. 'How can you hope to get back in time to catch the boats to Ireland? You'll be on foot and they'll have troop carriers and tanks. They'll cut off your escape route, then hunt you down like animals.' She was glaring at him now, her jaw rigid and her lips drawn in a tight, determined line. 'If you were further back at least you'd have a chance. We could even use these trucks to get away.'

They faced each other without speaking. Alex could sense the faint spark of hope in her eyes.

He lowered his head.

'SHIT! ALEX!' She drew a deep breath and averted her head suddenly. 'Why do you have to fight at the front? One less person, what difference would that make? Who would know?'

'I would know,' Alex replied sternly. 'I would have to live with it.' They had been over the same ground so many times.

'But there can be many ways of fighting. You don't need to be at the front to fight.'

'That's my place...that's where I'm going.'

'I don't believe you're really fighting for the defence of the survivors at all,' she said after a pause. 'I think the real reason is that you want revenge.'

He shrugged. 'Revenge is part of the reason.'

'More than part.'

Alex thought for a moment. 'I'm fighting for all the people the military have killed,' he said. 'I'm fighting to stop them from doing the same thing again.'

'You're fighting for yourself, Alex,' she corrected. 'You want to kill. You love it. You want to see them die. You don't care how many. Can't you ever think about life, about me, about the future?'

'Don't be ridiculous!' He turned away suddenly and walked over to the fire, feeling angry and not knowing how to reply.

'Well, I'm not going to watch you die,' she called after him bitterly. 'If we lose the battle, I'll return to the Welsh community and catch one of the boats for Ireland.'

He nodded without looking around.

'If you change your mind about the fighting, I'll be here,' she added, striding off.

He saw no more of her that night.

The next day, at dawn, the column shunted forward on the last twenty-kilometre hop to the city. Alex was riding on the back of one of the Lorries, next to Cliff and Roy. Cliff had guessed from Alex's face that the night before things had not

270

gone well with Elaine. Roy, however, lacking Cliff's perception, had asked bluntly what had happened. With equal bluntness Alex had filled in the main points of their disagreement.

For Roy it had never occurred to him not to fight. The subtlety of Elaine's argument was therefore lost on him. 'They want to wipe us out; we've got to stop 'em,' was his verdict. As far as he was concerned that was the end of the matter.

Cliff agreed with Roy, but he also understood Elaine.

'I think she realises that you need to fight,' he said. 'What she's not so clear about is why you have to be in with the front-line assault groups.'

He was watching Alex intently when he said this, and Alex knew it was a question and not an explanation. 'I need to be in the front line,' he said, frowning heavily. 'I could never live with myself otherwise.'

Cliff nodded; clearly, he had expected this. 'I guess I haven't been through the sort of traumas you have,' he shrugged. 'I haven't been interrogated or had to watch helplessly as the people who have tried to help have been dragged off by the military. It doesn't touch me nearly as deeply as it does you, but if Elaine was my girlfriend, I wouldn't be in such a hurry to throw myself into the front line.'

Cliff had had his say and never mentioned the subject again. His words, however, did not fade quite so quickly. They reverberated within Alex, setting up a doubt and conflict, which he could not easily resolve.

At midnight two hundred men massed in a small valley, hidden between two long lines of hills. They had been divided into two squads. Jeff would lead the assault on the armament supplies with one hundred and twenty men and Terry would be in charge of the remaining eighty men which he planned to split into two squads to blow-up the train links either end of section seventeen. Each squad was equipped with ropes, cutting equipment, explosives and a map of the city. In dry runs the plan had been practised many times. Two surface ducts would be dismantled, and the men lowered down the shafts on ropes. When they passed near the position of disused tunnels marked on the map, they would cut through the shafts and enter them. The force would then divide to attack their assigned targets.

Terry walked quickly up and down the lines of men, flashing his torch as they went. He had strapped to his waist his favourite hunting knife; hand grenades, a revolver and he had an automatic rifle lashed to his back. He radiated confidence and already he was looking forward to the spoils of victory. From Alex's description, the city was the equivalent of a gold mine; it could be ransacked almost endlessly to provide all that would be required to rebuild the country. And he had every intention of being one of the leading architects of that new society. With this victory would come the recognition he so badly needed. No one need ever know about his pre-holocaust days. So, it was with pride that he strode along the ranks of all these men under him. Command seemed to come so naturally to him. He always felt cheated if he wasn't in control.

The end of his parade brought him to Jeff, who was crouched over a map.

'Are they clear on their orders?' Jeff asked, without taking his eyes off the map.

'Perfectly,' Terry replied.

Jeff grunted and put the map away. He stood up.

'Well...' he said, 'ready or not we can't waste any more time. Give the order for them to move out.'

Terry wheeled sharply round. 'FORM YOUR SQUADS AND MOVE OUT QUIETLY,' he called.

The ranks closed, then bunched into two subunits, which quickly and silently began moving forward.

CHAPTER 16

Terry waited until the vibration of the train thundering along directly underneath had died. He flashed his torch on to his watch, then gave the signal to his men to start laying the charges. So far, the operation had gone like clockwork. They had met no military personnel on the surface, the ventilation ducts were where they had expected them to be, and the disused tunnel system was at the exact depth specified on the map. They were still at full strength and on schedule. Yet not everything was going to plan. Most worrying had been the discovery that the tunnel system above section seventeen was far more extensive than the map indicated. Once the train link to the sector had been cut, the plan was quickly to seal all remaining points of access into the sector. But it was now clear that the map had only shown the larger tunnels. In fact, they were interlaced with a network of smaller passageways, any one of which could provide an alternative route into the sector for the military.

The man in charge of laying the explosives called quietly; 'What time delay do you want set on the timers?'

Terry hesitated, again checking his watch. The other half of his command was at the other side of sector seventeen. The agreed time for detonating their charges was three o'clock. 'Set the timer for ten minutes,' he ordered.

The man nodded, conveyed the message and hurried off. In the shadows Terry could hear him whispering harsh orders to his men. Soon everything was set and Terry led his troop to shelter some distance off, in case the shockwaves from the blast caused cave ins.

As it turned out, the blast made the whole tunnel system shake and brought down several roof struts near the company, but no one was hurt. Several seconds later an answering rumble indicated the other party had also been successful.

The destruction of the rail link was the signal for Jeff to begin his attack on the armaments. Within minutes the sound of gunfire and explosions could be heard coming from somewhere beneath them. It wouldn't be long now till the waking military realised what was happening. Terry called on his men quickly to complete their work. According to his map, three tunnels converged into one just before entering sector seventeen. His orders were to seal this tunnel as close to the sector as possible, but now also they would attempt to shut down as many of the smaller ones that branched off it as their limited supplies of explosives would allow. He led his men past the point of convergence until they were nearly over the sector. Here, finding an area where part of the roof had collapsed, he ordered some of his company to lay charges, while he took the rest further on. Each time they passed side tunnels men dropped back and began preparing for demolition. Within half an hour they had successfully sealed the main tunnel and eleven minor ones. But their explosives had run out with another four tunnels left open. Terry had no choice but to station guards at each of these to watch for signs of the military.

Now all they could do was to wait for some news from Jeff. It came just before four o'clock in the form of a runner. He was completely exhausted and reeked of gunpowder and sweat, but his face told of a hard-fought victory. 'We've won,' he said triumphantly. 'We've sustained casualties, but we are now in complete control of the armaments.'

The news was greeted with cheers and much excited talk. The men appeared to think the whole thing was going to be a walk-over. Terry had to growl at them to keep their voices down. Immediately he sent news of their success to the surface. Other men from his company were waiting at the top of the ventilation shafts with two-way radios, precisely to relay such information back to headquarters.

Below ground, Terry ordered his men to resume their guard along the tunnels. This was the most difficult time, the waiting. Terry felt like a tightly wound spring ready to snap.

'There's still no reply,' said the radio operator, looking up.

'Keep trying, keep trying,' Marcus urged. He saw the pale faces of Dimitri and Matthew at the other end of the van and knew they were sharing his anxious thoughts. Sighing to himself, he walked over to a window and stared out into the blackness of the night. Suddenly he felt an overwhelming need to escape into that blackness. On impulse, he flung open the door of the van and stepped outside. The night air was crisp and refreshing. A slight breeze ruffled his clothes and cooled his face. His watch showed five thirty. The military had agreed to meet the survivors at the main entrance to their city half an hour before. What could be keeping them? And what kind of brinkmanship could this be, putting the lives of so many people at risk? He found their behaviour incomprehensible. He only had to give the order and half the city would be destroyed. Dimitri and Matthew would have done it already, saying that a dangerous enemy needed to be given just enough rope to hang himself with. But Marcus still held out; he didn't want the deaths of all those civilians on his conscience. They may have been naive in turning a blind eye to the military's activities, but they were hardly collaborators. And who's to say the survivors wouldn't have done the same thing in their place?

Frowning, he turned to look toward the east. It would be dawn in a few hours. Already a faint glow of purple outlined the hills. He could just make out the silhouettes of the tanks of the Scottish community perched high up, like blunted serrations of a saw. Everybody was waiting; he had only to give the signal. What fools the military were. Did they think he was bluffing?

Finally, he could take it no longer. The dreadful possibility that something had gone wrong made it imperative that he should move. He strode back to the van.

'We've waited long enough,' he told the radio operator. 'Give the order to destroy sector seventeen.'

The operator flicked a few switches on his radio set and began relaying Marcus's instructions. Dimitri and Matthew came up behind Marcus.

'You were both right,' he said before they could question him. 'We can't wait any longer. It could be a trick.'

The operator turned back to Marcus. 'They report that they can't reach Terry.' He narrowed his eyes as he continued to listen to his headphones. 'They say they can hear the sound of gunfire coming from some of the ventilation shafts.'

'Gunfire?'

'And explosions,' the operator added.

'Tell them to keep trying,' Marcus ordered.

'Yes, Sir.'

Marcus turned to Dimitri and Matthew, feeling the perspiration prickling his face. 'And tell all the tank units to move up immediately and cover all the entrances to the city,' he added.

For the next few minutes, the radio operator was frantically busy. Marcus stood by the door of the van and stared out in the direction of the city. He felt totally useless; he had made a fatal miscalculation. He thought of the fighting that must be going on in the tunnels over sector seventeen at this moment. Now everything relied on the abilities of Jeff and Terry.

As the dust and smoke cleared it was obvious that the roof had held. Terry swore viciously under his breath. The tunnel was too wide and too well constructed to be sealed with hand grenades. Without explosives, their hands were tied. Already the military could be seen creeping through the rubble toward them again. A few rounds were enough to send them diving for cover, but their answering volley was devastating; no one could hold out under that onslaught. Once more Terry and his men were forced into full flight.

276

The confident Terry was now at a complete loss to know what to do. The military had burst out of two of the unsealed tunnels almost simultaneously. Nearly half his company had been cut down before he knew what was happening. From then on they had been forced back and back. Each time they made a stand they lost more men; now only a handful were left.

They came to an intersection of three tunnels. Terry chose the most dilapidated of these, hoping to cave it in if the military followed. Driven by their own terror, they ran a long way before slowing down to listen for signs of pursuit. By now their strength was all but spent. The men collapsed where they stood, into the mud and slime, and lay there for many minutes, but there were no pursuing footsteps. Only the sound of water could be heard, as it spilled and gurgled its way from a hundred different cracks and crevices. Terry shone the beam of his torch over the roof and walls. Everywhere there were decaying props and cross-beams. They had been splashing through water for some time, now they could see that they had come to a halt on a spit of accumulated mud and silt between two pools. The impression was of workings that had been abandoned long ago.

He shone his torch on the remainder of his men. Only six were left. Soaking wet, covered in mud and panting heavily, they were a pitiful sight. Their ammunition was almost exhausted; they already looked defeated and bewildered. But this was not the time to give up. Jeff, he knew, would have no qualms about blowing the whole place up if he was threatened. It wasn't a comfortable position to be in, to feel one was sitting on top of a huge powder keg. After giving his men a few more minutes to recover, he set off again at a rapid pace.

For much of the next half-hour they laboured to clear a path through numerous obstructions. In places, the roughly hewn floor dipped into pools of evil smelling water, which reached to their waists. At other times, rock falls had all but sealed the tunnel and they had to call on more inner resources than they thought they possessed to dig their way ahead. But Terry remained cheerful; he thought he had found where they were on the map. According to him, this part of the system would eventually lead them to the surface over two kilometres away.

After some time, the tunnel began to climb steeply. The walls dried out and there was less cave-ins. Further still, its shape began to change, becoming broader and higher, with thick, evenly spaced roof struts. Even lengths of electric cable and light bulbs hung from the rafters. There were also many more side tunnels, some of a considerable size. But along these tunnels they caught the faint sounds of gunfire and explosions. Terry called a halt and strained his ears to hear. The battle was raging somewhere behind and below them. Jeff must still be holding out against the military. He felt a pang of sympathy for him. Although the men he had with him were the best the two communities could offer, they lacked the enemy's sophisticated weaponry, and had had little training in small arms. Their resistance could only be temporary. With renewed vigour, he set off again, his men dejectedly tagging along behind.

At another junction, where several tunnels intersected, Terry paused briefly, pointed to the furthest left tunnel then immediately began jogging down it. But by the time the rest of the company had caught up with him he had stopped again and was staring at a wall of broken rock that was barring their way. The sight made him groan aloud. He sprinted back past them to the intersection and tried another of the forks. From this also he soon emerged shaking his head. The men watched him as he waved them impatiently into the third tunnel.

This tunnel climbed steadily upward in a series of sharp twists and curves, then straightened out. Terry was slightly ahead as usual as they rounded the last bend. Suddenly, with an exclamation, he halted and his torchlight played over the ground. They had stumbled on the bodies of a number of

278

military personnel, recently dead, their chests ripped open by bullet wounds.

Fifty metres further along, this tunnel also ended in a pile of broken rock and rubble. Against it, were all that was left of the other half of their company. They lay in the attitudes of violent death, as though in the last few moments of their lives they had been trying furiously to burrow through that impenetrable wall.

The men could not understand the scene at all, but Terry could, and all the energy seemed to drain from him as he slumped against the side of the tunnel.

Eventually a spokesman for the others asked, 'What does this mean, chief?'

The man had to repeat his question before Terry looked up.

'Can't you see what's happened?' Terry demanded, in a voice surprisingly calm and composed.

'No, you tell us,' the man replied angrily. 'You have the map, and you know where you're leading us.'

'Quite true, quite true.' Terry shone his torch in his face. 'Well, for your information, we are now at the other side of sector seventeen. This is the last of three tunnels leading out of the sector. It appears all three have been sealed by our dead comrades. Yes,' he continued grimly, 'it seems that instead of chasing us through some old tunnels, the military decided to travel straight through and attack Jeff. They must have found these men on the way. And, of course, there was no way out for them because they had already closed all the exits from the sector. Caught in their own trap, so to speak. Now do you understand?'

'But there are probably some smaller tunnels they missed,' one of the company suggested.

'I didn't see any, did you?' Terry answered casually. He gestured towards the bodies. 'It's obvious they didn't either, or they wouldn't have been trying to claw their way out of here.'

'So, what are you going to do about it?' said another man asked. 'Where do we go from here?'

Terry smiled at his serious expression. 'Go' he said. 'We don't go anywhere. Even if we could dig our way out of here, it would take us hours. I reckon Jeff will be blowing up the dumps any minute now. Ironic, isn't it, we came through the holocaust only to be blown up by our own bombs! Oh God, it's so funny!'

And he cackled insanely as they stared at him in horror.

Jeff sat against some fuel drums, his head bowed, his rifle lying on the floor next to him. He was hopelessly trapped. Most of his men were dead and he was running low on ammunition. Things had gone terribly wrong; it was a total disaster. Only a few hours before they had been celebrating at taking the sector and finding a huge arms store. But there had been no larger weapons - artillery, tanks and rocket launchers were all missing. When they questioned one of the soldiers they had captured, he told them that most of the heavy stuff had been moved to sector eighteen for maintenance some months before. What they had seized were the small arms, ammunition and a fuel dump, and even these only amounted to half the city's supply. More of all these categories were also located in sector eighteen.

This failure, the result of inadequate intelligence, had only just been explained to them when all hell had broken loose. Suddenly one wall of the sector had blown apart and the military had swarmed in. His men had put up a tremendous fight and killed many soldiers. But they were facing hopeless odds. In the end they had to retreat amongst a huge supply of diesel fuel stored in the basement of the sector. The military had not pressed them too hard there, but had resorted to negotiations, fearing they would blow the place up if they fired.

So here they still remained. He checked his watch.

It was nearly six thirty. The stalemate had been going on for nearly fifty minutes. He was giving the military valuable time to clear the area. For the first time ever he was feeling physically sick with fear.

'Now, listen to me,' a rather tired voice called for the fifth time. 'Give yourselves up. This is the end of the line for you. You've fought well, but the battle has gone against you. Already our army is on the surface. Blowing up a fuel dump isn't going to change that. Come out with your weapons, and I personally will guarantee your safety.'

Jeff looked at the determined faces of his men. There was only nineteen left. A few metres away one of them held a small detonator. He only had to touch two wires together and the whole place would go up. He signalled to the man to come over and took the detonator from him. The others looked on grimly, finally realising Jeff was about to make the decision that would claim all their lives. But not one of them complained or showed any sign of emotion.

'At this minute we are driving back your forces on the surface,' the voice started up again. 'You're wasting your time and ours. Come out and give yourselves up.'

Jeff leaned across to his men. 'They won't risk firing with the fuel dump at our backs. I'll set the timer on the detonator for five minutes. I propose we charge straight for them. If we break through, we just keep on going, we may be able to escape through the same tunnel.'

They solemnly nodded their approval of his plan. He doubted any of them really believed a word of it. Even if they reached the tunnel, there was enough fuel and ammunition here to blow this whole sector out of the ground. They would go up with everything else.

When he was sure that everyone was clear on his instructions, Jeff turned his attention back to the military. There were possibly thirty men in the storeroom, huddled behind a number of small concrete walls next to the door. The rest, he assumed, were waiting in the corridors outside. His men checked their rifles and shared out their last supplies of ammunition. Then they looked towards him.

A moment's grace and then he gave the signal. Instantly they leapt from their positions and went rushing forward. They were met with no spray of fire. Instead, the military made a mad scramble for the door, where many were shot as they tried to squeeze through the narrow opening. The community soldiers were at their heels and immediately threw hand grenades into the passageway beyond, racing on straight after the explosions. For maybe a minute Jeff heard the sound of intense fighting in the network of corridors and then everything went quiet.

Another minute passed before the military came back, creeping over the bodies of their dead. Jeff watched the scene with an almost morbid fascination. He was very calm now, his mind clear and certain. He mused to himself that he was living the very last seconds of his life. The thought held no horror or anguish for him, for at that moment he had never hated anyone or anything more than the military. He re-set the charges to explode in twenty seconds, flicked off his safety catch and positioned his rifle on one of the drums. They came to within ten metres of his position still unaware of his presence. Impassively he emptied his last clip into them. The last memory he ever had was of soldiers running for their lives amid the slaughter of their comrades.

CHAPTER 17

In a dozen different locations came the grinding back of huge iron doors. And into the night, through the growing gaps, swarmed the heavy armour. Within minutes they had linked into a line, making one unbroken chain several kilometres wide.

Every second tank in the line had a powerful searchlight, a cyclops eye that moved ceaselessly. With hardly a pause, the wall of steel rolled forward, sweeping north at speeds of up to fifty kilometres an hour. Their target lay only fifteen kilometres off - another army, less well equipped, advancing toward them more slowly and completely unaware of the hammer blow about to fall.

When Marcus guessed that the saboteurs had failed, he had wasted no time in ordering all company commanders to mobilise their units and advance on the city. The foot soldiers were to move ahead of the armoured units in a series of arrowhead formations. The object was to scour the land for any hidden tunnels that were not marked on their maps. Nothing was to be left to chance. Every exit they found was to be destroyed, denying the military access to the surface. They would be sealed in and effectively defeated without firing a shot.

Alex was at the head of one of these arrowhead formations, in charge of a brigade of five thousand men and women and doing his best to restrain the over eager and encourage the more reluctant by means of a limited range walkie talkie. All commanders were equipped with radios, which were only to be used in the case of extreme emergencies, as it was assumed that any broadcast this close to the city would be monitored. So far none of the forward units had broken radio silence.

As they advanced the country began to break up, becoming hillier and increasing the difficulties of keeping the regiments under his command in touch. Alex called a temporary halt to check his compass bearings and look at the map. Due south lay the tunnel exits his brigade had been assigned to guard. Slightly to the left was the village of Box. Bath was some eight kilometres further away. It was at this moment that one of his aides spotted what looked like searchlights in the clouds above accompanied by a rumble. Alex felt sure it was powerful engines he could hear. He flashed his torch at the radio operator at the same time as Cliff came running up.

'It's confirmed, guv,' he panted. 'Tanks, and plenty of them.'

Alex nodded. 'Shit,' he said quietly.

'The radio's gone wild,' Cliff continued. 'Everyone's on the channel at once. Apparently, there's a whole line of them sweeping this way.'

'Where are ours?'

'They've already been given orders to move up, but the reports I've heard suggest they could have as many as four hundred tanks. We don't even have half that number.'

'Can our tanks catch up with us in time?'

'Afraid not, guv. Too far back. They're over ten kilometres behind. These bastards are only a few kilometres away and closing fast. Probably they are hoping to wipe out our main forces before any support arrives.'

'So, they have been monitoring us all along,' said Alex despairingly.

'Seems that way,' Cliff agreed. 'Our strategy seems to have been flawed from the start. I never thought much of it.'

Alex nodded, but didn't answer. The beginning of a plan was forming in his mind. He turned to the eastern horizon. The sky was turning a dark purple, but the sun would not rise above the dust burden for some time. Several hours of

284

twilight still remained. The land was a multitude of featureless black shapes, and to the military, who had no experience of the surface, it could not be more than that.

'All right,' he said finally. 'I want the whole brigade to dig in and get out of sight. Use the natural cover, but not a shot is to be fired until the tanks have driven right over the top of us. There are bound to be soldiers and back up artillery following up behind. We'll concentrate on knocking them out.'

Cliff nodded and ran off in a hurry.

'I don't want the radio used, the military are too close,' Alex called after him.

Alex repeated his instructions on the walkie talkie, then sent off runners to the squadrons on the flanks who might have difficulty in receiving his transmission. He also sent off a number of drivers with the same message, hoping the other commanders would also adopt his plan.

Alex turned back to the lights and tried to gauge the speed of their advance. The volume of sound had already markedly increased. And now from his vantage point he could see for the first time the sources of the lights. A long unbroken line of blackness appeared for an instant over a hill, then dived immediately out of sight. Behind it were hundreds of smaller headlights, each probably representing a rocket launcher or some mobile artillery unit. He checked his watch. It was nearly six. Marcus had not explained what had happened in the tunnels, but he had said enough for it to be obvious that the enemy's war machine was vastly superior to their own. Certainly, they had picked their battleground well. If the survivors lost, their only retreat would be across the open ground, there would be nowhere to regroup.

As they waited, the enemy opened up with a concentrated bombardment of the land. Tank shells and artillery pounded the armoured units over the survivors' heads. The advancing tanks selectively strafed any places that looked as if they could conceal hostile forces, for as yet, the military had not made contact with the survivors. Like

Alex's division, all the forward units had gone to ground. Once in position they blended into the surface as naturally as the rocks, becoming virtually invisible to the untrained eye. The military, finding themselves in the eerie twilight of a strange land, rolled over their positions, missing them completely.

Alex was with Cliff and several other men, covered in soil, behind a series of large boulders. A few minutes after the tanks and support artillery had passed, the first foot soldiers appeared. Alex could see them looking around nervously, their heads darting from side to side, their hands gripped tightly on their rifles. He waited until the first wave was almost upon them before he took up his walkie talkie and gave the final order for the assault.

From hundreds of covered burrows and hidden crevices the ground erupted in survivors. They fell on the soldiers like the rush of an angry sea, tearing into their ranks with anything to hand, from automatic weapons to primitive knives and clubs. The soldiers fought back desperately, but the surprise was total and they were not prepared for an enemy who fought with the viciousness of a wild beast. Panic spread through the ranks as thousands of survivors sprung, it seemed, from nowhere.

Alex was swept up in the slaughter around him. He focused all his rage on the smooth faced soldiers with shiny weapons and terrified faces. The animal within triumphed, breaking down the barriers of restraint he had tried to build up since the holocaust. Like his men, he recklessly attacked soldier after soldier. Bullets sang around him but he never crouched or paused. Having emptied his revolver, he picked up a rifle from one of the dead soldiers and continued the attack. Soon enemy soldiers were fleeing wildly past him, abandoning their weapons in their haste to escape.

To the left a dozen soldiers were set upon by half their number of survivors. There was a brief exchange of fire before the survivors ploughed into them with knives. Only two escaped towards Alex. He shot one of them and drew his knife on the second.

The victim saw him coming and tried to fend him off, but Alex weaved around his outstretched arms and guided the blade under his ribcage into the heart. The soldier's eyes bulged, he groaned and then dropped to the ground. Alex jerked the knife out and looked around for another victim to plunge it into, but the battle was already almost over. Pockets of remaining soldiers were being hewn down and killed. An army of survivors fifteen thousand strong was now poised between the armoured column and their base.

Ten kilometres further on the battle raged in the military's favour. Their superior firepower and skill were already forcing back the second-rate armour of the survivors. Their tanks were being rounded up like sheep into a shallow valley, the left and right arms of the military swinging around to cut off any retreat.

Marcus, several kilometres further back in his communication van, was going half-crazy with anxiety and frustration. His observation posts in the field kept screaming at him to tell the tanks to break free of the circle before it closed, but his communications with them had broken down. Already over half the tanks were destroyed and much of the supporting artillery had either been silenced or had run out of ammunition. In one last desperate effort, the remaining tanks massed near the bottom of the valley and rallied to try to break through the tightening noose. They drove quickly along the valley floor, destroying the eight tanks that tried to bar their way, but immediately more of the enemy moved up to take their place. Then the rear of the column came under attack and their retreat was hampered as they tried to defend their flanks. In the vital minutes that were lost, the circle had clamped shut in front of them. The military's artillery at once began firing into their ranks until in the end all that was left was twisted metal.

Meanwhile more tanks were sweeping forward to take out what remained of the survivors' artillery. The darkness of total defeat closed over these units also, and they fell silent.

The communication van was perched high on a hill with an overview of the unfolding tragedy. Marcus had abandoned the radio when the last tanks had been destroyed. He now stood motionless, staring down through the thick, tinted glass windows of the van. The enemy, advancing like a crashing wave, was driving all before it. That tide now washed the base of the hill and swept round either side. A few pieces of artillery stationed near him kept lobbing shells into the masses of surging tanks, pinpricks which would only delay the inevitable.

Marcus looked around. Of the two Scottish commanders, Dimitri was calm, his face a perfect mask, revealing nothing of the turmoil and shock he must be feeling. The other leader, however, had gone completely to pieces. He was still by the radio screaming orders at the few gun emplacements still operative. His whole body was bathed in sweat and his voice had become nothing more than a hysterical bark. Marcus turned back to the battle. The tank column had pierced to within two hundred metres of their position and was crunching over the burning hulks of artillery and rocket launchers. As they advanced they destroyed all the vehicles that still remained intact, whether defended or not, while the tanks at the rear maintained a constant shelling of the upper slopes. The smoke of desolation hung over the grim scene.

But Marcus, standing by the window, had long ceased to acknowledge what his senses told him. In his mind he was a small boy again, wandering through the woods, happy, contented, fully absorbed in a scene of beauty. He saw a girl's face, picnic things strewn on the green grass, a quiet river murmuring by…

Suddenly the back doors of the van were ripped apart and Dimitri was killed. Marcus was thrown against the radio and landed on top of the other commander, who was already unconscious and bleeding profusely from a gash down one side of his face. Marcus staggered out into the open. The ground vibrated with explosions, his lungs and throat were burning from the acrid fumes. The first black hulks of tanks made their appearance through the smoke, their turrets spinning round like tops, spitting out flame at whatever their searchlights fastened upon. The van exploded behind him and suddenly his shoulder was hurting, his right arm useless. When he touched the place with his left hand it became covered in blood. The smoke started to make him cough and he dropped to his knees, his sight becoming blotchy and his head beginning to spin. A tank halted on the crest of the hill, fifty metres away. Marcus could see the nozzle of the machine gun sweep towards him, cutting up the ground as it went. Then he was hit and for an instant everything came into perfect clarity. He could feel and hear the bullets smash through him as he was flung backwards onto the van. But seconds later it all faded as he slumped to the earth and quickly died.

The tanks did not pursue the few escaping survivors or attack the fleeing supply column. Reforming into a line they turned back towards the city, finally responding to the anguished appeals of their infantry.

Alex wandered amongst his men grim faced. Everywhere he looked he could see nothing but bodies and blood. His own troops, although largely unwounded, looked as if they had been bathing in blood. A bloated mosquito landed on his nose and lifting his hand to brush it away, he conveyed more blood, not his own, to his cheeks. He stared at his hands and then at his clothes that were already beginning to stiffen and darken with dried blood. Suddenly he was overcome with the urge to clean it off. He knelt down and tried to wipe it away on the shirt tails of one of the dead soldiers. The man only had a small, neat hole in the back of his head, but his whole face had been blown away. Alex got to his feet, feeling sick. He managed only a few unsteady steps before he had to sit down again. His stomach felt as though it had filled with acid. He leant forward, lowered his head and immediately started vomiting, continuing long after his stomach had emptied of food.

'I'm not surprised,' came a familiar voice from behind.

Alex looked up to find Cliff standing in front of him. The little carpenter smiled briefly at him.

'Can't say I blame you, though,' he continued solemnly. 'I wish I could get rid of my emotions as easily as you.'

Alex attempted to rise but became nauseous again and had to sit down.

'Leave it awhile,' Cliff said gently, putting a hand around his shoulder. 'No one's going anywhere for the moment.'

'What happened to you?' Alex asked, when the vomiting fit finally passed.

'I got by,' his friend said. 'I ended up by shooting a lot of those poor bastards while they retreated. But I didn't go after anybody with a knife. Haven't got the heart for that type of thing, no matter how mad I get.'

'You saw that?'

Cliff nodded. 'I was trying to keep an eye on you.'

Alex sighed and rose shakily to his feet. He managed it this time and felt his strength returning. But his heart had gone right out of the fight. All he wanted now was to crawl into a hole somewhere safe and let the battle wash over him.

Together they walked up a hill some short distance off. Far away they could see the military frantically trying to reform their ranks.

'It's all rather crazy, don't you think?' Alex said. 'I mean, we wouldn't have asked for much.'

Cliff agreed. 'I think if the military had known this was coming they'd have negotiated. I'm sure they had no idea we were capable of such a united response.'

'So, it was all a big mistake,' Alex laughed sourly.

'Yes,' Cliff nodded. 'Would you have gone to war, without putting out some feelers first?'

290

The question was not lightly put and Alex realised that Cliff was probably right. Even the military would not be so callous as to sacrifice this many men. Indeed, they had probably made a very stupid error. They had begun to believe in their own propaganda and discounted the survivors as a serious threat. In fact, both sides had been disastrously ill prepared.

'It's gone too far to stop it now,' Alex said bitterly.

Cliff nodded and there was a long silence between them as they watched the continuing battle at a distance, the military furiously combating the onslaught of the survivors.

'Have you heard any casualty counts?' Cliff asked.

Alex shook his head.

'Bad news, I'm afraid. About a quarter of our brigade has been either killed or injured.'

'A quarter!'

'It may well be more.'

'What about the other brigades?'

'The same. Although it does appear that we inflicted three or four times that number of casualties on the enemy.'

'But to what end?' Alex groaned; their eyes met and Cliff shook his head.

'Alex Carhill?' A stocky, dark coloured man was trotting up towards them. 'We've just received instructions from the remnants of our artillery units over the radio. About two hundred enemy tanks are still operative and are heading this way in an attempt to break through to the rest of their ground forces. You have immediate orders to advance towards the city and engage the enemy before their tanks arrive.'

His message delivered; the man started back down the slope to the radio operator.

Alex and Cliff exchanged glances. The implications of that cryptic message did not need spelling out. The fact that the tanks were returning pointed to their overwhelming victory.

'They must feel that if we break through the enemy's lines before their tanks arrive, we stand a better chance,' he mused softly.

'Chance of what?' Cliff asked. 'What are they asking of us? To invade the city?'

'It could be the only place left to run,' Alex said thoughtfully.

'True enough,' the little carpenter replied. 'There's nothing left out here for us.'

The blood of the dead was already losing its brightness as it dried. But the blood red sun was preparing to come up from the underworld and all along the east the first streaks of colour invaded the night.

'So, it will all come down to one last battle,' Alex said, and it annoyed him to hear his voice wavering slightly.

It was a slow process trying to marshal the survivors after the battle. There were new sophisticated weapons to master, taken from the bodies of the military, and the wounded to attend. The dream like calm was frustrating Alex, who started issuing orders to speed things up. Then, he in turn, was instructed by his commander to reorganise the remains of his brigade into three smaller regiments and bring them close together so as to be able to maintain contact with them by hand signals or runners. Other brigades appeared from all directions and were slotted in either ahead or behind Alex's brigade. This drew the survivors into five fighting units, each numbering several thousand men and women. Together these units formed part of a much larger, loosely knit arrowhead formation.

But Alex's expressions of impatience were soon overshadowed by the sudden reappearance of the tank column still some distance away. The survivors at once began to rush about in near frantic disarray. Groups of survivors arrived without commanders, and no one knew what to do with them. Instructions were lost or misinterpreted. In the end, something resembling an

292

arrowhead was formed. Alex's brigade took up position on the left flank of the arrowhead. Alex had drawn all his men close together and given a regiment to Cliff and the other to Roy, who seemed to have come through the last ordeal stronger and fitter than ever.

They were ready to move off when an explosion, apparently a big one, was heard some kilometres away, near the underground city. It was not, however, on the surface. It had a deep throaty sound, as though it came from far underground. Some of the men started to cheer as the word was passed around that sector seventeen had finally been destroyed. This news seemed to restore the failing morale and the foot soldiers now strode on eagerly.

The first obstacle they faced was a strong enemy position, strung out along a series of ridges over a kilometre across their path. The slopes of these hills were criss-crossed with mounted machine guns and hastily laid mines. Every boulder, bush or cover of any kind was bristling with soldiers. In places where cover was not available shallow trenches had been filled to capacity with men.

The survivors reached the valley in front of these defences and paused only long enough to regroup. Then they swarmed, hurling themselves forward, backed up with mortars and rocket propelled grenades. The speed of the advance seemed to weaken the spirit of the military. Many of their strong holds were overrun before they could fire more than a few hundred rounds. Others they abandoned voluntarily, rather than face the vengeance of survivors. Within ten minutes the first hill had fallen and the rest were steadily crumbling as the sides of the arrowhead drove deeper into their ranks.

Alex's troops, however, encountered stiff resistance. The hill to their right had already fallen, but to their left the battle see sawed as the military clung stubbornly to their positions. To break the deadlock, Alex decided to try to slip past the main concentration of the enemy by leading his men through a narrow cleft between two hills.

At first, dense scrub and a wood of stunted oak and beech trees concealed their passage, but the woodland petered out some two hundred metres further up the valley and they came under heavy gunfire as soon as they moved. Alex abandoned the idea of a costly frontal attack and sent out scouting parties to find a safe route up the hill. They returned with news of finding a dried creek bed that led up to the upper slopes. The creek offered the protection of thick scrub and trees along the whole of its course. Alex, with two hundred men detached from his main force, decided to attempt it.

The going was not easy, but after a while it levelled out and wound its way through smooth boulders. Ahead was a grassy meadow, which ended in another small wood. Behind the wood the land rose in a series of broken cliffs. Alex ordered his men to spread out through the boulders and sent a scouting party across the meadow. When they approached the wood, however, they were immediately fired upon. They fell back at once, but only four made it back alive.

Alex, crouching among the rocks, was using a powerful searchlight to try to see into the wood. The cliffs behind and the thick undergrowth, however, effectively concealed the numbers and the disposition of the enemy. There was still over half an hour of twilight left before he would be able to see clearly. He would be forced to lead his men into the blackness without knowing how many soldiers were waiting for them. Cursing his luck, he quickly brought up all his mortars and, on his orders, they blanketed the wood with mortar fire, but there was no response, no returning mortar or rifle fire, not even any detectable movement. After waiting for a few minutes, he decided that the enemy must have already deserted the wood. He signalled his men to start advancing across the meadow, while his mortars maintained covering fire from the boulders.

The line was spread out about halfway across the meadow when the whole wood suddenly erupted in gunfire. Alex started yelling at once for them to retreat, but events were already beyond his control. Half-a-dozen machine gun nests clattered out together, criss-crossing the meadow with bullets and cutting down wave upon wave of survivors as they tried to scramble over the last few metres to the wood. Mortars also began to rain down on the survivors' positions amongst the boulders, and the place became a death-trap as ricocheting shrapnel tore his men to shreds. Within minutes over a third of Alex's company were cut to pieces before his eyes.

When Cliff found Alex, he hadn't moved from his position overlooking the meadow. Already a large force of military had started to emerge from the wood.

'Come on!' Cliff screamed above the explosions. 'We can't do anything for them now!'

When Alex still didn't react, he tugged at his arm.

'You can't stay here!' he bawled in his ear.

His voice finally penetrated. Alex nodded and collected his rifle, and together they quickly descended the dried-up watercourse, sometimes having to clamber over many bodies, so recently their comrades.

They had reached a narrow passageway between two boulders when Cliff suddenly stopped and sank to his knees. He was kneeling beside the torso of a large man. The eyes stared dully into space; the mouth was slightly open as if the man had been in the middle of saying something when the mortar landed. With sudden, terrible apprehension Alex realised he was looking at Roy. The shock brought him to his senses. He pulled Cliff to his feet and they ran on.

Behind them the skirmish was drawing to a close. The military advance was continuing, careful and systematic; they reached the boulders and killed all the wounded survivors, nothing was left alive in their path.

In the valley below the main battle raged. The military's tanks and supporting artillery had now arrived and formed into a rigid wall of armour, pounding the hills already taken by the survivors and re-taking them one by one. With armoured personnel carriers in support they began carving large inroads into the rear of the arrowhead. The battle still hung in the balance.

Alex and Cliff were still in the dried-up creek bed, accompanied by the remainder of Alex's forces. Their positions having been overrun, the continuous bombardment had stopped, allowing them now to hear the shouts of the military as they moved through the boulders behind. Cliff and Alex came to a rock ledge where a small trickle of water tumbled into a large, shallow pool. Both men tried to jump over the pool, but only Alex managed to reach the rock platform beyond. Cliff landed awkwardly in shallow water and fell to his knees. Alex hauled him up and together they ran to join their men who had taken up positions along the riverbank. In the brief time before the military arrived, Alex ordered his men to dig in along the bank.

When they appeared, the soldiers were carelessly yelling and shouting at each other as the crept forward. Alex and Cliff exchanged a brief smile as they saw how recklessly they advanced, as though they already expected the survivors to be somewhere ahead running for their lives. It was much lighter now and to the survivors, whose keen senses were well attuned to the twilight, each soldier stood out like a beacon. As before, Alex waited until the soldiers were almost on top of them before he gave the signal to attack. The survivors shot and hacked their way through the advancing soldiers with a type of cold efficiency that quickly turned the arrogant advance into a terrified retreat.

The back of the arrowhead was now completely destroyed. The valley floor, flat and featureless, offered no protection for the survivors as the tanks advanced like a vast armoured wall, spitting fire. With little ammunition and only their rifles left, rank after rank broke and scattered. The soldiers accompanying these tanks seemed to relish this opportunity to take their revenge and quickly killed all who stood against them.

At the front of the arrowhead however it was a markedly different story as the survivors continued to surge on, overrunning and slaughtering the hapless foot soldiers in their path. As these soldiers abandoned their positions, or were killed, the survivors quickly collected their weapons and ammunition and turned them on the advancing tanks. Mortars, anti-tank rockets and armour piercing bullets were suddenly unleashed at the advancing column. With the destruction of the forward tanks, the tank column slowed as the advancing tanks had to plough their way through the wreckage of their comrades.

With the slowing of the tanks, the arrowhead surged toward the city with renewed vigour. A gaping hole left behind by the destruction of section seventeen had partly destroyed several closely linked sections of the city and exposed these sections to the surface. As the first survivors reached the city they poured into these sections meeting little or no resistance from the terrified remnants of the military.

Alex's company was advancing quickly now. The ambush at the riverbed had drained all of the military's taste for battle; they were fleeing recklessly ahead discarding their weapons in their haste to escape back into the city. Alex and Cliff were leading the company at a jog collecting the best weapons as they advanced. Behind, hundreds of spirals of black smoke greeted the rising sun as most of the tanks, both military and survivors, burned. The remaining wall of tanks was still lobbing shells into the survivors' ranks, but this quickly slowed as they were close enough now to see the survivors gleefully leaping down into the open wound that was once section seventeen.

When they reached the blast hole Alex and Cliff found they were amongst several thousand survivors who were pouring into the exposed tunnel system. Dead army-

297

uniformed soldiers lay in several clusters near some of the entrances. There was no sign of any further resistance, although muffled sporadic gunfire could still be heard in some of the tunnels. Alex took one last look behind. There was no more tank fire. He seriously doubted all the military's tanks had been destroyed. More than likely they had realized that, with the survivors pouring into the city, they had all but been defeated. He figured the military, in their arrogance, had committed nearly all their forces to the battle, assuming they would wipe the survivors out completely. There would be few soldiers left to defend the city. At close quarters the survivors would be more than a match for any remaining pockets of resistance.

Cliff and Alex followed the stream of survivors down through the blast hole toward a large concrete tunnel. Alex recognised it immediately as the underground train tunnel that linked all the sections of the complex. There would be no stopping the survivors now. They could follow the train tracks to all sections of the city. He turned back to the remains of the tank column behind him. The sun had now risen above the horizon, revealing a landscape dotted with burning hulks. Less than a kilometre away were the last of the military's tanks, now silent. He could see the survivors streaming over them and the military soldiers climbing out with their hands in the air. Closer at hand the same scenario was playing out. The military were surrendering. They had won an unlikely victory. At least, he thought, the rightful owners of this miserable world would inherit it.

Thank you for reading my book. If you liked it, please take a moment to leave a review at your favourite retailer.

Rob Cole

Other Books by Robert Cole

<u>Adult</u>

The Ego Cluster

In a future world strafed with economic inequality, religious wars and climate extremes scientists discover a gene cluster that appears to govern the human ego. By suppressing these genes much of the ego-driven nature of the human decision process could be converted to a more empathetic, logical and considered approach, devoid of racial, religious and economic bigotry.

Visionary scientists Ethan Hendersen and Amelia Holt form both a romantic partnership and a working one in which their characters will be tested to the limit when they are employed by a mysterious cartel to develop a treatment to eliminate the human ego. Professional colleague's Dr Doug Ashton and Caleb Fuller are also swept up in the action as the real potential of the ego cluster treatment becomes evident. This is a story of an epic battle between scientific progress and its potential to change the human mind and the entrenched mind-set of the powerful elite.

Mytar series: older children to adults

The Last Portal
(Book 1 of Mytar series)

Severe weather patterns - storms, floods and strong winds - are sweeping across planet Earth. Against this backdrop, three high school students, known and tormented for their strange abilities, fight their own battles against school bullies. The discovery of a strange key by their leader Chris Reynolds, plunges all three through a portal into a sister world, Cathora, in another dimension. In this world their behaviours, that labelled them as misfits on Earth, turn out to be the seeds of extraordinary powers.

They soon meet Batarr, the Guardian of the portal; he tells them they are not normal children, but are part of a group of six beings, called Mytar, who are periodically seeded throughout the dimensions to fight planetary invasions across these portals. Cathora has been invaded by an alien army, led by a creature known only as Zelnoff. After conquering Cathora, his next target is Earth. The Mytar alone have the power to stop him if the other Mytar on Earth can be found. There ensues many struggles and battles as Chris, Susie and Joe seek to evade Zelnoff's forces long enough for their powers to develop so they can detect the remaining Mytar back on Earth.

The Flight of the Mytar
(Book 2 of Mytar series)

Chris, Susie and Joe are transported back to Earth to find the remaining Mytar. To their horror, they find that two of the three Mytar were the bullies that had tormented them at school. With the agents of Zelnoff closing in, they are forced to transport them back to the underworld of Cathora against their will.

Once there, these new Mytar refuse to help and reignite old hatreds and conflicts. Hunted by the Nethral and the Taal, the Mytar children, guided by the Guardian Kaloc, are chased relentlessly through the underworld. When one of them is captured, it becomes a desperate struggle to rescue him and find the sixth Mytar before the forces of Zelnoff seize complete control of Cathora.

The Battle for Cathora
(Book 3 of Mytar series)

After many battles with a creature only known as Zelnoff, the children Mytar finally discover and transport the sixth Mytar from Earth to Cathora, completing the last member of their group. However, the Mytar powers are still underdeveloped and require intensive training to reach their true potential. In contrast, Zelnoff has gained more of the Mytar powers and his armies roam the planet unopposed. When a circling Zentor finds their hiding place, the Mytar children are forced to flee to the mistlands where they are ambushed and scattered.

With the situation seemingly hopeless, they discover critical information which points to a potential weakness in Zelnoff. With this information, one last desperate plan is devised. The Mytar must pool all their powers to fight an alien army and penetrate deep into Zelnoff's territory, if they have any chance of defeating him.

Printed in Great Britain
by Amazon